CW00547578

Best w

Judith Mather

VENGEANCE VISITS CORNWALL

The Dickens Fellowship

———— ESTABLISHED 1902 ————

The Worldwide Fellowship
of Admirers of Charles Dickens

 **The Dickensian**

For further information about The Dickens Fellowship
and The Dickensian apply to:

The Honorary General Secretary
The Dickens Fellowship, The Dickens House
48 Doughty Street, London WC1N 2LF

VENGEANCE
VISITS
CORNWALL

A Sanders and Wade Trilogy

Judith Mather

UNITED WRITERS
Cornwall

UNITED WRITERS PUBLICATIONS LTD
Ailsa, Castle Gate, Penzance, Cornwall.
www.unitedwriters.co.uk

British Library Cataloguing in Publication Data:
A catalogue record for this book is
available from the British Library.

ISBN 9781852002008

Printed and bound in Great Britain by
United Writers Publications Ltd.,
Cornwall.

For Phil

Contents

Book One

The Moving Finger

The moving finger writes; and, having writ
Moves on: nor all your piety nor wit
Shall lure it back to cancel half a line,
Nor all your tears wash out a word of it.

Rubaiyat of Omar Khayyam – second edition, 1868.

Chapter One

Today has started well. I had a very satisfactory bowel movement – I would love to say 'shit' but my status as a woman forbids such expletives, even alone in my own bathroom. As I had given my bathroom a top class clean yesterday, the room smelled of lemons with an undertone of my favourite perfume – lovely. Anyway, back to the BM. It did not require any straining, which is always a good thing, and the product was substantial and not too smelly. I carried out three flushes to make sure the poo and paper was well and truly expelled from my soil pipe (recommendation of my emergency plumber when I had a severe blockage recently) 'I bet you use that quilted paper,' he had said scornfully. 'Shocking stuff.' I blushed and mumbled something about not having a bidet. 'Double flush,' he said. 'Triple, if it's substantial.'

Anyhow, the BM was followed by a thorough hand-wash. My last boyfriend said I washed my hands as if I was about to perform open heart surgery. 'No, just making your breakfast,' I would retort. This usually shut him up. I always use proper soap and a nailbrush. There's something really satisfying about clean nails. I remember my mother once told me that 'in the old days' housewives would make bread and use the kneading of the dough to clean their nails. This gave me a whole new perspective on home-made bread. When I used to make bread, before I became gluten-free, I had a processor with strong dough hooks and a bread baker.

After my morning cuppa I walked down to the coast for a

morning swim. I'm lucky enough to live within walking distance of a spectacular bay and today the sun glistened off the water like diamonds scattered on the sea. I struggled into my lightweight wetsuit and rubber bootees and backed into the water. This manoeuvre is necessary because of the sharp rocks that fringe the beach. The idea is to lie on one's back as soon as possible, staying as stiff as a plank, and push along with one's hands until there is enough depth below to roll over. The inward journey would be easier today as the tide was receding and there would be a channel to walk through by the time I returned from my swim. As I said, it was a good day. I swam strongly out to the white buoy, 500 metres away, and then just lay on my back luxuriating in the cool water and watching the white fluffy clouds scud across the blue sky. A good day. I took my time swimming back and timed my arrival perfectly. Standing upright, I strode confidently between the rocks, feeling the squish of seaweed under my rubber bootees. My towelling robe was where I had left it at the top of the beach and, after rubbing myself down gently, I snuggled into it and flip-flopped back to my little apartment.

My breakfast was a heel of cheese (I love that expression – why a *heel* of cheese? Well, I think a leftover bit of cheese going a bit flaky round the edges looks a little like an uncared-for heel, not one that's bothered the pedicurist over much), grated onto toast and grilled slightly with a fried egg on the top. Fabulous!

My life was going quite smoothly at the moment. Mum says that life is like a domino push. Starting with the baby being pushed out into the world, the first tile falls and hits the second as the baby is smacked on the bottom (do they still do this?) and announces her arrival with a loud wail. Thus set in motion, nothing can halt the relentless click of tile on tile until the doctor closes the now old lady's eyes gently (do they still do this or is it just something I've seen in movies?) and announces life extinct.

It hasn't always been like this – smooth that is. I was an awkward gawky child with an almost savant-like ability in maths. This, as any teenage girl will tell you, is a sure way to alienate your classmates, especially if, like me, you have unruly red hair and are a foot taller than any girl your age. No matter how often I told them that I couldn't spell for toffee, and didn't know what longitude was, the blonde slim girls would call me a swat and ignore me, sniggering behind my back that I was probably a boy – being good at maths and all.

Still, the domino push goes on, *and all your wanting or regret can never reverse its progress, nor all your anger and frustration set it on a different course* (apologies to Omar Khayyam). Inevitably, I had to resit English and History, but having a grade A in Maths alongside my B's (eventually) in the others, I was practically guaranteed my three A levels and a university offer. I chose Manchester because everyone said it was best for maths, and graduated with a first class degree. I launched myself hopefully onto the world of work and spent two years in various waitressing jobs before realising that my degree was worthless. A small legacy (thank you Great Aunt Beryl) allowed me to do something more job-worthy. I had always enjoyed building things so, with little more evidence than this, I decided on a degree in architecture, with a side order of civil engineering. Casting off all advice to the contrary, I went for Plymouth University, because it was by the sea. Now, seven years later, I am living in Cornwall, working for a small team of architects specialising in renovating old tin mines and such. Smashing!

And today is a very good day. How could I know how it would end?

Chapter Two

DI Peter Sanders pulled up outside the large Victorian terrace. Blue and white 'police' tape cordoned off the entrance. Although somewhat dishevelled in his slightly too large grey suit, crumpled blue shirt and grey tie pulled loose at the neck, the DI cut an impressive figure. His six foot three muscular frame would look very at home on a rugby field, where it could be seen on as many Saturday afternoons as his busy work schedule allowed. Although not a conventionally handsome man, with mousy hair, cut short, and a nose which had been broken more than once, courtesy of the aforementioned rugby, Peter Sanders attracted more than his fair share of admiring female glances. The fact that he was totally unaware of this only added to the attraction and, if one was lucky enough to receive the attention of his pale blue eyes and devastating smile, it would take a long time to put this man out of one's mind. However, today there were no twinkling eyes or broad smile, the detective inspector was all business.

He closed his car door and covered his shoes in the obligatory plastic covers. A uniformed officer stood on duty at the doorway. 'Mornin', sir. Nasty one this. Paramedics are not hopeful.'

Peter snapped on his latex gloves. 'Where are they taking her?'

'Trevan, sir.'

'Who found her?'

'Lady in the flat below. She was coming off a night shift at the old folk's home, saw the mess on the stairs and went up to investigate. Found Miss Parks in the doorway of her flat. Mrs Jenner, that's the lady, sir, has some medical training so was able to detect a weak pulse and called for an ambulance.' The constable indicated indoors with his head. 'She's waiting in her flat, with Constable Walker.'

'Thanks. I'll check the scene and see her when I've finished. Where are the other tenants?'

'All interviewed, sir. Two have gone to work and an elderly couple on the ground floor are available if you want to see them. Apart from Mrs Jenner, no one heard or saw anything.'

'Good work, Constable. . ?'

'Green, sir.'

'Right. When my DS gets here, send her up, will you.' The DI looked around him briefly and started for the stairs.

There was no mistaking the metallic smell of blood that mingled with an undertone of lemon as he ascended the stairs, carefully stepping over scattered objects and plant debris which trailed across the steps. As he reached the top landing it became clear where the debris had originated. A small hall table had been overturned and its contents tipped off down the stairs. DI Sanders' eyes were scanning the scene and logging what he saw meticulously. He had an almost photographic memory. He could recall every aspect of a crime scene and had found that, in past cases, it could be the smallest detail that made a case stick. He bent slightly to look at the leg of the overturned table. *Blood here. A handprint.* Opening the door he took in the whole room before mentally sectioning it off into areas. As this victim was still alive, hopefully, there were no medics to get in his way, but they had left their own disturbance. Bloody footprints and marks where they had obviously made space to get the stretcher in place and secure the victim. This had been done quickly, as it should, and with no regard for preserving the scene, as could be expected. Nevertheless, DI Sanders was irritated slightly.

Walking slowly into the room, he took in the overturned chair by the attic window, gaffer tape hanging off it in places. A bookshelf with books and CDs scattered on the floor around it, a coffee table with a selection of design books artfully placed on the top. The blood trail led from the chair to the door. It appeared that Miss Parks had dragged herself across the floor. *Probably left for dead,* the DI thought, *so that must have taken some strength.*

In the small, neat kitchen nothing seemed to have been disturbed except for a supermarket sandwich wrapper on the draining board with a half-eaten sandwich inside. *Perhaps he disturbed her having a snack?* The bathroom led off a small hallway and smelled strongly of lemons, the scent he had noticed on his way up the stairs. The shower curtain and bath were wet, as was a towel which had been tossed over a clothes basket in the corner.

As he stood in the bathroom, a shout came from the living room. 'OK to come through, sir?'

'Yes, come on in, Rachel. Just be careful, SOCO's not been yet.'

'Any clue as to what happened here?'

DI Peter Sanders wore a puzzled frown. 'It doesn't fit, but I don't know quite what's wrong yet.'

'How d'you mean?' Rachel said, surveying the scene.

'Oh, I don't know. It's just that some bits are extremely tidy and then there are the CDs and books.' He looked at Rachel quizzically. 'Do you see? And it's the same in the bathroom, everything shining and clean – and then the wet shower and the towel just thrown in the corner.'

'Maybe a messy boyfriend?'

A knock on the door announced the arrival of SOCO. 'Alright to come in?'

'Sure, we've just about finished.'

As they carefully descended the stairs, Peter asked Rachel to organise a door to door. 'Somebody must have seen something, a car maybe. And check for CCTV, domestic and official.'

'Right, sir. Anything else?'

'Yes, could you interview Mrs Jenner, the lady who called for the ambulance. I'll be at the hospital if you need me.'

DS Rachel Morris pulled out her phone and made a few quick calls. Two uniformed officers were summoned to carry out the door to door interviews, and DS Kevin Sharp, one of the other members of the Serious Incident Squad led by DI Sanders, was asked to track down local CCTV footage.

While she was doing this, she was watching the DI remove his shoe coverings and gloves before swinging into his Range Rover. She ran her hands through her long black hair and gathered it up into a tight ponytail. Rachel wore no make-up and didn't need to. She was considered amongst her peers to be a beautiful woman, more suited to the catwalk than the police. Her long dark lashes framed intense brown eyes, which revealed her half Chinese origins. Her slim athletic figure moved gracefully even at a crime scene, and people were always amazed that, at thirty-five, she was still single. Rachel would say she was choosy, but was beginning to think that she liked her own space too much to let anyone in. The exception could be the man who had just driven off, but he didn't seem to see her as a woman, just a valued member of his team. She watched until the Range Rover was out of sight then, giving a sharp tug to the lapels of her smart black suit, went off to find Mrs Jenner.

The paramedics who brought Sandra Parks in had stayed behind to speak to the DI, and were drinking coffee in the waiting room. DI Sanders thanked them for waiting and asked if there was somewhere private for them to talk.

'The chapel's usually quiet at this time of day.'

'Lead the way, then.'

As they settled themselves at the back of the empty chapel, the first thing the DI wanted to know was how Miss Parks was now.'

'She's in a bad way but still alive. Lots of cuts and bruises. Her face is a mess and her right tibia is broken, but it seems that a blow to her head caused the most damage.'

'Can you tell me what happened? When did you receive the call?'

'Six-thirty. We weren't far away, so got there about six-forty. She was half in and half out of the door. Her eyes and mouth were gaffer taped, with remnants of it on her wrist also, but somehow she'd managed to drag herself to the doorway. I'd say the door must have been left open because she couldn't possibly have reached the lock with her leg in that condition. She was unconscious but had a weak pulse. If the lady downstairs hadn't found her when she did, I doubt she would have survived.' The paramedic conferred with his colleague. 'That's about it, wouldn't you say, Angie?'

'Yeah, I think so.' Turning to DI Sanders she said, 'You'll get more info from the doctor, but this is the worst beating I've ever seen. You just catch the bastard that did it.'

'I'll do my best, and thanks again for staying. You've been very helpful. Now I must get off and see the doctor.' Peter was aware as always of the burden placed on him by the public. *Catch the bastard.* Well, he had an exemplary record of arrests, but most people expected quick results and, in Peter's experience, it was slow methodical police work – with a little intuition, perhaps – that solved most cases. He was used to being berated by the press for lack of progress until the culprit was eventually apprehended, and then he was the best thing since sliced bread.

The doctor confirmed what the paramedics had told the DI. 'Her skull has a depressed fracture. Looks like it was a small round weapon, maybe a hammer? The tibia was fractured by a different weapon though, possibly something like a baseball bat. She has numerous cuts to her face and torso and her face has been punched repeatedly. There are cuts under her eyes and she has some teeth missing, also some hair has been pulled out.' The doctor shook his head sadly. 'He gave her a real going over. It's hard to tell, but I would say that the injuries were inflicted over time. Some of the cuts had started to heal slightly. I'd say he spent a few hours with her.'

DI Sanders had many years' experience of investigating the most violent and vicious attacks but was still able to be shocked by the inhumanity that one human being could display against another. But, however distasteful the litany of abuse was to hear, it was important to get all the facts and not leave anything out. 'What about sexual abuse, doctor?'

'No obvious signs of any penetration vaginally or anally or bruising on the thighs, so I'd say no at this point. We haven't done a rape test yet, due to her condition, but we will, maybe tomorrow, and I'll get the results to you.'

'Can I see her?' Despite having the full details from the doctor, Peter wanted to see Miss Parks for himself so that he could hold her image in his head. Not that he needed any motivation to pursue the culprit but he found it helped him to keep the victim in mind.

'I don't see why not, but you understand she is in a coma?'

'Of course, I don't expect to talk to her. As she survived it's possible that the attacker will want to finish the job. As well as seeing Miss Parks for myself, I want to ensure her security. We'll have a constable stationed outside her room at all times but, until that's arranged, I'll stay, if that's alright.'

'Yes, I understand. She's just through here at the end of the corridor.'

As the two men walked along, DI Sanders surveyed the corridor and rooms off. Indicating towards a fire door at the end he asked the doctor where it led to.

'The fire escape. If it's opened an alarm goes off.'

Peter nodded. 'Is there a way to disable the alarm?'

'I don't know, to be honest. I'll get one of the porters to come up and talk to you about that. They seem to know everything.'

'Thanks doctor, you've been very helpful. I'll let you get on now.'

The doctor smiled gratefully and hurried away as Peter stood on the threshold of Miss Parks' room. She was surrounded by machines monitoring her condition. Her head was bandaged and her arms, which were straight by her sides above the thin hospital blanket, had tubes inserted feeding the necessary drugs and nutrients into her frail body.

The DI pulled up a chair and sat down by the bedside, examining the features of the prone woman that he could see. Though the DI was sure that Sandra Parks had been a pretty young woman before this happened, she showed no resemblance to the photograph he had noticed in her apartment. She was pictured on a beach, the wind blowing her red hair so that it caught the sun. She looked healthy and happy, having apparently just emerged from the sea. The face he saw now was swollen and bruised, her eyes puffy and closed up and her lips, which surrounded the breathing tube, were stitched where the beating had torn the flesh. Being intubated, her breathing was steady but, although he knew she could be kept alive this way for some time, the damage to her brain could not yet be assessed.

19

As Peter started to think about where to begin the investigation, someone called from the doorway. 'You wanted some information, sir?' A young man, whose voice revealed an Eastern European accent, waved a hand, an enquiring look on his face.

'Yes, perhaps you could tell me where that fire escape door leads to.' The DI rose from the chair and joined the porter.

'To the fire escape.' The young man said sarcastically. This did not amuse Peter.

'Okay, lad, less of the wisecracks. Where does this fire escape lead to?'

The young man looked sheepish. 'Sorry, sir. It comes out at the back of the building, by the waste bins outside the kitchen.'

'Right. And is it always alarmed?'

'It is supposed to be, sir, but I happen to know that some of the fire alarms have been disabled so that staff members can smoke out on the fire escape. This is not permitted you understand, but it happens.' He shrugged awkwardly.

'And this one?' Peter said, indicating the door.

'I think so. It is a long way from here to the outdoor restroom and this is a shortcut.'

Peter went over and pushed the bar on the door. Sure enough it opened with no alarm sounding. 'Hmm,' he said. 'Okay, that's all for now. Your name is . . ?'

'Paved, sir. Paved Yaneccec.'

'Right, off you go lad.' Peter watched Paved stride confidently down the corridor as a uniformed constable passed him coming the other way.

'Ah. Constable Green, isn't it?' the DI said as the tall young man approached him.

'Yes, sir. I've been instructed to guard this room.'

'You were at the scene, weren't you?' The young constable nodded. 'Right, well this is a very important duty, Green. No one, and I mean no one, gets in here without checking who he or she is. All IDs must be checked, no exceptions, is that clear?'

'Yes, sir.'

'Right, I'm off to get someone to reset the alarm on that fire escape, and you don't leave your post for anything. I take it you've had a pee?'

'Yes, sir,' the constable grinned, 'first thing they teach you at bobby school.'

'Okay.' Peter patted the younger man on the back. 'I'll be back later tonight. If you need relieving for any other reason, call the station for backup.'

When Peter returned to the ops room, DS Rachel Morris had already set up the incident board. The other members of the team were gathered around paying rapt attention as Rachel outlined the case. She had been busy. Names of friends and colleagues with contact details were itemised around a picture of Sandra Parks. It was the same one Peter had seen in her room.

'I don't need to tell you how urgently we need to find the individual responsible for Sandra's injuries. This was a particularly vicious beating which may yet turn out to be more serious. The hospital reckons she has a 70/30 chance of recovery and, even if she survives, she may not have full brain function.' Rachel handed out assignments to the team. 'The DI and myself will go to see Sandra's best friend.' She checked on the board. 'Andrea Reynolds – known as Yaz. Then do you want to see the parents, sir? They're on their way from Manchester, should arrive late afternoon.'

'Yes, thanks Rachel.' He glanced around the room, taking in the other three members of his team. They'd all been here before. He'd picked them for their experience and enthusiasm for the job. Peter knew that they would give one hundred percent in the pursuit of this perpetrator. He smiled at them. 'Let's get on with it then. You can reach me anytime day or night, you know that. I want to know everything, no matter how insignificant it may seem, so reports in on time and complete. Okay, off you go.'

As the room emptied, Peter turned to Rachel. 'Good work, Sergeant, let's go see this best friend.'

Peter and Rachel pulled into a gravelled yard where a large barn stood. The building looked derelict but there was a van parked by the entrance door and loud music coming from inside. Rachel consulted her notes. 'My info says she's an artist, so I guess this is her studio.'

As the two officers entered the building, they took in the size of the space before them. The barn was cavernous, extending maybe thirty metres with rough benches along each side holding a variety of tools. In the centre of the space was a metal construction of a figure about three metres tall. On top of a ladder was a person in coveralls and helmet wielding a blowtorch. The music was loud in here and the DI wasn't sure how he would get the person's attention until Rachel turned the CD player off. The person on the ladder stopped suddenly and turned. 'What the. . ?'

'Andrea Reynolds?' Peter shouted. 'I'm DI Sanders and this is DS Morris. We'd like a word.'

'Right. And it's Yaz, I haven't been Andrea Reynolds for a long time. No name for an artist that.'

Yaz climbed down from her perch and removed her helmet to reveal a cap of short pink hair and a multitude of piercings. She was tall for a woman, Rachel thought about six two or three, and looked muscular under her coverall. Putting her welding torch down she smiled warmly at the officers. 'Can I get you a drink? Only tea, I'm afraid, but several varieties of that.'

'Tea would be great,' said Rachel. 'Just builder's will do.'

Whilst Yaz busied herself with the tea, Peter took a look around the studio. The piece that dominated the space was the metal figure which seemed to loom over him.

Yaz noticed the DI's interest. 'It's an angel,' she said as she placed three chipped mugs on an upturned box. 'I'm a bit obsessed with Anthony Gormley – you know? The Angel of the North?' Peter nodded as he pulled up a rickety chair. 'Well,' continued Yaz, 'I want to make something like that. Nowhere near as big, of course. I don't have the space for that.' She looked around her studio. 'I was lucky to find this place.'

The three of them sat and sipped their tea. 'What's this about then? Has something happened?'

'I'm afraid so, Miss,' said Peter. 'Do you know Sandra Parks?'

'Sandy? Yeah, I know her well. Has something happened to Sandy?'

'I'm sorry to have to tell you that she was attacked last night.' The DI watched for Yaz's reaction. People gave a lot away when they heard this sort of news. Yaz merely looked curious, a slight frown on her face.

'Is it serious? I guess it is if you're here.'

'She's in hospital. The attack was severe.' Rachel had her notebook out. 'Could you tell us where you were from 6pm yesterday to 6am this morning.'

'What? You can't think. . ?'

'Just procedure, Miss,' said Peter. 'We'll be asking everyone she knew that question, so that we can eliminate individuals from our enquiries.'

'Sounds like one of those police dramas on telly. I was here, where I always am.'

'The whole time?' Rachel said, looking up from her notebook.

'Well, I went to the shop for a sandwich, but that was around five and I came straight back here.' Yaz looked over at the sculpture. 'It's a hard taskmaster, the avenging angel.'

The DI changed the subject. 'Tell us about Sandra, what sort of a person is she?'

'Oh, a lovely person. I've known her since uni. We shared a flat in Plymouth for a while. She's very neat, and when I say *neat* I mean a neat freak. OCD, you know? Not badly. She did go out, held down a job, swam a lot. She was a fussy eater though – gluten free, plant based food, all that. She did, er – record her bowel movements. Food intake and output, so to speak.' Yaz smiled wanly. 'Needless to say, we didn't share for long. I'm a messy person and eat anything that's going. We weren't compatible in that way but we shared a drive, you know, sense of purpose? She was passionate about architecture and preserving old buildings. We used to drive around the coast looking for disused property, tin mines, count houses and the like. We also shared an interest in the environment – saving it, that is – I work with discarded bits of metal and she saves old buildings.'

'She works for a firm of architects now?'

'Yes, 'Vision', that's what they're called. Mike and Paul. Mike's the leader, at least in name, but they're a team really. Oh, and there's

23

Polly who's the IT whizz. They've got a place above the tea room in Fore Street. Sandy's been there about three years now. Oh, and she's a genius.'

The DI cocked his head quizzically at Yaz.

'Maths,' Yaz said in answer to the unspoken question. 'She was one of those people who can multiply two massive numbers in seconds – in her head. She can tell if something is a millimetre out of line and tell you how tall a building is. Genius, like I said.'

Peter looked over at Rachel who gave a slight nod. 'Well I think that's all for now, Miss. We may need to talk to you again. Are you planning to go anywhere?'

'No, I'll be here. Me and the angel.'

'Right then. Thanks for the tea.'

When they were in the car, Peter looked over at Rachel. 'What do you make of that then?'

'Interesting. Did you notice she didn't ask how Sandra was? And the past tense? Could be just a slip of course.'

'Mmm, shock takes people all ways, we know that, but there's something. And no alibi. We'll definitely need to speak to her again, perhaps down at the station.'

Rachel started the car. 'Hospital then. See if the parents have arrived.'

Mrs Parks sat beside the hospital bed, holding onto Sandra's hand whilst dabbing her eyes continuously with a tissue. She was a small round woman of about fifty or so, Peter estimated, although he wasn't good at guessing women's ages, especially older women. In contrast, Mr Parks was tall and wiry looking. He stood by the window, his hands behind his back, his whole body rigid.

DI Sanders spoke to the constable on duty outside the room. 'You can take a short break now, Constable, but before you go, do you have anything to report?'

'Not much, sir. No visitors except for the parents, but I asked to be kept informed of phone calls asking about Miss Parks.' He consulted his notebook. 'Just the one, sir. Someone called Yaz called to ask if she could visit. She was told 'not at the moment' and

24

became a bit offensive by all accounts. Other than that it's been quiet. I've got to know most of the staff attending to Miss Parks and I'm checking IDs like you asked.'

'Good work, Constable. Now off you go and get something to eat. DS Morris and I will be here for an hour or so. By the way, did they fix the fire escape alarm?'

'Yes, sir. All secure.'

Peter knocked and entered the room where Sandra lay unmoving. 'I don't want to intrude but I need to ask you a few questions.' Peter and Rachel took out their warrant cards. 'I'm DI Sanders and this is DS Morris.'

Sandra's father turned quickly from the window, his face etched with anger. 'How could you let this happen?' he shouted. 'Look at her, what sort of monsters do you allow to roam about down here?'

'Now then, Terry,' said his wife. 'It's not their fault.' Looking directly at the inspector she said, 'But you'll find him. Who did this to our girl.' It wasn't a question.

'We'll find whoever attacked your daughter.' Sanders pulled up a chair for Mr Parks. 'Please sit down, sir, we need to ask a few things about Sandra to help with our enquiries. We won't take up any more of your time than is necessary.'

Mr Parks sat grudgingly. Mrs Parks held her husband's hand and said, 'What do you want to know?'

'Just general things. A bit of background really. What sort of a girl is she?'

Mrs Parks smiled and looked at her daughter. 'She's beautiful, Inspector. You wouldn't know to see her now,' tears rolled down Mrs Parks' cheeks, 'but she's really lovely.'

Rachel took up the questioning. 'Why was she living in Cornwall?'

Mr Parks answered. 'Couldn't get work up North. A first class degree and couldn't get work, it's ridiculous. Waitressing she did. Bars, cafés, tried to get a proper job but nothing doing. I asked her to work with me – doing the accounts, you know. I'm a builder you see, but no, she didn't want that. My son, *our* son Martin, he works with me. We're doing okay, she could have been well set up instead of. . .' He looked at his daughter and rubbed his eyes with the back of his hand.

25

'Did she have any boyfriends, Mrs Parks?' Peter knew it was best to remain on task and not get drawn into family dramas.

'No one special,' said Mr Parks.

'Yes, don't you remember, Terry, that lad who wouldn't let her alone?' Turning to the DI, Mrs Parks said, 'There was this one lad, Mark, she met him at Manchester University where she was studying. Wouldn't leave her alone, would he Terry?'

'Little squirt! Short scraggy thing he was. Nice as pie at first but pushy, you know? Wanted our Sandra to get engaged. Bought a ring and proposed in front of all her mates. Got nasty when she turned him down.'

Mrs Parks took up the story. 'She finished with him after that, but he didn't take it well. Followed her around, phoned her at all hours, even went to the places she was working – just sat there, she said. She left a couple of places because of him.' She looked again at her daughter. 'I was glad when she left Manchester to study in Plymouth. Got away from him.'

'Has he contacted her since?'

'I don't think so, Inspector, not that she told us anyway. She say anything to you, Terry?'

'No, love. I think he got the message.' Mr Parks looked at his daughter. 'He couldn't have done this though. Could he? He was a little squirt like I said, nasty mouth on him, but I can't see him doing this.'

'And did your daughter mention any other boyfriends, anyone here?' Rachel said.

'There were boys, well men I suppose, that she dated. She mentioned someone at work. Paul I think his name was, but it didn't last. Ended friendly enough I think. They still work together, don't they, Terry?'

'I don't know love. She talks to you more than me about that sort of thing. You could ask our Martin though. He's looking after the business or he'd be here. Very close they are. He'd be mad as hell to see his sister like this. He wanted to go after that Mark when he was making a nuisance of himself, but I stopped him. Wouldn't have been a fair contest anyway, our Martin's six foot three and strong as an ox.'

'Well, I think that's all for now. I may need to check a few things out with you another time. Are you staying locally?'

'Terry has to get back, but I'm staying at a B&B just down the road. He'll be back tomorrow though, won't you love?'

'Aye. Our Martin will probably want to come too, no doubt.'

'If you could give DS Morris your contact details then. I'll keep you updated with progress as much as I can, and try not to worry, this is a good hospital and your daughter seems like a fighter to me.'

Constable Green was back at his post as Peter and Rachel came out of the hospital room. 'That was quick, Constable,' Peter said.

'Just had a sandwich, sir.'

'Who's relieving you later?'

'I don't know, sir. I'm due to stay until ten but I won't leave until my replacement comes.'

'Good lad. I'll be back myself later.'

The two detectives set off back to the station to see what the rest of the team had managed to find out. This was a fast moving investigation and the DI wanted to get all the reports in before the end of the day. 'Just make a detour to the crime scene would you Rachel? There's something itching at the back of my mind.'

Rachel was used to the DI's *itches*. He rarely missed a clue. Even when it was lodged in his subconscious, he worked at it until it came to the surface. Rachel took the shortcut across country to Falmouth. Making her way to the beach, she turned off the seafront into the side road leading to Sandra's flat. 'Will you need me, sir?'

'No, I won't be long. Just want to see the place again now that SOCO's finished. And we could do with surveillance here. Organise that will you.'

'Yes, sir.'

Peter stood in the middle of the room taking in the scattered books and CDs. *She didn't make this mess*, he thought. Moving to the bathroom he took in the discarded towel and the untidy shower curtain. *Nor this*. Moving to the kitchen he realised that something

27

was missing, *the sandwich – I hope SOCO bagged that*. There was fingerprint dust everywhere, but despite that, Peter could tell that this was a neat and tidy space normally. *Someone spent some time here, worked on her over a few hours then left her for dead*. He shook his head and turned to leave.

Rachel was waiting beside the car. 'Cover's been organised, sir. A car is on its way.'

'Right, let's get back to the station.'

Chapter Three

As the team briefing progressed, Rachel copied the information onto the incident board. All the work colleagues had been interviewed. They all seemed appropriately shocked at the news about Sandra. Maggie Williams spoke up. 'They seemed genuinely devastated, sir, couldn't think why anyone would want to hurt her.'

'What about alibis?'

'All together, sir, in the Miner's Arms,' said Kevin. 'Some sort of works outing. They'd just got a new contract and were celebrating.' He consulted his notes. 'They apparently called Miss Parks several times during the evening but there was no reply.'

'Check the phone records will you?'

'Already done, sir,' said Maggie. There were calls at 6.50, 7.35, 9.10 and again at 9.45, after that there were no calls to her mobile. She didn't have a landline. Mobile's missing, by the way, so we got that from phone records.' Maggie was young but had the makings of an excellent detective. On the outside, she epitomised a 'dizzy blonde'. She had the hair and make-up, as well as manicured and polished nails, green today, Peter noticed, but she had a razor-sharp mind and could think 'outside the box' as management speak would have it.

'Did anyone leave the pub during the evening?'

Kevin spoke next. He pushed his shaggy, dirty blonde hair out of his eyes. Kevin looked like a typical Cornish 'surfer dude' and, if time allowed, he could be found catching waves down at

Porthtowan, but he was police through and through, dedicated to his job. Turning a page in his notebook he said, 'Mike Travis left to let his dog out for a pee around 7.30. Wasn't away more than fifteen minutes, but then he left early – 9.30ish complaining of a headache. The party broke up soon after that, around 10.30.' The DS looked again at his notes. 'Oh, and Paul Collins arrived late, 7.30 or thereabouts.'

'So, apart from Polly, one of the other two could have gone to Miss Parks' flat around 7.30, tied her up and returned later to finish the job.'

'We've had a report from the hospital that they found traces of a sedative in Miss Parks' blood, sir,' said Maggie, waving a sheet of paper.

The DI looked annoyed. 'When did that come in? I need everything as soon as it comes in. Is that clear?'

'Only just come through, sir,' said Maggie. 'I've just this minute printed it off.'

'Okay. But chase it up will you Maggie, find out how long it would have been effective for.' The DI smiled apologetically. 'And what about IT? Did she have a laptop do we know?'

Kevin Sharp raised his hand. 'The workmates said yes, although she preferred to draw her plans the old fashioned way with graph paper and pencil.'

'It wasn't at the scene,' the DI mused. 'Have Uniform do a search of the area Rachel.'

'Sir.' Rachel acquiesced.

'What about the SOCO report? Anything yet, Kevin?'

'No, sir. I'll get on to them, see if I can hurry them up.'

'I'm interested in a half-eaten sandwich. It was there this morning and then not there when I called in an hour ago. See if they have done a DNA test on it.'

'Wouldn't that have been Miss Parks', sir?' Maggie asked.

'No, she was gluten free and wouldn't have eaten a supermarket sandwich by all accounts. It must have been a visitor from earlier in the day, or it just could be our attacker.'

Rachel added, 'Her friend Yaz said that Miss Parks was 'a neat freak' – had OCD, so I can't see her leaving a half-eaten sandwich around. I've got a friend with Coeliac Disease and she wouldn't even allow a wheat based sandwich in her house.'

'What's Coeliac then?' enquired Maggie.

'Gluten intolerance Maggie. Can be quite serious.'

'Alright, let's stay focused, Rachel,' interjected the DI. 'But it does make it likely that it was the attacker, which is good, if we can get a DNA analysis.' He turned to DC Sharp. 'Kevin, organise DNA samples from all the main suspects.'

Peter turned to DS Saroj Kapoor. 'You're quiet Saroj, anything to add?'

'I've been looking into the family, sir. Mr and Mrs Parks seem like an ordinary couple. He's a self-employed builder, she's a primary school teacher. One son Martin, older than Sandra by five years. He works with his dad.' She consulted some paperwork. 'Got some form with Manchester Police. GBH seven years ago. Bust up outside a pub, broke the lad's arm. Got six months suspended, and been clean since.'

'Thanks Saroj, I'll probably see him at the hospital tomorrow. Don't really fancy him for this but I'll check where he was anyway.' The DI rubbed his hands together. 'Okay. Good work today. Let's start bright and early in the morning.'

Sanders hadn't always been an insomniac, only since becoming a detective. Now he habitually woke in the early hours thinking about a case and was unable to get back off to sleep. Normally he would either check case notes or walk the streets thinking, before going into the station around six or so. This morning he decided to go to the hospital.

A uniformed constable was on duty outside Sandra Parks' room. 'Morning, sir,' she said, as she sprang to attention.

'Relax, Constable. Any change in her condition?'

'Not that I know, sir. She's still in a coma according to the nurse on duty earlier.'

'Visitors?' The DI gazed through the room window at the still figure in the bed.

'No, sir. Nurses and a doctor coming and going, that's all.'

'Right. I'm going to sit with her for a while, so you can stretch your legs if you like. Get a coffee maybe.'

'That would be most welcome, sir. Shall I get you one?'

'No, I'll be fine. Off you go, and take your time, no need to rush back.'

The DI watched the young constable walk away down the corridor. He took a moment to notice that she was very attractive, realising that he hadn't had what you might call a *date* for a long time. Turning reluctantly away, he entered the side ward where Sandra Parks lay in the same position as she was earlier. He pulled up a chair and sat at her bedside.

'Hello Sandra,' he said to the sleeping figure. 'I hope you don't mind me coming at this hour. I'm Detective Inspector Sanders, the person in charge of finding whoever did this to you.' As expected there was no response from Sandra, but the DI was of the opinion that, just because a person was in a coma, it didn't mean they couldn't hear you. He carried on. 'You were very brave and your strength saved your life. I believe that whoever did this meant for you not to survive, and that makes me think you must know who it is.' He shrugged. 'Of course you are unable to tell us anything at the moment, but I believe you can hear me and I'd like you to think about what happened last night. I know that will be painful, but it's imperative that we catch whoever did this and I know you can help.'

There was no change in the bleeping of the machines or the rise and fall of Sandra's chest, as the ventilator first inflated her lungs and then relaxed, keeping a steady rhythm. Nevertheless, Sanders continued to talk, going through his thoughts about the attack and the suspects he was considering.

At last! Someone talking to me rather than about me. I've realised that I'm in hospital and in quite a bad way if the hushed tones and my mother's sobbing is anything to go by. But now this nice inspector chatting on about what he calls 'my case' and asking for my help. Well, if only!

I'm thinking about what he's saying, but my mind's a bit of a blank. The last thing I remember is a knock on the door as I was just about to set off for the pub to meet the team. I remember thinking it

32

must be one of them come to get me. They know I can be a bit antisocial but there was another reason I was delaying last night, I was about to burst their bubble about the wharf-side development. I opened the door. I was hit by a smell – pungent and sharp – then nothing. As much as I try to search my memory, there's a complete blank until a few hours ago when I started to hear voices talking about me. I know I can't open my eyes or move at all so I must have been knocked out. Deliberately I guess, with medication. I can smell the usual hospital smells and I find that reassuring. I've always liked hospitals, unlike a lot of people. It's probably the antiseptic atmosphere that appeals to my love of cleanliness.

The inspector is still here, I can smell his aftershave, something light and spicy. He's not talking now though, but I can hear the rustle of paper occasionally, like he's reading through notes. I can feel myself drifting and give in to the sensation. Something is there at the back of my mind – just out of reach. Maybe I could just. . .

DI Sanders stretched and yawned. He was just putting his notes back into his briefcase when Mr and Mrs Parks appeared at the door with a tall, well-built young man. Mrs Parks stopped in surprise. 'Inspector Sanders! I didn't expect you to be here at this time, it's barely six am.'

'Good morning Mrs Parks, Mr Parks. I'm just on my way out actually but, if this is Martin, I wouldn't mind a word after you've visited with your sister.'

'Yes, I'm Martin. I'm a bit shattered though, been driving all night.'

'That's okay, I won't keep you long. I'll be down the corridor in the day room when you're ready.' With that, the DI left the family to spend time with Sandra and went in search of a strong coffee.

'Right, Inspector Sanders, how can I help you?'

The DI looked at the man before him. Martin Parks was indeed a large man. Must be six three or four, he mused, and all muscle. Good looking too, though his eyes looked tired and his red hair tousled. 'Can you tell me when you were last in touch with your sister?'

'Yes, very recently in fact. I spoke to her about a week ago to see how she was getting on with my mate Robert.' The inspector looked quizzically at Martin. 'Robert Munroe, Munroe Construction and Development. I put them in touch with each other when I found out that Robert was developing a site in the South West. I hoped to put a bit of work her way.'

'And how did she seem when you spoke to her?'

'Excited. She and her team were about to sign a contract with Robert to draw up the plans for the development of a wharf-side building in Penthavern. Just up their street it is. Conservation, you know? Using environmentally friendly construction methods and materials.' Martin fidgeted. 'D'you mind if we go outside to talk? I'm in dire need of nicotine. Mum won't let me smoke and drive and she rushed me straight in here when we arrived.'

'No problem, sir. I'm in need of fresh air myself.'

Outside the hospital grounds, Martin offered the inspector a cigarette and then, when that was politely refused, he lit one and took a long drag. He coughed slightly and smiled ruefully, holding the cigarette out and looking at it. 'I keep meaning to give up. My girlfriend would appreciate it for sure.'

The DI fell into step with Martin. 'Could you tell me where you were between 6pm and 6am on Friday into Saturday?'

'You can't think I'm. . ?'

'Just routine, sir. We have to eliminate people from our enquiries.'

'I suppose so, but to be considered even for a moment. . . well. I was in Manchester with my girlfriend, Stella. We went out about seven o'clock to meet friends for a drink and then onto a restaurant. We got back to my place around eleven-thirty, had a nightcap and went to bed. Had a lie-in and got up at ten-ish, then went out for breakfast.'

'Thank you, sir. If you could give me your girlfriend's details?'

Exasperated, Martin replied, 'Yes, if I must. Stella Peterson. Here's her phone number.' Martin scrolled through his phone and offered it to the DI.

Peter continued, 'Do you know of anyone who would want to hurt your sister? Any enemies or rivals? Boyfriends?'

Martin sucked on his cigarette and exhaled. 'No Inspector. She's a lovely person, everyone likes Sandy. She can be difficult to live with. Very high standards. But there's no side to her, you know? She'd help anyone out. I can't think who might have done this.'

'What about her old boyfriend? Mark, wasn't it? Your mother mentioned him yesterday.'

'What, that little runt? He wouldn't have it in him. Sly he is, more the pestering type than violent I'd say. Followed her around for weeks you know, making a nuisance of himself, but her moving South got rid of him I'm sure.'

'And no one since?'

'She had a bit of a fling with Paul, her workmate, but it ended amicably enough. He's going out with Polly now, another workmate.' Martin laughed. 'He likes to play close to home. That can come unstuck though, in my experience – what if you fall out? It can get really uncomfortable then.'

'No one else?'

'Well, she might not tell me everything. We're close though, and I'm sure if there was anyone serious I'd get to know about it.' Martin stubbed out his cigarette. 'Is that everything, Inspector? Only I'd like to get back to Sandy and then get my head down somewhere.'

'Yes, that's all for now. You've been very helpful, sir. If I want to speak to you again, what's the best number to find you on?' Martin gave the inspector his mobile number and turned away towards the hospital entrance. The DI watched him go. *He knows more than he's saying. I'll get Rachel to talk to him, she's good at winkling information out.*

Turning back to where his car was parked, Peter didn't notice the man standing smoking a few cars away. If he had, he would surely have found the man's body language suspicious and made an attempt to approach him. As it was, he got into his car and sped off to the station unaware of the interest shown in him by the stranger.

Chapter Four

The SIS (Serious Incident Squad) office was empty when Peter arrived. He busied himself adding information to the incident board. *Robert Munroe, Munroe Construction and Development* and *Stella Peterson,* he wrote and turned to see Rachel coming through the door with five takeaway coffees. She placed the cardboard tray on her desk and unwound the scarf from around her neck, hanging it and her coat up. 'Mornin', sir,' she said brightly. 'A bit chilly out for August. The great British weather, eh? Coffee? The others are on their way up.'

'Great Rachel. We need to crack on with this. Re-interview Mike Travis and Paul Collins and get Yaz in. She's hiding something I'm sure.'

Kevin, Saroj and Maggie came in chatting and laughing. 'Morning, sir,' they all said together. 'Thanks for the coffee Rachel,' said Saroj, gratefully sipping the hot brew as she took her seat.

The DI called for their attention. 'Thanks for the early start everyone. I've been at the hospital and there's no change in Miss Parks' condition I'm afraid, so, until she regains consciousness we revisit our suspects, there's more information than they've divulged so far. I met the brother, Martin, at the hospital. He seems to have a strong alibi but it'll need checking. Kevin, can you do that?' Kevin nodded and made a note of Stella Peterson's details from the board.

'Rachel, will you interview Martin Parks here at the station, informally of course, but I want him a bit nervous. I think he knows more than he's letting on about his connection with Robert Munroe.' The DI looked thoughtful, tapping his teeth with his pen. 'But before you do that, have a chat with Munroe himself. Miss Parks was his contact with Vision Architects and we need to know what their relationship was.'

'Kevin, bring Paul Collins in and go through his movements on Friday again. And chase up the DNA results on that sandwich.'

'Yes, sir. And we found Miss Parks' laptop, it was in a bin on the seafront.'

'That's good news Kevin. Any sign of her phone?' Kevin shook his head. 'Still looking, sir.'

Maggie, check out the laptop will you. You know the drill, emails, contacts and so on. Anything concerning Robert Munroe in particular.'

'Saroj, you're with me. We'll bring Yaz in and put a bit of pressure on. She's got no alibi and her reaction to Miss Parks' attack was a bit off.'

The DI nodded briefly at his team and checked his watch. 'It's eight o'clock now. We'll meet back here at one.'

The team dispersed, Saroj hanging back to wait for the DI. 'You got a favourite, sir?' She said looking over at the whiteboard.

'Based on what we know so far, Yaz has to be a suspect. No alibi, and she's certainly strong enough, working with all that metal, and she has access to tools.' The DI joined Saroj, pointing to the names on the board. 'Either Mike Travis or Paul Collins could have done it, they were in and out of the pub and had time to incapacitate Sandra and come back later to work on her.' He tapped the board with his pen. 'But it's motive. Who had enough of a grudge to do that to her?'

'What about the old boyfriend, sir? The one from Manchester.' She flipped through her notepad, 'Mark Askin'.

'Good point, Saroj. He needs eliminating. Find out where he is now will you. Ask Manchester police to track him down. Right, let's go and get Yaz.'

Martin Parks' mobile had gone to his messaging service twice, so Rachel tried the hospital. Sure enough, the ward sister said that

Martin was at his sister's bedside. Deciding not to leave a message, Rachel set off for the hospital. It was a busy morning, with traffic around Truro particularly dense at this time of day. 'Bloody commuters,' she said out loud, 'and why would holidaymakers want to be on the road at 8.30 in the morning?' Rachel honked at a camper van whose driver was crawling along whilst consulting a map, indicating that he should pull into a layby. Thankfully he did, looking sheepish. 'Never heard of SATNAV!' she shouted.

The traffic eased a bit and Rachel soon pulled into the hospital car park. *Peter thinks Martin's not telling us everything,* she mused. *He is in regular contact with his sister by all accounts and he was involved in setting up the deal about the renovation project, with. . .* ' She flicked through her notes, *Robert Munroe.* Having noted the property developer's phone number earlier, she decided to chance catching him now before seeing Martin.

The mobile rang out and was eventually answered by a man with a pronounced Scottish accent. 'Munroe.'

'Mr Munroe, this is DS Rachel Morris of Devon and Cornwall Police Serious Incident Squad.'

'That's a bit of a mouthful. How can I help you DS Morris?'

'I understand you have a contract with Vision Architects to renovate an old building in Penthavern.'

'Not exactly, detective, the contract hasn't been signed yet. I'm meeting with the team tomorrow to finalise the deal. We're all very excited.'

'Were you aware that your main contact with the team, Sandra Parks, is in hospital after being attacked on Friday night?'

'Yes, well I didn't realise she had been attacked, but Mike Travis did ring to say Sandra wouldn't be at the meeting as she was in hospital. It's a great pity because she has tremendous vision, if you'll pardon the pun, and was to be pivotal to the whole project.'

The past tense was not lost on Rachel. 'I do want to speak to you further Mr Munroe. If you could tell me where you are staying, I could call later this morning or early afternoon if it's convenient.'

'I'm taking my family out for lunch, detective, so no, it's not convenient.' His voice was less friendly now, Rachel noticed.

'I will need to speak to you, sir. Could you call in at Truro police station after your lunch?'

Robert Munroe sighed dramatically. 'If you insist, Detective Morris, I could be there around three. But I really can't see what this has got to do with me.'

'We're interviewing everyone who had a connection to Miss Parks, sir. I'll look forward to seeing you at three then.'

Rachel hung up and went off to find Martin Parks.

Saroj stole a glance at DI Sanders as he weaved his way through the morning traffic. She'd heard a lot about him at Police Training College. He was destined for high office by all accounts, but had a bit of a breakdown a few years ago. The word was that he had started drinking after his wife left him and became unreliable, leading to at least one incident where he let a suspect slip through his fingers allowing him free to kill again. Had a couple of other run-ins with the superintendent leading to a suspension, she'd heard, but managed to make his way back to DI eventually. It was such a cliché – police having domestic problems, she wondered if there were any happily married officers on the force.

She had no intention of marrying yet, despite her family's best efforts. Fancy, in this day and age, them expecting her to submit to an arranged marriage. Her parents had wanted her to be a doctor and, indeed, she did obtain a medical degree even though she knew it was not for her. It was during a rotation in forensic psychiatry that she became fascinated by police methods and decided to apply to Police College. Needless to say, her parents were very angry and it was then that they found a *suitable* husband for her and put pressure on her to accept him. Saroj remembered how her parents, brother and sisters, and even distant aunties, had pestered her, saying that her mother was ill and would probably die from the shame. It was unbelievable that they would go to such lengths, but Saroj remained firm, resulting in an estrangement, which was only now softening to the point where she could see her mother occasionally for coffee or a meal, always away from the family home, of course.

The DI slowed and pulled up outside Yaz's studio and Saroj brought herself back into the present.

Martin clasped his sister's hand. 'Oh sis, this should never have happened to you of all people,' he sobbed. 'I can't imagine who would do this, and why. It's not as if you mix with gangsters or anything, especially not here in Cornwall. Manchester maybe, but not a sleepy town in the West Country.' He hung his head as the tears rolled down his cheeks. Hearing a sound at the door, he quickly collected himself. Turning he saw an official looking woman, not his mother as he expected. Wiping his eyes he said, 'Hi, have you come to see Sandy?'

Rachel pulled out her warrant card. 'DS Morris, sir. Of course I would like to know how Miss Parks is getting on, but I would also like a word with you.'

'No change in Sandy's condition and I can't think why the police want to talk to me again, I've nothing to add, Detective Morris.'

'This is how we work, sir, methodically going over statements until we eliminate people from our enquiries. So I will have to ask you to come to the station with me so that we can get your statement formally.'

'It's ridiculous. I was in Manchester with my girlfriend on Friday night. I told you that, you can check with her.'

'We have checked with her, sir, and she supports your alibi.'

'Well then, what can I possibly have to contribute to your enquiries?'

'We won't take up too much of your time, sir. I'll wait until you've finished your visit with your sister and take you to the station myself.'

Martin sighed exasperatedly. 'Then please wait outside for me. This is private.'

The rock music was playing at full volume as DI Sanders and DS Kapoor entered the hangar-like space that was Yaz's studio. The artist was on top of the ladder, wearing a face shield and using a welding torch, singing at the top of her voice. There was no way to be heard above the din, so DI Kapoor moved over to the CD player and switched it off. The sudden silence stopped Yaz immediately. She turned, cutting off her equipment and lifting the visor from her head gear. 'What the. . ?' She shouted, before realising who the visitors were. 'Inspector,' she said, 'how long have you been there?'

'Just arrived Miss, er Yaz,' the DI replied turning to Saroj. 'And this is DS Kapoor. We need you to come down to the station to make a statement so, if you could leave what you are doing, we'll take you there.'

'What? Now? I had that other detective here just half an hour ago. I'm cooperating with your enquiries – gave a DNA sample, told you where I was on Friday night. I've nothing else to add.'

'Yes, now Miss.' The DI nodded and indicated towards the door. 'So if you could come down from there and jettison your equipment, we'll be off.'

'This is very inconvenient, Inspector, I'm at a crucial point here.' Seeing that there was no acknowledgement from the DI, Yaz shook her head and started down the ladder. '*Very* inconvenient. I was in the zone there, Inspector, if you have any idea what that is.'

'We shouldn't keep you long, Miss. Just a few things to clear up.'

Martin looked around the dismal interview room. The walls were a shade of green that could only exist in a police station, he thought. A sort of pea soup colour with streaks of brown here and there, the origin of which Martin didn't want to dwell on. And the lingering smell of stale urine and sweat, mixed with a musky perfume, added to the discomfort he felt. But it wasn't just the ambience of the room that set him on edge. Martin was scared. He'd had a sinking feeling ever since he saw his sister in the hospital, lying there all battered and bruised. If he was right, and he suspected he was, he was going to deal with it himself, not leave it to the cops to bungle it. He cleared his throat as DS Morris entered the room. 'How long do I have to stay in this shit hole?' he said with as much assertiveness as he could manage.

The DS smiled and, switching on the recording machine, said, 'It

41

is 10.30 am on Sunday 9th August. Present are DS Morris, DS Sharp. Could you state your name for the tape, sir.'

Martin sighed. 'Is all this necessary?'

Rachel nodded. 'For the tape, sir, if you don't mind.'

'I'm Martin Parks.'

'Thank you, sir. Now could you tell us where you were between 6pm and 6am on Friday the 7th to Saturday 8th August.'

'I've been through all this before. I was with my girlfriend in Manchester. That's 400 miles away from here if you are unsure, detective. We had drinks with friends, then a meal out, and finished up at my flat for a nightcap and bed. Is that enough, or would you like details of what we got up to in bed?'

Changing tack suddenly, Rachel said, 'And how well do you know Robert Munroe?'

'Robert? What's he got to do with anything?' Getting no reply, Martin continued. 'I know Robert slightly. He's a business colleague.'

'Could you tell us the nature of that business, Mr Parks?'

'Yes, if I must. He's a property developer and I'm a building contractor. As you might suspect, our paths cross occasionally when he needs work doing on a property he has acquired.'

'Do you meet socially?' Rachel noticed that Martin was becoming tense. He had beads of sweat on his upper lip.

Martin shifted slightly in his seat. 'On the odd occasion, yes. Most business of that sort is conducted over drinks or a meal. Not that I'd expect you to understand how the business world works, detective.'

The sarcasm wasn't lost on Rachel and she knew that Martin was becoming rattled. She smiled and looked at her notes for a few seconds, which seemed like a long time to Martin.

'When did you last see your sister?'

Martin shook his head. The rapid change of tack was unsettling him, just as was intended. 'Erm. . . I haven't seen her for a while. A couple of months or so.'

'Have you had any contact with her in the last couple of weeks?'

'Er. . . yeh,' Martin stammered. 'We spoke recently. Always do, you know, we're close. She told me that Munroe's property is probably a guildhall. She was very excited about it.'

42

'And did you discuss your friend, sorry, colleague, Mr Munroe on any of these occasions?'

'What if we did? It isn't a crime is it?' Martin realised he was speaking more loudly and moderated his tone. 'Robert had bought a derelict building down here somewhere and was looking for a firm of architects to draw up some plans for him, get it through local planning regulations and so on. I recommended Sandy's firm and put them it touch. That's all.' Martin looked from one DS to the other. 'You can ask any of them; Mike, Paul or Polly, they can fill you in on any arrangements they might have had.'

'How much was your sister involved in the 'arrangements'?'

'No more than the others, I think. But I don't know. She might have been. . . well was, the initial contact, but it's Mike's practice, so I guess he took the lead. You'd have to ask him.'

'Are you aware of any private meetings between your sister and Mr Munroe?'

'No,' Martin said, a little too quickly. 'I am not my sister's keeper though, detective.' Martin was becoming increasingly uncomfortable. 'Look, can I go now? I'm due back in Manchester today and want to call on Sandy before I go.'

Rachel nodded. 'We may want to speak to you again, sir.' She consulted her notes. 'Is this the number we can reach you on?' showing Martin the mobile number she had for him.

'Yes, but if I'm on site I often switch off. Too noisy to hear properly.'

'We'll leave a message, sir. Interview terminating. . .'

In the car, sat behind the two detectives, Yaz had been quietly thinking as they drove to the police station. On that Friday evening, she realised that she had left the remains of her sandwich in Sandy's flat as soon as she got back to the studio, but saw no reason to go back for it, except that Sandy would do her nut at having a sandwich containing gluten in her kitchen. She decided she would apologise later. Sandy would give her a lecture on cross contamination, but would forgive her eventually. Now her main worry was that she had lied to the police about being in Sandy's flat and, if they could connect her with the sandwich, she was in trouble.

Now, sitting at the metal table in the interview room, Yaz was becoming increasingly nervous. The two detectives had left her there an hour ago and she could feel the perspiration prickling on her scalp, even though the room was cool. She sipped water from the bottle a constable had brought her as she waited impatiently, her right leg jiggling constantly. *I suppose this waiting is supposed to set people on edge,* she thought, *and it's bloody well working.*

DI Sanders was preparing to conduct the interview, *she's had enough time to get nervous now,* he thought, when his phone rang. He answered with a brief 'Sanders,' listened intently, then said, 'Well, that's interesting. We're just about to interview her now so that information is very timely. Anything else? Fingerprints?' He listened for a few seconds. 'Wiped clean, eh? Sounds like a professional job or someone who's watched a lot of CSI. Thanks Kevin.'

The DI turned to Saroj. 'The DNA analysis on that sandwich matches that taken from Yaz.'

'Making her our prime suspect, sir?'

'Well, she has no alibi and this puts her at the scene, so she has some explaining to do at the very least.'

Suddenly the detectives entered the room and sat opposite Yaz. The woman, Indian, Yaz thought, spread out some papers from a file whist the one in charge, Inspector Sanders, fiddled with the recording equipment. Neither of them looked at her.

'Interview commencing 11.30am, Sunday August 9th. Present are Detective Inspector Sanders, Detective Sergeant Kapoor and Miss Andrea Reynolds, also known as Yaz.

Drumming up all her reserves of courage, Yaz said, 'Why am I here? I've told you everything I know.'

The DI nodded and looked straight at her, his ice blue eyes piercing hers. 'So you say Miss. . .'

'Call me Yaz. I haven't been Andrea Reynolds for years. Andrea isn't very rock and roll, if you know what I mean.'

'You say you've told us everything, Yaz, but you see, I think you've been lying to us.' He checked the file. 'In your statement you told us that you hadn't been to Miss Parks' flat on Friday7th August.' The DI raised his head and looked at Yaz, his face a blank. 'Are you still saying that, or would you like to tell us the truth now?'

Yaz visibly crumpled, her head dropping into her hands on the table. 'I was there,' she whispered.'

'A little louder for the tape, Miss.'

'I was there! But I didn't do anything to Sandy. She wasn't even in.' Tears rolled down her cheeks.

'Right, Miss. Let's start from the beginning, shall we? And the truth this time.'

Yaz told the detectives how, after she had bought her sandwich at the local shop, she thought she'd call on Sandy as she hadn't seen her in a while, being so caught up in her sculpture. 'She wasn't in though, but I have a key – for emergencies – and so I thought I'd wait. I got hungry and started to eat my sandwich, but then realised that she might be still at work or something. I couldn't ring her because I'd left my mobile at the studio and I thought it was silly to hang about on the off-chance, so I left.' She looked frantically at the two detectives. 'That's the honest truth.'

'What time did you leave?'

'It must have been six-ish.'

'Did you see anyone else as you left?'

'No, I was rushing then, eager to get back to the Angel, you know? No wait, I almost bumped into someone at the corner of the road. He was coming around one way and me the other. We practically collided, but he jumped back and hurried off. No apology or anything.'

'Could you describe this man?'

'Stocky, not very tall, dark clothing. Strange, come to think of it, all bundled up on such a warm night, he was wearing a hat, too, I'm sure.'

'Would you recognise this man if you saw him again?'

'No, don't think so. I only caught a glimpse of his face.'

'What did you do next?'

'I went back to my studio, stayed there all night. I have a sofa that I sleep on when I'm too tired to go home. And I was exhausted – working on the Angel non-stop.'

'Can anyone vouch for you Miss?'

'You mean did I see anyone? No, just me all night.'

*   *   *

45

'You not buying it, sir?' Saroj said, as they watched the uniformed constable lead Yaz away.

'She's jumpy as a kitten and she lied to us. Still not telling us everything, I'm sure. No alibi either, and she's certainly strong enough – all that working with metal. But as for motive? Let's get a warrant and search her studio and home, see what that throws up.'

At one o'clock the team met up in the squad room all eager to hear the result of interviews and aware that a suspect was in custody. They were a disciplined group though, and knew that the DI liked to lay things out his way and not have questions thrown at him. So they waited whilst the inspector made a few notes on the incident board then turned towards the team.

'Okay, we have now arrested Miss Reynolds, aka Yaz, and she's in the cells at the moment. Saroj has obtained a search warrant and will be conducting a search of Miss Reynold's studio and home after this briefing. We are looking for any weapons which may have been used in the attack and anything that may point to a motive for this vicious act. We'll confiscate her laptop and phone too, see what they can tell us.'

'Maggie, anything from Miss Parks' laptop?'

'Just the usual work type emails sir. Contact with Robert Munroe was all about the Penthavern project. All very business-like, arranging meetings and so on. Then there were several tos and fros between Polly Thomas and Sandra Parks. Sandra had asked Polly to check out the possibility of the property at Penthavern being an *ancient structure*. Polly replied later attaching a copy of an old map. Sandra seemed very excited by it, telling Polly not to say anything to anyone. There were several contacts with the other team members about bidding for other projects. Nothing personal. She may have used her phone for private emails, lots of people do.'

'Thanks, Maggie. Get them printed off.' Maggie waved the already copied documents in the air. Peter nodded. 'Leave them on my desk, I'll look at them later.'

The DI paused examining the board, pointing to names in turn. 'Other persons of interest. Martin Parks is keeping something back. He was in regular contact with his sister and he introduced her to this man – he pointed again – Robert Munroe. I believe that both

46

these men have more to tell us.' How did we get on with the Vision team members? Maggie, Kevin?

Kevin spoke up. 'Mike Travis admitted that he called at Miss Parks' flat when he left the pub at 9.30 but got no reply. He said he called her mobile and heard it ringing in the flat. He says she often goes out without her phone, something he's had words with her about before, he says. Anyway, getting no response he went home. He claims he called at a local shop for headache tablets. We checked this out and the shopkeeper did remember him dropping in at about ten o'clock. He's a regular customer so the shopkeeper was quite certain.'

Maggie consulted her notes. 'I interviewed Polly Thomas, sir. She and Paul Collins left the pub together around ten-thirty. Went back to her place and stayed together all night. She did tell me about the email from Sandra Parks asking her to look into the history of the old property that Robert Munroe had bought. Her searches revealed that the building might have been a guildhall dating back to the 1500s. She confirmed that Sandra was very excited about it but didn't really understand why.'

'Know anything about guildhalls anyone?' The team shook their heads in unison. 'Find out what was so exciting about it, will you, Maggie. And Rachel, speak to Robert Munroe again, see if he knows anything about this.'

'I'm seeing him later today, sir. He's coming to the station around three.'

The DI nodded and looked at Kevin. 'What about Paul Collins?'

'I interviewed him, sir. He confirms Polly Thomas's version of events after they left the pub. He says he arrived late because he went round to a mate's house to borrow some cash. His credit's maxed out apparently. He's relying on this contract with Munroe to put some more coffers in the bank. I have spoken to the friend and he confirms that he lent Paul fifty quid, and it's the last time he says. Paul is hopeless with money, gambles a bit – online stuff, poker mostly.'

The DI nodded. 'Good work everyone. Eliminations then.' He turned to the whiteboard again. 'I think we can cross off the Manchester boyfriend. Manchester police have interviewed him for us. Mark Askin works for an estate agent now and is engaged to be married. He admits being a bit obsessed with Sandra Parks for a while. He felt she threw him over because she got a first at Uni and he had to do a resit and finished up with a third. He was angry and embarrassed, he says, and followed her around to make her feel some of what he was feeling. He's happier now, having a good job and a girlfriend. The engagement checks out and his employers rate him highly. So I'm confident he needn't feature in this enquiry.

'Paul Collins and Polly Thomas give each other an alibi, so unless they're in it together, which I doubt, they can be cleared too.

'I don't believe that Mike Travis was our assailant, but he knows something, so we'll keep an eye on him and interview him again.

'Maggie, get on to that guildhall stuff as soon as. This feels important. Find out who else knew – Kevin, you're with Maggie on this, okay?

'Right, I'll be at the hospital if anyone needs me. It feels like we're getting somewhere so let's keep the energy up.'

The team dispersed, chatting as they went out. Rachel hung back. 'You fancy some lunch, Peter?'

'Well, just a quick one. Thanks Rachel, be good to talk it through.'

Rachel was thinking that they could have a pleasant lunch without talking about work, but she'd take what she could get. Sometimes she thought that Peter must be aware of her feelings towards him, and at other times she was sure he was oblivious. Rachel had been in love with her DI almost from the moment she met him. His brooding good looks attracted her and she had hoped that he might feel the same, but he always treated her as just another member of the team – a valued member who he shared his thoughts with – but a team member and nothing more. At times she was tempted to find another position, promotion perhaps, but there was something about this team, the energy it generated, that kept her here. She sighed and picked up her bag.

Chapter Five

Rachel and Saroj faced Robert Munroe across the interview room table. He looked relaxed and immaculate in a grey linen suit and blue shirt, open at the neck. His shoes alone would have cost Rachel a week's wages. He was a tall man, ruggedly handsome, with fair hair worn a little long but beautifully cut. His manner was of a person very much in charge of his emotions and used to being in control. *I'll have to shake him up a bit, show him who's in charge here*, Rachel thought.

After recording the introductions, Rachel said, 'What do you know about this guildhall?'

She thought she recognised a glimmer of shock in Munroe's eyes, but it was fleeting and he regained his composure rapidly. 'A *guildhall* you say? I am aware of guildhalls generally. Very rare buildings, Inspector, just one or two have survived in the country as far as know.'

'And the guildhall you own in Penthavern?'

This time he looked a little more rattled. 'I own? Ha! I don't know where you are getting your information, Inspector, but I own no such property, not in Penthavern or anywhere else.'

'Tell me about your relationship with Sandra Parks.'

Munroe shook his head, bemused by the change of direction. 'I. . . I had no *relationship* with Miss Parks, at least not in the sense that you're implying.'

Rachel studied the file in front of her, not meeting Munroe's quizzical gaze and allowing a silence to develop.

'Look, Sergeant Morris. . . '

'Detective Sergeant Morris,' Rachel corrected him.

Munroe pulled himself together and spoke quietly. 'Look, Detective Sergeant Morris, I knew this young lady only slightly. I'm sorry she's. . . unwell, but I had nothing to do with that. Now if that's all?'

'Tell me about the guildhall, sir.'

'What bloody guildhall? You're making a fool of yourself detective. Making ridiculous accusations and fishing for information. If I ran my business like this I'd be bankrupt in no time.' He looked from one detective to the other. 'So, if that's all, I'll be on my way.' Robert made to stand.

'Sit down, sir,' said Rachel, fixing him with a steady stare. 'I have one or two more questions for you.'

'Well you can ask them with my solicitor present. I'm not answering any more of your questions without taking legal advice.'

'That's your right, sir. We'll leave you to make that call.' Rachel signed off from the recorder and she and Saroj left the room, leaving Robert Munroe red-faced and fuming.

Sandra was aware that the nocturnal DI was back in the room. His aftershave was quite distinct and his presence somehow moved the air about in a different way to her mum or dad.

Strange how you get to use senses you weren't aware of when you're like this. I wonder what he'll tell me today? I've been thinking hard about things and I still can't remember. He's talking about my friends and family and ruling them out one by one, he says. He even brought up Mark Askin of all people. He was a complete nuisance for a time but I haven't thought about him in years. I'm sure he's ruled out the team, too, but he hasn't said so outright.

'Afternoon Sandra,' the DI said as he took a seat by her bedside. 'I bet you didn't expect me so early, but I want to run something by you.' The papers shuffled before he spoke again. 'What do you know about a guildhall?'

Sandra's pulse suddenly quickened and the monitor set off a loud alarm. A nurse hurried into the room and inspected the equipment before taking out a stethoscope and listening to Sandra's heartbeat. 'You'll have to leave, Inspector. I want the doctor to check her over.'

No, don't go. It means something, a guildhall. Just stay and tell me more.

'Right you are, Sister. I'll come back later. Please let me know if there's any change in her condition.' Turning to Sandra he said, 'Keep fighting, I'll be back.'

The search of Yaz's studio revealed a number of tools which could have been responsible for Sandra's injuries. After a thorough inspection of the neat rows of hammers, chisels, saws and assorted mallets, the search team took away a number of items for further examination by the forensic team.

Moving to the artist's flat in Bar Road, Rachel was taken aback by the total mess of the place in contrast with the tidiness of the studio. In the main room discarded clothes were draped over chairs and a pile of shoes littered one corner. There was a small desk covered in papers and unopened letters, some of them unpaid bills by the look of the envelopes. If the living room was a mess, then the kitchen was a health hazard. It seemed that every piece of crockery had been used and piled in the sink, mould growing on the scraps of food left on plates. Cupboards were left open, their shelves revealing opened packs of cereal the spillage from which could be seen on the worktop below. Rachel dreaded opening the fridge but did so and found some hard scraps of cheese and curled-up ham alongside an open margarine tub.

When this lady said she was messy, she wasn't kidding, Rachel thought as she moved towards the bathroom. This room, however, was relatively clean but had none of the usual lotions and potions prevalent in most young women's bathrooms. A large bar of soap and a tube of toothpaste seemed to be the limit of cosmetics, and the cabinet over the sink was completely empty. *Unusual not to have headache tablets at least,* thought Rachel. Moving back to the living room, Rachel started a search of the paperwork on the desk. Nothing of interest, apart from evidence of debt building up through unpaid accounts. The small drawer in the front of the desk was more fruitful. A number of letters carefully tied with ribbon were the only contents but were very interesting indeed. Finishing up with a desultory rummage through the rest of the flat, Rachel called it a day and, locking the door carefully behind her, set off back to the station.

Half way back Rachel received a phone call. 'Rachel, it's Peter. We've got a body washed up on Castle Beach in Falmouth. Meet me there.'

'Sir,' said Rachel. Turning the car around, she turned on the 'blues and twos' as she headed back the way she had come. When she arrived, the ambulance was just pulling up and a young constable was directing onlookers to keep away from the slip. Rachel grabbed a pair of wellingtons from her boot and, showing her warrant card to the constable, ducked under the police cordon and down the slip to the rocky beach.

The tide was well out and Rachel could see the body of a woman in a swimsuit half hidden by the kelp on the rocks. Another constable was standing by the body. He shook his head slightly as Rachel approached. She nodded and moved over the slippery rocks to get a closer look. A young woman, she said to herself, then moving round to the other side realised that she knew who it was. Polly's blonde hair spilled over the seaweed giving the impression of a mermaid sleeping on the rocky shore. Rachel knew better than to disturb the scene but could see, from her vantage point, a large bruise on Polly's pale face. Rachel heard footsteps crunching over the pebbles on the beach and turned to see DI Sanders making his way over.

'Sir,' she said, by way of greeting.

'What do we have, Rachel?'

'I think it's Polly Thomas, sir. Seems to have taken a blow to the head.'

The DI moved around the body, being careful not to disturb the locus. 'Doc's on his way, but I think we can dispense with the ambulance.' Bending to examine Polly's face he could see her eyes open and fixed, drops of seawater clinging to her lashes. 'Could have been accidental. Out for a swim and got caught in a strong current or rip.' Looking up he saw the familiar gait of Doctor Samuels walking unsteadily across the rocks. 'Afternoon, Ben,' said the DI.

The doctor nodded gravely. 'What do we have, detectives?'

Rachel and Peter moved aside to let Ben through. He knelt gingerly by the body, gently moving her hair from her face. 'She's very cold, but that's to be expected. Flexing her arms he said, 'Rigour mortis has all but gone so I'd say she's been dead for at least twenty-four hours. I'll be able to tell you more when I've done the PM.'

'So that puts time of death around three pm yesterday.' Helping the doctor to his feet, Peter asked, 'What time can we expect the PM?'

'Shall we say 9.30 tomorrow?' Receiving a nod from the two detectives, Doctor Samuels brushed himself down and started back up the beach.

Chapter Six

Peter and Rachel arrived back at the station to find the squad room empty. Rachel added today's sad information to the incident board and turned to see Peter slumped in a seat, his head in his hands. Looking up he shook his head. 'Poor girl. Do we have any information about next of kin?'

'Not at the moment, sir. Probably Paul Collins or Mike Travis will know something.'

'Okay. Put a call out to the others and tell them to get back here. You and I will go and see Paul Collins.' Peter looked grimly at Rachel. 'It could have been an accident, of course, but that would be a big coincidence given the circumstances, and you know how I feel about coincidences.'

'Yes sir. Oh! Almost forgot. I found some interesting letters at Yaz's flat. It seems she had romantic feelings for Sandra Parks which were not reciprocated. The letters clearly show that Sandra wanted nothing more to do with Yaz if she continued to pursue her. It looks like she had been making a bit of a nuisance of herself.'

'Mmm. Gives motive for Yaz to have attacked Sandra. However, she couldn't have had anything to do with Polly's death as she was in custody at the time.' Peter picked up his jacket. 'Let's see Paul Collins, then we can take the new findings up with Yaz when we get back.'

* * *

Paul Collins was shocked when the DI broke the news about Polly's death. He told them that Polly was planning a swim at around 3pm yesterday. He insisted that she was a good swimmer and would never put herself in danger. He added that he had been at his mate's house all Sunday afternoon watching videos and drinking. 'Had a bit too much actually and crashed at his place. I should have been meeting Polly but couldn't reach her and I was too drunk to care much.' Paul sat heavily on his sofa, head in hands. 'I tried again today but her phone was off, or so I thought, and I was getting angry with her. Oh God! Me being angry when she was. . . ' He sobbed loudly.

'Is there anyone who can stay with you, sir?' The DI asked kindly.

Paul pulled himself together. 'No, I'll be alright. Have you told her dad?'

'Not yet, do you have an address for him? And it's just her dad is it?'

Paul rummaged through a magazine rack by his sofa and brought out a battered address book. 'This is Polly's,' he said, waving the book. 'Her mum died when she was twelve, it's just been her and her dad since. He'll be devastated.'

Arriving back at the station, Peter saw a man waiting. He looked agitated and kept glancing around as if looking for help. The desk sergeant beckoned the DI over. Nodding towards the waiting man, he said, 'He's here about that young woman we have in custody sir. Wants to see whoever's in charge.' Peter glanced over towards the man who caught his eye, and raised his eyebrows. He was small and thin with sparse hair combed over a balding patch. His eyes moved around wildly, reminding Peter of a cornered rat. His clothes were smart, but closer inspection showed a frayed collar and a stain on his tie. He smiled tentatively at Peter.

Peter nodded in return, then turning back to the sergeant he said, 'Put him in an interview room and I'll see him after I've spoken to the team.'

Peter found the team subdued after hearing of the death of Polly

Thomas. He took up a position at the front of the room and quietly said, 'Rachel's giving Mr Thomas the news now, and then she'll take him to the morgue to formally identify the body.' He looked at the serious faces in the room. 'We don't know whether this was a tragic accident or murder at the moment. She was confident in the water, according to Paul Collins, but these things do happen, so we'll keep an open mind until we have the results of the PM.'

'Right now I want to know where everyone connected with the Sandra Parks' case was in the twenty-four hours up to three o'clock today. If this wasn't accidental, I'll put odds on it being something to do with Miss Parks' attack.' Peter gave out the assignments and then went to see what the man waiting downstairs had to say about Yaz.

As Peter entered the interview room, the man jumped from his chair. 'Are you in charge here?' he demanded. His voice was cultured and sharp, a man used to giving orders.

'Sit down please, sir. I'm Detective Inspector Sanders and I've been told you have something to tell us about Miss Reynolds.'

'Miss. . . you mean Yaz? Yes, well rather I have some questions I'd like answered.'

The DI sat down opposite the man. 'First off, sir, could you tell me your name.'

The man took a deep breath. 'Sorry, I'm going about this all wrong, only I've been so worried. I'm Harry Spinetti, a friend of Yaz's. She uses the barn next to the theatre as a studio. I'm the theatre manager. We let her have the space rent free and, in return, she builds the scenery for some of our productions. She's very talented.'

The DI made a few notes and allowed the silence to develop. Harry spoke again. 'I believe she's here, at the police station. One of our neighbours told me they saw her being led away by the police yesterday and she hasn't returned. I've been round to her flat but she's not there either.'

'And what is your relationship with Yaz, Mr Spinetti?'

Harry pulled his shoulders back and raised his voice a little.

'Professional, Inspector.' He then conceded, 'We're friends as well, I suppose. To be honest, I think she's amazing. I like to watch her when she's working, she's so strong and confident, it takes my breath away.'

'She allows you to watch her working, you say?' Peter thought this didn't ring true from what he knew about the artist.

'Oh no, Inspector, she doesn't know I'm there. She's very secretive, likes to work in private.' He smiled smugly. 'There's an old door at the back of the barn. Overgrown with brambles and nettles, so people wouldn't know it's there. At night, when she's working, I sneak in. She doesn't hear me because of that awful rock music and the hammering and such.' Seeing that the inspector looked surprised, he continued, 'It's not creepy, if that's what you're thinking. I'm not a stalker, I'm just fascinated by her talent, and a little bit in love with her too, if truth be known, but she's oblivious to that. We get on okay, but I have to live in hope on the romance front.'

'When was the last time you watched her, Mr Spinetti?'

'Well, that's just it, I went to the barn last night but she wasn't there. Very unusual that. And her things were disordered. She is generally what you might call untidy except when it comes to her equipment. She treats her tools with a lot of respect. Things were in the wrong places, you see. I notice these things.' He looked thoughtful for a moment, then continued. 'The last time I saw her was Friday night. I went round to the barn at about 9pm. She was working on her new piece – The Avenging Angel, I think she calls it. The music was blaring as usual and she was singing and welding, looking magnificent in her overalls and welding mask.'

The DI cut in. 'That would be Friday 7th, would it, sir?' Harry nodded. 'And how long were you *watching*?'

'Till about two in the morning. She finished then, tidied up and went to sleep on the sofa. I waited a few minutes then went over and covered her up with a blanket.'

'Right, sir. If you could just wait here, I'll be back to take a statement soon.'

* * *

57

Peter wandered into the squad room shaking his head. Rachel was busy updating the incident board. She was still sad after her meeting with Polly's dad and his subsequent tearful identification of his daughter's body. His world had been completely shattered. 'Since her mum died it's been just the two of us,' he sobbed. 'Now what will I do?' He had insisted that Polly could not have drowned by accident. 'Swims like a fish, she does. . . did.' He broke down again and Rachel had sought the assistance of a uniformed constable. 'Stay with him until he's ready to go home, and then get someone to take him,' she said. Then, turning to Mr Thomas. 'I have to go now, sir, but the constable will stay with you. Take as long as you like. I'll come to see you tomorrow when I may know more about how Polly died.'

Shaking herself out of her sad reverie, she turned to see the DI entering the room. 'Something troubling you, sir?' she asked.

'I feel like I need to take a shower, Rachel.' He sat heavily at one of the desks. 'That man is beyond creepy. His whole demeanour says psychopath or at least a major league stalker.'

'Who are you talking about, Peter?' asked Rachel, perplexed.

'We have a witness who can put Yaz in her studio for the greater part of the night on Friday. If you can believe this, he creeps into Yaz's studio through a door in the back and spies upon her all night. He is besotted with her, says she's *amazing* and *magnificent*, the only problem being she doesn't know he's there, and would surely be disturbed if she did know.'

Rachel blinked, an incredulous look on her face. 'That can't be legal, surely? We must be able to arrest him for breaking and entering, at least. Not to say being a complete arsehole.'

'He's the manager of the whole site where her studio is so, I guess, technically, he can have access, but not without her knowledge or permission.' Peter shrugged. 'We'd have to check that Yaz didn't give him carte blanch to invade her space any time he chose. However, the main point is, if he is to be believed, Yaz has an alibi for Friday night.'

'And do we believe him?'

'He seemed not to have a clue why she had been arrested, and that at least seemed genuine enough, so yes – I guess we do,' Peter

58

concluded. 'Have her brought into an interview room Rachel. We'll check this out and then I suppose we'll have to let her go.'

'He's been doing what!' a seriously pissed off Yaz exclaimed when the DI filled her in on her rescuer.

'The point at the moment is, do you want to make a complaint against Mr Spinetti?'

'Well, that would be a bit churlish seeing as how he's the one who can get me out of here.' Yaz examined her fingers. 'But, I'm telling you, Inspector, I had no idea that that creep had been watching me, and it really freaks me out.' She paused. 'He did approach me once, asking me out to dinner and drinks, but to be honest he repulsed me. I knew that he could stop me using the barn as a studio, so I was kind to him and didn't say, *why should I want to do that, you freak?* Which is what I felt like saying, believe me.'

'Well, based on his evidence, we are going to release you without charge. However, don't think about leaving the area, we may need to talk to you again. What you do about Mr Spinetti is your affair.' The DI stood and opened the door. 'You're free to go.'

'I'll be around for a while, but as soon as I've finished The Angel I'm giving up the studio. I'll have to stay in my flat until I can find somewhere else to go but, when I do, it'll be a long way away from Mr Spinetti.'

As Peter watched Yaz striding away, Harry Spinetti hard on her heels, he realised that he wouldn't like to be in Mr Spinetti's shoes if he tried anything on again with Yaz. 'I think we can be confident about that creep getting put in his place, Rachel.'

'I agree, sir. She's a strong woman all right, and she bats for the other side, so I think he's in for a rude awakening.'

'Couldn't happen to a nicer bloke,' Peter chuckled. 'But you realise we're back at square one now?'

'Want to go for a drink?'

'Yeah, perhaps a drink would help. Let's finish up here first then hit the pub.'

Rachel smiled happily. '*Maybe more than one,*' she said to herself.

After their third drink Rachel suggested food. 'I think it would be a good idea to get something solid inside me,' she said. Realising that what she said could be taken another way, she quickly added, 'Shall we try that new Indian down the road?'

Peter checked his watch. 'Good idea. I want to go back to the hospital later but I should eat first.'

That wasn't what Rachel wanted to hear. Oiled by alcohol, they had been getting along really well. After a brief discussion about the case, they had agreed to change the subject, and things took a more personal note. Rachel was sure she was getting through to him as they discussed each other's likes and dislikes, finding that they had a lot in common. Now he was all business again. *Back to the bloody hospital,* she thought, *I should book myself in, then I might get some attention.*

Immediately she regretted thinking this way. *That poor girl, at death's door. And Polly in the morgue. Perhaps when this case is over we can pick up where we left off.* Rachel smiled and followed Peter out, chatting about her favourite Indian food.

Ah, here's my favourite policeman. He smells different though, sweaty and hot. He's been working hard, I'll bet, trying to find who did this to me. Well detective, I think I know what the guildhall means. If I could tell you I would, but not right now, eh?

Peter approached the bed and took Sandra's hand. 'Hi Sandra, it's DI Sanders. I've got some sad news for you, I'm afraid.' He looked at the still figure in the bed, not knowing, but suspecting that she could hear him. 'Your work colleague Polly is dead, I'm afraid, drowned it seems.'

No! Polly? She can't have drowned, detective, she was a great swimmer, did triathlons and everything. Damn this. . . this. . . situation. If I could talk to you, I'd tell you that Polly was the other one who knew about the guildhall. There has to be a connection.

The DI carried on. 'We'll know more after the post mortem tomorrow, but everyone we speak to says Polly was a good swimmer and unlikely to have drowned accidentally.'

Good. Stay with that.

'As for your case,' Peter continued, 'we had a suspect but have had to let her go. Not enough evidence. But I'm not finished with Yaz yet.'

Yaz! No Inspector, you're barking up the wrong tree there. I'm getting some flashes of memory now, and it was definitely a man. Smelled manly, strong and rough too. He whistled and muttered under his breath, but I don't recall him speaking to me. I don't remember much at the moment, but it's coming back slowly, and painfully. And Polly – poor, poor Polly. I can't bear that she was mixed up in this because of me.

Peter looked up from his notebook and saw a tear rolling down Sandra's cheek. He took a tissue from the bedside table and gently wiped it away. 'You *can* hear me. I'm so sorry about Polly, Sandra. If someone did this to her I'll get him, I promise.' He squeezed her hand. 'You have my word on that.'

Peter noticed the doctor standing in the doorway. 'It's good that you're talking to her, not everyone gets it, even when I tell them that coma patients very often hear what's said to them.'

Peter turned and nodded. 'She seemed to be crying doctor. I gave her some bad news and. . .'

The doctor checked the instruments. 'It's not unusual to see tears. The eyes are still lubricated and will tear up from time to time. Nevertheless, I'll ask the nurses to check her more regularly. It could just be a sign that she's coming out of it.' Pointing to the monitor, he said, 'Everything looks fine here, though. Sorry about the bad news. Something to do with her attack?'

'Maybe,' said Peter. 'It's the way these cases go sometimes. One step forward and two back, so to speak.'

The doctor nodded. 'Well, I'll leave you to it. Good luck with finding the monster that did this.'

Peter sagged back into his chair. 'Well Sandra, it's back to the drawing board for me. Now, I need to lay this all out again.'

Back to his notebook, making lists, I expect, things and people to check out. I can't help you, Inspector, but I would put the guildhall at the centre. Not everyone is thrilled by old buildings, especially those which would have protected status. Robert Munroe would not have been happy about it for one. Only I'd planned to tell him after I told the team, so, unless he knew from another source, he was in the dark. Of course, Polly knew, but I told her not to say anything to Mike or Paul. I wanted to surprise them with it myself. It was a great find, a Fifteenth Century guildhall – rare as hen's teeth, and in Penthavern. English Heritage would have been as excited as I was. This was a find of national importance. The restoration would be the most wonderful thing, Inspector. It would mean that the work would be taken out of our hands, of course, but that's a small price to pay, and we'd get some publicity for finding it.

Sandra became aware that Peter had moved. 'I'll be off now, Sandra.' Peter closed his notebook and stood, placing the chair back by the window. 'I'll be back very soon.' He moved over to the bed. 'You're making progress, I'm sure of it, so keep fighting.'

Peter went back to the station, not expecting that anyone would be there at this time, so was surprised to see Rachel and Saroj deep in conversation. They both looked up as he entered. 'Evening, sir,' said Saroj. 'We're just going through the statements from Mike Travis and Paul Collins that Kevin and Maggie took.' She referred to the paperwork in front of her. 'Mike Travis was at his mother's place in Redruth for Sunday lunch. She confirms this, saying she was surprised to see him as he doesn't call very often.' Turning the page she continued. 'Paul Collins, as I think you know already, was at his mate's flat, and this was confirmed also.'

Rachel noticed that Peter was looking distracted. 'You okay, sir? she asked.

He scratched his head, ruffling his thick hair. 'Yes thanks, Rachel. I've been at the hospital – had to tell Miss Parks that Polly Thomas was dead.'

'Surely she isn't aware enough to understand?'

'I think she is, very much so. The doctor said he believes coma patients hear and understand a lot of the time, unless, of course, they are too badly brain damaged, and they don't know that about Sandra yet.'

He smiled at the two women. 'Anyway, why are you two still here?'

'Just taking a fresh look at the case sir, now that our prime suspect is off the hook.'

'Very commendable, but it's late and we've got the PM tomorrow at 9.30, so get off to your beds, I'll tidy up here.'

Saroj yawned. 'You're right, sir, feeling sleepy already. Goodnight.' Rachel waved and followed Saroj out, looking back over her shoulder to see Peter already engrossed in the statements.

Chapter Seven

Slumped behind his desk several hours later, Peter realised that he was too tired to put the pieces of this troubling jigsaw together. Looking at the clock, he realised it was well gone midnight. *Should get off home,* he thought, but was disturbed by the image of the tear rolling down Sandra Parks' cheek. *I'll call at the hospital on my way, make sure everything's alright.*

He left the building in darkness, relishing the fresh night air. Feeling a little more alive, he drove the few miles to the hospital. He felt, against everything that had happened to set them back, that there was a breakthrough coming. *Copper's intuition,* he thought, *never underestimate it.*

As he approached the ward, he noticed more activity than usual around Sandra's room. A doctor and nurse were in deep conversation in the corridor and the lights inside the room glowed brightly.

He approached the medics cautiously, showing his warrant card out of habit. 'Has something happened?' he enquired.

'Ah, hello Inspector,' said the doctor. 'Nurse Higgins and I were just discussing Miss Parks' condition.' He smiled briefly. 'Nothing to be alarmed about, or to get too excited about either, but we're getting signs of improved brain activity, which often precedes awakening in some patients. As I say, don't get your hopes too high at the moment, Inspector, there's still a long way to go.'

'Alright if I see her doctor?' Peter looked anxiously through the window at the still motionless figure.

'Of course, we're all finished now. Keep talking to her, Inspector, it helps a great deal at this stage.'

Sandra noticed the change in the air and the unmistakable smell of the detective. *Oh good, you're back. I'm remembering so much more, Inspector. It's so frustrating that I can't tell you what's going on in my mind. I keep thinking about money. It sounds strange, even to me, but I'll never forget my dad saying 'follow the money' whenever he suspected wrongdoing in his clients. 'It's a shady world, building, our Sandra' he told me. 'More criminals in business suits than overalls, and it's always about money.' So here's my thinking. Robert Munroe would be greatly put out, let alone well out of pocket, if it became known that he was sitting on a truly ancient building. The consents, schedules of work, not to mention archaeological surveys that English Heritage would require to be carried out, are seriously complicated and time consuming. And all the work is at the owner's expense too. He could write off the next two years, at least, and would probably never see the development he set out to achieve. But here's me rambling on and you can't know what I'm thinking. Just follow the money, Detective Inspector – follow the money.*

Peter had taken up his usual position by Sandra's bed. He took her hand. 'Hello Sandra, it's DI Sanders, but you probably know that by now. The doc says your brain is more active. I hope this means you're coming back to us, I just know you have a great deal to tell me. Sandra's pulse quickened slightly. Noticing this, Peter said, 'Is that you? Are you telling me you can hear me?' He looked at the monitor, her pulse again increased slightly. 'I'll take that as a yes then.' Peter was excited by this new development and thought about calling the doctor. Instead he squeezed Sandra's hand. 'I tell you what, you sleep on it tonight, and I'll come back tomorrow with some sensible questions, and we'll see if we can work something out.' Peter was beaming. 'You beauty!' he said laughing. 'I'll be off then, Sandra, but I'll be back.'

Peter was so excited that he didn't think he would sleep. However, he was also exhausted, and collapsed on his bed the moment he arrived home. *Just forty winks then*. He thought as he drifted off.

You never get used to it, the smell. Some police use 'Vick' under the nose, others chew gum, but it still gets through. The pathologists and morgue workers seem unaffected by it, but they are probably immune by now, or just see no point in complaining. Peter and Rachel donned their protective clothing and stood by the table on which Polly Thomas's body had been placed. It was something less than human now, with the chest cavity exposed and all the major organs removed. Everyone present still gave the corpse the respect it deserved, understanding that she was once a living, breathing, life-loving young woman.

The pathologist spoke. 'Death by drowning, certainly. Seawater in the lungs and stomach.'

'What about the bump on the head?' Peter asked.

'Almost definitely caused by the rocks on the shoreline. See here,' the pathologist pointed to the part of Polly's head that had been shaved, 'particles of grit and seashell deep inside the cut.' He smiled knowingly. 'This, however,' drawing Peter's attention to Polly's arms, 'is not accidental.'

Peter and Rachel bent forward to get a closer look. The pathologist continued. 'The bruising was caused by fingers gripping the forearms, like so,' and he demonstrated a grip from behind holding the upper arms very firmly. 'This young woman was held under the water, quite forcefully.'

'So it's murder then.' Peter looked at the pathologist who nodded confidently.

The squad had been in early and were busy writing up reports and collating information, a tiresome but essential part of police work. Peter and Rachel took up a position by the incident board. All eyes looked up expectantly, knowing where the two detectives had been this morning.

'We now have a murder enquiry,' said the DI. 'Perhaps not the one we have been expecting though.' He pointed to the picture of Polly Thomas. 'The pathologist has confirmed that she was drowned by someone holding her under the water.'

A short silence pervaded the room, seemingly out of respect for the dead young woman. 'Do you think the two cases are linked, sir?' Asked Maggie.

'Be a hell of a coincidence if they weren't. And I don't like coincidences.' Peter looked around the room. 'Apart from the obvious, that they both worked for Vision, we need to find anything else that links these two women.'

'The MO's are very different though, sir.' Kevin said what most of the team were thinking. 'With Miss Parks it seems like it was planned, he took his time, came prepared. But with Miss Thomas it's more opportunistic.'

'It could have been planned, Kevin, just a different setting.' A few heads nodded. 'Let's say he waited for her to set off swimming then took out a boat or canoe, followed her and attacked her when she was far out. This would give him time to escape before she was washed ashore.'

'I can see how that would happen,' said Rachel. 'It almost seems professional.'

'A hit man, you mean?' Peter said with interest.

'Well it's not impossible sir. Just think about it. All our main suspects have strong alibis, which is, in itself, unusual. One of them, or all of them, could have paid someone to murder the women.'

'A conspiracy? I can't see it myself, Rachel. Seems so cold and calculating,' Saroj commented.

'No, wait a minute, Saroj,' Kevin said. 'We have three main suspects, now that Yaz is out of the running, and they're all connected to Vision Architects in some way.'

'That's true, Kevin,' Saroj continued. 'But what about motive? Both women were well liked by their colleagues by all accounts, we haven't uncovered any feuds or jealousies, so why?'

'Have we ruled out the brother?' Maggie asked.

Peter answered. 'Not entirely, but he has an alibi for Sandra's attack, and he didn't even know Polly as far as I'm aware.' The DI was suddenly all business. 'Right, enough speculating. It's good to put theories forward and we'll bear them in mind, but it's solid police work that will get us our answers. So, Kevin and Saroj, I want you to go through these women's backgrounds and interests again, see if you can find anything that links them, apart from Vision.'

'Maggie, search HOLMES for any similar murders or murderous attacks.' This police data base gave up-to-date case-related information and could save many weeks of fact gathering. 'Also, Yaz gave us a description of a man she saw near Miss Parks' flat on the night of the attack, see if she can firm that up into a photofit image. Rachel, go and see Polly's dad again and give him the news. We'll see if he can throw any more light on why his daughter would have been murdered, now that it's been confirmed.'

'Let's meet back here at one o'clock. I'll be at the hospital.'

The DI hurried out.

'Spends more time at the hospital than in the squad room,' muttered Kevin. 'I don't know what he expects to get out of a comatose woman.'

Saroj raised her eyebrows and Maggie turned to her computer. Rachel didn't hear the comment or she would have given Kevin a mouthful. Instead she said, 'Okay, you all know what you're doing, let's get on with it.'

Chapter Eight

Peter took up his usual position at Sandra's bedside. He was just about to start a conversation when the constable came into the room. 'I don't want to be disturbed, Green,' the DI said sharply.

'Sorry, sir, but I think this may be important.' Peter nodded for him to carry on. 'Well, just now, sir, a man in a porter's uniform came along the corridor, someone I've not seen before. He was checking out Miss Parks' room and didn't see me at first. He clocked that you were in there and, turning to see me as well, scarpered, quick like, down the corridor. I didn't want to leave my post so thought I'd tell you.'

'Just now, you say?' Constable Green nodded. 'Well man, I think you could have given chase seeing as how I was here, don't you?'

The constable blushed. 'I suppose so, sir, didn't think.'

'Well go now, see if you can catch up with him. Go on!'

The young constable ran down the corridor, checking with the nurses if they had seen anyone hurrying away. A man had been spotted behaving strangely, not stopping when a ward sister asked him to fetch something from the stores for her. By the time Constable Green had reached the main entrance, the man was nowhere to be seen. Of course, he could have taken another route out, or still be in the building, it was hopeless in a place this size. On his way back to the ward, Green asked the sister for a description of the man who was acting strangely, it tallied with his recollection.

The constable reported back to Peter, who had calmed down a

little. 'I'm really sorry, sir, if I'd chased after him straight away I'm sure I would have caught him.'

'Don't worry about that now, Green. Get down to the station and get a photofit made of the man you saw. Ask for a replacement constable to come here while you're doing that. I'll stay here until then.' Peter saw the glum look on the constable's face. 'It's okay, Constable, happens to the best of us, especially when you've been on a duty like this for hours. When were you last relieved?'

'I've been on duty all night, sir.'

'Then you're entitled to make the odd mistake. When you've organised that replacement, go home and get your head down.' Peter made a mental note to have a word with the sergeant in charge when he got back. *You can't expect officers to work on top form if they're exhausted,* he thought. Now back to my experiment.

'Right Sandra, you'll have heard all that. Do you have some recollection that fits with a short and stocky man? Yaz saw someone that fits that description outside your flat the night you were attacked, and it could be the same man who was lurking around here just now, so think about it would you.

'Now, I'm going to start with some general questions to see if I can set a baseline, so, if you're ready. Is your name Sandra Parks?' Peter watched the monitor for any signs of change.

Well obviously it is, but I don't know how to raise my pulse rate just like that.

Seeing no change in Sandra's pulse, the DI continued: 'Do you have a brother Martin and parents Terry and Margaret?'

Poor mum and dad, and Martin, how must they be feeling?

The feelings that this question generated in Sandra did lead to a slight corresponding pulse increase. 'Now we're getting somewhere,' Peter said. Next question. 'Did you know the person who attacked you?' No response from the monitor. 'Okay, Do you know why you were attacked?'

I think I do, yes. It was something to do with the guildhall. Maybe someone didn't want it known. My dad always said 'follow the money.' Could be Robert Munroe perhaps?

The monitor flickered as her pulse increased again. 'So you might understand the motive. Well, let's go through them.'

'Revenge?' Sandra's pulse rate settled down.

'Love?' No change.

'Money?' A definite quickening.

'If I can trust this, Sandra, I might have that elusive motive, and it narrows the field considerably.'

'Sorry sir, I don't buy it.' Rachel was the first in the team to voice this opinion, but the others nodded along. 'So Sandra's pulse rate quickened. There could be a lot of reasons why that happened. Also, why should she know the motive? I can't see her attacker explaining his reasons to her.'

'I'm not saying it's a fact, but it gives us somewhere to start. Lord knows we've got nothing else.'

Maggie raised her hand tentatively. 'I've been looking through HOLMES sir and there are some interesting unexplained murders each involving a short, stocky man with a swarthy complexion. The murders seem random except for the description of the man. I've printed off a photofit from one of the murders.' Maggie held it out for the DI to see.

'Good work, Maggie. Did you get a photofit from Yaz?'

'It's with the technician now, sir.' She turned to her computer. 'I'll email him to see if he's finished.'

'Constable Green is also giving a description. Ask if he's finished too, will you?'

Peter made a note of the HOLMES information on the board. Turning back he said, 'Right, where does that leave us?'

'Where were the other murders, Maggie?' Rachel enquired.

Maggie checked her notes. 'Two in London and one in Halifax, oh, and one in Scotland.'

The team went quiet. 'Bloody Hell!' said Kevin, breaking the silence. 'London, Halifax and flaming Scotland! It can't be the same man. How many short, stocky, swarthy men must there be anyway? What about MO? Is there a link there?'

Maggie sighed. 'Different things, she quoted, knife attack, shooting, two beatings inflicting multiple wounds. That at least is similar to Miss Parks.'

The DI wanted more. 'Did the forces involved have any theories about this man? When did the offences occur? How much time elapsed between them? Get me more detail, Maggie.'

'Right, sir.' Maggie's computer pinged. 'Photofits back sir. I'll print them off.'

The team waited whilst Maggie collected the pages from the printer and handed them to the DI.

'Well, would you believe it? It's the same man, I'd stake my reputation on it. Looks like we've got a serial killer.'

'Or a gun for hire, sir,' Rachel said as she pinned the photofits onto the board. 'Has all the hallmarks of a hitman to me.'

'Fair point, Rachel. So we've got two lines of enquiry. Firstly, we need to see if we can find other unexplained murders in the last four years, say. Maggie you're still in charge of that. Secondly, let's look at the motive suggested to us by Sandra Parks.' The team looked sceptical. 'Oh, I know you don't give much credence to it, but it would support the hit man theory.' Rachel nodded. 'Okay Rachel, you find out who among our suspects would hire a hit man. They're not listed in the phone book, so who would know such a character?'

Chapter Nine

Martin drove into the hospital car park. He parked and turned to his girlfriend Stella. 'Do you want to come in with me, or will you wait here?'

'I'm not being funny or anything, Martin, but I don't know your sister and she's a vegetable, isn't she? Hospitals give me the creeps anyway.' Stella pulled a face. 'How long will you be though?'

Martin turned, an angry look on his face. 'She is not a *vegetable,* Stella, she is in a coma.'

'Same thing in my book,' she replied, examining her nails. 'She can't talk to anyone and wouldn't even know we're there, so what's the point?'

'The point is she's my sister. Are you coming or not?'

'Oh alright. I don't want to be sitting here like a lemon, do I? But can we be quick, we're supposed to be on holiday, after all.'

Martin paused outside Sandra's room to speak to the constable on duty. 'How is everything?' he asked politely.

'Not my place to say, sir. There's been no new developments as far as I'm aware, but you'd have to ask the doctor about that, or the inspector, DI Sanders.'

Thanking the constable, Martin entered the room with a bored looking Stella in tow. 'Hi sis! I see you're still bothering the NHS.'

Stella laughed derisively. 'What you talking to her for you daft sod? I told you, she's a vegetable, Martin. They'll probably be asking your mum and dad if they can switch her off soon. I've seen

d

it in films. Very sad and all that, but you can't keep them like that forever.'

You've surpassed yourself this time, Martin. I'll bet she's blonde with legs up to her armpits and nothing between her ears. Why do you keep going for bimbos, eh? I'm sure you could find someone with at least a modicum of intelligence. Anyway, I'm glad you've come, but if you could send Miss Insensitive away I'd appreciate it.

'Look Stella, you don't have to be here if you find it difficult, but the doctors said it helps if we talk to her. Why don't you go to that café near the entrance? Get yourself a coffee and a magazine and I'll come and get you when I've finished.'

Well I never, I seem to be getting through to people these days.

'Mmm, I'll do that, but don't be long, I want to go to Land's End and that Eden place today, and I need to get my nails done, don't forget.'

Give me strength! It's worse than I thought. She thinks the Eden Project is near Land's End and she can fit in a quick visit to a nail bar in between.

'We won't be able to go to both places today, love. It's two o'clock already and we've not had lunch.' Martin smiled indulgently. 'Anyway, I've got a surprise for you later.'

'Oh, Martin, really? What is it?'

'Well, it wouldn't be a surprise then would it? Off you go, love, and I'll see you soon.'

Stella tottered out in her tall heels, her firm backside encased in tight jeans. Martin watched, thinking about pulling those jeans off. *Perhaps have the shoes on though,* he thought lustfully.

She must be a wow in bed Martin, otherwise how could you stand her?

Martin stayed for a further fifteen minutes. He filled Sandra in on the work he and their dad had on. 'The business is doing really well love, we've got that contract dad told you about, you know, the new estate in Salford? Thirty houses in all. We've taken on more workers and are just cracking on with the first foundations now. I had this holiday booked, so Dad said it was okay for me to be away. Anyway, Stella was looking forward to it, so I couldn't disappoint her.'

She must be REALLY good in bed. Or is she an heiress or something? I'm glad you're doing well though. I wish I could tell you about my inspector. I look forward to his visits now. We're communicating, Martin! A bit rudimentary, and frustrating at times, but he seems to be able to understand me. The doctors say I've got more brain activity too, probably due to the inspector asking me questions. So you can tell Stella that this vegetable isn't cooked yet.

Sandra could hear Martin quietly sobbing. 'I don't know, sis, what's going to happen? You look so helpless lying there. If I could find out who did this, and I've got one or two ideas, I'll put them in a coma and see how they like it.'

Martin love, don't do anything daft. If you've got ideas about who did this, tell Inspector Sanders.

I'm seeing someone today who might be able to help, but I have to park Stella somewhere first. She'll like it though, in fact she'll love it.'

Martin was awestruck by Land's End. Not so much by the attractions, which he thought were a bit tacky, but by the coastline itself. The enormity of the sea and waves crashing on the rocks below was breathtaking. He turned to Stella, who was clutching her thin coat around her. 'It's fabulous, isn't it?'

'It's bloody windy, and I've just had me hair done. Look at it, it's like rats' tails. Can't we go into the souvenir shop?'

Martin smiled indulgently. 'You're not an outdoors sort of girl, are you? You go over to the shop then, I just want to take a few photos.' He wandered down the coast path away from the attractions towards the small animal farm. The crowds were less here and he got some good shots of a couple of seals playing around the rocks. *I can see why Sandra loves Cornwall,* he thought. The thought of Sandra made him think about the appointment he had later. *I'll have to tread carefully though. I want answers, and I'll get them but, 'softly, softly, catchee monkey', as they say.*

The Major-Domo touched his hat and opened the entrance door of the hotel as Martin and Stella approached. 'This is a bit of alright,'

Stella whispered to Martin, as she sashayed past the waiting doorman. 'Are we staying here, then? Is this my surprise?'

Martin tipped the doorman as he ushered Stella into the foyer. 'No love, but the next best thing.' He smiled at her puzzled face. 'I've booked you in for a pamper session. The works. Massage, facial, hair and nails.'

Stella was delighted. 'Oh thanks, Martin.' She stood on her tip toes to kiss him. 'I love a pamper.'

I'd never have guessed, he thought. 'Anyway, I've got someone to meet about work and I knew you wouldn't want to hang about. Go and book yourself in at the desk and I'll see you later. Have fun!' he shouted as she tottered away, still beaming.

Martin signalled for a waiter. 'I have a meeting with Mr Munroe, he's a guest here.'

'Do you know which room, sir?'

'No, I'm to meet him in the bar.'

'Very well, sir. This way please.'

Martin spotted Robert Munroe at the bar nursing a whisky. He turned instinctively and spotted his guest. 'Martin! Over here.' He signalled to the barman and ordered two more whiskys. As Martin came closer, Robert stood to shake hands with his friend. 'Shall we take our drinks over by the window? It's a great view and a bit more private.' The waiter put the drinks on a tray and followed them over to the full length windows overlooking the sea.

'Very nice, Bobby. You know how to look after yourself. Business must be good.'

'Business is great, Marty. I've just signed a deal on a property in Plymouth, well, several properties actually. Ex-Navy buildings, just ripe for development.' Robert sipped his drink. 'Sorry about your sister, by the way. Dreadful thing to have happened. How is she?'

'Holding her own, Bobby. In fact, the doc says she's showing signs of recovery.'

It was easy to miss the frown that briefly crossed Robert's features but Martin picked it up. 'That's great news, Marty, your mum and dad must be relieved.' Robert eyed Martin cautiously. 'You know she was leading my Penthavern project, don't you?' Martin nodded. 'It's a great pity she won't be able to oversee the work, but Mike's competent and we'll be using some of Sandra's ideas, of course.'

'She may surprise you yet, Bobby old mate. Our Sandra's a fighter.' Martin paused and grabbed a few nuts from the dish on the table. 'I was hoping to see the Penthavern property, if that's possible?'

'Sure thing mate. I need to go over there myself today so we can go together. But where's that girlfriend of yours? Wasn't she supposed to be here too?'

'Being pampered in the spa. Should give us plenty of time to get to Penthavern and back.'

'Right, no time like the present, old son. You'd better drive though, I've had a few too many of these.' Robert held up his glass and then drained it.

Rachel and Kevin were going through the files for the umpteenth time. 'Mike Travis seems to have lead a very quiet life, Kevin. He was born and raised here and, except for four years at Exeter Uni, has lived here all his life. Paul Collins is much the same. He also went to Exeter, but two years after Mike. Proper home birds the pair of them.' Rachel closed the file and sat back in her chair. 'I really don't like either of these two for hiring a hit man.'

'You're probably right,' said Kevin. 'It seems out of character and, more's the point, when would they have met anyone like that? They only go to work and the pub.'

Rachel laughed. 'Not exactly gangster material, are they? Him, on the other hand,' picking up the file on Robert Munroe, 'I could believe anything of. He's very slick and quite ruthless I'm sure. Property development is a cut-throat business and, for anyone to succeed the way he has, they would have to cut some corners. Maybe bribe a few people.' She tapped her pen on Munroe's photo. 'We need to dig deeper into his past, Kevin, see how much dodgy dealing we can pick up.'

Martin pulled up outside what looked like an old warehouse door. The paint was peeling on the wooden façade but there was a bright new padlock on the small entrance door. Taking out a key, Robert unlocked it and ushered his friend in. Martin was completely taken aback. Standing amid man-high weeds and small shrubs was an enormous barn-like building, obviously very old and in need of repair, but it had majesty. It immediately put Martin in mind of a cathedral, not on the same scale, of course, but in its presence. He was awestruck.

Robert came up behind him. 'What do you think, Marty? Superb, isn't it?'

'It's certainly that. How big is it? Must be forty metres at least.'

'Your sister looked at it and said "thirty-eight point six metres" and, by God, she was right. Marvellous talent that. Same inside. She told me the volume, and saw a plan in her mind of how the space could be split up. She just seemed to gaze into space and see it – like it was a diagram in front of her. Incredible, really incredible.'

'She's a special person,' Martin said quietly.

Stepping inside, Martin looked around the dimly lit interior. The wooden frame construction was evident from here, and between the timbers Martin could detect a wattle and daub infill with the remnants of strange markings in the limewash. Martin had seen pictures of similar markings in archaeological magazines. They were meant to ward off evil spirits, and were very ancient.

Robert suddenly grabbed Martin's arm. 'Want to see the roof?' He laughed. 'I've had a scaffolding tower built round the back. Had to see what state the slates were in. Come on, I'll get you a hard hat.'

As the pair climbed up the scaffold, Robert was like a child at Christmas, talking non-stop about the apartments and shops which would be accommodated by the space. 'Of course, the roof space would be reserved for the penthouse. The views are something else from up there, and I am putting in a roof terrace so that it can be enjoyed to the full. I'm hoping for 1.5 million, and I'll get it, too. Lots of Russian oligarchs eager to spend money, cash, if you take my drift.' Roberts tapped the side of his nose and smirked.

They reached the top of the scaffold and looked across the roof. Slates had shifted here and there and Martin could see, even with the obscure view he had, that the supporting roof timbers were very old indeed. Some trusses looked like whole tree trunks as they curved in a natural form over the void. Martin knew that what Sandra had told him was right. This wasn't just an old building but an *ancient* one and probably of some significance.

Suddenly, Martin's anger boiled up. 'You didn't want anyone to know about this place, did you Robert?'

'I don't know what you mean, Marty.' Robert looked puzzled. 'I want everyone to know about it, that's why I'm developing it.'

'Not *really* know about it, I mean. Sandra thought it was something special, something worth finding out more about. But that takes precious time, doesn't it Robert, maybe hold up your build altogether.'

'Nonsense man. Sandra was with me all the way, it was our project.' However, Robert looked edgy.

Martin shook his head and moved towards Robert, his fists clenched. 'You had to stop her, didn't you?' Martin pinned the smaller man against the scaffold rail. Robert looked down nervously. 'I know all about your deals Robert, bribing planners, using sub-standard materials. As long as the building stays up for a year or two that's all that matters to you isn't it? By then you're long gone.'

Martin pushed Robert harder against the rail. 'You've used some shady characters in your time to make sure you had the edge in a deal, haven't you? You're quite capable of silencing a young woman or two if they got in your way, aren't you? Robert was being bent backwards over the rail now and was visibly scared of the larger man.

'Marty, Marty, you don't know what you're saying.' Robert tried to placate Martin. 'You're sick with grief about your sister, I understand that, but you can't go around throwing accusations at innocent people.'

'Innocent! I don't think so. I can see the greed in your eyes. Well you won't get away with it, I'll drop you off this scaffold, I swear I will.' Martin's eyes were wild and Robert knew he stood little chance against the size and strength of the larger man.

'Look Marty, there's a lot of money in this job, some of it can come your way. . . '

'Don't you dare try to bribe me!'

Just then Martin heard steps on the ladder, and a shout came up from below. 'Who's up there? This is private property. I'll get the police on to you!'

Robert shuddered with relief. 'It's okay, John, just me showing a client around. We'll be down directly.' He smiled smugly at Martin. 'Best let me go, old boy, don't you agree?'

Martin shoved Robert aside and half fell down the ladder in his anger and haste. 'Not finished, Robert!' he shouted. 'Not by a long chalk.'

Chapter Ten

Peter entered the squad room on Tuesday morning looking a little more dishevelled than usual. He had clearly not shaved that morning and Rachel was sure he was wearing the same clothes as yesterday. 'The chief wants to see you, sir' she said, looking up from her computer and smiling. 'Rough night?'

'You could say that. This case is going nowhere fast Rachel. Just when I think I'm getting to grips with it I find myself down a blind alley again.' He straightened his tie, which didn't make a great deal of difference to his appearance. 'Did her majesty say what she wanted?'

'No, just as soon as you got in.'

'Keep the team here when they arrive. I want us to go through all our evidence again then re-interview persons of interest. We've got to get a fresh start.' He set off towards the door, touching Rachel lightly on her shoulder as he passed. 'Wish me luck.'

She smiled. 'She likes you. You won't need luck, just charm.'

DCI Angela Morton did indeed like her DI, but as a colleague, nothing more, and charm never worked with her anyway. At fifty-five Angela was dreaming of retirement. She knew that some of her, mostly male, colleagues carried on in the job until they were forced out or had a heart attack, or worse, but Angela preferred 'riding a desk' as they called it, and saw herself as a strategist rather than a hands-on cop. She was hoping that Peter Sanders would be her successor. There was that period a few years ago when he went off the rails, but Angela had supported him, even when he was demoted to DS for a while. He had certainly pulled his socks up and she was pleased to recommend his reinstatement to DI within a year. Since then he had coasted a bit, in her opinion. Oh, very good arrest and conviction rates, but he seemed to lack the enthusiasm for the job that had impressed her so much in the early days. She inspected the sheaf of reports in front of her. This latest case was nasty and troubling. Two young women, one dead, one as good as, and, although there seemed to be a plethora of suspects, no one had been charged. She understood the complexity of these cases, and the pressure to get results didn't help, however she expected a lot of Peter and wanted results.

'Come in,' Angela called as she heard the light tap on her door. 'God, you look awful. Anyway, sit down. Coffee?'

Peter smiled ruefully. 'Thanks ma'am, coffee would be great.' He sat heavily in the chair opposite to the DCI. Peter watched her as she poured the coffee. Angela looked young for her age, he thought, what my dad would have called a *handsome woman,* and there was no doubt that she had her admirers, but she had remained single. Married to the job, some would say. Peter liked and admired his boss though, she had a way of cutting through the dross and focusing on what mattered. He found this helpful, and hoped it would be now.

'Okay, Peter,' Angela said as she settled down with her coffee and tapped the file in front of her. She looked relaxed, although Peter knew she was anything but. 'Where are we up to with this case? Just fill me in on your thinking.'

Peter took a large swig of coffee which was hot and made him choke. 'Sorry, ma'am. . . '

'Angela will do, we've known each other a long time.'

'Right. Well, Angela, this is a very frustrating case. We have one young woman in a coma and another on a slab. Two different MOs, and very little on motive.' Peter paused to think. He knew that Angela didn't like excuses. 'One promising lead is a description of a man seen close to the first scene and again at the hospital where our first victim is. His photofit matches that of a man wanted in relation to a number of murders around the country. We're checking CCTV to see if we can get some clue as to his current whereabouts. He is distinctive in appearance and shouldn't be too hard to find if he's still in the area. We have an APB out on him so we should catch him if he tries to leave the country. We have other lines of enquiry. . . '

Angela held her hand up to stop Peter. 'This man looks promising. Focus on him for the time being. Don't spread your resources too thinly, Peter. Bring this man in and he may be able to fill in the blanks that are making this case messy.'

Peter smiled. 'Yes ma'am. I'll make finding this man a priority. However, I want to reserve the right to pursue a couple of additional leads.' He continued cautiously, 'It's possible that this man, let's call him Jack, has been hired by someone closer to the victims, and we may yet shake that person up enough to make a mistake.'

'Alright, Peter, but bring Jack in. I want to see results by the end of the week. Oh, and have a shave and tidy yourself up. You look like you've slept in that suit.'

Spot on, thought Peter. 'Yes, ma'am. . . Angela.' He waved over his shoulder as he left the room.

The team were assembled when Peter returned to the squad room. He stood in front of the incident board and took a deep breath. 'Okay, we have a prime focus.' The team looked attentive, notebooks in hand. 'The man seen at the crime scene and at the hospital is our priority, let's call him Jack. He is quite distinctive looking, so, if he is still in the area, someone will have seen him. Kevin, you check CCTV in a radius of five miles of Miss Parks' flat, and the same around the hospital. Maggie, he must be travelling around somehow, so you are on car hire and bus stations. Both of you let me know as soon as you have something.'

'By the way, sir,' said Maggie. 'I've had a look at Polly Thomas's laptop and phone. Nothing unusual. Same sort of emails as Sandra Parks, mostly concerning work. Her phone shows missed calls on the night she died, all from Paul Collins, so that ties in with what he said.'

'Okay, thanks Maggie. I suspect you've printed them off?'

Maggie laughed. 'On your desk, sir?' Peter smiled and nodded.

'Rachel, you're with me. We'll see how our other suspects respond to Jack's image. Get them all down here today. And it wouldn't hurt to re-interview them while we're at it.' Peter checked his watch. 'Back here at one.'

Three interview rooms held three very disgruntled people, four if you counted Robert Munroe's solicitor. Peter and Rachel were in the squad room. 'We'll leave Munroe till last, let him stew a bit. 'Let's start with Mike Travis. You lead. Usual routine of going over the same ground as before, then introduce the photofit, see how he responds. I'll let you know when I want to take over.'

Rachel liked the way that Peter set out the interview process. When she interviewed with some other people, she found their jumping in with unprepared questions unsettling. It may also have the same impact on the interviewee, but it often led to having to go over the same ground again and again. Interviewing with Peter was a calm affair for the officers, but had a more powerful effect on the suspect in her view.

Mike Travis was visibly nervous, beads of sweat forming on his upper lip. In itself, this could mean nothing, as innocent people often felt nervous in this situation, but it was always worthy of note. He protested about having to repeat what he had told them before, but Rachel stayed calm and asked the questions without responding to his comments. Just as Mike thought the questions were coming to an end and had started to relax a bit, Rachel showed him the image of Jack.

'Never seen him before. Is he the one? You know, the one who beat up Sandra?'

Peter couldn't detect any flicker of recognition in Mike's response, so he was either a great actor, or didn't know Jack. Peter signalled to Rachel that she should draw the interview to a close, which she did, telling Mike that they may wish to speak to him again.

A relieved Mike Travis left the station shaking his head.

The interview with Paul Collins followed much the same pattern, except that he was keen to know if any progress had been made in tracing Polly's killer. He was tearful through most of the interview, which made recognising behavioural changes difficult, but he showed no response to the picture of Jack.

Yaz blustered as usual, insisting that all this police involvement was interfering with her artistic process. 'I haven't been able to put in a good session for days now. What with this, and that creep Spinetti, I'm right off my game. I've boarded up the back door though, and sent him packing if he comes in the front, so I think he's got the message. Haven't seen him for a few days, anyway.'

Getting back to the interview, Rachel went through Yaz's whereabouts on the significant dates.

'Well, you had me locked up when Polly. . . you know. . . died. So I couldn't have had anything to do with that. And I've been through where I was when Sandy was attacked.'

'You were in love with Sandra.' Rachel made this a statement, not a question.

Yaz was visibly shaken. 'What makes you think. . ?' Rachel remained silent. 'Okay, I liked her a lot but she made it clear that she wasn't interested. I got my wires crossed. It happens.'

The two detectives studied their notes. Yaz looked from one to the other. 'You can't think I'd beat her up because she didn't fancy me? Lordy, if I did that every time I was turned down I'd be leaving a trail of bodies in my wake.'

'Turned down often are you?' Rachel said.

'Well no, I mean not often, but it's not easy being me. I seem to attract the wrong sort, men that is, women just don't seem to. . . they just don't. Alright?'

'You more than fancied Sandra though, didn't you? You were in love with her.'

'Yeah well, I was a bit cut up at first when she wasn't interested, but I liked her as a friend as well. I hoped we'd be able to hang out like we did at uni. I wasn't angry. Just a bit sad and sorry for myself.'

Rachel changed tack and showed Yaz the photo of Jack. 'Do you recognise this man?'

'Course I do. I did the photofit.' Yaz laughed out loud. 'This some kind of trick?' she continued when the detectives didn't answer. 'I bumped into him outside Sandy's flat. I told you that. But I don't know who he is. Never seen him before or since, okay?' She sat back in her seat. 'Can I go now?'

Kevin was in the squad room when Rachel and Peter returned. 'Munroe's solicitor has been creating hell about being kept waiting, and the chief looked in, wanting to know where you were. Didn't seem too pleased to be told you were interviewing suspects.'

Peter sighed. I'll go and see her. Rachel, you calm Munroe's solicitor down. Tell him we'll be with them soon.' He turned to go but Kevin called him back.

'A bit of good news, sir. Caught a man fitting Jack's description on CCTV near the docks in Falmouth. Maggie and I are going to do some house to house in the area when she gets back.'

'Fantastic Kevin. Got something to placate her majesty with now. Any other sightings?'

'Not so far, but I've not done the hospital area yet.'

'Keep it up. And good work Kevin, could be a breakthrough.'

Peter and Rachel waited patiently whilst Robert Munroe and his solicitor protested *in the strongest possible terms* for being kept waiting. 'You have kept my client here for two hours now and he's a busy man, so we'd appreciate it if you could keep this interview pertinent and speedy. My client has, after all, made a statement to you previously and he wants you to know that he has nothing to add.'

Ignoring the solicitor, Peter made introductions for the tape and opened the file in front of him. He addressed himself to Robert Munroe. 'Thank you for coming in today, Mr Munroe, we just have a few more questions to put to you.'

'Don't think I'll be saying anything different, Inspector. I know how you people work. Keep asking the same thing until someone says something different and then you pounce on it.'

'Had a lot of police interviews, sir?'

'No, Inspector. I just know how you work, that's all.' Robert's solicitor whispered something into his ear. 'Yes, okay Michael,' he replied irritably, taking a deep breath.

Peter went through the times and dates of the two incidents, asking about Munroe's whereabouts. Robert occasionally conferred with his solicitor, but gave the replies he had given in earlier interviews. He had been at Newquay airport when Sandra Parks was attacked and with his wife and daughter when Polly Thomas died.

'Polly Thomas was murdered, Mr Munroe.'

'When Polly Thomas was murdered then, Inspector. Gives me alibis for both occasions just the same.'

The solicitor spoke up then. 'If that's all, Inspector, my client has wasted too much time here already and, as I said, he's a busy man.' He pushed his seat back as if to stand.

'Sit down, sir. I have a couple of things to clear up yet.' Peter placed the photofit in front of Munroe. Robert's eyes moved quickly from side to side and he leant over to consult his solicitor.

'My client has nothing to say.'

Looking directly at Munroe, Peter said, 'It's a simple question. Do you recognise this man?'

The solicitor put a hand on Robert's arm. 'My client has not seen this man before.'

'He could tell me that himself.'

Robert waved his hand at the solicitor. 'It's alright, Michael. No, Inspector, I do not know this man. Now, if that's all. . ?'

Peter terminated the interview by saying that they may wish to speak to Robert again, at which both Robert and his solicitor sighed. 'This is tantamount to harassment, Inspector.' The solicitor said. 'Don't think we won't make a complaint if it continues.' And with that the pair left.

As the door closed behind them, Peter turned to Rachel.

'Well. What do you make of that?'

'He's lying, of course.' She gathered up her papers. 'I doubt we'll break him, though. We need to find Jack.'

* * *

87

'Any news from the door to door, Kevin?' Peter was hopeful that something would turn up that would give them a solid lead.

'Nothing so far sir, but there were several non-responses. Maggie and I are going out again tonight.' Kevin looked expectantly at Peter. 'Anything from the interviews, sir?'

'Shaken a few trees, that's all. Munroe's a cool customer and, of course, he's got a solicitor on board so we'll have to tread carefully. I thought he was evasive about recognising Jack. It may be something or nothing but he's still on my radar.'

Maggie caught Peter's attention. 'Nothing from the car hire places sir, and I've asked for the CCTV from the bus station.'

Peter nodded. 'Right. Finding Jack is still our priority so keep me informed about the door to door. Someone must have seen him.'

Peter went into his office and closed the door.

It was five o'clock before Peter decided enough was enough. He had been over and over the information they had gathered and was getting nowhere. He was just about to leave when the phone rang.

'Sanders,' he said wearily.

'It's Kevin, sir. You need to get down to Falmouth. We've got a body which may be Jack.' He gave the DI the address.

'I'll be right there, Kevin. Secure the scene and any witnesses, and call Dr Samuels and SOCO.'

Peter put the receiver down and cursed. 'A dead body is the last thing I wanted,' he said to the empty room.

Chapter Eleven

Arriving at the terraced house on Market Street, Peter was pleased to see the police cordon in place and Dr Samuels' car at the kerbside. Pulling on his shoe covers and gloves he passed the uniformed officer at the door and entered the gloomy house. The first thing he noticed was the smell. An obnoxious mixture of stale food, urine and body odour pervaded the atmosphere, so much so that he gagged. A solitary dim light bulb illuminated the nicotine stained ceiling where a colony of flies were circling. The room was furnished with battered chairs and a sofa, missing its cushions, so that the bare wooden slats were visible. The floor was covered in a dirty linoleum which stuck to the soles of Peter's shoes. He had seen deprivation many times in his career as a policeman, but nothing worse than this. Perched on the edge of one chair was a woman of indeterminate age. She was wearing a grubby dress, several inches too short for her large frame, and what appeared to be cut down wellington boots on her feet. Her chubby white legs were pale and hairy. The face that tilted itself up towards him was expressionless and drugged looking, and was framed by matted brown hair. Peter turned his attention to the corner of the room where Kevin stood by the staircase.

'Up here, sir,' Kevin said, and motioned towards the stairs with his head. 'Doc's already here.'

As Peter moved gingerly up the stairs, the smell intensified to include the unmistakable odour of dead body. The flies were thicker here, too. As he entered the room at the top he saw Dr Samuels coming to his feet and backing away from the prone figure on the bed. 'Evening, Inspector. Want to take a look?'

Peter moved closer and could see the body of a man naked except for a pair of dirty boxer shorts. His face was turned towards the room and Peter was in no doubt that this was the man they had been calling Jack. 'Cause of death?'

'I would hazard a guess at our old friend *blunt force trauma to the head*, but I'll be able to tell you more after the post mortem. He's been dead for some time though, twenty-four to thirty-six hours probably, but this room's like a sauna so could be less.'

'Thanks doc. PM tomorrow?'

Dr Samuels nodded as he packed his bag. 'Shall we say ten-thirty?'

Peter moved carefully around the room. The single bed was the dominant feature, with a small chest by the window, its drawers half opened with items of clothing spilling out. The thin flowered curtains were closed. Peter took out a pencil and deftly lifted the contents of the drawers to look underneath. No obvious sign of a wallet or other papers which might give them an identity for Jack. Being unable to glean anything further from the room, Peter made his way down the stairs to where the woman was still sitting in the same position. He motioned to Kevin to meet him outside.

'What's the story?'

'She didn't answer the door when we knocked at first, sir. I'm sure she was in earlier too when we made the first visit. I could see her through the letter box though, so I announced myself and told her to open up, and held my warrant card through the opening for her to see. She opened the door a crack and almost overpowered me with the smell.' Kevin grimaced at the recollection. 'Anyway, when I showed her the photofit of Jack it was obvious she recognised him. She looked scared and started to shake but didn't say anything. We came in and followed our noses to find him upstairs. Maggie has been trying to talk to her but she hasn't uttered a word.'

Peter glanced into the living room at the woman. 'She's either in shock or has some sort of learning disability, I'd say. Call social services, see if they know anything about her. In the meantime we'll take her down to the station and interview her there.'

* * *

'Teresa Anders, social services.' The woman held out her hand to Peter who shook it warmly.

'Thanks for coming so promptly, Miss Anders.'

'It's Mrs, but please call me Teresa.'

'Right. I'm DI Sanders, Peter, and this is DS Morris.'

Rachel waved. 'Rachel,' she said.

Having got the pleasantries out of the way, Peter said, 'What can you tell us about this lady?'

The three sat down around Peter's desk as Maggie brought in some coffee. 'She's well known to us, Peter,' said Teresa, nodding thanks to Maggie. 'Well before my time Tracy Walker was known to children's services. Her mother died when she was seven and it was just her and her dad after that. We put in lots of support, but to be honest, things were far from satisfactory. Reading the case file now you can see that she should have been brought into care early on, but she sort of fell through the net. We picked her up again as a referral from Women's Aid. Their enquiries, Tracy's version of events that is, revealed that she had been sexually abused by her father for several years and he then sold her to a friend of his to pay off some mounting debts.'

'Sold!' said a shocked Rachel. 'How do you mean, sold?'

'Just what I said. If Tracy is to be believed, her dad's friend paid him a hundred pounds for her. They were married, though Tracy had little say in that, and had two children. That's where we became involved. The children were taken into care and Women's Aid tried their best to *rescue* Tracy from her husband. You can see she has severe learning difficulties and wouldn't, or couldn't, bring herself to leave. Eventually, her husband had a heart attack and died. She went into a refuge where, over a period of time, a story of abuse by many men, who paid her husband for the privilege, came out. No prosecutions were ever brought as the police considered Tracy to be an unreliable witness, which is probably right.'

Rachel was as shocked by the casual manner that the story was relayed by the social worker as by the actual abuse. 'That's terrible, Teresa. She's still obviously a mess, so how has she ended up like this?'

91

'Women's Aid found her the house and we put in support where we can, but there's little more we can do officially, I'm afraid. Of course, we'll have more involvement when the baby is born.'

'She's pregnant?' Rachel thought that it was going from bad to worse.

'Yes. About six months. We'll take the baby at birth, naturally. There's no way she'd be able to care for a child.'

With the help of Teresa Anders, an interview of sorts was held with Tracy Walker. It was clear that she didn't understand the questions and looked like a frightened child most of the time. When shown the picture of Jack, she cried out and clutched at Teresa, but wasn't able to tell them how he came to be at her house. Seeing that Tracy was getting very upset, Peter decided to end the interview. Teresa volunteered to take her home and make sure she had some food in the house, promising to keep an eye on Tracy and make sure she was alright.

Rachel was visibly shaken. 'I've never heard such a sad story, Peter. A whole lifetime of abuse and deprivation. Children born and taken away, and no hope of things getting better, it's criminal.' Rachel's eyes teared up.

Peter put his arm around Rachel's shoulders, feeling the vulnerability of her slight frame. He pulled her into him and she gratefully laid her head on his chest and sobbed. After a moment or two, she broke away. 'Look at me, tough cop, eh?' Rachel dried her eyes.

'Come on,' said Peter. 'Get your coat. I think we both need a drink after the day we've had.'

Rachel's first gin and tonic went down quickly, and Peter immediately went to the bar to replace it. Rachel looked apologetic. 'Sorry. That wasn't very lady-like, necking a drink like a docker.'

Peter laughed as he sipped his beer. 'You should have seen me a few years back. I'd have downed three whiskys in the same time, and you had more excuse than I had.'

'I hope you don't mind me asking, but was that after your wife left?'

Peter thought for a moment. 'I don't mind, it's all water under the bridge now.'

'What happened?'

'Julia was an unusual woman. We met at a rugby dance, she was with someone else but I was mesmerised from the moment I set eyes on her. On the attractiveness scale, she was a ten, whereas I class myself as a six at best. That's why I was stunned when she suggested we leave and find somewhere quieter. We moved in together six months later and married a year after that.'

'I'm guessing that things went downhill?'

'Not at all. We had a great time. She was ambitious for herself and for me. She was an education inspector but had her eye on higher office. She pushed me to look for promotion at every opportunity, and I did. She was very persuasive, and I was still a little in awe of her.'

'What about kids? Didn't you want children?'

'She didn't, and I just went along. She spent more and more time away. Became a government advisor on education and had a flat in London. I was proud of her, proud to be with her. We had long weekends in five star hotels as often as we could. Julia liked luxury, and exotic holidays that she would book. I just fitted in as usual.'

'Sounds great, didn't you enjoy it?'

'At first, yes. I bought into the lifestyle and everyone saw us as a golden couple.'

Peter had stopped talking, staring into his drink. Rachel should have left it there but, emboldened by the alcohol, wanted her curiosity satisfied. 'So what went wrong?'

'Julia spent more and more time in London, but I didn't mind that, work was demanding and it gave me time to dedicate myself to the job for a while. You know what it's like. We still went on luxury weekends and she seemed as affectionate as ever.' Peter noticed his drink was finished. 'I'll just get more drinks,' he said, making to stand.

'No, it's my round. Same again?'

'Thanks, whisky and water, please.'

Peter took the opportunity to nip to the gents. He caught sight of himself in the mirror and sighed. Should he be unburdening himself to a junior officer like this? It felt good though, to talk about it after all this time, to put that ghost to rest.

When he returned to the table Rachel smiled up at him. 'I'm sorry, Peter, I shouldn't be quizzing you like this. You really don't have to tell me anything.'

'No, it's okay. I've not told anyone what happened, and it's time I did.' He picked up his drink and took a long draft. 'We had been away to Bath. Great hotel, lovely days out. She shopped for clothes and I browsed the antique shops. We were in her car. She always had a classy car, this one was a Jaguar. When we arrived home it was late evening. She stopped outside the house and just waited.' Peter scratched his head. 'I had no idea. She just said that she wouldn't come in, she had everything she wanted in the car. It still didn't dawn on me that she was leaving me, so she spelled it out. She had met someone else, an MP. She didn't even say she was sorry, just shrugged as if to say 'that's life'. I got out and collected my bag from the back and just stood there on the pavement. I was dazed. It all felt surreal. She drove off and, eventually, I went in and had a few drinks.'

'The heartless cow!' Rachel couldn't help herself. 'Sorry, but that's the worst dumping I've ever heard of.'

Peter gave a hollow laugh. 'It's okay, you should have heard what I called her when it struck home that she had gone for good.' He swirled the rest of his drink and downed it, holding the glass up. 'That's when this became more than an occasional tipple. I carried on working, if you could call it that, until they suspended me. What hurt most was that the rugby team didn't want me any more either. I would turn up drunk and I was a liability on the field, so they dropped me.'

'That must have been an awful time for you, Peter. How come you're back to DI now? If you don't mind me asking.'

'I don't mind. My big sister Jane is in the Navy, well RNAS to be accurate. She's a flyer – jets. She stayed with me and put me on a strict regime of diet and exercise for four weeks. She was very frank, told me that she never liked the snobby bitch in the first place,

94

and made me laugh for the first time in weeks by doing impressions of Julia at her most offensive. She also persuaded the rugby team to give me another go, and I found myself back in the fold. Work followed, except I wasn't DI anymore, demoted to DS. That was okay though, I was back and very eager to prove myself. Angela helped.'

'The Chief!'

'I owe her a lot. She believed in me and told me I'd make DI in a year if I applied myself. She was right.'

Peter brought more drinks. Both of them were getting a bit tipsy now. Rachel asked the question that was top of her agenda. 'So has there been anyone else since?' She actually fluttered her eyelashes.

'Are you flirting with me?'

'I could be.'

Peter looked puzzled. 'Do you not have anyone at the moment?'

'A series of Mr Wrongs I'm afraid.'

Peter looked startled. '*Mr* Wrongs? But the word around the station is. . . '

'What?' Rachel said with a lopsided smile.

'That you, er, aren't fond of men.'

'Bloody Nora! Is that what they think?'

Peter nodded slowly. 'Have they got it wrong then?'

'Too right they've got it wrong. Just because a woman doesn't have a man in tow doesn't mean she's a lesbian.' Realising she was talking loudly and attracting attention, Rachel lowered her voice. 'I'm choosy, is all. And yes, if you want to know, I was flirting with you.' She smiled seductively. 'Shouldn't I be?'

Peter leaned across the table. 'You know as well as I do that it's frowned upon for officers to have relationships, especially with junior ranks.' Seeing her disappointed face, he took her hand. 'So we'll have to keep it quiet, won't we?'

Peter's house was in a leafy suburb of Truro. Originally a small bungalow, it had been tastefully extended to form a split level house surrounded by neat gardens. He and Rachel walked up the drive, having paid off the taxi they sensibly took from the pub. Ornamental lights came on as they passed, revealing raised beds made from railway sleepers inset with blue spotlights.

'Very nice indeed,' said Rachel, stumbling over her words.

'Mmm. Julia had good taste, I'll give her that. I don't know why I bother with the upkeep, shame to let it go to ruin I guess.'

Peter put his arm over Rachel's shoulder, partly to hold her up, and ushered her into the hallway. Pushing the door closed with his heel, he pressed her into the wall and kissed her long and hard, his hands sliding down to cup her bottom cheeks. Rachel returned the urgency of the kiss, her arms around Peter's neck.

'Let's go somewhere more comfortable,' Peter muttered into her neck.

'Mmm, good idea,' Rachel slurred, just before she slid down the wall.

The smell of bacon wafted into the bedroom, accompanied by a tuneless whistling. Rachel pushed herself upright and looked around her. It could have been a five star hotel room. The bed was super-king with a grey silky coverlet which must have cost a small fortune. Sunlight was slanting through the shuttered windows revealing beautiful décor in shades of grey, white and pale green. The effect was neither manly or girly, but tasteful, with a good eye for design.

She looked down to see that she was naked and blushed, imagining what went on the night before. Noticing a white fluffy robe behind the door, she jumped from the bed, instantly regretting the sudden move. She slipped the gown on and walked unsteadily into the en-suite bathroom, the bright spotlights dazzling her. Looking at her face in the large mirror over the washbasin, she sighed. *Not looking my best* she thought. She splashed water on her face and ran her fingers through her hair. *That will have to do*, she said to herself, and, tightening the robe, she set off to follow the delicious smell.

Peter was in the kitchen frying bacon in one pan whilst making pancakes in another. He looked at home by the cooker and was clearly an accomplished cook. 'Good morning,' he said looking

96

over his shoulder. 'Coffee's on the table, help yourself. This'll be just a minute or two.'

Rachel slid onto a dining chair and poured herself a coffee. The kitchen was as immaculate as the bedroom, and, she imagined, the rest of the house. 'Mmm, great,' she said sipping the coffee. 'This is delicious.'

'I confess I'm a bit of a coffee nut. Grind my own beans and all that.' He smiled over at her. 'Glad you like it.'

'Peter. . . last night. . . did we?'

'Not that I didn't want to, but you were a tad drunk, and I wouldn't take advantage. I slept in the spare room. Don't look so worried, I sleep there all the time now.'

Rachel looked down the front of her gown. 'But I'm. . . '

'Not down to me, that. You must have been on auto pilot. Happened to me a lot in my drinking days. I'd come home, not remembering how I'd got here, but still undress and fold my clothes. Remarkable! I did look in on you a couple of times, but you were sleeping like a baby.'

'Ah, good. I mean, good that I behaved myself, not so good that I missed sleeping with you.'

Peter beamed as he brought the pancakes and bacon over to the table. 'Plenty of time to put that right. Only if you want to, of course.' Placing a plate in front of Rachel, he kissed her lightly on the lips. 'Help yourself to maple syrup.'

'Oh lovely. I could easily get used to this.'

'Don't get too excited, it's your turn next time.'

Rachel smiled at the thought of a next time. 'I'll do my best.' She poured a pool of maple syrup onto her pancakes and tucked in. 'This is delicious, by the way. Who taught you to cook?'

'That would be Julia.' Peter smiled wryly. 'She kind of took over my life for a while. Controlled me, if you like. It's taking time to get back to being me, if you know what I mean.' He looked over at Rachel who was licking maple syrup off her lips. He felt a surge of desire. 'Last night helped a lot. I haven't felt so relaxed in ages, and I slept through, which is very unusual.' He stood to clear the table. 'Right now, though, we unfortunately have to get to work.' Peter leaned over Rachel's shoulder and kissed her neck, lingering while

e

she pressed her head into his shoulder. 'I'll call you a taxi while you get dressed. There are clean things in the wardrobe, Julia's stuff, but it should fit you nicely. You should find something suitable if you want to change after your shower. It might look odd if you appeared in yesterday's outfit.'

'You don't mind?'

'Should have got rid of her stuff years ago but I don't use that room now so never got round to it. You're welcome to anything.' He stacked the dishes in the dishwasher and wiped down the worktop. 'I've got this post mortem at ten-thirty and I want to call in at the hospital before that. Probably best if we don't arrive together, anyway.'

'The advantage of them thinking I'm gay is that they won't suspect a thing.' Rachel left the room, seductively dropping the gown off her shoulders and laughing.

Chapter Twelve

Rachel attracted admiring glances as she entered the squad room. Kevin actually whistled, and Saroj gave her the thumbs up. 'You been shopping? That outfit must have cost a pretty penny.'

Rachel was suddenly embarrassed. She had chosen a cream linen pants suit from Julia's wardrobe which she had teamed with a coffee coloured silk shirt. She thought that she always dressed smartly so no one would notice the designer clothes. 'Had this stuff for ages, if you must know. It's getting a bit dated now so I thought I'd start wearing it for work. Anyway, are you suggesting I don't usually look good?'

There was a chorus of, 'not at all' and 'you always look great.'

Rachel shrugged and sat at her desk. 'Okay. Anything new?'

Saroj nodded. 'Yes. This may be interesting but it could be nothing.'

'Spit it out then.'

'Andrea Reynolds, aka Yaz, was brought up in a children's home in Leeds. Of itself, that's not remarkable, but when I spoke to a member of staff who was there at the time it became more interesting. Andrea and a boy called Stephen Crookshank were implicated in the death of another resident. A girl called Mandy Harris, who was found at the bottom of the stairs one morning. Her head was cracked open on the marble hall floor. She'd been there most of the night. She was said to have had a run in with Andrea who threatened her. Stephen Crookshank was not very bright but strong, and dedicated to Andrea. The staff member said he often lost his temper with anyone who crossed Andrea and, after she had had her fun out of it, she would step in and stop him. The thinking at the time was that Andrea failed to stop him this time. She said he was with her all night, and the pair of them were punished for that, but there was no evidence that they had been involved in Mandy's death so it was deemed an accident.'

'How old were they at the time?'

Saroj checked her notes. 'She was fourteen and he was sixteen. He was discharged from care soon after this event and he disappeared, didn't keep social work appointments.'

'What about Andrea?'

'She ran away at fifteen and couldn't be found.'

'It could be nothing, but it's an interesting pairing. A violent young man in thrall to one of our suspects.'

'Did you find out why she was in care?'

'Single parent on drugs. Andrea's behaviour was described as wild, and her mother couldn't control her, so much so that she was referred to a child psychiatrist when she was ten. Care Order when she was eleven. No details other than that.'

'Track down the psychiatrist if he or she is still around, will you? Let's find out a bit more about Andrea Reynolds. That's great work, Saroj.'

'Maggie, see if you can find Stephen Crookshank. He's bound to have left a trace somewhere. Send Jack's photofit to the children's home. You never know, we could get lucky.'

The post mortem was straightforward, revealing a blow to the head causing a subdural haematoma. 'One interesting thing is that he seems to have had a meal, fish and chips by the look of it, and a great deal of whisky. I could have become inebriated from the fumes when I opened his stomach.'

'Thanks, doc,' Peter said, smiling at the usually reserved pathologist's attempt at a joke. 'Type of weapon?'

'The indentation would suggest a hammer or possibly a crowbar. Used with some force, I would say.'

'A man then?'

'Not necessarily. The weight of the instrument and a good swing could mean almost anyone might have struck the fatal blow. No hesitation marks though, so someone confident in handling the weapon.' The pathologist pointed to the injury. 'I'd say he was standing, or at least sitting, upright, and the blow was on the left, so a right hander, if they were facing each other, and that seems most likely, considering the position of the injury.'

'Thanks, doc.' Peter looked over at the gurney at the other side of the room, a covered body awaiting Dr Samuels' ministrations. 'Busy morning?'

'Oh him? Suicide, most probably. Found at the bottom of the cliffs, somewhere appropriately, but not very imaginatively, named lover's leap.'

'Do we have a name?'

Dr Samuels consulted a flip chart. 'Spinetti, Harry.'

'Mind if I have a look?'

'Help yourself. You know him?'

Peter pulled back the sheet covering the body. Harry Spinetti's face was battered but there was no mistake. It was Yaz's unwanted admirer. 'He was a witness in a case. Could you let me know if you find anything unusual doc?'

'Certainly, Peter. Can I say you're looking very chipper today. I've thought you were looking a bit dismal, if truth be known. Upturn in your personal life?'

'You could say that, Ben.' Peter headed for the door, smiling like the Cheshire Cat.

Rachel looked up as Peter came into the squad room. Her heart gave a flutter and she was sure everyone would notice the blush that spread up her cheeks. Peter showed no difference in his demeanour than at any other time. However, when he spoke, his voice seemed lighter and a smile played about his lips.

'Morning. Anything new?' He looked around the room expectantly. 'Rachel?'

'Morning, sir. Saroj has found some interesting information

about Yaz, and we're waiting on a communication which may put her and Jack together.'

Saroj filled the DI in on the new findings. A ping on her inbox interrupted the discussion. 'Right. My contact at the children's home has tentatively identified Jack as Stephen Crookshank.' She looked up beaming. 'She's emailing over a photo of when he was sixteen.'

'Kevin and Saroj, bring Yaz in straight away, and this time we're arresting her on suspicion of the murder of Stephen Crookshank.' Peter's energy levels took a leap. *Now we're getting somewhere*, he thought, and his mind strayed to the body of Harry Spinetti lying battered in the morgue. *Too much of a coincidence? Maybe not.* 'I'll be with the Chief.' He left the room with a spring in his step.

As Peter was on his way to see Angela, he received a message from the duty sergeant that Martin Parks wanted to see him, and was waiting in reception. 'Put him in an interview room and I'll see him when I've finished with the DCI.' Then, thinking that Martin may not wait, he decided to ask Rachel to start the interview. 'No, hold on, DS Morris will see him. Oh, and give him a coffee, will you.' Peter was interested in what Martin had to say and didn't want him getting restless. He quickly phoned Rachel and arranged for her to conduct the interview. 'I'll join you when I've finished with Angela.'

'Right, sir.'

Just as he rung off, his phone buzzed again. 'Yes?' he said, a little too sharply.

'Caught you at a bad time?'

Recognising the pathologist's voice, Peter apologised. 'Sorry Ben, just a bit hectic here at the moment.

'I just thought I'd let you know that I found an injury on the head of my suicide, Harry Spinetti, that I thought you might be interested in.'

'Go on, don't keep me in suspense.'

'An indentation which looks man-made rather than the result of falling onto rocks. And here's the interesting bit, it matches the injury to Stephen Crookshank. I'd say, with some certainty, that the two blows were from the same instrument, possibly a hammer.'

'Very interesting, thanks Ben. Report on its way?'

'As we speak. Sorry to add to your workload.'

'Not at all. It could help considerably.'

After asking Maggie to liaise with the local police who dealt with Harry Spinetti's case and secure the scene, he continued to the DCI's office, now with extra news to impart.

Angela waved for Peter to take a seat whilst she finished some paperwork. Looking up, she smiled warmly. 'Help yourself to coffee,' she said. Peter poured two cups. He didn't really want a drink but it made for a more relaxed atmosphere.

'Now, tell me where you are up to with your current cases. It seems you've got more than usual on your plate. They are connected?'

'Almost certainly, and getting more complex by the day.' He filled her in on the latest developments.

'So you think that Andrea Reynolds killed Stephen Crookshank. To do what? Silence him?'

'He may have tried to blackmail her, that's one possibility, or she's just tidying up loose ends. She may think he's unreliable and, knowing that it was only a matter of time before we caught up with him, decided to take him out of the picture.'

'She's not killed before though, as far as you know? It's not easy to take a life, Peter. Do you think she's capable?'

'Anyone's capable in the right circumstances. And then there's Harry Spinetti.'

'Yes, interesting development that. What would be her motive for killing him?'

'Well, we know he was pestering her, perhaps it got out of hand and she lashed out.'

'Just happened to have a hammer to hand on a cliff top?'

'Yes, I know there are things as yet unexplained, but she has a temper, and she's a cool customer, so I wouldn't put it past her.'

'Okay, keep me posted. Oh, how's Sandra Parks by the way? Still in a coma?'

'Her brother's here in an interview room with Rachel. He came in asking to speak to me, so I'll find out. I haven't been to see her for a couple of days myself, and was planning on doing that today sometime.' Peter admonished himself silently for his neglect of Sandra Parks, and felt a bit guilty for his time spent with Rachel. Then he immediately shook himself out of it mentally. *I wouldn't have missed a second of it,* he thought, recalling the picture of her leaving his kitchen this morning, her robe sliding off her lovely smooth shoulders. 'I'll let you know what I find out, ma'am. . . Angela.'

'Okay, Peter. And may I say you're looking better than I've seen you in ages.'

'Getting more sleep ma'am, that must be it.'

Chapter Thirteen

Rachel had completed the preliminaries with Martin and fixed him with a steady stare. 'What can we do for you, Mr Parks?'

'I've been less than frank with you, Detective, concerning Robert Munroe.'

'Go on.'

'I have suspicions that he may be responsible for what happened to Sandra.' Martin thought for a moment before continuing. 'I don't have anything concrete but I know things about him. He's a ruthless character and I think he'd not stop at murder if it helped his cause. Oh, he wouldn't do it himself, of course, but he knows some shady people who are quite capable at a price.'

'Why do you think he would want to hurt your sister?'

'Because of the guildhall, Detective. You see, he paid a lot for that building, an awful lot, and he has to make it pay. The only way he can do that is by developing the site – he has plans for commercial and domestic properties within the building which would net him a tidy profit. If English Heritage were involved, inspecting the building and so on, it would, at best, mean delays, and delay in the property development field means big losses.'

At this point Peter entered the room. Rachel asked Martin to repeat his suspicions.

Peter nodded his understanding. 'And why have you just decided to tell us this now, Mr Parks?'

Martin looked directly at the DI and spoke softly. 'I'm not a violent man, Inspector, but I don't know my own strength sometimes. I tried to take matters into my own hand. you see, and very nearly did something I would regret for ever.'

'Something concerning Robert Munroe?'

'Yes, Inspector. No harm done, but it gave me a jolt, you know? I'm going to leave it to you now. Just look into the bastard, will you? If I can help, I will, contact me any time.'

'So does that put Robert Munroe back in the frame?' Rachel asked as she walked alongside Peter. They had decided to go for a coffee and discuss developments. It also meant that they could be alone and away from eyes that might detect a change in their relationship. They worked with detectives, after all.

'We'll have to look into it. Perhaps there's a connection between Munroe and Stephen Crookshank. It's a long shot, but Crookshank has travelled around, maybe their paths crossed.'

'Long shot alright, and extra work based on what? Martin Parks' suspicions?' Rachel preceded Peter into the café and found a quiet table in the back. When they were seated and coffees ordered, she continued, 'He could be trying to discredit Munroe for his own ends, it certainly seems like there's no love lost.'

Peter had been listening attentively, but changed the subject. 'Are you going to let me cook dinner for you?'

Rachel relaxed her shoulders and leaned across the table. 'Did we come here to talk about us or the case?' She smiled seductively. 'I do want to repeat yesterday, but there's more than dinner on the menu.'

Peter raised his eyebrows in mock disbelief. 'You're very forward, Miss Morris.'

'It's Ms, and I think we should go back to talking about the case before we're forced to get a room.'

Peter laughed out loud, his blue eyes twinkling. 'That's what I like about you, *Ms* Morris, you're all business.' He sat back in his seat and took a sip of coffee. 'Okay. Two lines of enquiry.' He counted off on his fingers. 'One, we'll look briefly into Munroe's background, check if he was ever in the locations where the murders that Crookshank is suspected of took place. Two, look at dealings that Martin Parks has had with Munroe, see where this animosity is coming from, and whether it gives him enough motive to implicate Munroe.'

'D'you think Munroe has any connection with Yaz?'

'*Three* lines of enquiry. Now I'm beginning to sound like Monty Python.' Rachel looked puzzled. 'Before your time? The Spanish Inquisition sketch?' He shook his head. 'Never mind, I'll have to educate you.'

Rachel laughed. 'So it's background checks again. The team will be pleased.' She checked her watch. 'Anyway, Yaz has cooled her heels for long enough now, and the duty solicitor, who I believe is Jackie Cameron, should have arrived, so, reluctantly, I say we head back.'

'Okay. Let's not wait too long before we have that dinner though. I want to get to know you a lot better, Rachel. I can't believe we've worked alongside each other all this time and I don't know the first thing about your life.'

Rachel squeezed his arm. 'That goes for me too. Is tonight too soon?'

Peter gave the team instructions regarding the background checks and noted their displeasure. 'I know, but I do feel we're getting somewhere, so one last push, eh?' The three team members nodded. 'Rachel and I will be interviewing Yaz. Get a message to me if anything turns up.'

In the interview room, Yaz was in deep discussion with Jackie Cameron, which ceased as the two detectives entered. Rachel turned on the recording equipment and asked everyone to introduce themselves. The preliminaries over with, Peter opened a file and, after a brief perusal of the papers, turned to Yaz.

'Tell me about you and Stephen Crookshank.'

Yaz had a whispered conversation with her solicitor, then faced Peter, her hands on the table, nursing a plastic cup of water. 'I met Stephen at a children's home in Leeds.'

'Go on.'

'My mother was a druggie and a slut. When I was little, I did everything I could to get out of the house. When I was four they allowed me to go to school and it was okay. I got fed and I liked stories and books. The teachers said I was well above average with reading and that. A high IQ apparently, though they never said how high. They let me read by myself a lot, nurturing my talent they said, but then they wanted me to mix more because they thought I was becoming *a loner,* and that would never do.'

Yaz sipped some water before continuing. 'Anyway, by the time I was seven, I was bored out of my head. School was crap, home was crap. I took to hanging around the town cadging money and food. Sometimes people would call the police and I'd get taken home. They could see how things were but still left me there. I never understood that. I was referred to a psychiatrist – me! It was the bitch of a mother who should have been referred. They were kind, let me draw and work with plasticine. It was called play therapy and I loved it, especially the modelling. But then it stopped. A report was written and I was sent to a special school. It's not just dumb kids that go to special schools. Who knew? That was alright for a bit but, naturally, they wanted me to *mix*. What is it with this mixing lark? I was happy on my own. Anyway, I started truanting again and they said I was out of control so, in the end, I got sent to a children's home.'

'The one where you met Stephen Crookshank?' Rachel asked.

Yaz nodded. 'I was ten, nearly eleven, he was two years older and had been there a while. He was a bit thick, you know, but he sort of latched on to me. He told me how things worked, how to keep your head down and such. He could wrap the staff round his little finger and showed me how to do the same. We got lots of perks and freedom whilst others were getting punishments, *sanctions*, they called them, or *consequences*. If you did something wrong they didn't shout or anything, just said, '*there will be a consequence to that behaviour*', and then you'd lose privileges or be grounded. It didn't happen much to me or Stephen though.'

Peter looked at his notes. 'Tell me about Mandy Harris.'

Yaz consulted with her solicitor again, then nodded and spoke directly to Peter. 'Little Mandy? She wanted to make trouble for me, couldn't stand that I got special treatment. She stole things and then, miraculously, found them in my room. She damaged things and said she'd seen me doing it, that sort of thing.' Yaz looked uncertain about whether to continue. 'You have to understand, Inspector, Stephen was not very bright and he was, how shall I say, *devoted* to me. I didn't ask him to harm her. He had given one or two others a smack when they'd upset me, but I didn't expect what he did to Mandy. I can tell you this now 'cause he's dead. I covered for him, of course, but things were never quite the same after. He was coming up sixteen by then, so the authorities decided to move him to more independent living. He said he'd come back for me when I was sixteen and we'd move away together. I wasn't having any of that, so I ran away when I was fifteen.'

Jackie Cameron asked for a break at this point, so Rachel drew the session to a close. 'We'll resume in an hour,' she said. 'I'll get you a sandwich, Yaz.'

The team had been busy in Peter's absence but had turned up nothing of interest. Kevin told them. 'Stephen Crookshank has been implicated in a murder in Glasgow, and Robert Munroe has carried out several developments in the city, but the date didn't overlap, and there's no apparent connection between Munroe and the murder victims or Crookshank. I also drew a blank with the London and Halifax murders, and Munroe had no dealings, as far as I can tell, in either location.'

Peter and Rachel listened attentively. 'What about Martin Parks' dealings with Munroe?'

Kevin checked his note book. 'According to his dad, Martin was angry with Munroe for insisting on sub-standard materials on a build that Martin's firm were working on. The planning permission stipulated a strict environmentally sound construction but Munroe didn't adhere to the stipulations, and Martin withdrew from the contract. There was animosity at the time, Mr Parks said, but he thought Martin had got over it now, although he never tendered for any work with Munroe Developments after that. That's why Mr Parks was surprised that Martin put Munroe in contact with Sandra. Perhaps he regretted it.'

'Hmm. Any luck with Yaz and Munroe?'

'Nothing,' said Maggie. 'I can't see how their paths would have crossed. There are a number of calls from her phone to an unknown number, probably a burner phone, but nothing to suggest it was Munroe's. More likely to have been Crookshank.'

'Thanks everyone. I still think Munroe had a lot to gain from burying the guildhall discovery, as Martin Parks said, but maybe not enough to commit murder. So our prime suspect for Miss Parks' attack and Miss Thomas's murder is still Yaz, with Crookshank as her accomplice. We're also holding her on suspicion of the murders of Stephen Crookshank and, because of the similarity of murder weapon, Harry Spinetti.'

'Want to grab some lunch and discuss tactics, Rachel?' Peter said, after telling the team to get something to eat and write up their reports.

After the pair had left, Kevin observed, 'They seem to be spending more time together these days.'

'It's this case, Kevin, we're all working longer hours. And besides, she's not into men, is she?'

'I'm only saying. . . '

'I could see it,' chimed in Saroj. 'There's no evidence that she's gay, and he definitely isn't.'

Maggie was insistent. 'All I'm saying is, let's not start a rumour, you know how they fly around here. Let's just do what we're told. The boss thinks we're getting somewhere, so let's not be distracted by tittle tattle.'

Kevin and Saroj burst out laughing. 'Ooh, *tittle tattle*. . . '

Maggie laughed along with them. 'Come on, let's get some lunch. It's fish and chip day in the canteen.'

Chapter Fourteen

Settled in the Harbour Inn with a pasty and a pint each, Peter and Rachel were focused on Yaz. If any of the team had seen them, they would have concluded that their relationship was purely professional, and all talk of romantic involvement would end. They would not have suspected the hidden feelings smouldering just under the surface, feelings that would be unleashed later that day. But, for now, the case was everything, as they discussed how they would handle the commencement of the interview with Yaz.

'We need a murder weapon, Rachel. Nothing from the search of Yaz's studio or the Spinetti murder scene?'

'Nothing sir. Blood found on the cliff top was Spinetti's, so it looks like he was hit over the head and then pushed over. We do know it was the same weapon in his and the Crookshank murder, so safe to say the same assailant.'

'Probably, and Yaz had motive for both. Spinetti was a nuisance and Crookshank, if we're right about him being the hit man, knew too much. We know that she had tried to get away from him once. Maybe this time she wanted rid of him for good.'

'We can question her about the CCTV footage showing her near to where Crookshank was staying.'

'It's something, but she lives close to there so could have been legitimately in the area. We have to get her to admit she visited him, at least.' Peter thoughtfully sipped his beer. 'I've been wondering what happened to the whisky bottle, and who bought the fish and chips. Get Maggie and Kevin to search nearby waste bins for the bottle, and take the photos of Yaz and Crookshank to local fish and chip shops.'

'It could have been Tracy Walker, sir. Perhaps Crookshank gave her the money to get the fish supper and whisky.' Peter nodded, so Rachel made a note. 'I'll get the team to check that out too.'

'We need this information to get to us during the interview, so impress on them the urgency, will you?'

'I think they're well motivated, sir. If it's out there, they'll find it.'

'Mmm. And I want that murder weapon. Tell Saroj to organise another search of Yaz's studio. I'd stake my reputation on it being there.'

'No pressure, then,' Rachel quipped.

Peter smiled warmly at her. 'Come on, if we box this off by the end of today, just think how much sweeter this evening will be.'

On the way back to the station, Peter received a call from the hospital. Sandra was coming out of the coma. 'I'll be right there,' he said and turned to Rachel. 'We'll have to keep Yaz in the cells for a bit longer.' He made a quick call to the station to arrange it. 'Want to come with me?'

'Of course. I hope she's able to tell us something useful.'

'Me too, but I'm not getting my hopes up just yet, she may not remember anything.'

Peter and Rachel bumped into Martin Parks coming out of the hospital shop with a large bunch of flowers. He was reading the front page of a newspaper and didn't notice the detectives at first. When he did, he gestured towards the headline in the paper. 'If that doesn't take the biscuit. Bobby comes up smelling of roses again.'

Property developer hands historic find over to National Trust.

Peter scanned the text and the photo of Robert Munroe standing in front of the guildhall shaking hands with *a representative of the National Trust.* 'I see what you mean. But why would he do that?'

Martin shook his head. 'Don't you understand, Inspector? The publicity he gets from this is worth hundreds of thousands to him. The projects will come rolling in. And to think I may have had a hand in it.'

Peter looked quizzical. Martin clarified. 'I threatened him with exposure, said I'd let English Heritage know of his plans to desecrate a historic building. He turned that around so that he became hero instead of villain.' He gave a hollow laugh. 'Got to hand it to the man.'

Peter handed the newspaper back to Martin, changing the subject. 'How's your sister? I heard she's come out of the coma. You must be relieved.'

'Yes, Mum and Dad are with her. Her eyes are open but she's not able to talk yet. Still seems a bit out of it actually, but the doc says it's natural to be confused at first. They're hopeful that she'll progress quite quickly now. Did you want to see her?'

'Yes, just a brief visit, we won't get in your way too much, I want to ask her a few questions if she's up to it.'

'Well, promise you won't tire her out though, we don't want any setbacks at this stage, Inspector.'

The three of them walked together to the ward. Martin was curious. 'Have you got the man who did this to her then?'

'We have a suspect in custody, I can't say more than that at the moment, sorry.'

'It's okay, I'm just glad to have Sandy back with us. Good luck with your suspect though. I hope you throw the book at him.'

Sandra's vision was still a bit blurry as she looked at the man stood next to her brother in the doorway. *There's my inspector.* She took in the tall muscular man with fair hair cut short, angular features with straight eyebrows and hooded eyes. His nose seemed to have been broken at some time but, rather than detract from his appearance, made him more attractive. *Not quite what I expected but a strong face, determined too.* He came closer to the bed, nodding briefly at

113

her parents. 'Hello, Sandra.' He smiled broadly. *A lovely smile.* 'Good to see you and, more to the point, good that you can see me.'

'I won't bother you too much but I wanted to see you and let you know that we think we're getting to the bottom of your attack. Mr and Mrs Parks and Martin had left the room to get some coffee, so Peter felt able to confide some details to Sandra. 'We're pretty sure that the man who did this to you is dead.' Sandra's eyes widened. 'I can see you understand me. We believe he may also be responsible for Polly's death, but we're yet to confirm that.' Sandra looked sad and tears formed in her eyes. Her brow furrowed questioningly. 'We don't fully understand why at the moment, Sandra, but it has something to do with your friend Yaz, we're pretty sure about that.'

Sandra shook her head. *Yaz? You can't be serious why would Yaz want to hurt me?*

'I understand that Yaz was in love with you, and that you let her know you weren't interested. Is that right?' Sandra nodded slowly. 'Did the man who attacked you mention her name?' Sandra shook her head. 'Did he say anything at all?' Sandra thought for a bit, then nodded. She tried to speak but the sound was just a groan. 'Could you write it down?' She nodded again.

Peter took out his notebook and pencil and handed it to Sandra. Her hand shook with the effort of writing but, in shaky letters, she spelled out *Avenging Angel,* and handed the book back. She slumped back, making an expression that Peter read as 'sorry'. 'That's great, Sandra. We'll leave you in peace now. Get some rest and I'll see you tomorrow.'

'So did Crookshank see himself as Yaz's avenging angel?' Rachel mused as the pair drove back to the station. 'Or was it a reference to Yaz's desire for revenge?'

'Either way, Rachel, it puts Yaz at the centre. He did it for her, I'm sure of that. We can use this new information, see how she responds when we put it to her.'

'But why Polly? She doesn't seem to have a connection with Yaz.'

'I don't know. Perhaps he was out of control. We believe he's murdered before, could be coincidence?'

114

'We don't believe in coincidence though, do we?' Rachel commented. 'She worked with Sandra. Did Yaz have a thing for her too?'

Peter shrugged. 'Can't see it myself. If she was really in love with Sandra, it seems a bit unlikely that she would fall for Polly as well. Unless it was to make Sandra jealous.'

'Not a motive to have her killed though. And Polly wouldn't have welcomed any advances surely, she was with Paul.'

'Let's not over complicate things with speculation. We've got a number of questions to put to Yaz yet, so let's see where that gets us. I just wish we could find the Crookshank and Spinetti murder weapon. If we can prove that Yaz was responsible for those killings, I'm confident she'll give us Crookshank for the others.'

Chapter Fifteen

The start of the interview was taken up with Jackie Cameron making it known that she was not pleased at the way her client had been treated so far.

'Ms Cameron, I'm sorry that you and your client had to wait, but we received a phone call telling us that Sandra Parks has regained consciousness and we went to check a couple of things out with her.'

Yaz looked up startled. 'She's okay now?'

'Miss Parks is making a good recovery, and she had some interesting things to say about her attacker.' Peter knew he was stretching a point but he felt he was justified in the circumstances.

Yaz was about to ask a question but Peter raised his hand to stop her. 'We'll get to that in due course. First I want to ask you about Stephen Crookshank. We have you on CCTV near where he was staying, can you tell us what you were doing there?'

'I live near there. I use the corner shop a lot so I'd have to pass. . . ' Yaz stopped and consulted her solicitor. 'I have nothing to say about that,' she continued.

'So you know where Stephen Crookshank was staying?'

'No comment.'

'We have a witness who can place you in his lodgings.'

'Hmm. I don't think so.' Yaz's solicitor whispered something to her. 'Okay,' said Yaz, clearly irritated.

'You brought fish and chips and a bottle of whisky, and were upstairs with Stephen Crookshank for quite a while, weren't you?'

'No comment.'

'Was Stephen becoming a liability, Yaz? Did you get him drunk and then kill him?'

'No comment.'

'We know that Stephen attacked Sandra Parks, and we have fingerprint evidence to show he killed Polly Thomas.' Again Peter was stretching a point because the pathologist had found only a partial print on Polly's arms, but that partial matched Crookshank.'

'Is that a question?'

'Did you incite Stephen Crookshank to attack Sandra Parks and also to kill Polly Thomas?'

'No bloody comment.'

Rachel took over the interview. 'You've had a sad life, haven't you, Yaz? Mother not there for you, brought up in care. . . '

'Care! That's a good one. They're only there because they get paid. They don't *care* for you.'

Jackie Cameron touched Yaz's arm. 'Oh, bloody shut up!' said Yaz, irritated. 'You're just the same. Paid to *represent* me. You don't care if I'm guilty or innocent, it's all in a day's work for you.

'No one knows about my life. I learned to look after myself very young. How would you feel coming home from school to find your mother in bed with one druggie and your own bed occupied by another?' I got *myself* taken into care. Bloody social workers kept giving that cow another chance. *The child is always best with its mother*. What a load of crap. They went home to their little families at the end of the day, like you all do, so don't talk to me about care.' Yaz smirked. 'It was convenient, though. I got a clean room, regular meals and an education, and they were easy to manipulate, these care workers, so I had an easy ride.'

Rachel thought she was getting through to Yaz, so continued on the same tack. 'Stephen Crookshank helped you, didn't he? He cared about you?'

'Ha! Stupid Stephen, yes he cared. Cared enough to do anything for me, like a little puppy dog. Wanted us to *be together always*, that's what he said, but I wasn't having any of that.'

'You ran away when you were fifteen, you said, what happened then?'

'I survived. Tossed a coin to see whether I would go North or South, South won. Hitched and did odd jobs on the way and ended up in Devon.'

'You went to Plymouth University. You had no qualifications, so how did that happen?'

'Did an access course. I'm not thick, you know. Breezed through it and decided to do a fine arts degree. I was good at art, and it meant I didn't have to sit behind a desk all day. I could be my own person.'

'And you are. Your work is very good.'

Yaz smiled. 'Glad you like it.'

'Then Stephen found you. How did that make you feel?'

Yaz looked troubled. 'He was all grown up. Same Stephen but stronger, you know, pushy. We got drunk one night and I told him about Sandy. He was jealous as hell. Then when I said she'd dumped me, he got angry, he was out of control really, I should have realised.'

'Realised what, Yaz?'

Jackie Cameron interrupted. 'My client needs a break.'

Yaz seemed to realise where she was. 'Yeah. I need a break.'

Damn, thought Rachel, turning off the recording equipment. 'Right, we'll get back in an hour.'

As the constable led Yaz away, Maggie was hurrying down the corridor in the opposite direction. 'Just coming to find you sir,' she said to Peter. 'We've found the whisky bottle and it's got Yaz's prints and Crookshank's prints all over it.'

Back in the squad room, the team took stock. Peter led the discussion. 'We can place Yaz in the vicinity of Stephen's lodgings, and we can show that they shared a bottle of whisky. If we can match that whisky to Stephen's stomach contents, then we can put her at the scene. But we still can't show that she killed him. We need that murder weapon.'

'Rachel was doing well taking Yaz back to her past. She's clearly a disturbed. . . '

Saroj jumped in. 'Sorry sir, slipped my mind. We had a call back from a Henry Small, Ms Henrietta Small, actually. She was the child

118

psychiatrist who treated Yaz when she was seven.' Saroj checked her notes. 'Ms Small described Andrea Reynolds as having tendencies to become a *high functioning sociopath*.'

'What, she could tell that at seven?' Peter was aghast.

'Apparently. And she said that Andrea was highly intelligent and manipulative.'

'Hmm. Damned at seven. It certainly fits though. Would Ms Small be willing to testify as an expert witness?'

'She said that would be difficult because personality disorders cannot officially be diagnosed in childhood. She was giving me her opinion only. Called Andrea *an unforgettable child*.'

'Right, well it's good to know, anyway. Kevin, did you get anywhere with the fish and chip shops?'

'One place remembered Yaz, but said she comes in quite often so couldn't pinpoint the day.'

'Right. I want the three of you to turn that studio upside down again. The murder weapon is there, I'm sure of it. Find it! We're running out of time.'

'Okay, Yaz, I want to talk to you about Harry Spinetti.'

Yaz looked blank, clearly back in control of her emotions. 'A question?' she said sarcastically.

'When did you last see Mr Spinetti?'

'Can't recall.'

'How well do you know Mr Spinetti?'

Yaz looked from her solicitor to the detectives. 'You know this. He vouched for me when you last had me in here, accusing me of lord knows what. You were wrong then, too.'

'How often have you seen him since then?'

'Not since I boarded that back door up.' She smirked. 'Spoiled his fun, that did.'

'Did you see him on the twelfth of this month?'

'No comment.' Yaz smiled at Jackie Cameron as if to say, *see – I can do it.*

'On the twelfth did you go for a walk with him along the coast path?'

'You must be bloody joking. Sorry, no comment.'

'Did you kill Harry Spinetti and throw his body over the cliff?'

'No comment.'

Rachel took over the questioning. 'Did Stephen enjoy his fish supper?'

Yaz's eyes darted left and right. 'No comment.'

'You went to his lodgings with a fish supper and a bottle of whisky, didn't you?'

Yaz remained silent.

'You see, we have a whisky bottle with both your prints on, and smudges of grease, very probably from chips.'

Yaz said nothing.

'We also have a positive identification of you at a fish and chip shop adjacent to Stephen Crookshank's lodgings.'

Yaz's solicitor jumped in. 'Where is this going, Inspector? Do you have any actual evidence that my client was in any way involved in Stephen Crookshank's murder? What you've given us so far is circumstantial at best.'

Chapter Sixteen

Kevin, Maggie and Saroj stood in the doorway of Yaz's studio. Kevin voiced what they were all thinking. 'This is a total waste of time. We've been through and through this place.'

'Well, we'll just have to go through again. Let's divide up and see if we can unearth anything.'

The search lasted about half an hour, with nothing new turning up. 'The boss isn't going to be pleased. Perhaps she threw the hammer over the cliff after Spinetti.'

'SOCO have combed the area and found nothing so far,' said Maggie, idly sorting through the tools on the worktop.

Saroj was dusting herself off at the doorway, ready to call it a day. The other two joined her and took one last look at the studio. 'She is a talented artist,' said Maggie. 'It looks like she's finished the Angel.' As they all stood and stared at the statue, a ray of late evening sun shone through a high window, illuminating the top of the statue. 'The face is bronze, isn't it, or brass? It's certainly gleaming in the sunlight. And it looks like Yaz.'

Saroj agreed. 'She's the avenging angel.'

The three were mesmerised for a moment, then Kevin said, 'Wait a minute, what's that in her hand?'

The statue's right hand was raised rather like the statue of liberty, and in it was what looked like a hammer.

f

Chapter Seventeen

The interview was becoming repetitive, and Peter was about to call a break when there was a light tap on the door. 'DI Sanders is leaving the room.'

In the squad room Kevin held up an evidence bag with the hammer in it. 'Yaz's fingerprints are on it and we're checking the blood now.'

Peter pumped the air. 'Bloody marvellous! We've got her now.'

After half an hour, Peter and Rachel were ready to continue the interview. The blood results had shown two different blood types which were a match for Crookshank and Spinetti. DNA analysis would take longer, but the blood types were enough, along with the fingerprints on the hammer, to charge Yaz with the murder of the two men.

Jackie Cameron started talking almost before the two detectives were in the room. 'Either charge my client or let her go. You obviously are just on a fishing expedition here with nothing but flimsy circumstantial evidence, and you are running out of time.'

Peter ignored the solicitor and began recording the session. 'Continuing the interview with Andrea Reynolds, six-fifteen. Persons present are the same as previously.'

Peter slowly opened the folder in front of him and slid a photograph across the table towards Yaz. It showed the post mortem shot of the head injury to Stephen Crookshank. Yaz looked across at the solicitor and then at Peter. She raised her eyebrows in silent query. Peter responded. 'I am showing Ms Reynolds a photograph of the head injury sustained by Stephen Crookshank.'

'Really, Inspector,' said the solicitor indignantly. 'Is this necessary?'

Ignoring the outburst, Peter pushed another photograph across the table. 'I am showing Ms Reynolds a further photograph, this one is of the head injury to Harry Spinetti.' Yaz looked from one image to the other, turning a little pale. Peter continued, 'Do you see the similarities? Both of these injuries were made by the same implement.'

Yaz remained silent but Jackie Cameron protested yet again: 'What is the purpose of this, Inspector? My client has denied anything to do with these murders, so my original comments stand. Either charge her or let her go.'

Peter continued to ignore the solicitor, which clearly irritated her. 'I am now showing Ms Reynolds a photograph of the weapon we believe was responsible for both these injuries.'

Yaz's eyes moved wildly around the room and she visibly shook.

'Do you recognise this item, Ms Reynolds? It has on it the blood of both of the victims and, more importantly, your fingerprints.'

Yaz shook her head nervously and turned towards her solicitor, who said, 'Detective Inspector Sanders, I would like a private consultation with my client.'

'Of course,' he replied, gathering up the photographs. 'Interview suspended at six thirty-five.'

The team members looked up expectantly as the two detectives re-entered the squad room. 'Not yet,' said Peter. 'But we're nearly there.'

'Her face said it all,' commented Rachel. 'She knows the game's up and so does Cameron. Who will no doubt be suggesting a deal or a lesser charge.'

As the team were discussing the possible outcomes, a light knock came on the door. Maggie, being closest, opened it and beckoned

Jackie Cameron in. Speaking to Peter, she said, 'My client would like to make a statement, Inspector.'

'Very well. We'll be there in a few minutes.' Peter let out a long sigh as the solicitor left the room. 'This is it, team. It's been a brute of a case but we've got there in the end. The next hour should answer our questions. Thank you for your dedication and hard work. Drinks will be on me later.'

After the interview had been restarted, Peter invited Yaz to make her statement. 'Take your time Yaz, and tell me what happened from the beginning.'

Yaz took a deep breath and began reading from some prepared notes. 'First of all, I want to say that I did strike Stephen Crookshank and Harry Spinetti, but it was in self-defence.' She looked up at Peter who remained expressionless. 'Stephen came after me years ago when I left the children's home at fifteen. He eventually found me through some advertising for a theatre production at the Minack Theatre where I had done the scenery. He tracked me down and wouldn't let me be. He said we should be together and he was very forceful in his demands.' Yaz sniffed away some tears. 'He followed me around and wouldn't let me alone. I tried to just be his friend, had drinks with him and even told him that I was a lesbian. He refused to believe me, so I told him about Sandy, how I loved her and how she had dumped me. He got that look on his face like he used to at the children's home, all fierce and trembling. Anyway, I stupidly told him where she lived. I was drunk and thought he'd just give her a scare, it was my revenge, I suppose.' Yaz sought a tissue which was supplied by her solicitor.

'Are you alright to continue?' Peter asked.

'Yeah. I want to tell you. I bumped into him when I was leaving Sandy's flat that night. I told him she wasn't there and to leave her alone. I went back to my studio, like I said, and I thought he'd gone too. When I heard about what had happened to Sandy I knew it was him. That's why I gave you his description, I wanted him caught.'

'Do you know where the weapons he used are?'

'In a rucksack in the loft at his lodgings. He's done this before, you know. He bragged about it to me, how he stalked women and killed them. He had tools and chloroform in his rucksack. He enjoyed it, you could see it in his eyes. Anyway, he wouldn't let up on me. He pestered me about other relationships I'd had, but I said it was only Sandy and that she had left me for Paul, where she worked. He's not the brightest tool in the box, Inspector, and it seems he misheard me and, believing Sandy to be gay, he thought I said Pol, short for Polly.'

'Did he tell you that he had killed Polly?'

'Yeah. He boasted about it. Said he hired a canoe and followed her out when she went swimming. He pretended he was in difficulties and she. . . ' Yaz choked back a tear, 'she went to help him. He held her under till she drowned.' Yaz shook her head sadly. 'He came to see me after, like a cat bringing a dead mouse to its owner. I was very scared of him but couldn't let him see that.'

'Why didn't you come to us with this information?'

'I don't know, I was scared he'd find out, I suppose. I planned to finish the Angel and leave, run away again. I went to see Stephen where he was living with the fat bird and I thought we could have a drink like old times and I'd persuade him to just be friends. He stripped off his clothes and came at me, throwing me onto the bed. I still had my tool belt on and he was unclipping it when I just grabbed the hammer from it and lashed out. He fell backwards and stopped moving. I wriggled from under him and rolled him over onto the bed. Then I left. It was self-defence.'

'Did you see Tracy Walker on your way out?'

'Who? Oh yeah, she was watching telly. I'd given her some chips and she was stuffing her face. I told her not to let on I'd been there. She's a bit dim but she understood.'

'Understood what?'

'I didn't threaten her or anything, just said not to let on.'

'Are you alright to continue, Yaz, or do you need a break?'

Jackie Cameron nodded, and Yaz said she would like something to drink and a short break.

* * *

125

Peter came into the squad room, running his hands through his hair. Rachel had taken the opportunity to freshen up as this was set to be a long session.

'Well, we've got a confession for Crookshank, but she's claiming self-defence. She's also told us that Crookshank was responsible for Sandra Parks' attack and Polly Thomas's murder. He told her that he'd killed other women as well. Kevin, I want you to go to Tracy Walker's place. There should be a rucksack in the loft containing items used in the attack on Miss Parks.'

'What about Spinetti, sir?' asked Saroj. Kevin halted on his way out to catch the answer.

'We'll put that to her next. My guess is that she'll persist with a claim of self-defence for that, too.'

Rachel entered, having splashed her face and tied her hair back neatly. She looked fresh and eager. Peter smiled warmly at her. 'You okay to ask Yaz about Spinetti?'

'Of course, sir, I'll look forward to it. It really feels like we're in the home straight, doesn't it?'

'We've got a result on Sandra Parks' attack and Polly Thomas's murder and a confession on Crookshank's murder. We'll get a lot of brownie points for helping to clear up Crookshank's other murders, that is if fingerprint and DNA evidence helps with them. So, all in all, I'd say we've had a good day so far.'

'Just Spinetti to go then. I think that, now she's started talking, she'll want to get it all off her chest.'

'You could be right, Rachel. So, if you're ready?' And Peter held the door open for her to walk through.

After the preliminaries, Peter asked Yaz if she was okay to continue. She nodded and looked down at her notes again.

Rachel pushed the post mortem photograph of Harry Spinetti across the table. 'As we told you previously, Ms Reynolds, this wound was caused by the weapon you have identified as the one you used to attack and kill Stephen Crookshank.' Yaz nodded morosely. 'Could you now tell us what happened with Harry Spinetti.'

Yaz looked nervously at her solicitor who nodded encouragingly. 'Harry wouldn't leave me alone. I told him I wasn't interested in men but he didn't accept it. He made crude suggestions about what he would like to do to me. I had found porn magazines at the back of the studio where he used to watch me and they were all S&M, so you can guess what he wanted. He was smaller than me and weedy looking, as you know, but he had the power to take the studio away, and I wanted to finish the Angel, so I strung him along.' Yaz took a long pause but Rachel waited her out. 'When I got back from Stephen, I was shaken and agitated. He was there, Harry, touching the Angel and leering. He could see that I'd made it in my own image, now that the face was finished, and I think it turned him on. I couldn't stand him being in the same room as my work so I suggested a walk. He looked disappointed at first, but I said we could come back later and have a drink, not that I had any intention.'

'What was your intention, Yaz?'

Jackie Cameron leaned over and whispered something into Yaz's ear. Yaz resumed. 'I wanted to talk to him, that's all, explain again that I wasn't interested and that I'd report him to the police if he didn't stop harassing me. I had almost finished my project now, so I decided it didn't matter if he threw me out. We walked up towards Pendennis Point along the coast path. He kept telling me how much he adored me and that he could make me happy, that sort of thing. I tried to explain that I was gay but he said he'd had gay relationships himself, and he could tell I swung both ways. We stopped to look down on a secluded cove. It's a beautiful spot. The tide was coming in and crashing on the rocks. I said something like how lovely it was and he jumped me. Grabbed my arms and tried to push me to the ground. I guess he caught me off guard and I stumbled backwards. He threw himself at me and I instinctively reached to my tool belt and found the hammer I used earlier. I hit him over the head and he slumped forward onto me. There was a lot of blood. I pushed him off and rolled him over the cliff.'

Yaz looked exhausted, she was totally spent. She dropped forward, resting her head on the table.

'Just a couple more questions,' said Rachel, holding her palm towards the solicitor who was about to protest. 'Was Harry Spinetti dead when you rolled him over the cliff?'

Yaz looked startled, as if she was waking from a dream. 'Dead? I don't know. He was bleeding and very still, that's all I know.'

'Why didn't you report these two incidents to the police, if they were self-defence as you say?'

'I don't know. Not in my DNA, I suppose. I just wanted to run.'

Peter took over. 'Thank you for being so frank with us, Ms Reynolds. I'll get the constable to take you back to the cells now. You will be charged in due course, do you understand?'

Yaz nodded wearily.

Kevin had found the rucksack where Yaz said it would be and, after photographing it in situ, had handed it over to forensics for analysis. He had been disturbed again by the conditions that Tracy Walker was living in. She had a new man living there who was clearly under the influence of something. Tracy was sat watching the TV and the pair hardly noticed as Kevin and the uniformed constable entered through the open door, introduced themselves and went upstairs.

Kevin was talking to Maggie about it when Peter and Rachel came into the squad room smiling triumphantly. 'There's nothing we can do about it, Kevin,' Maggie was saying. 'They're not breaking any laws and, if people want to live like pigs in shit, then I guess it's their business.'

Then all eyes turned expectantly on Peter and Rachel. 'Ladies and gentleman, we have a result!' Peter said to the team who gave a resounding cheer. 'Yaz has confessed to murdering Spinetti. She claims it was self-defence but we expected that. We'll have to put our evidence to the CPS, but I'm confident we'll get the go ahead to charge her with murder. We only have her word that she was afraid for her life when she struck them, and she did have the hammer with her, by chance, she says, but it could point to premeditation.'

'Do you believe her, sir?'

Peter thought for a moment. 'No. I think she intended to kill them, get them out of her hair. I believe she is also guilty of incitement for the attack on Sandra Parks, and accessory to Polly Thomas's murder, but that may be difficult to prove. We know she's a highly intelligent and resourceful woman. The child psychiatrist believed that she would become a high functioning sociopath and my bet is she was right.'

Rachel agreed. 'I bet Jackie Cameron asks for a psychiatric report, preparing for a plea of diminished responsibility.'

'That's possible, Rachel, but out of our hands.' Peter turned to Kevin. 'How about the rucksack, was it where Yaz said it would be?'

'Yes sir. I've dropped it off at forensics, but a quick glance inside showed a number of tools and there was a strong smell of chloroform.'

'Well that was true at least. If we find Sandra Parks' blood on the tools, we have a clear result. I'm sure the family will be relieved to know we have confirmed who her attacker was.' Peter looked weary but pleased. I'll go and fill the Chief in and contact CPS. You get some coffee and have a well-deserved break.'

Chapter Eighteen

Angela Morton was at her desk, eyes glued to her computer screen. She waved Peter in absentmindedly and held up a hand to signify that she would just be a moment. Closing the laptop lid she turned to him and smiled. 'Tired but happy, seems to be a good description. You have news for me?'

Peter managed a wry smile. 'Yes, ma'am. We have a confession based on self-defence for both murders. I've spoken to the CPS and they're happy for us to charge Andrea Reynolds with two counts of murder.'

'Not manslaughter?'

'There are holes in the self-defence claim. The lawyers can fight it out in court. There's a possibility that there will be a request for psychiatric reports, and that may be appropriate. She's an unusual individual, to say the least.'

Peter filled Angela in on the other results concerning Sandra Parks and Polly Thomas, as well as the possible clear up of old cases.

Angela was impressed. 'That's a great result, Peter.' She looked thoughtful. 'I have just got them to agree to my early retirement.'

'Congratulations, ma'am.'

Angela held up her hand. 'Only on the understanding that I can recommend a replacement.' She paused briefly. 'You've shown yourself to be a great leader, Peter, and I detect a renewed enthusiasm for the job.'

'I'm flattered, Angela. You know I like to be hands on though. Being a desk jockey doesn't suit me.'

'Horses for courses, to extend the metaphor. Lots of DCIs continue with hands on work Peter, that shouldn't be a problem.'

'In that case, ma'am, I'm delighted to accept.'

Sandra was sitting up in her hospital bed, looking a lot better than the last time Peter saw her. She smiled as he walked through the door. Her voice was still a little croaky, but improving. 'Good to see you detective. Do you have news, or is this a social visit?'

'Both. How are you feeling?'

Sandra indicated her position with a wave of her hands. 'As you see, I'm sitting up and taking notice. It'll be a couple of weeks before they let me out, but I can cope with that.' Sandra observed the serious look on Peter's face. 'Is it bad news?' she said, suddenly feeling concerned.

Peter brightened. 'No, not at all, though you may find it surprising.'

'Don't keep me in suspense.'

'Yaz has confessed to killing two men, one of whom was the perpetrator of the attack on you.'

Sandra's eyes widened. 'Yaz, but why?'

Peter gave Sandra as much information as he felt able to, stressing that what he was telling her was, for the moment, confidential. Sandra was quiet for a few minutes, as she considered the events of the last weeks and the surprising outcome.

Peter changed the subject, and talked for the rest of the visit about Sandra's remarkable recovery and her plans for the future. By the time he left, she was her usual smiling self, though Peter knew that the thought of her friend having a role in the attack on her would haunt her for a while yet.

Chapter Nineteen

The Harbour View was packed at eight o'clock, but the team had managed to find a table and were lining up the drinks as Peter fought his way through the crowd. He pulled up a chair next to Rachel and gave her a resounding kiss. The team exchanged looks and Kevin said, 'Told you so.'

Rachel looked flushed and happy and returned the kiss with enthusiasm. The pair ignored shouts of 'get a room' and simply raised their glasses. 'To a successful outcome on several fronts,' said Peter beaming. 'Cheers!'

The team joined in as Peter whispered in Rachel's ear. 'There's a bottle of champagne with our name on it back at my place.'

She smiled and said, 'Feeling tired myself, actually.'

Peter downed his drink. 'There's enough behind the bar for a good night, so enjoy yourselves, and well done again.' Eyebrows were raised as Rachel accompanied Peter out of the door. 'Should have had a bet on that,' said Kevin glumly.

The gourmet dinner that Peter had planned was abandoned and he stopped for a take-away on the way back. However, when he and Rachel arrived, Peter placed the food in the oven, picked up the champagne and two glasses and headed for the bedroom, his arm around Rachel's shoulder. Stopping in the doorway, she reached up and kissed him passionately. 'I think the champagne can wait,' she said, and Peter needed no encouragement.

Epilogue

Six months later. . .

Rachel spoke into her phone. 'Peter, where are you? We're going to be late. Give me a ring as soon as you get this. Love you.'

Peter looked at his phone. *Love you too*, he thought as he examined the three rings he had selected for his shortlist. Picking up a square cut diamond solitaire, he held it to the light. 'This one,' he said decisively. 'All class, with a bit of attitude.' *Just like the woman who I hope will be wearing it*, he thought.

'Couldn't have put it better myself, sir,' said the jeweller, finding a velvet lined box.

After paying the eye-watering bill, Peter returned Rachel's call. 'I'll be with you in fifteen minutes. We'll be in plenty of time, don't worry. Love you.'

Now a well-established couple, Peter and Rachel had been invited to see work starting on the guildhall. Sandra had been retained by the National Trust as a consultant, and it was today that she would oversee 'breaking ground' on the project, a cause for celebration after months of investigations and archaeology. The fact that this January day was bright and sunny made for a festive atmosphere, even though the ground was rock hard for the small digger. A team of specialist builders and stone masons had been commissioned, and they were all there waiting with their plastic cups for a toast in champagne to acknowledge that work had begun.

Rachel and Peter parked the car and ran up to the site just as the digger lifted a ceremonial sod from the ground at the side of the building. Sandra popped the cork on the first bottle and, with a cheer from the assembled crowd, filled their cups.

It was a lovely event made all the sweeter for Peter seeing Sandra back to full health and smiling broadly. Spotting him, she came over. 'My lovely inspector,' she said, kissing his cheek. Then smiling at Rachel, she said, 'I know he's really your lovely inspector, but a girl can dream.'

'You really helped me though, Peter. All those long nights listening to you examining my case, it gave me lots to think about.' She smiled ruefully. 'I wouldn't make a good inspector though, would I? Suggesting it was all about money and Robert Munroe.'

'Can't blame you for suspecting Munroe, Sandra. Martin reckoned that he was relieved when you were in hospital, and he could get on with his plans without interference. It would be too late to stop him once he'd started demolition, and he could plead ignorance, of course.' Sandra nodded as Peter continued. 'He's a smart man though, his generous *gift* to the nation gave him maximum publicity for his other bids.'

Peter ran his fingers through his hair. 'I still don't understand what Crookshank was looking for, though.' Sandra looked puzzled. 'The CDs and books on the floor? It suggests he was searching for something.'

Sandra smiled knowingly. 'I've been thinking about that, Inspector. I'm pretty sure that was Yaz – her protest against what she saw as my reason for rejecting her. Her messiness, Peter. And she left that sandwich deliberately, I'm sure of it. She knew how I would react. I'd have to spend hours cleaning every trace out of my kitchen.' Sandra shook her head sadly. 'She's such a damaged person, Peter. I didn't know all about her early life and, now that I do, I can sort of understand her better. What do you think will happen to her?'

'The trial's been held over for psychiatric reports. I think that she'll be found guilty of manslaughter, and they'll take her mental state into account in the sentencing. I still believe that she knew exactly what she was doing when she told Stephen Crookshank about you, and the mix up between Polly and Paul's names sounds too bizarre not to be true. But she wanted Paul to have the same treatment as you, I don't doubt that.'

'So it was all about revenge?'

'The Avenging Angel? Why not? I don't think it was all about you, though. With a past like hers, she had a lot to be angry about. I hope she gets help, but I can't forgive her for her actions, she was responsible for three deaths, after all.'

Rachel placed her hand on Peter's shoulder. 'Enough gloomy talk. Today is about Sandra's success.'

'Yes, my guildhall was saved.' Sandra looked proudly at the old building. 'I can't wait to see it returned to its former glory.' She looked teasingly at the couple before her. 'I think the Trust has plans to use it as a wedding venue, amongst other things.'

Peter was about to comment, when an official looking man from the Trust called to Sandra. 'I'd better go,' she said. 'Photo opportunity. Munroe's not the only one who needs publicity. Have some more fizz, you two.'

Peter put his arm around Rachel as they watched Sandra weave her way through the crowd. 'I've booked us a lunch at Romano's and there'll be more champagne if you can manage it.'

'We celebrating something?' Rachel asked.

Peter patted his pocket. 'I certainly hope so.'

Book Two

Dust to Dust

Ah, make the most of what we may yet spend.
Before we too into the Dust descend;
Dust to Dust, and under Dust, to lie,
Sans Wine, sans Song, sans Singer, and – sans End!

Rubaiyat of Omar Khayyam – First Edition, 1859

Chapter One

'What can I say about Angela Morton?' Peter Sanders stood on a chair in the packed pub, surrounded by colleagues from the Truro branch of the Devon and Cornwall Police. A few ribald comments were shouted out by way of suggestions. Peter held up his hand to request quiet. 'I've known and respected Angela for many years now. I won't say how many years as I don't want to give away her age – or mine for that matter. But in that time, I've come to respect her quiet good sense and her calm approach to, what we can all agree, are often tragic and challenging situations.' Peter glanced over to where Rachel stood, drink in hand, smiling encouragingly. Peter had rehearsed his speech that morning as they were having breakfast. He continued. 'Angela was not only my DCI but, I hope she will agree, my friend, and she has always been encouraging and positive when I've needed it. So, thank you Angela, and the very best of luck in your retirement. Please raise your glasses to our DCI as she bows out. The Chief!'

The toast was echoed by the assembled crowd, followed by a round of applause and shouts of 'speech' aimed at Angela Morton. 'Well, just a few words then.' She said. 'But I'm not standing on that thing,' indicating the chair. 'Thank you, Peter, for your kind words. If I knew I was that good, I might have stayed.' General laughter rippled around the room. 'I've been very happy here at Truro. . . '

Peter's phone vibrated in his pocket and he made for the quiet of the exit to take the call. 'Sorry to bother you, sir,' said the duty sergeant. 'We've had a report of a body over near St Just.'

Peter took the details and turned to see Rachel at his elbow.

'What's up?' She enquired, knowing it could only be work.

'We've got a body, out on the cliffs. Give my apologies will you.'

'I wish I was coming with you. Be like old times.'

'Me too.' He kissed her lightly on the cheek. 'I'll find out what we've got and call for back up if I need to. Could be anything at this stage.'

Rachel watched him go. When they had started their relationship several months ago, she had volunteered to move out of the Serious Incident Squad where they had been close colleagues. Even closer now, with their engagement in January and a wedding planned for September, things had moved quickly but neither of them saw a reason for delay. Both wanted a family and Rachel was all too aware of her biological clock ticking.

Now that Peter had been promoted to Detective Chief Inspector there would need to be a new DI to take his place. Under normal circumstances, that might have been Rachel, as his Detective Sergeant, and she bristled slightly at the thought of someone else taking that position. She was happy enough in her new role as DI heading up the Child Exploitation Unit, but still missed the collaboration that excited her about working with Peter, his sharp mind and her thoughtful analysis had worked well together, she thought. She also missed the team. Kevin, Saroj and Maggie were friends as well as colleagues, each bringing their own particular strengths to the squad. Who would it be now, she wondered? She'd heard rumours that it was to be someone from outside the county. Rachel just hoped that whoever it was would fit in. After all, Cornwall could be a difficult place to fit into.

Chapter Two

Peter pulled up on the dusty track leading to the cliffs. Despite it being a beautiful June day, the wind still whipped off the Atlantic, causing the sea to churn and crash against the rocks. The sound became louder as he approached the scene where a group of police and fire officers stood in a small knot around a cordoned off area.

He checked his pocket for his plastic shoe coverings and latex gloves as he strode purposefully towards the group. A woman detached herself from the others and marched over to him, waving her arms. 'Please leave the area sir, this is a police crime scene.'

Peter fished his warrant card out of his pocket and held it towards the woman. He had never seen her before, but she seemed to be taking control of this situation. The first thing he noticed was that she was a black woman, small in stature but heavily built. Her jacket was flapping in the breeze and it looked to Peter like she was struggling to keep her feet on the uneven ground.

'Detective Chief Inspector Sanders,' Peter said, by way of introduction. 'And you are?'

'Detective Inspector Wade,' Cassandra Wade flashed her warrant card, 'and this is my crime scene.'

'It's only your crime scene if I say it is, DI Wade, and at the moment, I doubt that will be the case.' Peter pulled on his shoe protectors and snapped on the latex gloves. 'Now if you could just follow me, you can fill me in on the situation.'

'With respect, sir,' Cassie said as she trotted beside Peter, trying to keep up with his long strides, 'I took the call and was first on the scene so, where I come from, that makes me SIO.'

Peter stopped suddenly, turning to face the startled woman. 'Just where you come from is not clear to me yet and, before I allow you to lead an investigation on my patch, I need to know a lot more about you.' Peter looked the woman in the eye. 'Now, what do you know about this body?'

Cassie bristled at the sharp way she had been dismissed. Holding Peter's gaze, she reeled off the information. 'Civilian reported a dog down a mine shaft. When the fire rescue officers made it to where the dog was, they found a body. Made a bloody mess of the scene as you can imagine.' Peter made no comment, still holding her gaze. Cassie continued. 'I've cordoned off the area and sent for the doctor and SOCO, though I doubt they'll find anything useful, the way the ground has been disturbed.'

'Right. I take it you are my new DI?'

'I'm attached to the Serious Incident Squad, sir, if that's what you mean.'

Peter nodded, distractedly looking over Cassie's shoulder towards the cordons. 'Okay, you go back to the squad room and wait for me there.'

'With respect, sir. . . ' protested Cassie.

'I find that when people start a sentence with, *with respect*, they mean anything but. Go back to the office and wait for me there. I don't want to have to repeat that instruction, DI Wade. We'll talk later.'

Cassie sighed loudly. 'Right you are.'

Peter looked at her expectantly.

'Right you are, *sir*,' Cassie said, belligerently.

Peter pursed his lips and nodded, then, turning away, strode towards the scene.

Detective Sergeant Saroj Kapoor walked into the squad room, a smile playing on her lips as she remembered the rendition of, '*why was she born so beautiful*' sung lustily at the departing chief. Saroj didn't know when or how this song had become a tradition for retiring officers, but it always seemed to hit the right note between respect and mickey-taking for which police officers were renowned. The room was empty apart from a stout black woman lounging at Saroj's desk, flicking through the files that had been left there.

'Can I help you?' Saroj enquired, none too happy with the intrusion.

The woman looked up. 'Milk, no sugar thanks,' she said distractedly.

'Let me start again. I'm DS Kapoor and that's my desk.' When the woman didn't respond, Saroj continued. 'I assume that you are our new DI?' Still no response. 'If so, there's a vacant desk over there.' Saroj pointed to the corner of the room.

At that moment Kevin Sharp entered. He took in the scene, glancing between the two women. He moved over to the desk, his hand outstretched. 'DS Kevin Sharp,' he said pleasantly.

Cassie extracted herself from behind the desk, accepting Kevin's handshake. 'DI Cassandra Wade.'

'Very pleased to meet you. Can I get you anything, ma'am? Tea, coffee?'

Saroj turned on her heel and left the room.

Arriving at the scene of crime at the same time as Peter was his old friend and colleague Ben Samuels. Ben had been the pathologist for this area for around ten years and, in that time, had got to know and respect the quiet and methodical detective he now saw striding out before him. 'Peter!' he shouted. As the other man turned with a smile, Ben jogged to catch up.

'What do we have?' Ben said as he drew level with Peter.

'Only just got here myself, doctor. It seems that a body has been dropped down a mine shaft. The fire officers are waiting with rescue apparatus for me to give the word.'

As Peter and Ben neared the scene, they could see the pulley system that had been erected over the mine shaft. There was a low granite wall surrounding the hole which had become overgrown with weeds and small shrubs. A faded sign warned 'Mine Shaft – Danger of Death', and Peter thought how appropriate that missive was on this sunny morning.

They continued to chat amicably. 'I'm sorry I didn't make Angela's retirement do. Dealing with a suspected suicide. Dreadful business. A young girl, apparently bullied on social media, hanged herself.' Ben shook his head. 'Such a tragic waste.'

'Definitely suicide?' Peter enquired.

'Oh, no doubt. Parents are devastated, naturally.'

They arrived at the cordoned area. Peter turned to the constable on duty there and introduced himself. He was known to most of the people present and especially Constable Green who had worked briefly with the DCI on a case last year. Peter spoke to the chief rescue officer. 'I think we can bring her up now. The scene is pretty much trashed by the earlier efforts with the dog rescue, so SOCO are unlikely to find any footprints or anything.'

'Right you are,' said the officer. 'Let's go, lads.'

While the recovery was being carried out, Peter learned that the dog, which had been the original cause of the activity, was alive but badly injured. The owners had taken the poor animal away to the vets for examination. Though Peter was not a dog lover, he could still empathise with the couple who must love their pet, and he hoped the dog would survive its ordeal.

A full two hours later, the body was raised the twenty metres from the bottom of the mine shaft after being strapped to a stretcher in the confined space below. Laying the human cargo gently down on a grassy verge, the rescue workers withdrew to allow Peter and Ben access.

Releasing the body from the securing straps, it became clear that this was a young girl. Dark skinned, with a mop of thick curly hair. The body looked in good condition and Peter guessed that she had not been dead for very long.

Ben moved over to examine her. 'Young woman, girl really, at a guess around fourteen or fifteen.'

'How long has she been dead?'

'No more than two days, I'd say. I'll be able to be more accurate after I've opened her up.'

'Cause of death?'

'Strangulation, almost certainly. See these marks here?' Peter bent down to see the purple bruises around the girl's neck and nodded.

'So it's definitely murder then?'

Ben nodded. 'Full work up tomorrow, we should find out more then.' He stood up and spoke quietly to Peter. 'Shall we say ten-thirty?' Peter nodded and shook the doctor's hand.

Peter spent a little more time walking slowly around the site to fix the scene in his mind, then he arranged for SOCO to make a wider search of the area. No bag or means of identification had been found with her in the mine shaft, so chances were that they had been disposed of locally.

Leaving two constables to guard the scene, he made his way back to his car.

Peter walked through the squad room without a word and entered his office, closing the door firmly behind him. Saroj and Kevin exchanged glances, neither of them being used to their DCI not acknowledging them. Kevin shrugged and continued his work. Cassandra, who had been out of the office using the ladies room, came in and went immediately over to Peter's office. Giving a sharp knock on the door, she went in.

Peter was talking on the phone and looked up when Cassandra entered. He held his hand over the receiver. 'Please wait outside, DI Wade. I'll call you in when I'm ready.'

Cassandra spun round and exited, none too happy at this sharp dismissal. She noticed the smirk on Saroj's face. Feeling the need to stamp her authority on the team, Cassie went over to where Saroj was working. 'This desk will do me fine,' she said, returning to their earlier conversation. 'I like the aspect better than the window one, and it's nearer to the Chief.'

Saroj thought of arguing but knew that the line of command put Cassandra firmly in charge of this situation. 'Yes ma'am. I'll clear my things out when I've finished this report.'

Cassie nodded, satisfied that Saroj had been put firmly in her place, and went over to the coffee machine. At that moment Peter opened his door and called Cassie in. She waved a cup at him. 'Coffee sir?'

'Thanks, DI Wade, black please.'

g

After they were settled with their drinks around a low coffee table in Peter's office, he smiled and addressed the woman opposite him. 'We didn't get off to a good start Cassandra, so shall we begin again?'

Peter had been on the phone to Liverpool CID, wanting to learn a little more about Cassandra Wade before he spoke to her. Her commanding officer had nothing but praise for the DI's work. Her clear up rate was exemplary. She was a hard worker, tough and uncompromising. That was good to hear, but Peter wanted to learn more about her personality. 'How did she get on with her team-mates?'

'I'd say she has a bit of a chip on her shoulder.' The Liverpool DCI said. 'At thirty she was young to be a DI, and tongues will wag about positive discrimination, if you take my point. She's a hard taskmaster with junior ranks, but good fun out of the work setting. Typical Scouse humour – may take a bit of getting used to, but no malice. She has a lot of specialist knowledge, DCI Sanders. She could be very helpful to you.'

Armed with this knowledge, Peter asked Cassandra how she felt about her placement with Devon and Cornwall Police.

'Bloody pissed off, if you want the truth.' Cassie eyed her senior officer. 'Can I speak plainly, sir?'

'That wasn't plain enough?' Peter smiled to take the sting out. 'Carry on, Cassandra.'

'With respect. . . er, sorry,' Cassie said remembering their earlier conversation. 'To be honest, I wanted another big city placement. London would have been great, but Birmingham, even Glasgow would have been better than Cornwall.' Cassie looked sheepish. 'No offence sir, but this feels like a sleepy backwater after what I've been used to.'

'What were your reasons for leaving Liverpool, then?'

'Not my choice, sir. I thought. . . well, in fact, I knew, I'd done a great job busting a major drug ring. Trouble was, the gangs involved had contacts who made threats against my family. If it had just been me I would have been willing to tough it out, but I've got two kids, sir, and it wouldn't have been fair on them.' Cassie sipped her coffee. 'As it turns out, they're not happy either. Obviously missing their mates, but as well as that, they complain that there's nothing to do around here, and I can't dispute that from what I've seen.'

'That must make it difficult for you, I can see that, but as far as the job goes, I think we may surprise you.' Peter brought out some statistics that he had been inspecting and passed the papers over to Cassie. 'Drug crime is on the rise in Cornwall and it seems to be going hand in hand with child welfare. It's well known in the team that my partner is heading up the new Child Exploitation Unit, so I get to hear about it first-hand.'

Cassie nodded as she read the reports in front of her.

Peter continued. 'Take this morning's case, for instance.'

Cassie jumped in. 'Yes, it occurred to me, too. I've had a quick word with the pathologist,' she consulted her notes, 'Ben Samuels. And from what he was able to tell me, the girl didn't look like she belonged here, if you see what I mean, and I am very aware of the 'County Lines' situation in rural districts.' She was clearly invigorated by this possibility. Peter had to admire Cassie's initiative, which he decided should be rewarded.

'We'll work the case together. Your expertise in the drug scene will be invaluable, Cassie, and I know the area, so we should make a good team. How do you feel about that?'

'Fantastic, sir. I won't let you down.'

'Tonight though, will be the traditional police welcome, if you're up for it?'

'Never been known to refuse, sir. I'll have to let my kids know, and I wouldn't want to stay late.'

'I wouldn't want that either. Lots to do tomorrow so we'll need a good night's sleep, and no hangovers.'

Cassie smiled, feeling better now that she had a case to focus on. She was sure the DCI would leave it to her once he got to know her capabilities. She had to admit, though, that the local way of doing things was a bit slow by her standards. She had heard it said that Cornish folk do it 'Dreckly', meaning directly, which was another way of saying, *when it suited them.* She would soon shake them up. She stood and picked up the empty coffee cups, keen to make a good impression.

147

As Cassie re-entered the squad room, she could see that Saroj had cleared her desk and was now ensconced behind the one by the window, as instructed. A small battle to win but important in Cassie's view. As a black woman, she knew that she had to work harder and assert herself more than her male counterparts. She hoped that the whole team would have learned that Cassandra Wade was a force to be reckoned with, and that she would now get the respect she deserved. Friendly relationships could come later when the pecking order had been fully established. Satisfied with the morning's events, Cassie left the room to get her belongings from her car. As she went, the whole room heaved a collective sigh of relief.

Chapter Three

The previous evening had been unusually quiet compared to the usual welcome given to a new team member in the police force. Saroj and Maggie had given their apologies after just one drink. Only Peter and Kevin were left to wish Cassie all the best in her new role. By nine o'clock no one fancied another drink, so the party broke up.

This morning, Cassie and Peter stood in their protective clothing at the side of the post-mortem table. Their young victim had been undressed and her clothing bagged for forensic examination. Dr Samuels was beginning his scrutiny of her external features before moving on to what lay inside.

'There's some bruising to her head and face that's consistent with the fall she sustained, and there are a number of scratches, probably from the brambles. And see here, there are finger bruises to the upper arms and wrists, indicating a struggle. There'll be no prints, of course, as it was over her clothing.' Ben examined her hands, running an implement under her fingernails and dropping the residue into a container. 'We may find some DNA evidence from this. It looks like she put up a fight.'

Peter glanced over at Cassandra, who was wiping her eyes. 'You okay?' He mouthed.

Cassie nodded. 'No problem, sir,' she replied, but Peter thought she looked upset.

Ben was busy making a Y incision and seemingly didn't notice the exchange. The girl's skin and muscle was peeled back and the ribcage cracked open to reveal her organs. One by one, these were removed and examined before weighing and bagging. Ben looked up over his glasses. 'She was pregnant. About four months, I'd say.'

Cassie let out a small gasp and asked to be excused. 'I'll see you outside,' Peter said. This show of emotion was the last thing he expected from his tough new DI. Ben looked up, a little startled to see the DI's departure, then continued. 'No obvious sign of sexual abuse,' he said, swabbing the girl's genital area. 'But we'll have this tested for semen.'

Peter stayed to the end of the physical examination, overseeing the taking of blood and tissue samples for further analysis.

'Thanks, Ben,' he said as he removed his protective clothing. 'Let me have the blood and any semen results as soon as possible, will you?'

'Of course, Peter. Is DI Wade alright?'

'Don't know, mate. I'll check up on her now.'

The two men shook hands, smiling warmly. 'Always difficult, children,' said Ben. Peter nodded his agreement, his mouth a grim line.

Outside, he found Cassie leaning against the wall. She smiled sheepishly at Peter. 'Sorry about that, sir. My girl is about that age,' she said. 'It could have been her, dark skin, slim build, curly hair. Made me think, that's all.'

'No need to apologise, Cassie. Shall we grab a coffee before getting back?'

Cassie smiled warmly. 'I'd like that.'

They found a quiet table in the coffee shop, a latte for Cassandra and a black coffee for Peter. 'You have two children?' Peter asked.

'Yeah. Micky who's fifteen and Tanya. She's thirteen going on forty.' Cassie's eyes teared up again. She sniffed loudly. 'Sorry, sorry, sir. It's just, what that poor girl must have gone through. I feel so ashamed that I complained about my redeployment. Tanya and Micky were threatened so, you see, that really could have been Tanny on that slab.'

'It's okay, Cassie, I understand. Make us all work harder to find out what happened, who she is, is there someone missing her?' Peter became more business-like, knowing that Cassandra would respond as a DI and not a mother. 'We need to get on to missing persons, here and nationally. I suspect she came from a large city.'

Cassandra nodded. 'That's my guess, sir. The first time I saw her I felt she didn't fit, if you see what I mean. My intuition says London, but could be Manchester, Liverpool, anywhere where there's established drug activity.'

'So you're thinking County Lines?'

'It's got to be a possibility. It'll be interesting to see the clothing analysis, whether there are any traces of drugs. And she should have had a bag or something. If we could find that it would be helpful.' Cassie was thinking out loud. 'We should get sniffer dogs involved in the search. You have them, right?'

'We're not as backward as you seem to think. Cornwall has over four hundred miles of coastline. We have regular drug seizures both in harbour and out at sea, so our sniffer dogs are well up to the mark.'

'Sorry, sir.' Cassandra blushed. 'I meant no offence.'

'It's alright, none taken. It's a good idea, nonetheless. I wouldn't have immediately thought of it. Let's get back to the squad room. If you're up for it, you could give the team a quick talk on County Lines and the drug scene in Liverpool and other big cities.'

'Of course, sir. If you think they'd be receptive.'

'They're a good bunch and very keen to have new intel.' It'll help break the ice too, Peter thought. The business with Saroj's desk had not gone unnoticed and Peter was keen to establish good working relationships as soon as possible.

Cassie nodded. 'If you think it would help.'

Chapter Four

Charlie heard the knock on the door. He was scared but knew he had to open up. The Community Police had installed a spy hole and a camera when they first found that a Somali gang of drug dealers had started to use Charlie's flat in East London as a base. Even though Charlie was of limited intelligence, he knew that this was no protection against the ruthless Mali Boys. He opened the door wide and several large black men pushed past him as if he wasn't even there. The gang leaders had keys, so Charlie knew that these men were lower down the hierarchy. Charlie didn't need to be asked before he went to the kitchen and came back with beers for the men, then he made himself scarce. He could hear the stilted, often violent, conversations from his bedroom. The men talked about a rival gang member being stabbed and impaled on railings as a warning. They laughed and joked about how the man had no pride. 'Fuckin' beggin' man! Like that was gonna make a difference. Should have taken his punishment like a man.'

'Too right, blood. See his face when he saw the railings? Ha! Shit scared man.'

Charlie heard the door go. Another man entered, this time using a key. *One of the bosses*, Charlie thought. He hurried to the kitchen for more beer.

'Got anythin' to eat, Charlie?' the new man demanded.

Charlie brought packets of crisps. The new man threw the packs on the floor and stamped on them. 'Somfin to eat, man. Not this crap!' He threw some notes at Charlie. 'Go and get us some curry an' stuff.' Charlie grabbed the money and left.

When Charlie returned with several containers, there were new people in the room. Two girls were draped over the men on the sofa, and Charlie could hear sounds from his bedroom which he knew meant there was a man and a girl in there doing dirty things. He was used to this now and simply sat on the floor in the corner waiting new instructions. He thought about how it was when his mum was alive. They didn't have much, but she loved him and looked after him. When she died, the council moved him into this flat. He had a 'supporter' at first, and she taught him how to shop and cook food for himself. But now there was no one. His supporter had told him on her last visit that the council had cut-backs which meant, as far as Charlie could see, that he was on his own.

Charlie first met Jamal at the take-away. He had been friendly and asked if he could come back with Charlie to his flat. Charlie was lonely and happy to have made a new friend. The next day a group of men came with Jamal. Charlie was scared and said they should go, but they hit him and pushed him into the bedroom. He told the community police officer about it and two men came and installed the spy hole and camera. He hadn't seen anyone since then. Jamal had threatened Charlie not to go to the police. Jamal had a knife and showed Charlie what he would do with it if he said anything to anyone about their 'friendship'. Since then, Charlie did as he was told.

'Hey, Jamal, man.' One of the gang members shouted. 'Who you got there?'

Charlie could see a thin black girl cowering behind Jamal. 'New recruit,' Jamal said, pushing the girl over to the men on the sofa. Charlie thought she looked very young, and scared like him, but she smiled at the men and squeezed onto the sofa. The two girls who were already there pushed at her. 'Hey bitch, this is taken!'

One of the men grabbed at the new girl. 'What's yer name, bitch?'

The girl mumbled, looking very scared. 'Neema.'

'Right, Neema. Let's see what you can do.'

The man stood up, pulling Neema with him, and they went through to the bedroom. Charlie could hear an argument from inside and then a man and a girl came out. The girl had no clothes on and Charlie hid his head. Mum had always told him that he shouldn't look at girls, especially their private bits. Everyone started laughing then, and the men in the room grabbed at the naked girl. Charlie put his head in his hands and cried.

Chapter Five

Cassandra stood at the front of the squad room, behind her was the white board with photographs and information about the dead girl, who they had temporarily decided to call Alice until they had a confirmed identity. Cassie's eyes flickered around the room while she took stock, then she began.

'I know I'm very new here, which is an understatement. I was unlucky, or lucky, whichever way you choose to see it, to land a murder on my first day, and you can see from the board behind me, the information we currently have on Alice. It's very little, and that needs to change quickly.' Cassie handed out a single sheet of A4 to each of the team members. 'I have made a few notes about serious drug crime which I believe may be relevant to this case. Of course, we may find that Alice is a local girl who had an argument with her boyfriend who then killed her and dropped her body down a mine shaft. If that's the case, we could solve this in a day or two.'

Kevin raised his hand. Cassie nodded to him. 'Ma'am. The perpetrator must have local knowledge to know where to find a mine shaft which was fairly accessible by car.'

'True, Kevin, or have a link to someone local. There could be more than one person involved in this crime.' Kevin nodded and Cassie continued.

'I'm thinking that there could be a drug element to the murder. I've given you some information about 'County lines'.' Everyone consulted their handout. 'You can see that this term refers to the mobile phone line which is the link for the drug gangs to sell drugs. Young people or vulnerable adults become couriers taking drugs and money across the county from the gang's base to customers across the region. I believe that Alice could have been one of these couriers.'

Saroj whispered something to Maggie. Cassie spotted her. 'Would you care to share that, DS Kapoor?'

'Ma'am. We know this. Why do we need a lecture on drugs right now?'

'I'm not sure what you know, Saroj. And it does no harm, in my opinion, to have a refresher if the topic relates to a current case.'

Saroj nodded, conceding the point.

'Right. We also know, following this morning's PM, that Alice was pregnant. Now unless an individual in the gang wants a girl to be his 'baby mama', you all know what that is?' Maggie expressed ignorance of the term. 'Well, Maggie, if an individual man has a relationship with a girl, and by relationship don't think I mean a loving one, he might want a baby to boost his standing in the gang, so he allows a girl to have his baby. Okay?' Maggie nodded.

'If there's an unwanted pregnancy, a gang member may pay for a termination, if this doesn't happen, the girl is banished from the gang as being of no further use, or, if she kicks up a fuss, disposed of in another way. Dropped down a mine shaft, for example.'

At this point, DCI Sanders took over the briefing. 'Thanks DI Wade, that was very informative, and gives us a definite line of enquiry. Before that, however, we have to explore the local links. Kevin, will you get a photo of Alice into the local papers and the nationals for good measure. Maggie, find CCTV footage from the rail stations and bus terminals in Penzance and Truro, see if Alice came in that way. Saroj, make a list of known drug dealers and their haunts for DI Wade, then the two of you can look into that together.' Saroj raised her head sharply, but then nodded.

'As we know, the first twenty-four hours of a murder enquiry are vital, so I'm approving overtime. Get sandwiches in. It's going to be a long one.

'I'm going back to the scene now to meet up with SOCO.'

* * *

The cliffs on the outskirts of St Just are spectacular, and Peter always loved walking the coast paths. Today, the sea pinks and the 'policeman's buttons' were out in force, their delicate looking flowers resisting the strong westerly wind that was the prevailing direction on this rugged coast. The blackthorn trees bore testimony to this, their branches sloping eastward away from the strong wind. Peter stood looking out to sea. He loved to look at the pounding waves, but had a fear of water which dated back to his childhood when his dad, being a Navy man and in love with the sea, tried to teach his young son of six years to swim. His daughter Jane, older by four years, had taken instantly to the element and swam like a fish, but Peter screamed blue murder when he was dunked under the waves. Being tired of this, Peter's dad carried him out into the water one day and, letting go of him, turned and walked towards the shore. Peter could still remember the terror of being tossed around, spluttering as he fought for air. Jane saved him, pulling him to the beach with apparent ease, but not before he had learned to hate and fear the sea. After that, his dad gave up on him. He had always wanted Peter to join the Navy but that was now impossible. Jane did join, and was currently a high ranking officer in the Royal Naval Air Squadron at Culdrose. She had hoped to get her dad's approval, but he seemed disinterested in her achievements. It appeared that a daughter was not as good as a son in this respect, and it made both siblings bitter.

That was a long time ago, thought Peter, but he always gave an involuntary shudder when watching the sea, remembering the fear, and the broken relationship with his dad. Both parents had been killed in a car crash on the A30 five years ago, without Peter ever hearing another kind word from his dad. No matter that he had made it to Detective Inspector or that he was a valued member of the police rugby union club, nothing made up for the disappointment his dad felt at his son not following him into his beloved Royal Navy.

Turning away from the cliffs, Peter strode off to join the SOCOs who had spread out with the sniffer dog to comb the brambles and the ruins of granite mine buildings for anything that may give them a clue as to how Alice had ended up in the mine shaft. Just then a shout and a wave came from Peter's right. One of the team had spotted something. Peter quickened his step to join the man.

He was standing in the lea of a stone wall. On the ground was a pile of cigarette butts. 'I think someone spent some time here, perhaps waiting for someone?' He said. 'There's a handy rock to sit on and, with your back to the wall, it's quite private.'

'Not your average picnicker then?'

'Too many cigarette butts for that, I think. I'll collect them up for analysis.' Peter nodded and strolled around the area. Noticing a flattened area of grass, he headed along it to a thicket. Seeing a piece of black material, he shouted out to the scene of crime officer. 'Over here!'

Peter parted the branches carefully and the other man extracted a rucksack which he bagged. 'Get the team over here, will you,' said Peter. 'See what else we can find.'

The sniffer dog showed a great deal of interest in the rucksack, but a further search of the surroundings revealed nothing new.

As the SOCO team were packing up, Peter phoned Cassie. 'DI Wade? Sanders here. We seem to have found a drugs connection. A rucksack with apparent traces of an illegal substance. We'll know more after analysis. I want you to bring in known local drug dealers, Saroj should have a list by now. Get a DNA swab from them if you can. If they refuse, arrest them on suspicion. I'll be back in an hour or so.'

'Yes sir.' Cassie smiled, having no doubt now that her hunch was right. She looked over to the window desk. 'DS Kapoor. Got that list yet?' Saroj nodded. 'Just printing it off, ma'am. It's not a long list, mostly small time pushers.'

'Okay. We'll have them in anyway.' Cassie collected her coat. 'See to that, DS Kapoor. I'm going back to the scene for a look around.'

'Ma'am,' said Saroj. 'What do you want us to do with them?'

'Keep them here till I get back, of course.' Cassie shook her head. 'You're interviewing them as part of a murder enquiry so it shouldn't be a problem. Surely you know that, DS Kapoor?'

'Ma'am,' said Saroj, looking flustered. 'I'll get onto it right away.'

Cassie left the room in a hurry, pulling her jacket on as she went. At the duty desk she requested a local constable to accompany her to the scene as she was unfamiliar with the area. Robbie Green was within earshot of the conversation. 'I'll drive you, ma'am.' He volunteered. 'Constable Green, ma'am.'

'Okay Green, but be quick about it.'

Chapter Six

Cassie and Constable Green walked slowly along the coast path which bordered the crime scene. 'It's very rugged,' said Cassie, surveying the rough path and the cliffs which fell dramatically to the rocky shore line below.

'Yes, ma'am. Tin mining country. See all the derelict granite buildings? They were engine houses and ventilation shafts. Tin capital of the world for a while, was Cornwall.' Robbie pointed further along the coast. 'The buildings and wheelhouse you can see there is Geevor Mine. Not in use now but a worthwhile museum if you're interested.'

Robbie carried on, liking the fact that he had the DI's full attention. 'And all along here is where Poldark is filmed.'

'Poldark the TV series?' Cassie asked.

'Yes, ma'am. Restricted access when filming is underway. Many locals have been used as extras.'

'Well I never. Poldark is my daughter's favourite programme.' She laughed. 'In love with Ross Poldark. Wait till I tell her about this place, she'll be queueing up to be an extra.'

Returning to the matter at hand, Cassie stopped and concentrated on the young constable. 'So, Constable Green, who would know about this mine shaft?'

'Any of the locals, ma'am. Regular visitors might have discovered it too. The coast path is very popular for walkers. Some of them come back every year. And there's the Poldark effect, of course. We get visitors from all over.'

'Hmmm.' Cassie mused. 'Are there guides who take parties out?'

'I believe so, ma'am.'

'And they might point out dangerous areas, like mine shafts?'

'Almost certainly, ma'am.'

'Food for thought, Robbie, don't you think?'

'I probably wouldn't have thought of it myself, ma'am, but I suppose that's why you're the DI and I'm just a constable.'

Cassie laughed. 'Too right, Constable.'

Robbie thought this might be a good time to make a request that had been on his mind for some time. 'Ma'am? Can I ask something?'

'Fire away.'

'Could you see your way to considering me for the DC post which is coming up in the SIS?'

Cassie looked the young man up and down. 'I don't see why not. I don't know you at all though, so I'll have to discuss it with the Chief, but you seem keen and that's always a good start. Put something in writing for me.'

'Thanks, ma'am. I'll get on to that right away.'

Chapter Seven

Charlie was waiting in the queue at the local Spar shop. Jamal had sent him out to get more beer and he was thinking about whether he should buy some chocolate for himself, when he spotted the headline in a newspaper.

HUNT FOR CORNWALL KILLER

The body of a young black girl was found earlier this week in a mineshaft in Cornwall. Police suspect that the murder was drugs related and want anyone who recognises this girl, or who has any information at all, to get in touch with their local police station.

But it wasn't the report that took Charlie's eye, it was the photograph. *That's Neema*, he thought. He picked up the paper and looked again to be sure. It was definitely her. *Murdered? Neema's dead*? Charlie ran from the shop, forgetting that he still had the newspaper in his hand. 'Oi!' shouted the shopkeeper. 'You have to pay for that!' Turning to the next customer, he chuckled, 'He's not all there,' pointing to his head. 'I'll get the money off him when he comes in again.'

Charlie was half way back when he realised he hadn't bought the beers. He panicked, standing rooted to the spot on the pavement. Charlie's hands shook as he looked again at the photo in the paper. Tears sprang to his eyes. He thought about showing the photo to Jamal, but something held him back. He turned around and started walking in the opposite direction to his flat. He didn't know what to do but he was scared to go back. Charlie was thinking about the last few months when Neema and he had become friends. She usually hung back when the gang left his flat, or she came to see him in the mornings when Jamal and the other men were still in their beds.

'Come on, Charlie, let's go for a bacon buttie.'

Charlie would smile and follow Neema willingly to the little café down the road.

Neema was great. She didn't treat him like the others. She asked him what he thought about things as if he was a normal person. Jamal had asked Neema to take a train to Plymouth with a package for one of his contacts there.

'What would you do, Charlie?'

Charlie was about to say, *I don't know*, when he saw Neema's eyes staring at him, expecting an answer. He made himself think. *What would I do*? he thought. Then he gave someone advice for the first time in his life. 'Don't do it, Neema. I think it's wrong.'

'I think you're right, Charlie, but Jamal might hurt me if I don't.'

Charlie hadn't thought of that. 'Run away, then,' he said.

'I've got nowhere to go, Charlie. I'll just do this one and then perhaps he won't ask me again.'

After that, Neema did go on train rides with packages, over and over again. When she wasn't doing that, the men who came into Charlie's flat took her into his bedroom. Sometimes one man and sometimes two or three. Neema was always sad and shaking after this and Charlie would make her a cup of tea. Then they would sit and talk until she felt better.

He'd been walking for a long time and was far away from his flat. He looked around but nothing was familiar. Charlie was still holding the newspaper and wondered about going to the police. Jamal had told him never to talk to the police, though, and he was scared of what might happen. He was too frightened to go back to his flat even if he could find his way. He hadn't got the beers and Jamal would be mad and hit him again. So Charlie kept on walking.

Chapter Eight

NEEMA'S STORY

Neema was taken into care when she was eight. Her mother had died when she was six and her mum's sister, Aurelia, had come to look after her and her dad. Neema liked Auntie Aurelia better than her mum, who she remembered as always ill and in bed a lot of the time. One day Auntie Aurelia left without saying a word to Neema. Her dad was angry and wouldn't answer Neema's questions about why her auntie had left them. After a few weeks, she received a letter from her auntie which simply said she couldn't live with Neema's dad anymore and she hoped that Neema would understand some day.

Things became very bad for Neema after that. Her dad came into her bed most nights and forced her do things to him that made her feel sad and confused. Neema became very withdrawn, and this change in Neema's personality was noticed by her teacher. After that there were other people who came to their house and talked to Neema and her dad. Dad got angry a lot and hit Neema for telling the teachers about what they did together. He wouldn't believe that she hadn't told anyone.

A little while later Auntie Aurelia came back to stay and Neema's dad left. Neema knew that she probably should have been happy, but she missed her dad and blamed her auntie for sending him away. The social workers said things like, *out of control*, and *behavioural problems*, and pretty soon Neema was taken away too.

After Neema had been in a children's home for three months with no possibility of a return to her dad, her social worker recommended placement with a family. The court made an adoption order and so began the protracted journey of assessing Neema and matching her with adopters. A long, drawn out process ensued. Adopters didn't want a disruptive eight year old, they mostly wanted a baby. However many times the social workers explained that there were no babies placed for adoption, or at least, very rarely, the couples still held out hope of having a little one to bring up as their own. Neema languished in the care system.

The children's care home organisation, *Transplace*, had several homes dotted around the Greater London area. It was their practice to move children between homes when staffing levels were down, and Neema was moved many times. Regular changes of schools and carers took their toll on Neema and she became, in the social worker's words, unmanageable and disruptive. Needless to say, records and transfer protocols were other victims of frequent moves and eventually Neema became lost in the system.

When she was twelve, Neema ran away. If anyone wondered where she was, which was unlikely, they would assume she was staying at another home. Such was the chaos that was the private residential care system. The frequently used misnomer, *lost in care*, applied very much to Neema, yet another victim of the underfunded and badly managed care system.

After living rough for several days, Neema met Jamal. He bought her food and clothes and promised to look after her. She very soon realised that nothing had changed. She was still pushed around and abused. The only one who seemed to really care about her was Charlie and she loved him like the big brother she never had.

Chapter Nine

Cassie arrived back at the office to find everyone busily working. Maggie was trawling through CCTV footage, Kevin was examining missing persons' reports and Saroj was making notes on the whiteboard. She looked up when the DI came into the room.

'We've got three people in interview rooms, ma'am. Known drug dealers or pushers, at least. And we've got the PM report back. It's on your desk.'

Cassie nodded. 'You're with me in the interviews, Saroj. We'll start in ten minutes. And we'll need some DNA swabs.' She picked up the PM report. Alice's pregnancy was confirmed and DNA analysis had been carried out on the foetus and the scrapings from her fingernails. The results confirmed that the source was the same, but no match had been found on the system. Needle marks on her arms suggested past drug use, but no drugs were found in her system. Her last meal consisted of vegetables, lentils and spices, possibly a vegetable curry. Time of death had been tightened up to fourteen hours between 10am and midnight on the Tuesday. Cassie was pleased to see that Saroj had noted the results on the whiteboard.

'Any luck with CCTV, Maggie?' Cassie said without lifting her eyes from the PM report.

'Nothing yet, ma'am. I've checked back three days for train and bus arrivals but I'm wondering how long Alice had been in Cornwall before she was murdered, so I'm going back further.'

'Of course, she may have arrived by car,' prompted Cassie. 'As far as I could see, St Just is a small place, probably with a tight knit community. Get over there, Maggie, with a photo and check out the neighbourhood. Door to door if necessary, and find out where she may have stayed if she spent time in the area before she was killed.'

'Mispers, Kevin?'

'No match so far, ma'am.'

'Okay, keep on with that, and don't forget missing from care, different recording systems.'

'Yes, ma'am,' said Kevin, exasperated that the DI thought he wouldn't know that.

'Right, Saroj. Who do we have?'

'Richie Elliot – the most high-profile. Known to have links with dealers in Plymouth. Shane McCoy – new to the area, operates around Camborne, and then there's George Pengelly. He's lightweight, as much a user as dealer. Local lad well known to us.'

'We'll start with him, then.' Cassie picked up her folder and followed Saroj out of the room.

Kevin looked over at Maggie and raised his eyebrows. 'Rather her than me,' he observed, and Maggie nodded. 'She's certainly got the bit between her teeth.'

Cassie and Saroj sat opposite George Pengelly. Cassie started the recorder and made the introductions, noting the time and date of the interview.

'Mr Pengelly. Do you mind if I call you George?'

George shrugged, picking at his fingernails which were stained brown with dirt and nicotine. His left leg jiggled nervously. George could have been anywhere between twenty-five and fifty. His thin face was lined and grubby, with a deep scar on his right cheek. His hair was in matted dreadlocks reaching to his knees and he occasionally scratched his head with a long fingernail.

Cassie continued: 'Thank you, George,' she said. 'Do you know why you're here?'

George shrugged again.

167

'We're investigating a very serious crime, George, and we're hoping you might be able to help us.'

George looked up then. 'Don't know anythin' about a crime.'

'You don't know what it is yet, George.' Cassie opened her folder and took out the photograph of Alice. She slid it across the table towards George. 'Do you recognise this young woman?'

George shook his head and turned away, his eyes swivelling around the room.

'Take a good look, George. This young woman was murdered. Do you know who might have done that, George?'

'Don't know her or anythin' about a murder.' George didn't look at the photo.

Cassie pushed the photograph nearer to George. 'Look at her, George. She was strangled and dropped down a mine shaft. She was only fourteen.'

George forced himself to look at the image, he could tell she was dead in the photograph and this disturbed him. He stammered. 'I. . . I'm sorry she's d. . . dead but I don't know her. Now can I go?'

'I'd appreciate it if you could help us for a little while longer, George,' said Cassie softly. 'Would you like some tea, a biscuit perhaps?'

George looked up and nodded. 'Thanks,' he said, a little bewildered.

Cassie signalled to Saroj and she left the room briefly to arrange for the tea and biscuits.

Cassie pointed to the photo again. 'She's very distinctive, isn't she, George? I bet there's not many girls like her in these parts.' George stared at the photo. Cassie continued. 'A black girl, very pretty, would stand out, wouldn't you say, George?'

'I suppose so. Not many black girls in Cornwall.'

'You're exactly right, George. Not many black girls in Cornwall. So what do you think she was doing here?'

Saroj came back, followed a few seconds later by a female constable carrying tea and biscuits. George munched down on a biscuit and gulped his tea. 'No sugar,' he said.

'I'm sorry, George.' Cassie looked again at Saroj who was looking very glum, but left in search of sugar.

'Now as you were saying George, what was a black girl doing in this neck of the woods?'

George seemed to relax as he sipped his tea. 'Only ones I see have come from up north or London.'

'And why would they be here, George?'

'Well, you know, bringing stuff like.'

'Stuff like drugs, George?'

George stiffened.

'You're not in any trouble, George. We're investigating a murder. We're not interested in drugs at the moment.' Cassie leaned forward over the table. 'Look, George, we could do with your help. I bet there's not much gets past you. You'll know everything that goes on around here. Am I right?'

George stroked his bristly chin. 'I might know a bit,' he said smugly.

'You see, George, I'm new here.'

George laughed. 'Yeah, I guessed that. That's a Scouse accent, isn't it?'

'You're very perceptive, George. So, I need some local knowledge, and I suspect you're the man for that.'

George nodded sagely. 'Is there any more tea?'

Two hours later George had laid out the local drug scene. Shane McCoy was a waster who was used occasionally by Richie Elliot to run errands. Richie had contacts in Plymouth who got supplies from other cities including London and Manchester. He used mules to transfer stuff around the county. 'Maybe this girl who's dead was one of them,' George said. 'Not that I know anythin' about her murder though,' he emphasised. 'Just might have seen her about.'

'Where might you have seen her, George? This is very important information. I just need a bit more from you.'

George raised his chin and looked across at Cassie, making up his mind. 'I might have seen her around St Just. Hanging about with those hippy types. Can't swear to it, but it looked a bit like her.'

'Can you remember when this might have been, George? Think carefully, it's very important.'

'Be about a week ago, I think. I was goin' in the Co-op for some milk and stuff as she was comin' out. One afternoon, about three.'

h

'That's incredibly helpful, George. Now there's just one more thing you can do for me and we can let you go. We'd like to take a swab for DNA analysis.' George looked alarmed. 'Nothing to worry about, George. Just so that we can eliminate you from our enquiries, okay?'

Saroj was holding court in the squad room whilst Cassie was with the Chief filling him in on developments.

'Honestly, she had him eating out of her hand. I was sceptical at first. She seemed to be going easy on him and giving him too much deference, if you know what I mean. But I was impressed at the end, I can tell you.'

'Does it take us any further forward, though?' Kevin said.

'Of course it does. We now know that Alice was in St Just a week ago, so we can intensify our search around that area. And the 'hippy types' should be well known enough for us to find them. Maybe Alice was staying with them.'

Maggie said, 'It means I can search CCTV a lot earlier too.'

Cassie strode back into the office, stopping in her tracks to see the team sat around talking. She was just about to reprimand them when there was a spontaneous call of 'Well done, ma'am,' from the three.

'Yeah, well, we've got a lot more to do yet so let's get on with it,' said Cassie, a smile playing on her lips. 'Use this extra information to inform your research and let's see if we can't nail down Alice's movements a bit better.'

She turned to her DS. 'Saroj. We need to prepare for the interview with Richie Elliot. He's been sweating for long enough now, so he should be good and ready.'

'Right you are, ma'am,' said Saroj happily, as she prepared herself for another master class in interview technique.

The interview with Richie Elliot couldn't have been more different. Cassie's tone was harsher and more business-like. After she had introduced herself and Saroj, she turned to Richie.

170

'Mr Elliot, you know why you're here?'

'Not a clue,' said Richie as he leaned back in his seat.

Cassie held eye contact with him until he looked away. She slid the photograph of Alice across the table. 'We know you have been using this girl as a mule for your drug business, Mr Elliot, and we now strongly suspect that you were involved in her murder.'

Richie glanced at the photo and looked away. 'No comment,' he said.

'I haven't asked you a question yet, Mr Elliot.'

'No bloody comment anyway,' he said smugly.

'Where were you on Tuesday the 10th June between 10am and midnight?'

'No comment.'

'She didn't come this far usually, did she?' Cassie continued pushing the photo further across and tapping on it. 'This girl was your Plymouth connection, wasn't she?'

Richie's eyes widened slightly before he looked away again. 'No comment.'

'What happened, Mr Elliot, did she refuse to go back this time?'

'No comment.'

'Look at her, Mr Elliot. Was she frightened? Had she had enough?' Cassie paused. 'Things had changed, hadn't they? She was pregnant now.'

Richie's body twitched and his eyes slid sideways.

'Oh, I see. You didn't know that.'

'No comment.'

'Let me tell you how this usually goes, Mr Elliot. A girl gets used until she is no more use. She becomes a liability. Of course, these girls are dispensable, aren't they? Then someone, someone like you, Mr Elliot, gets the order to eliminate a girl. No skin off your nose, just another tart, after all.' Cassie paused. 'And, in any case, you know it would be the worse for you if you didn't do as you were told.'

'No comment.' Richie was looking detached and anxious.

'See, that's what surprises me, Mr Elliot.'

Richie looked up.

'You're quite a big wheel yourself. Why you let these London mobsters control you is beyond me.' Richie was listening. 'They give the orders and you get the shitty end. You mustn't be as tough as you look.'

'I know these people, Mr Elliot. They've got girls queueing up to join their gangs. God knows why, but they have. One little tart here or there is no big deal. So what I'm thinking is that you, Mr Elliot, *you* wanted her dead, and I'm going to prove it.'

'I had nothing to do with it. And you can't prove I did,' Richie was rattled.

'We'll see. Stand up, Mr Elliot.' Richie staggered to his feet. 'Richard Elliot, I'm arresting you on suspicion of the murder of a young woman as yet unidentified. You do not have to say anything, but it may harm your defence if you do not mention when questioned something which you later relay on in court. Anything you do say may be given in evidence. Do you understand?'

Richie protested, 'You can't do this!' he shouted. 'I want a solicitor.'

'One will be provided for you if you can't provide your own. Now we're taking you to the cells and we will require a DNA swab for analysis.'

After the constable had lead Richie away, Cassie turned to Saroj. 'Get a warrant to search his place.'

'Ma'am. What about Shane McCoy?'

'Let him go for now, but tell him we'll want to speak to him later.'

'Yes, ma'am.'

Cassie strode off, satisfied that she was on her way to solving this case. Perhaps she could prove that she was wasted in this rural backwater and the powers that be would send her somewhere more worthy of her talents.

Chapter Ten

Cassie entered the squad room to be told that the Chief wanted to see her as soon as she had finished interviewing. She was excited and looking forward to giving him the very positive update.

Peter answered her knock with a brisk, 'Come in.' He looked up to see the smile on his new DI's face. 'Looks like you've got good news for me, Cassie.'

Cassie nodded and took the chair that Peter indicated. 'I've arrested Richie Elliot. Saroj is organising a warrant to search his place.'

'Lay out the evidence for me, Cassie.'

'He was evasive, of course. *No comment* all the way, but his body language said *guilty*. I'll have another crack at him tomorrow. I'm confident I'll get a confession.'

'You've checked his alibi?'

'Again it was *no comment* but he obviously had something to hide.' Cassie was becoming less sure as she faced the scrutiny of the DCI. 'He knew Alice, I'm sure of that, and he can't, or won't, account for his whereabouts when she was killed.'

Peter was unconvinced. 'I'll give you tomorrow to question him further, but don't abandon other lines of enquiry just yet.' He could see that Cassie's demeanour had become less confident. 'Perhaps the DNA results will help. If he is the father of Alice's baby, that would go a long way to nailing him.' Peter stood to show Cassie out. 'Good work so far, DI Wade. I'll see you tomorrow.'

'Right, sir.' Cassie thought that Peter was being over cautious. In her old job she would have had the full support of her boss. Cassie didn't like being micro-managed, she didn't like it at all.

Peter's phone rang as Cassie was leaving. It was Rachel. 'Can you pick up another couple of bottles on your way home?'

Peter gave a brief laugh. 'Hello, sweetheart, lovely to hear from you.'

'Sorry, love, but I'm in the middle of this recipe and I now know why Gordon Ramsey swears so much.'

'It's only your mum and dad, Rachel. I'm sure they'll be happy whatever you give them.'

Rachel sighed. 'I know. But, as they say, I've started so I'll finish. The wine?'

'Of course, love. I'm leaving now so I'll be back to help. I'm looking forward to seeing your folks again, although your mum might just continue her interrogation. She's not sure I'm good enough for you yet.'

Rachel laughed. 'Don't worry, she likes you Peter, but I know she can be a bit fierce. Look, I have to go, I'll see you soon.'

Peter cast his mind back to the first time he met Rachel's parents. Her dad was a very pleasant man, enthusiastic and welcoming, and he and Peter were chatting away like old friends in no time. Su-Lin was quite different. Peter could see where Rachel got her beautiful oriental looks from, though she was taller than her mother. Su-Lin was a dynamo. Never still for long and constantly fussing over her daughter, asking questions and giving advice, most of it unwanted. Over that first dinner, Su-Lin held Peter's gaze and extracted information about him and his family like a pro. There were things he hadn't even told Rachel, but he felt compelled to reveal all to this feisty Chinese woman.

Su-Lin had come to the UK after meeting Raymond, Rachel's dad, at a world banking symposium. She was from the National Bank of China and he from Lloyds of London. Raymond said it was love at first sight, but it took many months before Su-Lin could leave China. The old communist regime had left some of its archaic rules in place and getting a travel visa was very difficult. Raymond recounted how he met her off the boat at Southampton. She looked so small and vulnerable, he said, but then she had spotted him and pushed her way through the crowds, carrying two large suitcases, beaming from ear to ear. He fell in love over again.

It was such a romantic story that Peter felt quite emotional when Raymond told it. Peter had looked at Rachel and smiled. Su-Lin was watchful, perhaps wondering if her daughter's romance could compare. Peter couldn't help feeling a bit insecure, but was determined that this second meeting, on his home turf, so to speak, would convince Su-Lin that he was the right man for her daughter.

He locked up his filing cabinet and turned off the lights in his office. As he entered the squad room, he could see that Saroj was still at her desk, a single lamp illuminating the document she was working on. She looked up as Peter approached. 'You off, sir?' she said.

Peter nodded. 'You should be too, you've put in a good day's work today, so I hear.'

'Can I be frank, sir?'

Peter leaned against the adjacent desk. 'Go on,' he said.

'I can't help thinking we're rushing this investigation. DI Wade is convinced we've got our man but I'm not sure. Richie Elliot is definitely hiding something, but it could be just his drug activity. I can't see his motive for murder, sir.'

'DI Wade is a very experienced officer, Saroj, and she may be right about Richie Elliot. We've got more evidence to gather yet, so let's see where that takes us, eh?' Saroj nodded glumly. Peter continued. 'How are you getting on with her personally?'

'She's quite prickly, sir, but I think I can learn a lot from her.'

'Well, I want my squad working together, so try to get on. Cassandra is new to this area and her kids are not too happy with the move by all accounts, so you'll need to cut her some slack. Okay?'

Saroj smiled and nodded. 'Sir,' she said.

'Right, if there's nothing that can't wait, you should be off home. Goodnight.'

'Night, sir.'

Saroj knew that Peter was right and that she should be more

understanding of her new boss, but there was just something about Cassandra Wade that she found hard to deal with. The woman obviously had a point to prove, but Saroj was determined that Cassie's agenda, whatever it was, would not undermine this team.

Chapter Eleven

The dinner had gone well and Su-Lin was more friendly than the last time Peter encountered her. She talked about her life in China and how she missed her family. Su-Lin's mother was a twin but, because of the one child policy of the old regime, one baby was given away to a childless couple. This was always a source of great sadness to Su-Lin's mother, and just after Su-Lin was born, her mother had set out to find her twin. She succeeded in tracing her to Shandong province, many miles from Shanghai where they lived, only to discover that her beloved sister had died three years previously. She found a nephew, though, and he gave Su-Lin's mother some jewellery that had been his mother's and made a promise to keep in touch. Peter was fascinated by this insight into a totally foreign culture. Su-Lin talked about the Cultural Revolution and how her father's relatives were stripped of their homes and belongings as they were considered to be academics. They were sent many miles away from their homes to work on farms and learn humility. Peter could see the sadness in Su-Lin, but also the strength of character which made her travel alone to a different country for a man she hardly knew. He was beginning to have a great deal of respect for his, soon to be, mother-in-law.

When dinner had finished, Rachel's parents had pleaded tiredness and decided on an early night. Rachel and Peter tidied the dinner things away, chatting about Su-Lin and her family, Rachel's family too, of course. 'Would you ever want to go to China for a visit?' Peter asked.

'I don't know. Probably not unless my mother would come with me, and I suspect that won't happen.' Rachel smiled up at Peter. 'Anyway, she seems to have decided you're okay, or she wouldn't have shared all that family business with you.'

'I'm glad, because I like her too, very much.' They settled on the sofa with a cognac each and considered the evening as a whole.

'Went well, I thought,' said Peter, his arm draped around Rachel's shoulder. 'That was a delicious meal. I think your dad was impressed.'

'What about you, chef? Were you impressed?'

'Now you're fishing.'

Rachel snuggled in. 'Of course I am,' she laughed.

Peter bent over and kissed her. 'I'm always impressed by you,' he said. 'And you looked particularly beautiful tonight, if you don't mind me saying.'

'Mmmm, I don't mind at all,' said Rachel, kissing him back. 'It's early but. . . '

'Is that an invitation, Ms Morris?'

'Aren't we beyond flirting?' Rachel laughed. 'Are you up for it or not?'

'Oh, definitely up for it, but can I just run something by you while we finish our drinks?'

An hour later, Peter had outlined the progress made in the mine shaft murder. Rachel had listened attentively, clearly interested in what her old team were doing and how the *new girl* was settling in.

'It seems to me like you are lacking motive and opportunity, at least until you can place this Richie Elliot at the scene, and you have a positive DNA match between him and the foetus. I wouldn't count your chickens just yet.' Rachel was also interested in the case from her team's point of view. 'Our work is overlapping with yours on these sorts of cases. If Alice is as young as you say, then she could have crossed our radar. Do you want me to look into it?'

'I'd be delighted if you can spare the time. Perhaps you could come and give a briefing to the squad.' Peter was thinking out loud and didn't notice that Rachel was losing interest.

Rachel yawned. 'Sorry, I think the day's catching up on me. I'll see if I can locate your Alice on our systems but I'm a bit tired now and ready for my bed. And anyway, I thought I was on a promise.'

Peter downed his drink and pulled Rachel up off the sofa. 'And so you are. D'you know how sexy you are when you're sleepy?'

Peter switched off the lights and followed Rachel up the stairs, being sure not to disturb the soon to be in-laws.

Chapter Twelve

Charlie had spent all of Jamal's money now and was hungry and thirsty. He had slept in a park and was cold and wet. He didn't know where he was and, anyway, he couldn't go back to his flat now, even if he could find it. Jamal would be mad at him for not getting the beers and for spending his money. He thought about Neema and looked at the photo again, stroking her image on the damp page. She would know what to do, he thought. She would say, *come on, Charlie, let's get some breakfast,* and she would take him to the warm, dry café with the smell of frying bacon, and he'd have a big mug of tea and a bacon buttie. Just thinking of this made his stomach rumble. Not knowing what to do, he lay down on the bench and cried.

It was several hours later when a community policewoman found him. He was breathing but unconscious. The policewoman called for the paramedics and Charlie was whisked away to hospital. When Charlie woke up he was in a bed with clean white sheets. There were tubes in his arms and a machine like a television making beeping noises next to his bed. *Perhaps I'm in heaven*, he thought. This thought was further enhanced when a woman in white leaned over him and smiled. 'Back in the land of the living, are we?' she said.

Charlie smiled back. 'Can I have a bacon buttie?' he said.

* * *

A constable was talking to one of the nurses in the corridor. 'Any idea who he is?'

'He says his name's Charlie, but either doesn't know, or won't tell us where he lives. He's clearly got learning difficulties, so it's hard to know what he understands. Physically he's well enough to be discharged so we can't keep him beyond today.' The nurse glanced over to where Charlie lay gazing at the crumpled paper that he refused to let go of. 'That photo in the newspaper, it's about a girl who was murdered. He seems to know her.'

'Alright if I go and talk to him?' the constable asked.

'Yeah, no problem, though I don't know what you'll get out of him.' The nurse bustled off down the ward, leaving the constable staring at the man in the bed.

The constable approached Charlie, smiling and holding his warrant card out. 'I'm Police Constable Taylor but you can call me Paul.'

Charlie was startled. Jamal had said never to talk to the police, they were no good, but Charlie remembered that Jamal had hit him when he said this, and this police man looked friendly.

Paul continued. 'Do you mind if I sit down, Charlie?'

Charlie simply smiled weakly.

Paul pulled up a chair. 'Now Charlie, let's try and find out why you were sleeping in the park. Have you left home, is that it?'

Charlie didn't know what to say. He had left home, so perhaps he should say yes. Charlie nodded.

'If you tell me where you live, Charlie, I can take you back in my police car. How would that be?'

Charlie shook his head violently. 'Not going back,' he said, looking agitated.

'It's okay, Charlie, I won't take you back if you don't want to go. Do you think you could tell me why you don't want to go back home?'

The young policeman looked closely at the man in the bed. He looked about thirty or so and was plump and disheveled. Obviously he had a mental health problem, so maybe he'd run away from an institution of some sort. Charlie was still clutching the newspaper. Paul reached for it but Charlie snatched it away.

'It's okay, Charlie, I just want to see what you're looking at in the paper.'

Charlie smoothed out the crumpled sheet and showed it to Paul. 'Neema,' he said.

Paul knew instantly what the article referred to, as his team had been briefed just yesterday about the murder of a young girl in Cornwall. 'I won't be a minute, Charlie, I just have to speak to someone.'

Constable Taylor called the station and told them about a possible identification of the murdered girl. 'We may need a specialist to help Charlie talk about what he knows. He's a bit mentally challenged, if you catch my drift, but I'm sure he knows her.' Paul knew that it would be a feather in their cap if they could identify the girl, and he would get a pat on the back for discovering the connection.

Paul looked over at Charlie who was drinking a cup of tea and dunking biscuits quite happily. He approached the nursing station. He waited until the ward sister had finished a phone call, then showed her his warrant card. 'We'll have to keep Charlie here until we can get a specialist interviewer over.'

The sister consulted the chart on the wall behind the desk. 'As you can see, we're short of beds, Constable. The best I can do is put him in the day room for a while, would that suit you?'

'Thanks, that's great, sister. I'm sure as long as he's fed and watered he'll stay wherever you put him. We'll move him when we know where he lives.' Paul smiled. 'And thanks again.'

Chapter Thirteen

Maggie was in the office early on Saturday morning. She had been thinking overnight about the case and wanted to search CCTV at Plymouth railway station, acting on her theory that Alice may have been travelling from there, or may have changed there. She started two weeks prior to Alice's murder and checked both the incoming and outgoing trains. Moving quickly through the footage, Maggie suddenly spotted a girl she thought could be Alice alighting from the London train and meeting with a woman on the platform. Although the younger female had her back to the camera, Maggie was convinced it was Alice. The other woman was older and dressed in hippy clothes, a tangle of blonde dreadlocks tumbling over her shoulders. The two women embraced warmly and then hurried off to board the Penzance train which was waiting on the adjacent platform.

Making a note of the date, which was ten days before Alice's body had been found, Maggie printed off stills from the CCTV to share with the team, before moving her search to the arrival of the train at the Penzance station later that same day. Sure enough, the footage showed Alice and the other woman disembarking and walking over to the bus station. Maggie lost them at this point, so couldn't tell which bus they caught. Still, a major piece of the puzzle, she thought, feeling very pleased with herself.

When everyone had arrived in the squad room, Cassie kicked off the team briefing with a summary of where they were up to with

Alice's murder. She felt confident that Richie Elliot would be more compliant today after spending a night in the cells, and it was obvious that she was looking forward to the interview that lay ahead. Asking for progress from the rest of the team, but not really expecting much, Cassie was surprised when both Maggie and Kevin raised their hands.

'Kevin,' she said. 'What do you have for us?'

'Ma'am. The duty desk have had a fax from the police in London. They have an ID on the photograph we put out.' Kevin consulted his notes. 'Apparently she has been identified by a homeless man who said her name is Neema. No more yet, but they are interviewing the man, who they say has some sort of mental health problems, today in the hopes of getting more information.'

'Excellent news, Kevin. Keep on that will you. Maggie, you have something?'

'Yes, ma'am. I trawled through earlier CCTV and found Alice arriving at Penzance station after leaving Plymouth with another woman.' Maggie handed out the print-offs. 'They seemed very friendly and apparently boarded a bus from the terminal outside the station. No footage of that, but I'll make enquiries today to see if I can find out where they went.'

Cassie was taken aback by the progress made. Aware that she may have underestimated the dedication and competence of this group, she clapped her hands together in acknowledgement. 'Great work Maggie and Kevin. Let's dig a bit more into a possible Plymouth connection, and go through mispers again now that we have a name.'

Cassie became aware that Peter was standing at the back of the room. 'Did you get all of that, sir?' she asked.

'I did, DI Wade, and I want to add my thanks to Maggie and Kevin. This takes us a good way forward, so well done both of you.' He looked at his team and smiled. Just what I wanted, he thought. Cassandra Wade now knows that she's not the only good detective on the block.

'DI Wade, my office please.'

'Sir,' said Cassie, wondering what the Chief could want with her. They entered Peter's office together. 'Take a seat, Cassie,' he said, as he settled himself behind the desk. Cassie waited patiently. 'I'll be leading the interview with Richie Elliot this morning,' Peter said, noting Cassie's raised eyebrows. She paused before replying.

'Of course, sir. Can I ask why?'

'Not a reflection on your competence, Cassie. I always intended to lead this case, but other work has got in the way up to now.' Peter could see that Cassie looked sceptical, so decided to take her into his confidence. 'Between you and me, I'm not comfortable taking a back seat with a desk job, and the super knows that. I will allow you to have free rein on most cases but reserve the right to lead when I want to.'

Cassie nodded briskly. 'Thank you, sir. I welcome your involvement. Is there anything we need to discuss before we see Elliot?'

'I've been through the transcript of your interviews with him and with Pengelly, and I think you made considerable progress. Armed with what we have learned since, I think I can build on that.' Peter stood to signal the end of the meeting. 'Shall we say 9.30? Just follow my lead. I'll let you know when I want you to step in.'

'Right you are, sir. I'll organise that now.'

'Oh, and Cassie, I may have a contact in Plymouth, if that line of enquiry takes off. Keep me up to speed.'

'Sir.' Cassie returned to the squad room deep in thought.

Richie Elliot was considerably jumpier this morning, probably due to having no access to drugs since yesterday. His left leg jiggled constantly, and his eyes darted around the room nervously. 'You can't keep me here,' he said. 'I've not done anything.'

Peter and Cassie sat opposite Richie and started the recording, introducing themselves and noting the time of day. 'You've been advised of your rights, Mr Elliot,' said Peter. 'I'll ask you again if you would like a solicitor present.'

Richie shook his head. 'I know I said I might want a solicitor, but I've been thinking. I've done nothin' so why should I need a brief?'

'You know that this is a serious matter, Richie, you don't mind if I call you Richie?' He shook his head. Peter took out the photograph and pushed it over the table towards him. 'Yesterday you refused to comment when DI Wade asked you if you knew this young woman. I'd like you to look at this photograph again.'

Richie glanced at the photo and shook his head. 'Take a good look, Richie. I think you do recognise her. Her name is Neema.'

Richie's eyes darted left and right. 'No comment,' he said, turning his body away from the table.

Peter persisted. 'You can continue to say *no comment,* Richie, and we can continue to hold you until we get some answers.'

'You can't keep me here. I know my rights.'

'Let me tell you, Richie. This is a murder enquiry, and you have not been able to provide us with details of where you were at the time this young woman was killed. We have taken a DNA swab from you and the results will be back soon. We will also be conducting a search of your flat.' Peter noted that Richie looked startled. 'What do you think we might find? Something that connects you to this girl?' Peter tapped the photograph before indicating to Cassie that she take over.

Cassie leaned over the table. 'Look Richie, you may not have had anything to do with this murder, but you know something, so why don't you help us now. Neema was a drug mule, wasn't she? She was seen meeting a woman at Penzance railway station.' Richie's head twitched nervously, and perspiration formed on his upper lip. 'She was heading for St Just, wasn't she? That's your patch, Richie. You know the woman who met Neema. She supplies you, doesn't she?'

Richie sighed and put his head in his hands. 'I want a solicitor,' he said.

Richie was led off back to the cells and Peter asked the duty sergeant to organise a solicitor. Cassie entered the squad room as Saroj was writing an update on the whiteboard. She turned to face Cassie. 'Morning, ma'am. I've just returned from Richie Elliot's flat. I found a stash of Class A and Class B drugs under his floorboards plus a substantial amount of cash. There was also a photograph of him with a woman who looks a lot like the one in the CCTV image seen meeting Neema in Plymouth.' Saroj pointed out the photo which was pinned to the board.

Peter caught the end of the conversation. 'Good work, Saroj,' he said. 'We can hold him on drug charges at least, but this just might be the lever to get him to tell us what he knows about Neema.'

Cassie butted in, still feeling that she should have a major role in this enquiry, and not willing to give up all the ground to the DCI. 'Saroj, take that photo around St Just. Someone will recognise her, I'm sure. Then you'll be able to pick her up and bring her in.'

'Ma'am.' Saroj glanced at Peter who gave a brief nod. Saroj was finding life a bit difficult, as Cassie seemed determined to score points at every turn. Sooner or later she would have to have it out with the Chief. He'd said he wanted harmony in the team, but it felt like he was avoiding confronting Cassie about her attitude. Maybe a conversation with Kevin and Maggie first, though. Better to present a united front.

Chapter Fourteen

Peter and Cassie were discussing how to handle Richie Elliot's interview when Maggie popped her head in the door. 'Sorry to interrupt, but there's a video conference call for you, ma'am, it's from London, Newham police.'

'I'd like to hear what they have to say, Maggie,' said Peter. 'Put the call through to my office please. Cassie and I can take it here.'

'Sir,' said Maggie, wondering if she had made a mistake in addressing Cassie first. It's getting hard to tell who's SIO on this case, she thought. Perhaps she should check out if the others felt the same.

The video call was from a mental health specialist with experience of interviewing individuals with learning disabilities. Her name was Janine Jackson. After introductions, Janine told them that she had interviewed a Down's Syndrome man called Charlie in connection with the disappearance and possible murder of a girl called Neema.

Peter gave Janine a brief outline of the case involving the girl they now believed to be called Neema. 'This tentative identification is based on Charlie's conviction that the photograph we placed in the national newspapers is his friend Neema. Were you able to find out anything which could help us confirm that?'

Janine nodded briefly. 'You have to understand that Charlie cannot retain information very well and has limited recall of events.

However, some things stick in his mind, especially if they've been traumatic. For instance, he was able to tell me about a group of men who seemed to have been using his flat as a base for drug related activities. He knew the leader's name to be Jamal. It seems Charlie is very afraid of Jamal who had been violent towards him on a number of occasions. Charlie also spoke about girls coming to the flat and describes what I understand to be sexual activities between young girls and the gang members taking place regularly. One of the girls was Neema. From what he was able to describe, the sex was often violent and sometimes involved several men with one girl.

'Charlie describes Neema as his friend, and I think they became close, like brother and sister. Not a sexual relationship as far as I can tell.'

Peter interjected. 'Was Charlie able to tell you anything about Neema's background, or her last name, for instance?'

'He told me that she lived in a big house with lots of other girls and boys. I took that to mean a residential care establishment of some sort. He didn't know her last name or if she had any family. She told him she ran away, if that's any help?'

'It could be. If she was a London girl, and in care, we may be able to trace her from her first name. Is there anything else he could tell you?'

'He told me that the last time he saw Neema she said she was going away for a bit but would come and get him when she had a place. She told him not to tell anyone.' Janine looked at her notes. 'Oh, and he said that she used to go to Plymouth a lot. He remembered the name because he thought it was funny, a place having a mouth.'

'That's very helpful, Ms Jackson,' said Cassie. 'It confirms one of our lines of enquiry. Can I ask you what's going to happen to Charlie.'

'Thanks for asking, DI Wade. The police raided his flat and have made a number of arrests and, as far as I am aware, Charlie can safely return to his place now. I'm going to make sure he gets some support. He's all alone in the world and incredibly sad. I think that's why Neema meant so much to him. It seems like she didn't take advantage of him and was really fond of him. It could be true that she intended to come and get him like he said. In which case, it's doubly tragic if she was murdered before she could do that.'

'What do you think?' Peter asked Cassie after they had ended the call.

'It opens up a new line of enquiry, certainly. There can't be that many girls called Neema in the care system around London. If we concentrate our efforts around the East London area and work outwards from there, I think we should get something.'

'Of course, it may not be the London area at all, Cassie. Many girls who run away from care head for London, so we will probably need to put out a country wide enquiry.' Cassie nodded, as Peter continued, 'The Plymouth connection is interesting, though. It looks like Neema was running county lines between London and Plymouth. She would possibly have met a Cornwall connection there to take the drugs on to this part of the country. Very possibly the woman she was seen with at Penzance railway station.'

Cassie agreed. 'We should check out CCTV at London Paddington station. Maggie has been particularly successful with CCTV so I'll get her to progress that.'

At the mention of a team member, Peter raised the question which was on his mind. 'So, how are you finding the team generally?'

'Well, like I said, Maggie is proving very efficient and I've been impressed by Kevin's work rate. Saroj is willing enough, but seems a bit slow for a DS. I've had to remind her about procedure a couple of times and I'm not used to doing that with officers of her rank.'

'That surprises me, about Saroj, I mean. If I'm honest, Cassie, I think you intimidate her a bit. I've always found her to be a very competent member of the team, inspirational even. The pair of you don't seem to be hitting it off at the moment and I don't like bad feelings in the squad, so do something about it, will you. Take her out for coffee, ask her advice, you know how it goes, gain her confidence. I'm sure things will work out.'

Cassie felt doubtful, but smiled her acknowledgement. Peter was her DCI and she knew that she had to make this work if she was to be left alone to manage cases in the future. 'Sir.' Cassie smiled.

'Will that be all?'

Peter held up his hand to delay Cassie's departure. 'Get Kevin to search local authority records for a girl called Neema. Could be a needle in a hay-stack job but we have to start somewhere.'

Cassie stood. 'Sir.'

'Oh, and get onto Plymouth Vice Squad. Find out what's happening in their area at the moment. There's a DI called Andrews, Mark Andrews. A good bloke, plays rugby.'

'Yes sir.' Cassie edged her way towards the door.

'And don't forget DC Green. He's starting with us on Monday and he's said to be a first-rate researcher. He could give Kevin a hand with the local authority stuff. We need a lot more information Cassie, and quickly, if this case isn't to go stale on us.'

'Yes, sir.' Cassie opened the door.

'We'll interview Richie Elliot at two. Let me have the results of the search on his flat before then.' Peter looked up to see Cassie hovering by the doorway.

'We have the results, sir.' Peter raised his eyebrows. 'Sorry, sir, slipped my mind.'

'Go on, then.'

'Class A and Class B drugs sir, plus cash. He was obviously dealing. And there was a text message on his phone from an unlisted number on Tuesday morning.' Cassie checked her notes. 'It said, *Willing to meet. Usual place. Let me know when.* That's it.'

'I should have had this information when it came in.'

'Sorry, sir.' Cassie felt a bit of a fool and didn't like the feeling.

Peter waved his hand at her by way of dismissal. 'That's all, DI Wade. No time to waste.'

'Yes, sir,' said Cassie as she closed the door, clearly exasperated. She was used to running the show in Liverpool, her DCI there being very much a *desk jockey*, and she bridled at being directed in this way. She had no choice but to go along with Peter, at least for the moment. She would allocate tasks as Peter suggested and see how that worked out. The Plymouth contact could be useful, though. She'd get on to that herself. As for Saroj, well – a coffee and a bun might do it, but Cassie was sceptical.

Chapter Fifteen

The search of Richie Elliot's flat had revealed that he was obviously involved in the drug scene in the West Penwith area. Probably a lone dealer with contacts in Plymouth for his supply and controlling a few local pushers, one of whom was probably George Pengelly.

The interview with Richie Elliot was predictably '*No Comment*' when questioned about Neema's murder, but, after a whispered conversation with his solicitor, he held his hand up to possession with intent to supply. Peter and Cassie agreed that he was frightened of someone. Peter pressed him hard for information about this person, asking him specifically about the text message. Richie said it was nothing, just a girl he'd met. Even though they were convinced he was lying, they couldn't shift him from this story or discover anything about Neema's murder.

Peter continued to press Richie on his whereabouts when Neema was murdered. 'You still haven't provided us with a satisfactory alibi, Richie. I have to warn you that, unless you do, we can hold you as a suspect in Neema's murder.'

Richie again consulted his solicitor and nodded glumly. 'I was in Newquay,' he said quietly.

'Now we're getting somewhere,' said Peter. 'If you have an alibi for the time of the murder, we can rule you out as a suspect.' Peter held Richie's gaze. 'You'd like that, I expect.'

'It's difficult,' said Richie. 'I could get into trouble, you understand?'

'Not as much trouble as you will be if you don't tell us.'

'I was meeting someone.'

'Name?' said Cassie.

'I was with Shane. We met this bloke about some pills. I don't know his name, but he was a black bloke.'

'Shane McCoy?' said Cassie.

Richie nodded. 'Only these blokes are seriously hard, you know. My life would be in danger if I said anything, honest.' Richie was sweating profusely.

'How do you contact them?' Peter asked.

'They contact me on a burner. I never had a number.'

'Describe the man you met,' said Cassie, who was realising that she had let Shane McCoy go.

'Well, he was black, like I said. Tall, well built, looked like he could handle himself, you know.'

'What sort of accent did he have?' Continued Cassie.

'Not from round here. London possibly. He had posh clothes. Leather jacket, boss trainers. He kept sayin' *I'm the man*. He said that a lot.'

Peter glanced at Cassie, who indicated that she had no more questions. 'Okay, we'll leave it there for now. We'll be checking your alibi, but right now there's the little matter of the drugs seizure from your home. Stand up please.'

Richie stood as Peter read the charges.

As they watched Richie Elliot being led away, Peter remarked, 'We know where to find him. Let him stew for a couple of days and then we'll give it another try. I think he knows more than he's saying about this black guy.' Peter turned to Cassie, who was picking up her papers. 'What did Shane McCoy have to say when you interviewed him?'

Cassie looked flustered. 'Truth is, sir, we let him go without interviewing him. We didn't think he would have anything useful for us at the time."

Peter raised his eyebrows. 'You let him go! Well I'd say you need to get him back, and quickly, DI Wade.'

'Yes, sir. I'll have him brought in right away.'

'You do that, and let me know when you have him.' Peter marched off to his office, leaving Cassie red-faced.

j

* * *

Maggie looked up when she saw the Chief entering the squad room. 'We've got the results of the DNA analysis from Neema's baby, sir and the skin under her fingernails. No match for Richie Elliot or George Pengelly. We know that the DNA from the fingernails is a match for the foetus, so we can be fairly sure that the father is also the murderer.'

'Disappointing that it's not Elliot, Maggie, but it narrows down the field. Now we just need to find him.'

'I'm doing a general database search now, sir.'

Peter noticed that Robbie Green was sharing Maggie's workspace. 'Nice to see you again, DC Green. You don't start with us until Monday, though.'

Robbie stood to attention. 'I hope you don't mind, sir, I thought I might call in to say hello. It's my day off tomorrow.'

'I don't mind at all, Robbie. I'd like you to work with DC Williams for a while anyway. Carry on.'

'Sir,' they both said in unison.

As Peter had gone into his office, Cassie came into the squad room looking displeased. She had her phone to her ear. 'Okay Kevin, just find him!' As she ended the call, her phone rang again. 'What?' she shouted. Then, looking abashed, she said apologetically, 'Sorry, DI Andrews, I thought it was someone else.' Cassie listened before answering in a much calmer tone. 'That would be fantastic, DI Andrews. . . right, Mark, and it's Cassie. Great ,I'll see you around ten tomorrow.'

'Got a result, ma'am?' said Maggie.

'Yes, at least I hope it leads to something. A contact of the Chief's in Plymouth. He has time to meet tomorrow.' She tapped her teeth with her phone. 'And that gives me another problem.' Looking at the two eager faces smiling up at her, Cassie decided to be cheeky. 'I don't suppose either of you have some time tomorrow, only I've got two teenagers who could do with a bit of company, if you see what I mean.'

Robbie was the one to speak up. 'It's Sunday tomorrow, ma'am.'

'Okay Robbie, here's your first lesson about the Serious Incident

Squad. If there's a murder enquiry on the go, weekends don't exist. Got it?'

Robbie looked sheepish. He should have realised that time was at a premium in murder investigations. 'Sorry, ma'am, I'll remember that.' Aiming to get back in his DI's good books, Robbie smiled and said, 'Your kids, do they like surfing, ma'am?'

'Probably never tried it. They can swim though. Why?'

'I'm an instructor at the surf school and I'm doing my stuff at Gyllyngvase Beach all day. The weather looks great, too.'

'And you wouldn't mind my two tagging along?'

'Be glad to help, ma'am. We've got all the gear, they'll just need swimming things.'

'You, Robbie Green, are a lifesaver.'

'Yes ma'am,' said Robbie smiling, 'I do that, too.'

Chapter Sixteen

It was indeed a beautiful day when Cassie parked her car and walked into the police station in Plymouth. She remembered the mixed reactions from her children the night before when she broke the news about the surf school. Micky had been pleased, excited even, but Tanya was less than enthusiastic. 'Can't I just stay here, ma?'

'Not possible, Tanny. It's going to be good weather, by all accounts, so just sunbathe. Take a book or something.' Tanya had sulked for a bit but eventually went up to her bedroom to find suitable swimwear. She had just started to wear a bikini and was probably in front of the mirror trying on different ones. Cassie had smiled remembering her teenage years. The angst and embarrassment. She had been a plump teenager though, whereas Tanya was slim and athletic. And with her light brown skin, Cassie had to admit that her daughter was growing into a beautiful girl.

They were good kids, her two. Again Cassie reflected on her decision to take the post in Cornwall. At least they're safe, and that's what matters. And this case is turning out to be interesting too. It's not forever, so I might as well relax and do my job. Just then a shout came from the reception desk. 'DI Wade?'

Cassie turned to see a slight man in a grey suit. His head was shaved, as a concession to oncoming hair loss, Cassie guessed, and he wore fashionable dark framed glasses. Not what she expected when Peter had told her that Mark Andrews was a rugby player. Her boss was more the type, tall and muscular with the remnants of a broken nose. Attractive for all that though. Cassie had told her friend on the phone when she'd asked about Cassie's new boss, that he reminded her of the statues they had seen when they were in Rome on holiday. 'Fully clothed, of course.'

Bringing herself back to the present, Cassie walked briskly over to DI Andrews. 'Cassie Wade,' she said, taking the offered hand. *Strong handshake*, she thought.

'Mark Andrews. I thought we might go out, seeing as it's a lovely day. Get a coffee and maybe some lunch while we talk.'

'Sounds perfect,' said Cassie happily.

'Have you been to Plymouth before?' Cassie shook her head in reply. 'Okay, we'll get a coffee down at the Barbican and then stroll along the Hoe to find somewhere for lunch. How's that sound?'

'Well, it sounds great as long as we remember why I'm here. I do need any information you might have on drug transportation, and exploitation of young girls, too.'

'No problem, Cassie. I've got some intel for you back at the office, but I'll go through the salient points as we walk.'

Mark held the door for Cassie and led her down the street.

'You're from Liverpool?' Mark said as they walked down the main shopping street.

'Why does everyone say that?' Laughed Cassie, 'Is it so obvious?'

'One of the best known accents in the country after Irish and Scottish. Probably thanks to the Beatles.'

'Yeah, I suppose so. What about you?'

'Born and raised a janner. That's Plymouth, like a scouser is Liverpool.'

Cassie chuckled. 'Not many people get away with calling me a scouser. I'm from Childwall, the posh bit.'

Mark nodded. 'I guess Liverpool is a bit like Plymouth – a maritime city.' He waved his hand around. 'This area was completely bombed out during the war and rebuilt. That's why it's a bit of a concrete monstrosity in parts.' Passing a ruined church, Mark told Cassie that this building had been left standing as a reminder of the destruction visited on the city by the Luftwaffe.

Eventually the maze of smaller streets led to the waterfront, where small cafés and shops bordered a wharf at which a three mast sailing ship was moored.

'It's lovely here,' said Cassie, admiring the old buildings.

Mark took her elbow and led her across the road to a café with tables outside. 'What can I get you?' he said, after pulling back a chair for her to sit.

Cassie was amused by the old fashioned courtesy, but allowed herself to be looked after for once. 'Americano with milk please.'

After taking a sip of his coffee, Mark became business-like. 'How can I help you?'

Cassie outlined the case. 'What I'm interested in establishing is the connection our victim had with Plymouth. We suspect that she was transporting drugs, possibly from London, and meeting up with another courier who took them on to Penzance.' She looked at Mark over her coffee cup. 'If you could confirm any of that it would be a great help.'

Mark nodded. 'I've shown the photo of your girl to my team and she was recognised. Petra, my DS, patrols the station here and has spoken to a girl matching Neema's description, but this girl gave her name as Jasmine. She said she was meeting with her auntie, and she was later observed talking to an older woman, so no action was taken.'

'Would it be possible for me to speak to Petra? You see, we're trying to establish Neema's background and any clues, like an accent, would be useful.'

'Perhaps; not today, but I could get her to ring you. Other members of my team said they might have seen the girl in the photo but couldn't be sure. I've asked them to look at CCTV from the dates you gave me, see if it jogs their memories.'

Mark looked thoughtful. 'Look, seeing as you've come all this way, I'll try Petra, see if she can meet you before you leave.' He took out his phone and speed-dialled a number. Mark moved away to take the call. Returning he said, 'She could find an hour or so later. Can you stay until three?'

'I'm really grateful,' said Cassie, nodding enthusiastically. 'I'll just have to make a call.'

*　*　*

Driving back, Cassie mulled over her conversation with Petra, Mark's DS. She was sure now that the girl Petra had spoken to was Neema and had established that she had a pronounced East London accent. Petra had also spoken to her colleagues who told her that the older woman was often seen at the station and believed she was a drug courier. Cassie was a little surprised that, knowing what the woman was involved in, she had not been pulled and interviewed formally. Petra said that her focus was on child exploitation and that her colleagues were after the bigger fish so, whilst wanting to understand how the trafficking of drugs was organised, they were more interested in tracking back to the source. Arresting the small fry didn't help much in that task, *it merely alerted the chiefs if the indians were picked off.*

Cassie was satisfied that the trip had been worthwhile and that she had made some valuable contacts. Her thoughts turned to her earlier phone call to Micky. '*No rush ma, we're okay. Robbie's lighting a fire and we're going to have a cook-out. If you're quick, you could join us.*' Cassie had not heard her son sound so relaxed in ages. It was five-thirty as she turned onto the beach road in Falmouth. The sun was sparkling over the water and the waves were gently lapping the shore. Cassie parked and walked down the slight slope onto the sand, feeling very over-dressed in her business suit. Glancing around she saw a group over to her left sitting around a small fire. Micky and Tanya hadn't spotted her yet, and they were laughing at something someone said. They looked happy. It was Robbie Green who noticed Cassie as she took off her shoes to walk over the sand. He waved and spoke to Tanya, who stood and beckoned her mum over.

'Just in time, ma,' she shouted. 'There's sausages or mackerel left. Tanya looked fresh and sun-kissed, her dark curly hair blowing in the gentle breeze. Cassie thought she had never looked so lovely. Micky made a space beside him on the blanket for Cassie to sit. 'Thanks for this, Robbie,' she said, nodding over at the young constable.

'No problem, ma'am. Micky's a natural surfer and Tanny's the paddle board queen. The two teenagers laughed. 'I was in the water more often than on the board, Robbie,' laughed Tanya.

Didn't mind getting your hair wet, then? thought Cassie. *That's a first*.

Tucking into a plate of mackerel, Cassie reflected that this could be a turning point for her family. The relaxed way of life here might suit them, for a while at least.

Chapter Seventeen

Monday morning saw the team assembled in the squad room looking tired and listless. The only exception to this was Robbie, who bounced around making coffee for everyone.

Peter stood at the front of the room, the whiteboard behind him. 'Okay, where are we up to? Cassie?'

Cassie stood and joined Peter. 'I had a useful day in Plymouth yesterday. I met a DS Petra Gutherson, who recognised the girl in our photo and had spoken to Neema, but she knew her as Jasmine. Petra said that this girl had a pronounced East London accent, so it's probable she was looked after in the London area.' Cassie looked over at where Maggie and Robbie were sitting. 'Start your search there, but bear in mind that children are often moved out of borough, so widen the search if you get no joy.' Robbie nodded enthusiastically, as Maggie made a note.

'Petra also confirmed that Neema was seen in the company of an older woman matching the description of our Penzance hippy, so it's really important that we trace this woman. Saroj, have you had any luck with that?'

'Yes ma'am. I'm told she's called Molly – Molly Malone, would you believe, and lives in a commune just outside Pendeen. I've been over there. It's quite well organised. The council have given them permission to live there on the understanding that they become self-sufficient in five years. One or two families are building houses, the rest are in caravans. They have a smallholding and sell vegetables, cheese, crafts and such. Molly Malone was not there when I called, but she was known. She has a daughter, Blossom, who was there, being looked after by other women.'

'Good work, Saroj,' said Peter. 'Get back there today. It's very important that we interview this woman.'

'What about Richie Elliot's alibi?' Cassie looked around the room.

Kevin raised his hand. 'I interviewed Shane McCoy with the Chief yesterday. McCoy confirms Elliot's story. Said they were in Newquay all day and overnight. He mentioned the Wetherspoon's pub. He said he saw Elliot talking to a black man but denies any involvement in drugs. We're searching his place today.'

Peter took over from Kevin. 'McCoy is shifty. I believe he knows more about this black guy. He looked scared, like Elliot did when he mentioned this man. Maggie, can you get CCTV from Wetherspoon's and the streets around there. This black guy should be easy to spot.'

'Okay,' said Peter, looking at his watch. 'We'll meet back here at four. My office, Cassie.'

Peter sat behind his desk and motioned Cassie to a chair opposite. 'How did you get on with my mate Mark then?'

Cassie smiled and shook her head. 'Not what I expected when you said he was a rugby player, sir.'

Peter laughed. 'Not big and brawny enough you mean?'

'No disrespect, sir, but he was a bit on the small side.'

'Watched much rugby, have you?'

'What, in Liverpool? It's football all the way there.'

'Well, rugby needs terriers and greyhounds as well as Rottweilers like me.'

'I wouldn't have you down as a Rottweiler, sir. Big and brawny, yes, but more of a gentle giant.' Cassie hoped she wasn't being too familiar, but Peter just laughed.

'Only on the rugby field, Cassie. Anyway, you can ask my partner, she's coming in at four to brief the team on Operation Capture. That's the operation her team are carrying out into child exploitation in the south west. I think there could be links with our investigation.'

'I'll look forward to meeting her, sir. She may know Petra Gutherson.'

'Perhaps. I really think that there's a wider aspect to our murder, Cassie. It seems like we have a lot of pieces but can't fit them together just yet. I want you to work closely with Plymouth and with Rachel's team, see if we can make some progress.

'Sir,' said Cassie. This was just what she liked. A complex case involving several forces. As long as she was in charge, of course.

As Cassie returned to the squad room she noticed that Saroj hadn't left yet to track down Molly Malone. Remembering that Peter had asked her to build bridges, Cassie walked over to Saroj's desk.

'Just finishing up here, ma'am, and then I'm off to Pendeen.'

Cassie could feel the woman's nervousness. 'No, I'm glad I caught you. I'd like to come with you, and I thought we could stop off for a coffee on the way if you know somewhere.'

Saroj brightened up. 'There's a nice café in St Just, ma'am. We can go through there on the way.'

'Right, let's be off and catch the elusive Molly.'

Once they had bypassed Penzance and left the A30, the countryside became more rugged. Wild moorland bordered the winding road with only the occasional wind-blown tree to add variety to the landscape. They passed a road to the right which was signposted *Pendeen,* but Saroj continued on, past a disused quarry and a riding stables on the left. After a couple more miles they went down a hill into a small town. The main street was narrow, with granite cottages and shops along each side. Saroj pulled in at a small square lined with pubs and shops. Cassie could see the square tower of a church. 'That looks interesting,' she said, indicating the ancient building.

'Do you want to have a look inside, ma'am? I believe it's quite old.'

'No time today, Saroj, but I wouldn't mind exploring a bit when I have the time.'

The two women found a window table in the small café which overlooked the square. The smell of baking pervaded the atmosphere and Cassie was tempted by the sight of newly baked scones. A round, jolly looking woman came over. 'What can I get you, me dears?'

'Just coffee for me,' said Saroj. 'How about you, ma'am?'

The formal address was not missed by the waitress. 'You on holiday or business?' She enquired nosily.

Cassie frowned at Saroj. 'No, just visiting. I'll have a tea and one of your lovely scones, please.'

As the waitress bustled away, Saroj whispered across the table. 'Sorry, ma'am.'

'It's okay, better call me Cassie though, when we're not on official business. I suspect this is the sort of place where everyone knows your business and gossip spreads like wildfire.'

'You're not wrong there, ma. . . Cassie. These small villages, especially around the *wild west*, are renowned for it.'

After their drinks had been served and Cassie was tucking into a warm buttery scone, a look of absolute bliss on her face, Saroj started the conversation. 'How are you settling in, Cassie?'

Dabbing her mouth with a napkin, Cassie smiled up at Saroj. 'Quite well, I think. I must admit I didn't want to be here. You know why I was moved?'

'No, not really. There's gossip, of course. Something to do with threats being made against you in Liverpool?'

Cassie nodded and filled Saroj in on the situation with the drugs bust at her old posting. 'It was the kids really, Saroj, I couldn't have them in danger. Can't say I wouldn't have chosen somewhere livelier myself, but Micky and Tanya seem to be settling in okay, and this case is lively enough for anyone, so. . . '

Cassie had a sip of tea and asked, 'What can you tell me about Rachel, the boss's fiancé?' Saroj looked questioningly at Cassie. Cassie continued innocently. 'She's coming in later to talk to us about Operation Capture, so I just wondered what you thought.'

'Well, you know she was a colleague, don't you?' Cassie nodded, munching the last of her scone. 'She was well liked, I certainly liked her, we did a lot of work together. Does Peter think she could help with our case?'

'I think that's it. The child exploitation angle. The Chief thinks there could be a link with our girl. Rachel works closely with the team in Plymouth, so there are connections.' Cassie finished her tea and walked over to the counter to pay.

'Thanks, Cassie,' said Saroj as they left. She felt better about her boss now that the ice had melted a bit. *Perhaps she just needed time to settle in*, she thought generously.

'Right, Saroj, let's track down our wayward Molly.'

Continuing through the small town in the opposite direction to entering, Saroj drove down a steep hill into a valley, then around a sharp bend and up the other side. 'I bet there's not a level road in the whole of Cornwall,' said Cassie good-naturedly.

'Too true, ma'am,' laughed Saroj, suddenly enjoying the ride in the countryside and the company of her boss, who seemed much more relaxed than normal.

'And these bends keep you on your toes too!' said Cassie, as Saroj swung the car around a particularly sharp curve. A sign read *Carnyorth*, which consisted of a small group of cottages running at right angles to the road, and then just a few miles further on was *Trewellard*. A few more houses and pubs here, plus a building which announced itself as a *Meadery*.

'And what's a *Meadery* for, then?' asked Cassie. 'They make mead there?'

'No, ma'am. It's a restaurant of sorts. Quite unique to these parts, are Meaderys. Rough food and even rougher wine, and mead of course. The kids love it. All dark and atmospheric.'

Soon they passed through Pendeen and the Geevor tin mine workings. 'That's a museum,' said Cassie.

'Yes, ma'am. You've heard of it?'

'Robbie told me. When we were up at the murder scene. Much further now?'

'No, ma'am, just down this track here.'

Saroj turned off onto a rough gravel road, slowing down to accommodate the dips and boulders. Over to the right could be seen a whisp of smoke and a flagpole with a Cornish flag and yellow banner with an orange sun in the centre. 'That's it,' said Saroj, pulling over into a layby.

She and Cassie climbed out, the wind immediately whipping their clothes around them. 'I'll let you lead,' Cassie said to Saroj, her eyes taking in the site. There were several caravans in various states of repair and two primitive construction sites where buildings were taking shape. Two men who were working, stripped off to the waist, shielded their eyes as the women approached. 'Can I help you?' shouted one, raising his voice against the wind.

Cassie and Saroj raised their warrant cards aloft. 'Is there someone in charge here?' said Saroj.

The man who had shouted looked at his colleague and shrugged his shoulders. 'Not as such,' he chuckled, as he climbed down his ladder. 'I'm Christian, how can I help?'

The two women picked their way across the uneven ground to where Christian stood, hands on hips. 'We're looking for a Molly Malone,' said Saroj. 'Do you know where we could find her?'

'What you want with Molly?' said Christian, guardedly.

'That's our business. Do you know where she is?' Saroj held eye contact with the man, allowing a silence to develop.

'Aye,' he said eventually. 'The green caravan yonder,' indicating with his hammer. 'She was there this morning and I've not seen her leave.'

Cassie led the way, dodging around piles of wood and children's toys. It was messy but not unkempt. There seemed to be an order to things here, she thought. Arriving at the green caravan, Saroj knocked on the door, which was standing ajar. 'Get that, Blossom,' said a voice, and a little girl clutching a worn teddy bear peeped around the door.

'It's two women, mam!' she shouted, and then dodged back inside.

A tall slender woman came to the door, wiping her hands on a grubby apron. 'Yes?' she said, raising her eyebrows.

'Are you Molly Malone?' Said Saroj, showing her warrant card. The woman nodded. Saroj continued, 'DI Wade and DS Kapoor, Devon and Cornwall police, can we have a word?'

Molly popped her head back into the van. 'You watch that dough,

Blossom. But don't play with it, you 'ear me?' She stepped down from the van, a nervous look on her face. 'How can I help you?'

Saroj took out the photo of Neema and showed it to Molly. 'Do you recognise this person?' she said, watching for Molly's reaction.

A small pause, then Molly said, 'I might do.'

'Might or do?'

'Yeah, I've seen her around.' Molly's eyes darted between the two women and alighted on Cassie. 'You a relative?' she asked.

'Because I'm black?' said Cassie incredulously.

'Well, yeah, I suppose. No offence.'

Cassie sighed and shook her head. Saroj continued. 'When did you last see her?'

Molly scratched her scalp through her dreadlocks. 'Don't know for sure. Week or two maybe.'

'Where did you last see her?'

Molly looked at the floor. 'Can't rightly remember.'

'Look Molly, we can do this here or down at the station. We have CCTV footage of you with this girl in Penzance just over a week ago. How do you know her?'

Molly looked around as if she was going to make a run for it. She was barefoot and her little girl was in the van, so Saroj reckoned she would think again.

'Come on, Molly. This girl, Neema, is dead, murdered, so if you know anything about it you should tell us now.'

Molly shook her head. 'I don't know nothin' about no murder, honest. I met her in Plymouth and she wanted to see Cornwall, so I brought her. Don't know any more.'

'Right. Come on. Get someone to look after your daughter and we'll talk at the station.'

'No, please, I don't know anythin'.'

'Do you want us to arrest you?'

Molly sighed and went into the van. She came out with Blossom and shouted over to a woman sat shelling peas outside her caravan. 'Marg, look after our Blossom, will yer?' The woman nodded and, with a small push from her mum, Blossom ran over to Marg.

Chapter Eighteen

Plymouth was sweltering under a mid-summer sun as DI Mark Andrews entered the police building. *Thank God for air con*, he thought as he flashed his warrant card and was granted admission through the security doors. He was there today for a meeting with Petra Gutherson for an update about Operation Capture. The undercover operation had been going on for several months now with nothing to show, and Mark was feeling the pressure from his superiors to make some arrests or bring it to a close. Petra was the controller of the undercover officer, who had so far given very little intel. She made excuses for him, saying that it takes time to win the confidence of the people he was embedded with, and Mark understood this. However, there was always the danger of undercover officers being drawn into the sleezy world they were investigating. The temptations in the form of financial rewards and a taste of the good life, albeit criminal, were sometimes too much for weak minded officers and, the longer this one remained under cover, the more likely that became. It's never easy to pull an operation, but Mark was tempted, if only to get the Chief Super off his back.

Petra was waiting for him outside the conference room. With her was one of the civilian admin people, Christine, he thought. To save the embarrassment of getting her name wrong, Mark simply nodded and opened the door for the two women. When they were seated, Mark asked Petra for an update and Christine took out her notepad.

Petra began with the customary excuses. 'It's not unusual for there to be very little to report on a job as sensitive as this one,' she said nervously, knowing that was not what Mark wanted to hear. 'However, DC 57 (the code name for the officer known as Deep Cover 57) reports that he has been given access to the names of some girls who regularly attend the *parties*, as they are known, where a number of men, names not yet known, have access to the girls for sex. Some of the girls are as young as twelve, he says.'

Mark held up his hand. 'Does DC 57 know where the parties are held?'

'Not as such, sir. He believes there are a number of venues.'

Mark continued. 'So, he knows some girls' names. He doesn't know who the men are, and he doesn't know where the alleged sexual assaults take place.' He consulted his file. 'It's been what. . ? Seven months? And we are still as much in the dark as when we started. We suspected then that girls were being used in this way and that a group of men, some possibly very senior officers in the police, as well as local business men and politicians, were involved.' Mark looked directly at Petra who was beginning to squirm a bit. 'We're no further forward, Petra. We expected evidence – photographs, venues, girls who were willing to make a formal complaint and give evidence, at least.' He paused. 'You know the pressure I'm under, Petra. I'm definitely of a mind to pull this operation and find another way, if we can.'

Petra shook her head slowly. 'DC57 feels he may be close, sir. He does have some photographs, which are in your file marked XC 11 to 19. They show some of the organisers meeting to discuss arrangements. We also have a photo, XS 15, taken from general surveillance, which shows our man with these organisers.'

Mark was exasperated. 'DS Gutherson, we already know who *these* men are, have done for months, it's the men who participate that we need to catch, with their pants down if possible. Do you understand?' Petra looked defeated. 'We went to a lot of trouble to set this up. DC57 was essentially eradicated from the police database expressly because we had suspicions about senior police involvement. DC57 has had all the support we could possibly offer and has still not obtained the information we need.' Mark shook his head sadly. 'I'm sorry, DS Gutherson, if DC57 hasn't produced the goods by now, I can't see how continuing with this will get us the evidence we need.'

Petra made one last ditch attempt. 'Can you give me another couple of weeks, sir? If we've not got anything by then. . . '

Mark sighed deeply. 'Two weeks, Petra, and then that's it. Okay?' Petra nodded.

'You have a list of the girls' names, at least. Can your general surveillance track them?'

'Not easy, sir. We don't know where they are picked up, or when. We may have names but not addresses. These girls fly under the radar.'

'Under the radar? Isn't DC57 supposed to be under the radar with them? That's why he's there, for God's sake!'

'Sorry, sir. I've got a meet with him tonight. I'll let him know of your concerns.'

'Yes, you do that. Okay, off you go, and thanks Christine.' Christine nodded and Mark was pleased that, at least, he had got her name right. Not much else positive had come out of this meeting. Now he had to face the Chief Super with nothing to offer but excuses. As he was gathering his papers together, his phone vibrated.

'DI Andrews.'

'Wow, do you look as bad as you sound?'

Mark gave a hollow laugh. 'Rachel, how the devil are you?'

'Better than you, by the sound of it. I was hoping we could meet. I think you're aware that a murder case of Peter's could have connections to our Operation Capture. If you have the time, I'd be grateful.'

'Can it be today? I'm trying to put off seeing the Chief Super. Be good to get some news for him if you have something.'

'Can't promise. I want info from you as well, but if we can find a connection it could help both of us.'

'How soon can you get here?'

'Already here, mate. Usual place? Ten minutes?'

Chapter Nineteen

The interview room was chilly despite the warm sunshine outside. Molly shivered, and not just because of the cold. She had been given a cup of tea some time ago and, being alone, not knowing what the officers were doing, was making her increasingly nervous. Molly knew that the police had ways of getting you to say things you didn't mean to, and she knew she had to stop herself from blurting anything out. The man who met Jasmine on the day she disappeared had threatened her and little Blossom, and she had no doubt he was as good as his word. Molly had come a long way from the life she had when she was into the drugs in a big way. Christian, the founder of the *Sacred Sun* commune, had helped her to find a new way for her and Blossom, and she had hope for the future for the first time in her life. But she knew that she was still fragile and, if she had to leave the commune because of this man, she could easily slide back into the old ways.

The door opened, startling Molly. The two women who brought her here came in looking serious. One of the detectives switched on the recorder. 'Interview started at fourteen-thirty. Present are DI Wade, DS Kapoor and. . . state your name for the tape please.'

Molly nodded at the instruction. 'Molly Malone.'

'Is that your real name, Molly?'

'No. I'm Molly O'Keefe, but because I'm Irish I get called Malone, like the song. I don't mind, I like it better than O'Keefe.'

Cassie continued. 'Okay, Molly, do you know why you are here?'

'You want to know about poor little Jasmine. I told you, I don't know nothin' about her being killed or anything.'

'How did you know her?'

Molly sighed. 'Look, this was my old life, okay. I'm clean now and doin' alright.' Cassie simply stared at Molly. She continued. 'I used to fetch stuff from Plymouth for someone.'

'Would that someone be Richie Elliot?' Molly looked down at her shoes, her leg jiggling nervously. 'Come on, Molly, we know about Elliot and his associates.'

'Yeah, well, it was Richie. But I just handed them over. Don't know what happened after that.'

'Presumably you were paid for your trouble?'

Molly leaned back, looking between the two women. 'He paid me in stuff.'

'Drugs, you mean?'

'Yeah, I sold them on to someone. Made a bit of money that way.'

'Who did you sell them on to?'

Molly shook her head. 'I don't want to get anyone in trouble.'

Cassie suddenly slapped her hand on the table, startling Molly. 'Come on, Molly. This is a murder enquiry. Your piddling bit of dealing is not of interest to us at the moment, but that can soon change. Do you understand me?'

'Okay, it was George Pengelly I sold them to. I don't do it no more though. I'm clean now, and me and Blossom are doin' alright at the commune.'

Cassie leaned back and made a note on the file. Saroj took over the questioning.

'Okay, Molly, tell us about Neema, or Jasmine as you know her.'

'I told you. I used to meet her at Plymouth station. Collect stuff from her and bring it back here.'

'By stuff, you mean drugs.' Molly nodded. 'What kind of drugs?'

'I never knew what was in all the packages. What Richie gave me was a bit of *blow*.'

'Cannabis?'

'Yeah. Nothin' heavy. I wouldn't touch anythin' like that now.'

'Okay, so you met Neema at the station.'

'Yeah. She was nice. We usually had a cup of tea while we were waitin' for our trains. She'd never been out of London, and I told her about Cornwall, how pretty it was an' all that. One time she just said she wasn't goin' back, to London, you know? I wanted to know about the cash I gave her, for the stuff, like, but she said they owed her.' Molly shook her head sadly. 'I thought she was mental, tryin' to swindle that London lot, but she said she'd be okay once she got to Cornwall. Disappear like.'

'So she came back with you. What happened then?'

'I took her to the commune. She bunked in with me and Blossom.'

'So she was living with you?'

'No, not living, just a few days. Christian, that's our founder, he has rules about who can stay. *All have to contribute*, he says. Once you start lettin' strangers doss at the camp it soon becomes a magnet for dropouts and druggies, he says. We have to become self-sufficient in five years and make a proper go of it, so Christian is very strict about these things.'

'But Neema stayed, what? Two, three days?'

'Yeah, I told her she had to go. She asked me to walk with her up to the cliffs. There's some *benders* up there. . . '

Cassie looked up. 'Benders?'

'Like a camp. Bent over branches covered over, like tents.'

Saroj continued. 'So you took her to the cliffs?'

'Yeah, and that's where I left her.'

'When was this Molly, what day?'

Molly thought. 'It was about a week ago. Monday, Tuesday, something like that. No, it *was* Tuesday. We have meetings on Tuesdays, and I was rushing to get back for it. I wanted to tell Christian that she'd gone.'

'This is important, Molly. Did you see anyone else on the cliffs that day?'

Molly frowned and shook her head. 'No. There might have been some walkers, there's usually walkers, but they was a long way off.'

'And have you seen or heard from Neema since then?'

'No, miss. Honest I haven't.'

Cassie folded her file and turned to the recorder. 'Interview suspended at fifteen-eighteen. Do you want another cup of tea, Molly?'

'Can't I go now? I said everything I know.'

'You have been very helpful so far. There's just a few more questions. Tea?'

Molly nodded glumly.

Cassie and Saroj walked down the corridor together and into the ladies room. When they were washing their hands, Saroj said. 'What do you think, ma'am?'

'I think she knows more than she's telling. I'm not convinced she went up to the cliffs to join the bender camp. It sounds like an arranged meeting to me. There's those cigarette butts by the old mine building. Someone was waiting. Molly knows more about that, I'm sure.' Cassie dried her hands and straightened her hair. 'When we go back in you ask her what she knows about Neema's background. They must have talked about something over those cups of tea. If we get her talking, she might let a few names slip. And we could do with the DNA analysis on the cigarette butts. See to that, will you.'

'Right, ma'am.' Saroj was used to the slow progress of interviews. Not like the telly would have you believe at all, she mused. Suspects breaking down and confessing, or telling all, didn't happen in her experience. It took patience and experience to wear someone down. At least Molly hadn't asked for a solicitor. One who might just advise her to go *no comment*. That was very frustrating.

Cassie continued. 'In the meantime, let's bulk out this file. Make it look like we've had more information.'

As the two entered the squad room, Cassie saw a very attractive, oriental looking woman talking to Kevin and Maggie. Saroj noticed Cassie's interest. 'That's Rachel Morris, ma'am. The Chief's partner. He said she was coming in at four to talk about her role in child exploitation.'

'Mmm,' said Cassie. 'I remember. It would be a pity to miss that. Let's see if she could wait while we finish our interview. I want to get back to Molly before she thinks too much.'

Saroj introduced Cassie to Rachel, who said she'd be more than pleased to delay if that was okay with everyone.

'Shouldn't be too long,' said Cassie smiling. 'If we can't get her to crack in an hour, we'll have to let her go and have her in again another day.'

Rachel watched Cassie with interest as she pulled out a sheaf of papers from her desk drawer and placed them in the file she was carrying. Not what I expected, she thought. But then Peter had said very little about his new DI except that she was very competent. *Well, that's men for you. Leave out the interesting details.*

Saroj began the interview with Molly Malone by reiterating what she had already told them. 'So, we know you knew Neema, we know she came with you to the Pendeen commune, and we know you walked with her to the cliff path on the day she was murdered. You claim not to know who she might have been meeting on that day, saying only that you believe she was going to the bender camp. You did not have any communication with her after you left her on the cliffs.' Saroj looked up from her notes as Molly nodded.

'Neema was with you for three days. What did you talk about?'

'What?'

'You must have spoken to her in that time. What did you talk about?'

'Er. Well, she told me a bit about London. I've never been, see. She said she wanted to get away.'

'Did she say why she wanted to get away?'

'People wasn't nice to her, she said.' Molly thought for a moment. 'Oh, except Charlie. She liked him.'

'Was Charlie a boyfriend?'

'Boyfriend?' Mollly laughed. 'No nothin' like that. She said he was a bit simple, but kind. He was the only one who was good to her.' Molly was becoming relaxed now that the questions were not about her. 'She said she wanted to bring him here, to Cornwall, once she got settled and had had the baby and that.'

'Neema was pregnant?'

Molly suddenly looked guarded again. 'Well, she said she was, but I don't know, she could have been lying.'

'Why would she lie about something like that, Molly?'

Molly became alert again, her eyes darting about. 'I don't know. People do, don't they? To get attention, like.'

'If I told you she *was* pregnant, what would you say?'

'Was she?' Molly didn't sound surprised.

'She was.' Saroj watched Molly squirm. 'Did she tell you who the father was?'

Molly was shaking now. 'Look, I don't know nothin'. I told you.' Molly desperately wanted to get out of this room now. 'All I know is that she said she'd be getting some money soon. Then she'd get a place for her and the baby and send for Charlie to live with her.' She turned away from Cassie and Saroj. 'That's all I know. Now I want to leave. You can't keep me here.'

Cassie glanced over at Saroj, then closed her file. 'Okay Molly, you can go, but we will want to speak to you again, so stay put. Is that clear?'

Molly jumped up. 'Yes, miss. I've got nowhere to go, anyway.'

Saroj said she'd see Molly out, and Cassie headed back to the squad room. She was formulating a theory as she walked. *Neema gets pregnant. She wants out, so she scarpers, taking the drugs money with her. A bit risky, that, but she is only fourteen, so perhaps she believes they would forget about her. Then she tells Molly that she's going to get some more money soon. Sounds like blackmail. The baby's father no doubt. That's who she was meeting on the cliffs. The DNA from the fingernail scrapings confirm that the father is more than likely the murderer too, so he's our prime suspect. We need to find that man and I think Molly knows who he is.*

It was the end of a long day and Cassie was feeling hot and sweaty. She pushed her unruly hair back from her forehead and straightened her jacket before entering the squad room. Rachel was leaning on a desk talking to Peter as Cassie entered. Rachel could have just stepped off the cover of *Vogue*, thought Cassie. Her graceful, slim figure was clothed in a fashionable pants suit in grey, with a white silk blouse. She wore no make-up that Cassie could discern, and her straight black hair was tied back with a simple bow at the nape of her neck. Altogether, there was no doubt that she was a very beautiful woman. Standing beside her, Peter seemed to glow, his face transformed with adoration.

I think I may be sick, Cassie whispered to herself, uncharitably, not realising that Robbie Green was right behind her. 'Ha. Sorry ma'am, couldn't help hearing.'

'No, I'm sorry Robbie, very wrong of me.' But Cassie had a wicked smile on her face. 'What's the story with these two, anyway?'

'Well she was known around the station as the ice maiden. No one could get near her. There was even talk that she didn't like men, if you know what I mean. The DCI had a bad divorce, they say, and kept himself very much to himself. Then suddenly they were an item. No one saw that coming.'

Cassie thought that Robbie Green must keep his ear to the ground. A good skill in a detective. 'And what about Saroj? What's the story there?'

'Well,' said Robbie conspiratorially. 'The word is that her family tried to force her into an arranged marriage, but she rebelled. I don't think she has much to do with them now. She's a trained doctor too.'

'You're quite the oracle Robbie. Anything on the others?' Cassie smiled.

'Only that Kevin is an ace surfer. Don't know much about Maggie but I'm working with her, so. . . '

'You amaze me. Now get me a coffee before you wheedle secrets out of me.'

Robbie smiled, but didn't say that spending time with Cassie's kids had been very instructive. Very instructive indeed. 'Ma'am,' he said and went over to the coffee machine.

Cassie was still looking at the romantic pair over by the window. It was a very long time, if ever, since anyone had looked at her like that. She'd always been a plain looking girl, her short stature becoming rounder as she got older. Her saving grace was her sense of humour and her self-deprecating nature, which drew more attractive people into wanting to be her best friend. The man she eventually married was one of these. Tony had just ended a relationship and said that Cassie was just the tonic he needed. They had been together for three months when Cassie got pregnant. Tony

k

did the right thing, at least that was what his mother said. Cassie had overheard her telling a friend at the wedding that it wasn't a love match, and she was sure that Tony would get bored soon enough. Cassie hated to admit it, but she was right. Tony loved Micky but he found parenthood constrictive. When Tanya was born he could barely stay in the house, making any excuse to stay late at his work as a lawyer. This turned into drinks after work, with the inevitable arguments when he rolled home. Cassie didn't wait for him to say he was leaving, she made that decision for him. That was twelve years ago now. The divorce was easy and Tony had remarried a year after. He lived in London now and the kids went to see him as often as he and they could manage it. By all accounts, Tony adored his new baby boy and was a doting father. Perhaps he needed to grow up, Cassie had thought when Tanya told her this.

Cassie's reverie was disturbed, as Rachel approached her. 'How did it go with your young woman?'

Cassie smiled. 'Oh, you know, she's keeping a lot back, but we can pull her again.'

'You look done in. Shall we leave this for another day?'

'No, absolutely not,' said Cassie. 'I'm okay, and you've been here for a couple of hours now, so let's crack on.'

'Right,' said Rachel, sensing something negative from the other woman, but not sure why or what. Smiling warmly, she turned on her heel and took up a position at the front of the room.

'Okay, what can I tell you about Operation Capture?'

After the briefing, Peter was the first to ask Rachel a question. 'So what has the undercover officer, DC57, been able to provide?'

'Very little it seems. The last time I spoke with Petra, she was about to have a meet with him, so maybe something came of that. The suspicion that senior police officers are involved in the abuse means that the operation is very tricky. They can't be allowed to suspect DC57 otherwise it could be very bad for him. For that reason, all data about him has been removed from the police database, just in case anyone with access decides to do a search.'

Rachel continued. 'We do have some photographs of the

organisers and that's possibly where your contacts could help.' Rachel passed out copies. 'I was thinking especially of your recent suspect, Molly. She has connections with Plymouth. She's a bit too old for our men to be interested in, but she may have noticed something, or been told something. Perhaps Neema had been approached and told her about it? She certainly fits the profile. Anyway, it's worth a shot.'

Cassie was interested in other girls who had been targeted. 'Have any of them spoken to police about their experiences?'

'One or two, yes. That's where the operation began in earnest. Two girls were interviewed after the care staff in their residential home became concerned. Apparently, the girls suddenly had new mobile phones and jewellery, and began staying out late, coming home drunk. When questioned, they said they had boyfriends who bought them the phones and stuff. They admitted going to parties with the men but said it was all consensual. They became less forthcoming when asked if they had had sex with men other than the boyfriends. Police interviewed them and found out that other men at the parties were older white men, whereas their boyfriends had been black, probably Asian. The police strongly suspected that sex had taken place between the girls and the older men, but the girls were too scared to talk about it. One girl, spoken to separately, said she was sure that a couple of the men were police. One had visited the children's home she was in, when a girl called Nicki had told staff she had been raped. Nicki was moved soon after and nothing else was heard about it.

'The interviewed girls were unwilling to give the names of the boyfriends, but the police confiscated their phones and traced the men to a taxi firm in Plymouth. The girls were moved for their safety and the operation was set up.' Rachel indicated the photographs. 'The men from the taxi firm feature in the photos. DC57 has infiltrated this group and is now working with them as a taxi driver.'

'Okay,' said Peter. 'If that's all, we'll re-interview our suspects tomorrow with these photos.' Turning to Rachel. 'That's been helpful, thanks.'

She smiled warmly. 'No problem, sir.'

Chapter Twenty

Petra Gutherson knocked on DI Andrews' door with some trepidation. It had been a week since he had told her that, unless DC57 could provide more information about the men involved in Operation Capture, he was going to pull the plug. Now she had to give him some bad news, probably some of the worst news possible from an undercover operation.

She opened the door as Mark called, 'Come in.' He waved her over. 'Take a seat, Petra, I'll just be a minute.'

Petra watched Mark signing a number of pages before gathering them into a neat pile and placing them in a folder. 'Bloody paperwork. Takes up more time than actual policing.' He smiled up at Petra. 'Coffee?'

'No thanks, sir. I've got some bad news, I'm afraid.'

Peter was in an interview room with Molly Malone and her solicitor, who was provided for her when she was arrested on suspicion of perverting the course of justice. He had a bundle of photographs in front of him. He looked up at Molly and pushed one of them across the desk towards her.

'Yesterday you told my inspector that you recognised this young woman.'

Molly glanced quickly at the image. 'Yes. I knew her as Jasmine.'

'You also stated that you accompanied Jasmine, aka Neema, to a spot on the cliffs outside St Just on Tuesday 16th of June. Could you tell me what time that was?'

Molly shook her head. 'I don't think so, not exactly, anyway. I don't have a watch, see. It was afternoon, probably about two o'clock or something.'

'That's very good, Molly. It helps us a lot. Now, I'm going to show you another photograph.' Peter took one of the photos supplied by Rachel and pushed it towards Molly. 'There are a number of men in this photo. Do you recognise any of them?' Molly looked at each man in turn, then glanced at her solicitor, who nodded briefly.

'I don't know any of them.'

Peter showed Molly a second photo. 'What about this group?'

Molly looked quickly at the image, then pushed it away. 'No.'

'Look at it again, Molly. Have you seen any of these men?'

Molly looked at her solicitor. He whispered something in her ear.

'No comment,' said Molly, nervously.

'Now, when you were so clear and careful about the first image, and then you hardly glance at the second, do you know what that tells me, Molly?' Molly looked down at the table and shook her head. 'It tells me that you *have* recognised someone from the second photograph but are not willing to tell me.' Molly's leg started to jiggle and she glanced between her solicitor and Peter. He continued. 'I want to remind you, Molly, that a girl has been murdered, and obstructing our enquiries into that is a very serious offence. Do you understand? You could go to prison for a long time.'

'I can't. . . I've got a little girl.' Molly started to sob quietly.

Peter gathered the photographs. 'You think about what would happen to her, Molly, and talk to your solicitor, I'll give you ten minutes.'

Peter left the room.

'You can't find him!' Mark was incensed. 'Tell me.'

'He didn't make the meet last week and I've been trying to raise him since. We can't get a trace on his phone. The general surveillance team have not seen him around the taxi office.' Petra shrugged her shoulders. 'He's disappeared.'

'I don't believe it. After all the time we've spent with nothing to gain, and now this!'

'I'm very worried about him, sir.' Petra was angry that Mark was thinking of the cost rather than the safety of one of his officers.

Mark was chastened by Petra's tone. 'Of course. You're right, we should be worried. When was the last contact?'

'Sunday the 14th of June, sir. We had our regular meeting. He seemed agitated but I put that down to him getting closer to the action. He assured me that everything was okay.'

'And he hasn't been seen since?' Petra shook her head. 'Right. Usual routine for a missing person. Check CCTV, rail and bus stations. Put out an APB on his car. You know the score. Find him, Petra.'

When Peter re-entered the interview room, the atmosphere had changed. Molly was sitting straighter and her solicitor was leaning back in his seat. 'My client would like to make a statement,' he said somewhat wearily.

'Okay, Molly. What would you like to tell me?'

'Could I see that photo again? The second one of the men.' Peter slid the photo over to Molly. She pointed to one of the group. 'Him. I've met him.'

'Where did you meet him?'

Molly glanced at her solicitor, who nodded encouragingly. 'On the cliffs, that day.'

'The day you went with Jasmine? Tuesday the 16th June?' Molly nodded. 'Please speak for the tape.'

'Sorry, yes, that day. He was waiting by the old mine workings.'

'Did you speak to him.'

'He spoke to me. He said if I ever told anyone about him, he'd kill me. Then I left. I left Jasmine there with him.' Molly sobbed.

'Okay, Molly. You're doing the right thing. I'm going to leave you for a moment, but I'll be back. Would you like a cup of tea or coffee?'

'Tea would be nice,' Molly said, wiping her eyes. She heaved a big sigh, and seemed relieved to have spoken out, Peter thought, as many people do when they finally get something off their chest.

Cassie looked up as Peter entered the squad room. She was just finishing a phone call, and beckoned Peter over. 'Mark Andrews has just contacted me to say that his undercover officer is missing, and their search has shown his car on the A30 approaching Penzance on the 16th June. Pinged at 10.20am.'

'Do they have a photograph of him they could send us? And his car registration.'

'I'll get on to that now,' said Cassie. After sending the email, she turned to Peter. 'Did you get anything useful out of Molly?'

'Yes. She's admitted to seeing a man waiting for Neema on the cliffs on the 16th. She ID'd the man from one of the Operation Capture photos.' Peter turned to Kevin. 'Do we have the results of the DNA analysis of the cigarette butts yet?'

'I'll get on to them, sir,' said Kevin, picking up his phone.

Cassie's email pinged. 'Photo through, sir,' she said to Peter, who came over to have a look.

'Wait a minute,' he said, as he pulled the images that he showed Molly from his file. 'Well I never,' he said. 'It's the same man, I'm sure of it.' He handed the photo to Cassie.

'Certainly looks like it, sir.'

'Get on to Andrews and verify that. This case is getting very interesting indeed.'

Chapter Twenty-one

Mark Andrews was livid. Not only had their undercover officer gone AWOL, but he was now the prime suspect in a murder case. The Chief Super was chasing Mark for answers, and quick. Not only that, but he had been ordered to conduct a joint investigation from now on, linking the murder investigation by Truro police with their own Operation Capture, with Peter Sanders as SIO. He liked Peter, but didn't like the thought of him taking over his case. He didn't like that one little bit.

Mark paced his office as he waited for Petra Gutherson. He had to tell her that she was suspended whilst the Anti-corruption Unit carried out an investigation into her handling of the undercover cop known as DC57. Mark was furious with Petra, but he also had compassion for any officer who found themselves subject to internal investigation. It could mean the end of her career and, as one of his most valued officers, he hoped she could avoid that outcome. Mark forced himself to calm down as he spotted Petra making her way across the office. She looked tired and drawn, and he suspected that she had had little sleep since the news about DC57. He smiled and waved her over.

Petra took the news well, Mark thought. She had probably been expecting it. Losing an undercover officer was very grave. Petra confessed that she had been worried about him, that he seemed distracted, and had very little information to share when she met up with him. 'I should have acted on that, sir, and I'm sorry. I let him convince me that everything was going to plan, but I could see that he was very worried about something.'

'Water under the bridge now, Petra. You need to focus on the AC investigation. Get your story right.'

'Sir. What about DC57? Is there any news?'

'I'm sorry, Petra, I can't share any of the investigation with you. You understand why?'

'Yes, sir. Sorry, I wasn't thinking. AC might suspect that I'm helping him. I understand. It's just that I wouldn't do that. You believe me, sir, don't you?' Petra was clearly upset, tears filling her eyes.

'Just let the investigation take its course, Petra. I'm sure you have nothing to worry about. My advice is to be honest and straight-forward with them. All officers make mistakes, they know that, but you must prepare. Think it through. You should be able to anticipate the questions they will ask, and have the answers ready. Your police rep will help you with that, too.'

'Thank you, sir. Good advice.' Petra stood and handed over her warrant card. 'Good luck with the case.'

Mark shook her hand warmly. *A good officer*, he thought as she left. *I hope she gets through this and gets the opportunity to learn from her mistakes.*

As Mark watched Petra walk through the office, shaking hands with her colleagues, who he knew wished her good luck, he spotted Peter entering with DI Cassie Wade at his side. He saw that Peter held the door for Petra and that Cassie shook her hand. Mark reminded himself that these were good people and that he shouldn't feel threatened by them. So what if he wasn't in charge of this case now, he could still contribute and prove his worth. They would be relying on him for the background of Operation Capture and his local knowledge, so he shouldn't be kept out of the loop. He walked out of his office to meet them.

'DCI Sanders, DI Wade, welcome to our humble abode.'

Peter spoke up. 'No need for formality, Mark. It's Peter and Cassie. We're looking forward to working with you.'

'Thanks, Peter. We'll be sharing an office, if that's okay. Very short of space here.'

'Absolutely fine, Mark.'

'Cassie can have the free desk over there,' indicating the desk that Petra had just vacated.

'Well, now that we've got the pleasantries out of the way, I'd like to have a staff briefing.'

'I'll get that organised. I think most people are here.' Mark opened his office door. 'But perhaps you and I could have a brief chat first?' Peter nodded. 'Right, I'll get some coffee, black isn't it?'

Peter sipped his coffee and put the mug down on the desk. 'First off, Mark, how are you feeling? It's awful when something like this happens in a team. It's not a nice job to suspend an officer, she looked gutted.'

'Thanks, Peter. Of course, she was gutted, but it's a serious business losing track of an undercover officer. We were relying on her to feed us intel about the operation and if she'd acted sooner, we may not be facing the situation we have now.'

Peter nodded. 'There's no doubt it's messy. I have a report now that the DNA from cigarette butts found near the scene of our murder also belong to the perpetrator. We have witness testimony that a man was waiting for Neema on the cliffs, and that man has been identified by the same witness as your undercover, DC57. Now that he's disappeared. . . well, it doesn't look good for him.'

'I have some information too, which, I'm afraid, confirms our suspicions.' Mark passed a sheet of A4 over to Peter. 'As you see, DC57 was caught on our CCTV accessing his HR file. I can only assume that he was removing something incriminating, possibly his DNA record. And then there's this.' Mark handed Peter an image taken from a CCTV camera showing a man boarding a ferry at Plymouth docks on the 17th June at 1.20pm. 'I know it's only half face, but I'm sure this is DC57.'

'Where was the ferry headed?'

'France, sir. Roscoff.'

Chapter Twenty-two

Sunil Jamdar pulled his backpack over his shoulder. The weather in Brest was hot and sunny and he thought what a lovely place it would be if he was on holiday. As it was, he was on the run, hoping to find a job on one of the large yachts that came and went in the busy harbour. He had some experience of sailing, having crewed for his friend Martin, who owned a fifty footer moored in Falmouth. That seemed like a lifetime ago. No, even worse, a different life altogether. Not for the first time, he wondered how he had allowed himself to be in this position. It had been tough at first, the suspicion never far from the surface when he was with the gang of taxi drivers. It was easy enough to get the job, they were always short of drivers, but he was aware of being kept at arm's length. Silence falling when he walked into the room, secret meetings late at night. Sunil kept his head down and just got on with his work. He had always been a cheerful person, which earned him his nickname, *Sunny*. After a while this attribute had won the others over and they started to talk in his presence, whispers at first, but growing more careless as time went on.

One evening the boss asked if he could take a group to an address and wait for them. There would be extra cash in it, a bonus, the boss said. The group had consisted of four girls. Done up to the nines they were, short skirts, make-up. But nothing could hide the fact that they were young, very young. Sunil estimated they would be twelve or thirteen, at most. The girls were accompanied by a large black man, who sat beside Sunil but didn't speak until they reached their destination. Sunil had set off north along the A386 towards Tavistock. The SATNAV was fixed and he wasn't quite sure where he ended up after leaving the A road and taking a multitude of left and right turns. Eventually the black guy said, 'Stop here,' as he approached a pair of stone gates set into a high hedge. The guy told him to pull in and Sunil drove slowly up a long gravel drive which led to a large house. Lights were burning from the downstairs and upstairs windows, and the front door was ajar, with another large black guy standing guard at it. Sunil's next instruction came. 'Pull in over there, then wait.' As the car stopped, the girls jumped out giggling and fixing their clothes, staggering on too-high heels. The minder ushered them to the house, herding them like a flock of sheep. When they were inside, the two black guys disappeared around the back.

Sunil thought this was a chance for him to look around. After the men had been gone five minutes, he ventured out of the car, an excuse of needing a pee ready in case he was spotted. Walking quietly around the side of the house opposite to the one the two black guys had taken, Sunil was able to look in through a downstairs window. The girls stood in the middle of the room, each with a drink. Around them were several men, aged around fifty or so, Sunil estimated, each dressed smartly in business suits. They seemed to be weighing up the girls, making Sunil think of a cattle auction. Then one man beckoned a girl over and took her hand. He led her out of the room. This was repeated until all four of the girls had been *claimed*, and the remaining men settled down to talk and drink.

Sunil took out his phone to take a picture, but heard a noise from over his shoulder and saw the two black guys approaching. He quickly unzipped his pants and had a pee into the border. As the men approached, Sunil smiled sheepishly. 'Couldn't hold it in, guys,' he laughed.

'Get back to the car,' said the one who had been with Sunil.

'No problem,' said Sunil. 'Is there a drink going? Coffee or tea?'

The men ignored him and watched as Sunil shrugged his shoulders and walked back to the car.

As he looked out over the gardens, Sunil tried to remember

when he had stopped being that conscientious officer and had become seduced by the illicit life he was supposed to be investigating. It was probably when he met Jasmine. He smiled at the memory of her walking bold as brass into the taxi office one day. A skinny little thing with tight jeans and a puff ball jacket. A small heart shaped face was topped with an explosion of curly hair, but her best feature by far was her smile. Large white teeth exposed from behind generous lips and lighting up her whole face. All the men in the room smiled automatically, you just couldn't help it with Jasmine, she won your heart the very first time you saw her. At least, that's how it was for him. He never thought about her age that first time he gave her a lift to the station. She had been *doing a special*, in her words. He later found out that a man had asked for her specially for a one to one. She'd stayed with him overnight in a hotel.

All the way to the station, Jasmine had chatted, asking Sunil questions and laughing at his cheeky answers. He had stayed with her while she waited for her train, he drinking coffee and she an enormous strawberry milkshake. After that he always tried to be the one to collect her from the station for the parties, and he began to hate the fact that she was taken to these addresses for the pleasure of the business suited men. When they were alone, he would ask her why she did it. She simply shrugged and said, *why not?* Then one night she came out of the party house early. Her face was bloodied, and she had bruises to her wrists. Sunil was lounging in the back of the car when she climbed in. She immediately snuggled up into his arms, sobbing quietly. He put his arms around her and held her. Soon she began to kiss his neck and run her hands over his thighs. He should have stopped her, he knew that now, but at the time, he was overcome with desire. He told himself later that she had started it and that he was the real victim, but that was nonsense. After that night, they started to make arrangements to meet each time she was in Plymouth. They went back to his flat, and these hours spent together were some of the happiest in Sunil's life. Jasmine was full of fun and sexually insatiable. They talked about going away together, Jasmine painting a picture of a life in the country, with chickens and goats. Laughing as she imagined Sunil milking a goat.

It soon dawned on Sunil, though, that this life she talked about was a dream. He was a police officer, he had a family and commitments. It would mean the end of his career, of the job he loved. But before he could end it, Jasmine had texted him to say she was pregnant.

Peter and Mark stood on the deck of the *Pont Aven,* watching as the French coastline got nearer and nearer. Mark had visited Roscoff before, taking advantage of the special offers that Brittany Ferries put on in the autumn months. Now it was the start of the summer season, though not quite the busiest, as the schools hadn't broken up yet. Nevertheless, the ferry was packed, and the two detectives had been lucky to get a booking for their car and two passengers.

Peter had visited France before, but his ex-wife Julia had always favoured the south, which meant a flight to Nice and a hire car. He had enjoyed the ferry trip, though, despite his fear of water, taking advantage of the on-board restaurant and its sumptuous buffet. They were arriving at 7.30pm French time, so planned to stay overnight in the little harbour town. The French police had contacted them after their alert to be on the lookout for Sunil Jamdar, telling them that he had been spotted on CCTV getting into a lorry at the docks. The lorry had been tracked to Brest, where gendarmes had been waiting. They had not approached Sunil yet but were keeping him under observation. Peter's plan was to spend the night in Roscoff and travel bright and early the next morning.

Driving up the incline from the docks, Mark took a right and then a quick left turn towards the town. They travelled along a road bordering the sea, and the smell of seaweed and the squawk of gulls reminded Peter of home. Parking on the seafront, the pair set off in search of overnight accommodation. Roscoff was an unexpected location for a seaport. A small and very pretty town with restaurants and shops bordering the road. There was the spire of a church in the distance, and the two men set off to explore. Winding their way through small back streets, they came upon a cobbled square where the church was situated. Almost opposite was a hotel, where the charming receptionist told them they unfortunately had only one twin room available. Without too much hesitation, Peter and Mark agreed that it would be no hardship to share, after all, they had shared a changing room many times during rugby matches.

Refreshed by a shower and change of clothes, they set off to look for a restaurant, deciding against the hotel dining room in favour of a more authentic French experience. The holiday atmosphere pervaded the narrow streets, with couples and families wandering around, checking out menus and souvenir shops. In the end, they settled on a Creperie, and squeezed themselves in on the end of a wooden bench. The pancakes were fresh and delicious, washed down with a generous carafe of the house wine.

'This feels more like the start of a holiday than an investigation,' said Mark, happily glugging his wine.

'I know what you mean, but you'll forgive me if I said I'd rather be sitting opposite Rachel than a fellow officer,' Peter laughed.

'Shall we take a drink outside and talk about tomorrow? That way it might feel more like work.'

'Okay. But let's go to that place by the water, where the boule pitch is.'

That agreed, Peter settled the bill, and followed Mark out onto the street, feeling rested and satiated.

The next morning, with Mark driving, the two set off for Brest. Passing the docks, they took a rural road through a series of roundabouts before turning onto the D788 towards Brest. After an hour or so, Peter got his first experience of a French motorway, the N12, which would take them into the heart of the coastal city. Once he got used to the driving being the opposite way round to home, he realised with some pleasure that the traffic was much lighter than on the UK motorways. 'I think I would enjoy a driving holiday in France,' he said.

'Indeed,' said Mark, 'and the rural roads are even less populated. I always think it's like England was in the 50s, not that I was around then, of course.'

Peter laughed, and relaxed, enjoying being driven by such an amiable companion. 'How long before we're in Brest?'

'A couple of hours or so should do it. It looks like our man isn't having any luck getting a job on a boat. Jean Baptiste said they had watched him spend the night at a small hotel and then return to the port this morning. He seems to be talking to anyone he can find coming off sailing boats, but is met with a firm shake of the head each time.'

'He must know we're onto him by now, and my guess is he's getting pretty desperate.'

'Jean Baptiste said he would call if Sunil made a move away from the port, and we could ask them to detain him if that happened. Otherwise, the gendarmerie would prefer us to apprehend him and take him back with us. Less paperwork and bureaucracy that way.'

Just then Peter's phone rang. He listened as Cassie told him that a search of Sunil's flat had found evidence of two people using the bed, and that swabs had been taken. Also that a sample of Sunil's hair had been bagged for DNA analysis. 'Thanks, Cassie,' said Peter. 'Rush that through, will you, and keep me informed.'

An hour later the SATNAV guided Mark to the rendezvous point, where two police cars waited. The air was fresh as the two men climbed out of their car and approached the French officers. Warrant cards were shown, and Peter was given a report of Sunil's current position in impeccable English. *Why is it that we Brits rely on other countries to speak our language*, he thought, feeling a little embarrassed.

Thanking the gendarmes for their assistance, Mark and Peter set off towards the harbour, and the official looking buildings around the port. They soon spotted Sunil on a bench, gazing at his iPhone. Splitting up, they approached him from two directions. They were quite close before Sunil spotted them and made to run, only to give up when he saw Peter bearing down on him. He slumped back onto the bench and waited for the two detectives to reach him.

Sunil was quiet as Peter read him his rights, cuffed him and told him that they were arresting him on suspicion of murder. Only then did he speak. 'I want to do a deal,' was all he said.

'We might talk about that when we get you back to England. For now, you should know that we have a great deal of evidence linking you to this crime, and that you are looking at a long prison sentence, as you probably know.'

Sunil simply hung his head. 'I want a solicitor straight away,' he said, as he was helped into the back of Mark's car.

Chapter Twenty-three

After a night in the Truro cells, Sunil was brought up to the interview room. There was a buzz in the team room, with everyone talking about the arrest of a fellow officer for the murder of a young girl. Not many people knew Sunil personally, as he had been brought in from out of county, but they knew that he had been supervised by one of their own, Petra Gutherson, and suspected that it was Sunil who had deceived her, rather than believe that she could be capable of duplicity.

Peter and Mark were well prepared for the interview, with all their evidence lined up. They had a witness to place Sunil at the scene. They also had DNA evidence linking him to the unborn child, the fingernail scrapings and the cigarette butts. So, to say they were confident was an understatement. Sunil had said nothing since his arrest, merely asked for his phone call when he contacted his solicitor, who was waiting in the interview room for a private word with his client before the interrogation began.

The interview started at 10.15 with all parties identifying themselves, the solicitor being John Baker-Stokes, well known to Mark as a top notch criminal lawyer. *He's cost a pretty penny,* he thought, as they settled down. Perhaps more evidence that Sunil had gone 'rogue' during the operation, having money to spend on a fancy brief.

Peter began. 'So Sunil, do you want to take us through what happened?'

Instead of Sunil replying, John Baker-Stokes cut in. 'My client wants you to know that he acted in self-defence when the unfortunate accident involving the young woman Jasmine, aka Neema, occurred.'

Peter and Mark showed no reaction to this statement, though inside they were each wondering how Sunil was going to play this defence.

Peter addressed himself to Sunil again. 'Talk us through it.'

The solicitor spoke again. 'My client has prepared a statement.' He passed a sheet of paper over to Peter.

'Thank you for that, but I'd like Mr Jamdar to tell us in his own words.' He looked at Sunil. 'In your own time.'

Sunil shrugged. 'I admit that I knew Jasmine and that we had a sexual relationship. I believed that she was seventeen.'

Peter stopped him. 'How did you meet Jasmine?'

Sunil glanced at his solicitor, who was making notes and didn't return the look. 'It was during an undercover operation.'

'That would be Operation Capture?'

'Yes. She was one of the young women suspected of being involved in parties where sexual activities took place.'

Mark butted in, speaking sharply, 'Come on, Sunil, what do you take us for? These parties involved *girls*, not young women, some as young as twelve, as well you know, and the sexual activities amounted to rape.'

Sunil looked down at the table. 'I know nothing about what went on at the parties, I was never inside. I was a driver, that's all.'

Peter took up the questioning. 'Let's get back to your relationship with Jasmine. She became pregnant?' Sunil nodded. 'And you were unhappy about that?' Sunil nodded again. 'Please answer for the tape.'

'Yes, she was pregnant, and no, I wasn't happy.'

'How old are you, Sunil?'

Sunil looked up. 'Twenty-two.'

'So you have a sexual relationship with a young woman who you believe to be seventeen years old, that's only five years difference. Why were you so unhappy that you decided to kill her? Why not stay with her and have a baby together, or not, but support her as any

234

responsible person would do? You are a responsible person, aren't you? Being a police officer.'

Sunil looked at his solicitor, who responded on his behalf. 'I've told you, Inspector, that my client acted in self defence when the young woman unfortunately died. Your questions and your tone are offensive.'

Peter ignored the solicitor and stared at Sunil intently. 'Tell us what happened on the cliffs.'

Sunil sighed. 'Jasmine called me and said she wanted to meet. She was living nearby, and the coast path was convenient for her.'

Sunil paused, his eyes darting around. 'Go on,' said Peter.

'She wanted money. I offered to pay for an abortion, I thought that would be what she wanted. But she just went mad. Came at me like a banshee, clawing and hitting out. I tried to restrain her, but she broke free and ran.' Sunil paused again and Peter waited. 'I chased after her. She was in a very volatile state and I was worried she might trip or get hurt, it's very rough there.'

Peter waited, as a silence grew. Eventually Sunil continued. 'She was backing towards a stone wall, screaming at me. I went to put my arms around her, but she scratched at my face. I tried to hold her off and my hand must have been around her neck, pushing her away. She twisted and struggled. I was trying to calm her down, but she suddenly went limp and fell backwards over the wall. I hadn't realised that it was the entrance to a mine shaft. She simply fell over and disappeared.'

Peter checked the time. 'It's 11.20am. We'll leave it there for now.'

Peter and Mark watched as Sunil was led back to his cell, followed by a somber looking Baker-Stokes.

'Well, he's got balls, I'll give him that,' said Mark. 'Can't say I expected a self defence plea.'

'There's a long way to go in this interview,' replied Peter. 'At least he's not going "no comment".'

'True enough. It could be different when we hit him with our evidence, though.' Mark shook his head. 'I just can't believe that a fellow officer could be so brazen and heartless.'

'Mmm. Survival, I guess. He knows what awaits him inside if

he's convicted. My instinct is that he'll go a long way to prevent that from happening.' Peter turned to Mark. 'Let's go through Petra's undercover reports again. My guess is that we can challenge his assertion that Jasmine was seventeen through his early observations.'

The two detectives poured over reports from the last seven months of undercover work as recorded by Petra Gutherson. Though they found nothing explicitly stating that Jasmine was younger than Sunil claimed her to be, the gist of his reporting was that the girls involved in the parties were 'under age', some estimated to be around twelve or thirteen. It would have been unusual, to say the least, if one of them, Jasmine, had been seventeen as he asserted. However, they didn't have concrete evidence of Jasmine's age, and wouldn't have until they established her true identity. They needed to find out exactly who she was.

'Let's make another effort with the children's homes. What do we have so far?'

Peter flipped through his file. 'Not much. Without a full name the local authorities can't check their records.'

'What about social workers who might have been around at the time? Jasmine or Neema was a striking looking girl, surely someone remembers her.'

Peter nodded. 'I'll get my team onto it. Maggie and Robbie are good researchers, I'll put them on it full time.'

After a break to make phone calls and get some refreshment, Peter and Mark asked for Sunil to be brought back to the interview room.

Robbie had received the call from Peter and was excited at being given such a crucial assignment. Maggie was at the canteen getting sandwiches so he made a start on setting up some searches. He found the thirty-two London borough councils easily enough and made notes of the main contacts for the children's service divisions for each. Maggie came back into the office and he filled her in on their task.

'Nothing I like better than talking to social workers,' said Maggie sarcastically, and Robbie laughed.

'My mum's a social worker,' he replied.

'Oh God. Me and my big mouth,' said Maggie.

'Don't worry, I know what you mean, but perhaps I could talk to them? I think I understand the lingo by now.'

'Feel free, Robbie. I'll get onto the care homes again. Check out staff who've been with them a long time, and from what I know already, that's a short list.'

Peter entered the interview room ahead of Mark. They introduced the continuation of the session and opened the files in front of them.

Peter tried a speculative question, knowing that Sunil was no novice and could probably lie convincingly. However, his reaction may give something away. 'What can you tell us about Jasmine's past?'

Sunil shook his head, looking from Peter to his solicitor. 'What do you mean?'

'Her last name, for instance?'

'No. She never told me.'

'What about when she ran away from the children's home?'

Sunil blinked rapidly. 'Children's home?'

Peter didn't repeat the question, but allowed Sunil to think. 'She told me she ran away from *home*. Abuse, I think, though she didn't go into details. No mention of a children's home.'

Mark slid a paper over to Peter and deliberately pointed at something. It was, of course, spurious, but Sunil reacted by looking again at his solicitor, who remained impassive.

Peter continued. 'You were supervised in your undercover work by DS Petra Gutherson.'

Sunil nodded, looking worried. Then realised he had to speak. 'Yes.'

'Your reports to her were impressive, very thorough. She records that you said the girls involved in the parties were all underage, by your estimation. Did this include Jasmine?'

Sunil looked uncomfortable. 'Erm, I didn't meet Jasmine until after that report.'

'You remember the date of this report, then?'

Sunil looked panicky. 'Not exactly, no. But Jasmine was one of the last to join. I do remember that.'

Seeing that Sunil was rattled, Peter changed the subject. 'When you said you held Jasmine off with your hand on her neck when she attacked you, which hand was that, exactly?'

Sunil shook his head, as if to clear his thoughts. He looked down at his hands. 'My left. No, my right.'

'Which was it, Sunil? Left or right?' Sunil glanced at Mark, who was avidly consulting a paper which looked like a forensic report. He ran his hands through his hair.

'I can't recall.'

'You are saying you don't know?'

'I'm saying I can't remember. It was difficult. She was scratching at me and I was defending myself. I may have used both hands.'

'Both hands together?'

Sunil was sweating slightly. 'Er, no. One and then the other.'

'So, in this *difficult* situation, you switched hands to hold her off?'

'Yes, I must have done.'

'Must have done? Why's that? Do you think we have evidence that supports that statement?'

Sunil looked down. Then he whispered to his solicitor, who whispered something back. 'No comment,' he said.

Mark took up the questioning. 'You say you didn't know that Jasmine was underage?'

Sunil sighed loudly at the change of topic. 'If you're trying to throw me with these rapid changes of subject, you won't. I'm telling the truth.'

'Can you answer the question, Sunil.'

'I did not know that Jasmine was underage. Is that good enough for you?'

'What if I told you that we have a witness who will testify that Jasmine told you she was fourteen when you first met?'

'I'd say that your witness was lying.' Sunil seemed to have regained some composure.

'Our witness will also testify that Jasmine intended to blackmail you because of that fact, and that was why she met you on the cliffs that day.'

238

'This is all nonsense and supposition. She wanted money, yes. But she had nothing to blackmail me about.'

There was a silence in which Sunil looked from one detective to the other. Peter eventually looked up from his file. 'Let's get back to your hands, shall we. I'm still confused as to what you are claiming. You say you held Jasmine off with one hand and then the other. At any time, were your two hands together around her throat?'

'Definitely not. I've told you, I was fighting her off, pushing her away. At some point I had my hand on her neck. That's all.'

'That's what's confusing me, Sunil. You see, I have a forensic report here that shows quite conclusively that Jasmine was murdered by manual strangulation. That's two hands together, with both thumbs pressing on her throat. I think you know enough about this type of incident to understand when I tell you that the hyoid bone was broken.'

Sunil said nothing, so Peter continued. 'This would only have been possible if two hands were around the victim's throat working together with some force.'

Sunil looked across at his solicitor, who gave a slight nod. 'No comment,' said Sunil, who was looking weary.

John Baker-Stokes leaned across the table. 'I'd like my client to have a short break now.'

Peter looked across at Mark, who nodded his agreement. 'Interview suspended at 12.45.'

'I would say we've got him,' said Peter to Cassie, who was waiting anxiously in the team room.

'That's great news, sir. We've also had a result on Jasmine or Neema's identity.' Cassie paused for effect. 'Maggie and Robbie came up trumps. They spoke to a social worker who remembered a client called Neema Sullivan. This woman had a sad life and died leaving a daughter, Jasmine Neema Sullivan, dob, Dec 17th 2005. That makes her fifteen this December.'

'Does the social worker remember anything else?'

'Apparently, Neema had a sister, Auriela Nkosi, who looked after Jasmine and her dad for a while after the mum died, but that arrangement broke down. That's all the social worker knows, except that Jasmine was in care at some time, probably with *Transcare*, a private care organisation they used a lot.'

'That's fantastic, Cassie. . . '

'Not finished yet, sir,' said Cassie, enjoying the moment. 'Maggie looked into *Transcare* and found reference to Jasmine Sullivan being admitted, aged ten, but records were sketchy after that, and *Transcare* doesn't exist anymore. One ex-worker, that Maggie managed to track down, told her that children were moved so often that paperwork was often lost. There was no record of Jasmine being discharged from care, and this worker said there should have been, as this was a legal requirement. She could only surmise that Jasmine absconded before she was sixteen, and that this went unnoticed. Apparently, this happened on a few occasions that she knew about.'

'Is there any way we can find this Aurelia Nkosi and get a swab for DNA analysis? With a positive familial match we could say for certain that our victim is Jasmine Neema Sullivan.'

'Onto it, sir.'

'Excellent work, Cassie. Pass that on to Maggie and Robbie, will you.'

'Of course. Can I ask where you are up to with Sunil?'

'Like I said, I think we've just about got him. I don't want to say any more at the moment, but he's struggling to maintain his version of events in the light of our evidence. This ID information will help us enormously too, especially if we make the DNA match. Keep on it Cassie, top priority.'

The interview resumed with a weary looking Sunil, but two invigorated detectives. The solicitor was the first to speak after the introductions for the recording were made.

'My client has information vital to uncovering a paedophile ring here in Plymouth. He is willing to give the police the details in exchange for a lenient assessment of his role in the tragic death of the young woman called Jasmine.'

'Your client has got a nerve,' said Mark. 'The information he has was gained during a police undercover operation in which he was the undercover officer. By rights, that information belongs to the police, and we want it handing over. No deals necessary.'

The solicitor continued. 'That may be so, detective, but you have no way of knowing exactly what my client has. As he sees it, his career with the police is over and he has no need to hand the information over. He is, however, willing to reveal the identity of abusers and places where abuse has taken place, if his terms are met.'

'You know as well as I do,' said Peter, 'that we are unable to make any deals of that sort. This isn't the US.'

'Ah, but you can make recommendations, detective.'

Peter looked over at Mark, who shrugged slightly. 'Let's say we could have an influence, what does your client want in return for his information?'

Peter noticed that Sunil brightened considerably. The solicitor continued. 'He wants you to view his actions as self defence manslaughter, which he feels is fair, and expects no custodial sentence.'

'I bet he does,' replied Peter. 'I might be willing to consider a charge of manslaughter, but the DPP would have to sanction that.'

Sunil couldn't resist speaking at this point, even though his solicitor gave him a warning look. 'Involuntary manslaughter,' he stated. 'I might accept that.'

Peter made a hard eye contact with Sunil. 'We have a weight of evidence which could put you away for life. Your information is an unknown quantity at the moment. At the very least we would need to see some of what you claim to have before we make a judgement. We have a warrant to search your flat. . . '

'You don't think I'm stupid enough to leave that sort of stuff lying around my flat, do you?' Sunil retorted angrily. Mr Baker-Stokes grabbed his arm. 'I need some time with my client. You have the details of his deal. Perhaps you would like to consider it. Maybe with a more senior officer?'

Peter ignored the barb and ended the interview. He was seething inside that this jumped-up, corrupt officer thought he could manipulate the system and get away with murder. However, he also

l

knew that the Chief Superintendent might take a more pragmatic view, and consider the deal if it meant clearing up a significant child exploitation operation. That would be a feather in his cap.

Suddenly Peter felt deflated. He was exhausted by the interview and wanted nothing more than to get home, have a long soak in the bath and a cuddle on the sofa with Rachel. He looked over at Mark, who looked every bit as weary as he did. 'What do you say if we call it a night?' He said to Mark. 'I think another night in the cells wouldn't do our man any harm and we can approach this with a clear head in the morning.'

'I thought you'd never ask,' quipped Mark, a grin on his face. 'We might have some news on the DNA match by then, too.'

'Okay, that settles it.' Turning to the team room he said, 'Right Cassie, it's home time. You can drive, but don't be surprised if I fall asleep on the way.'

Chapter Twenty-four

Cassie and Peter had arranged to meet in the Truro office at 7.30am the next day, and were pleased to see that Maggie and Robbie were there also. Peter went over to the pair as they sat glued to their respective PC screens. 'Very well done, you two,' he said. 'Have you any more news for us?'

Maggie beamed, delighted to be praised for her efforts. 'We have the birth certificate for Jasmine Neema Sullivan. The father, Terry, died last year of a heart attack. The aunt, Auriela, still lives in London and has provided a swab to the local police for analysis. We may get the results today. If there's a familial match, we have a certain identity for our murdered girl.'

Peter nodded. 'I'm pretty confident it will be her. Did the aunt have any photographs we could compare with?'

'I asked her that. She only had baby photos, taken with her mum, Aurelia's sister. I figured they wouldn't be much use.'

Just then Saroj walked in. 'Well, the gang's all here, I see,' she said amiably.

'Hi there, Saroj,' said Cassie. 'What's new?'

'Well, I haven't been idle since you've been away,' replied Saroj, taking off her jacket. 'I have taken the statement from Molly Malone confirming that Jasmine confided in her that Sunil was in no doubt about her age. She said that that was the reason she was so confident about getting money from him. Molly also identified the man on the cliffs as Sunil Jamdar from the photo you provided.'

Saroj helped herself to a coffee. 'What about you, sir?' she asked Peter. 'How did the interview go?'

Peter gave the team a summary of the interview, admitting that he was torn between pressing for a charge of murder, and having the opportunity to clear up a major child exploitation ring.

'Your man's got a nerve, wanting a deal,' said Saroj. 'He must have provided some evidence to his handler in all those months. Isn't that enough to crack the paedophile ring?'

'Apparently not, Saroj.' Peter shook his head sadly. 'He seems to have lead Petra Gutherson a merry dance. It now appears that he got sucked in quite quickly and played her along while he reaped the benefits.'

'A nasty character, then?'

'Certainly unscrupulous. Mark Andrews is meeting with the Chief Super this morning. I hope he can suggest a way forward that doesn't mean capitulating to Jamdar's demands. I really would feel angry about that.'

Saroj caught Peter's attention. 'Another thing, before you leave, sir.' Peter nodded. 'When can we expect to release Jasmine's body? The aunt was asking.'

'If the DNA result confirms what we think it will, I see no reason to delay.'

'Thanks, sir. Oh, and Janine Jackson, the mental health officer who interviewed Charlie. You remember him, sir?'

'Of course, he gave us our first proper lead.'

'Well, she's kept in touch with him, and apparently he's not doing too well. He's asking if he can see Neema, as he calls her, and Janine thinks it would help him.'

'Well, I can't see the harm in it. You may want to check with the aunt first, that is if the DNA result confirms that it is his Neema.'

'Right, sir. I'll get on with that.'

Peter looked around the room. 'Well done everyone. Cassie and I will be off now, but if anything new comes in, let us know immediately.'

Chapter Twenty-five

Chief Superintendent Simon McKenzie considered the two men sitting opposite him. DI Mark Andrews he knew. The other man, who looked like he could take on a mob of villains single-handed, he hadn't met until this morning. He did know that he was expected to make a decision about this rogue police officer who, quite apart from now being the subject of an anti-corruption investigation, along with his handler, had also been arrested on suspicion of murder. He sighed as he looked again at the report provided for him that morning by DI Andrews.

'Tell me, DCI Sanders, how strong is your case against DC Jamdar?'

'Enough to get a conviction, sir.'

'Of murder?'

'We'd charge him with that, naturally, but his brief could argue manslaughter.'

'And now he wants to make a deal which, by all accounts, could net us a very nasty gang indeed. A gang we have been investigating for some months now and, I don't mind telling you, DCI Sanders, I want these men arrested and this paedophile ring broken up. Even if, as has been suggested, it includes some very prominent figures. In fact, I'd say *because* of that.' The Chief looked over his half-moon glasses at Peter. 'What do you have to say?'

'Thank you, sir. I have been giving this some thought. It grieves me to see anyone, especially a police officer, get away, literally, with murder. However, if we did accept Jamdar's deal, I could see a scenario where he would be required to give evidence in court, after which, if what we know about the organisers of the paedophile ring is true, his life would be in danger. In such a case, it would be our responsibility to protect him. Long term.'

The chief smiled, and Mark looked over at his colleague in admiration. Simon McKenzie was known amongst his fellow senior officers to be a man with a strong sense of irony. 'Naturally you are speaking of the witness protection service?'

'I would say we'd be irresponsible not to relocate him somewhere well away from the UK. Australia perhaps?'

'Ha! Well I never. Good man, good man. Let's waste no more time, then.' The Chief was all seriousness now. 'Tell that solicitor fellow, Baker-Stokes, that he can have his deal, providing the evidence that Jamdar has comes up to the mark. After, and *only* after you're happy with it, you can lay out the conditions. Understood?'

'Yes sir,' smiled a happy Peter. 'I'd be delighted.'

As the two detectives left the chief's office, he could be heard laughing and muttering, 'Witness protection. . . good man, good man.'

It turned out that Sunil Jamdar had hidden his stash of evidence, along with a substantial amount of money, at the care home where his grandmother was being looked after. Making an unexpected visit to his slightly confused relative, Sunil introduced Mark and Peter as colleagues and they each had a cup of tea with the old lady before Sunil retrieved a large bag from inside her wardrobe. 'Thank's for looking after this, Granny,' he smiled, and kissed the old lady on her forehead. It turned out that Sunil had a large and close-knit family, and it gave Peter some satisfaction to know that this corrupt officer would be estranged from them for a very long time. Witness protection can be tough even with some family members accompanying you. It is purgatory to go through alone. Maybe Jamdar would even have chosen prison had he known what was awaiting him. Well, he would know soon enough, thought Peter. Just as soon as we have assessed this little lot. He swung the bag of evidence into the boot of the car, handcuffed Sunil Jamdar and assisted him onto the back seat.

John Baker-Stokes was looking smug as he talked with his client about the upcoming interview. 'I think we can be assured of a deal if the evidence you provided meets with their approval. And I can't see why it would not.'

'Yeah. I'm home free,' said Sunil bitterly. 'I've lost my job, and I'll be a marked man as far as the police are concerned.'

'Better than prison though, surely?'

'I don't know. With a conviction of manslaughter, I could have served as little as two years, maybe even suspended.'

'You could still take your chances with that if you wish.'

Sunil put his head in his hands. The enormity of his situation was only just dawning on him. It had seemed like an exciting game up until now. Outwitting the police, seeing the smug looks wiped off their faces; he admitted to himself that he had enjoyed that. Whilst he was still immersed in the gang culture, his behaviour had mirrored theirs, it had to in order to be an effective undercover. Now that he was away from that life, he found himself coming back down to earth with a bang. Seeing his grandma yesterday, and thinking about what she and the rest of his family would think when the full story came out, sobered him. He could imagine the shock and disappointment from his mother and father, and the derision from his brothers, who would probably think he got what he deserved. And what was it all for? Sure, he had enjoyed the extra cash. He had not had so much money at his disposal in his life. And the girls, well, one girl in particular. He had been mesmerised by Jasmine. She seemed older than her years, certainly sexually experienced. He had been the one feeling gauche when she had come on to him. He couldn't pretend, though, that he didn't know she was a child. A sexy, funny child, but too young for what they were doing, what *he* was doing.

Sunil let out a long sigh, and looked up sadly as the two detectives came into the room. The larger one, DCI Sanders, was a tough nut, for sure. Despite his training in interview techniques,

Sunil couldn't work out what the DCI was thinking, couldn't guess his next move. The other one, DI Andrews, was familiar to him. Sunil had even interviewed with him before, and he felt on solid ground with this detective, but there was no doubting the apprehension he felt now, as the DCI started the recording.

'Mr Jamdar, we have examined the evidence you have provided, and we believe it goes some way towards giving us what we need to make a move on this group.' Peter paused and made eye contact with Sunil. 'However, it doesn't go far enough.'

Sunil looked panicky and turned to his solicitor, who shook his head slightly. He leaned over the table. 'What do you mean, not far enough? There's photos and addresses, as well as names of the girls involved.'

Peter took out a photograph from his file and turned it towards Sunil. 'What this shows is a room with a number of men drinking and talking to some girls. Young girls, admittedly, with older men, but what it doesn't show is any sexual impropriety taking place.'

Sunil looked shocked, his eyes darting between the detectives and his solicitor as if looking for answers. 'You could raid the premises. Catch them at it. It's obvious what they're up to.'

'Not obvious enough to justify a warrant, I'm afraid. We need actual testimony from the people involved, or a reliable witness.' Peter placed both his hands on the table and leaned forward slightly. 'What I want to know is, were you ever in the house when the alleged abuse took place?'

Sunil looked down at his hands. 'What if I was?'

John Baker-Stokes put his hand on Sunil's arm. 'My client and I need to talk.'

Peter did not want to lose the momentum. Ignoring the solicitor, he pressed on. 'If you *were* in the house, and witnessed any of these men having sexual relations with these girls, that would be very helpful to our case. You understand that, Sunil?'

'I think you are badgering my client,' said Baker-Stokes. 'He needs a break.'

'All in good time, Mr Baker-Stokes. We've only just started.'

Sunil shook his head sadly. 'I wasn't supposed to go in, but I managed to sneak in through a back door and up some rear stairs.'

Baker-Stokes sighed. 'I have to advise you to say no more until we have had an opportunity to talk.'

Ignoring him, Sunil continued. 'It was early on, soon after I started the undercover work. The second or third time I was asked to drive the girls. I was keen to do a good job, you know?'

Peter nodded, but said nothing.

Sunil carried on. 'Anyway, I peeped into a bedroom and saw two men leaning over a girl. She was tied to the bed and looked very unhappy. One man stripped off and had sex with her. He also hit her several times. She was sobbing but not struggling.'

Mark signalled to Peter that he wanted to take over. Peter nodded and leaned back in his seat. Mark was trying very hard to control his anger at his undercover officer. 'Did you report this to your handler?'

Sunil shook his head. 'I wanted to get more evidence. I had to get back to the car then, but decided to photograph the action next time. I wanted to impress Petra.'

'What happened?'

'I was caught lurking about on the landing. I said I was curious and that I thought that the men were lucky to have fun with these girls. Pretended to be interested, you know?'

'Go on.'

'They laughed and took me into a room where a girl was still tied to a bed where the men had left her. She was naked and crying to be untied. The men told me to have my fun with her. I protested, saying I didn't like *sloppy seconds*. Sorry to be crude, but that's the way they talked. Anyway, they wouldn't take no for an answer. It was sort of a test, you know?'

'So you abused this poor girl?'

Sunil put his head in his hands and sobbed.

'Please speak for the record Sunil.'

'Yes! I did, and I've never been more ashamed in my life.'

Baker-Stokes spoke up. 'I really must insist that I have time alone with my client.'

Peter nodded and brought the interview to a close, saying that they would return in one hour. In the meantime, he would arrange for tea to be brought in.

Peter, Mark and Cassie sat around the table in Mark's office, a tray of coffee and biscuits in front of them. Peter had brought Cassie up to date with the interview, whilst Mark sat silently, looking morose.

Peter patted him on the back. 'I know how I would feel if this was my operation. How do you want to handle things now?'

Mark nodded briefly. 'Thanks for asking, Peter, but I think it best if you and Cassie take it from here. I could be seen as too involved.'

'Fair point. We've got a confession of rape of a minor. He should be going away for a long time for that. However, we also want him to testify against the men involved.'

Cassie raised her hand. 'There are mitigating circumstances to the rape. He was working undercover and was coerced into the act during that operation, maybe in fear of his life?'

'That's very probable, Cassie, and that may cut some sway with the DPP when considering charges. There's no doubt that he has behaved very badly and committed a crime in the course of his undercover work. I am aware that there is a school of thought that believes undercover officers should never be convicted of crimes committed whilst working. And, as much as I dislike the man for what he did, we do have a duty to our undercover officers. It could be argued that Sunil should have been pulled out long before it got to this point.'

Peter turned to Mark. 'How's it going with Petra Gutherson?'

Mark shrugged slightly. 'You're right about the support, Peter. There's no doubt we let Sunil down. Petra has admitted as much. She suspected Sunil had gone rogue, but chose not to act, hoping he would come good in the end. It was the first time she had handled an undercover operation, and she should have come to me with her concerns. On the other hand, maybe I should have questioned her more deeply. It's a real mess, Peter.'

'Okay,' said Peter thoughtfully. 'We have to make a decision, so I'm going to suggest that we can make the charges go away in return for Sunil's testimony in court. After which, we could offer him witness protection which could work out to be a worse punishment than a prison sentence.' Peter looked at the other two who were looking sad but not disagreeing. 'I hate to say this, but we also have the reputation of the force to consider, especially as public confidence in us is low at the moment. It would do us no good at all to have this mess dragged through the courts. On the other hand, breaking up a paedophile ring would undoubtably boost our standing with the public.'

'To be honest, I want him to suffer, but I get the point about public confidence, and I can't even believe I'm saying that.' Cassie smiled ruefully. 'But here's how I see it.' She counted off on her fingers. 'One, Sunil's brief has a good chance of getting him off with manslaughter for the death of Jasmine, anyway. Two, Mark and his team, sorry Mark, definitely had a duty of care towards their officer which it looks like they neglected. And three, we have an opportunity to make this mess go away, with a good result for the force as well.'

Peter nodded. 'None of us is happy with the way this is panning out, but we must make a decision. If we're all in agreement?' The other two nodded. 'Right, let's take it to the DPP.'

Mark nodded. 'I'll set up a meeting for you with the Chief Super. Thanks, Peter, Cassie, for all your support. I'll be glad when this is over.'

Chapter Twenty-six

Molly stood in the garden of the commune with a small box held reverently in her hands. She looked up and smiled at the group gathered around her. It was only a week ago that she, Aurelia and Charlie had stood in much the same way to formally identify Jasmine Neema Sullivan's body in the cold, unwelcoming morgue. Today the sun was shining, and the setting couldn't have been more different. Molly was pleased when Aurelia had agreed to this ceremony taking place here. Aurelia had said that Jasmine had never been happy in London so, as this was the place she had chosen to live, it was fitting that her ashes remained here. Christian had agreed that Charlie could stay with Molly whilst this was arranged, and he clearly loved being here.

Early one morning, Christian had come across Charlie in the vegetable garden. He watched in amazement as Charlie expertly weeded the plot, thinning out some carrots as he went. When eventually Christian approached Charlie, he learned that the man had attended a gardening scheme for people with mental illness and learning disabilities. Charlie said his teacher thought he had a natural affinity with plants. He didn't understand what that meant. All he knew was that he loved growing things.

Since that day, Christian had been thinking about Charlie and the contribution he could make to the commune. Christian's house was nearly finished now, and he and his family would soon be moving in. His intention was to sell his caravan, and he could definitely use the money, but until he did, he had an idea of letting Charlie use it. Snapping out of his reverie, Christian came back to the moment.

Molly was standing by the prepared hole in the garden. A sapling of an apple tree rested on the ground nearby. Molly began to speak. 'Although we didn't know you for long Jasmine Neema, you touched our hearts, and we were all saddened by your death and the loss of your unborn child. You loved this place and wanted to stay here, so here you will stay.' Molly opened the box and took out a handful of ash, dropping it into the hole. Offering the box to Aurelia, she did the same, then Charlie, Christian and the others, one by one until the box was empty. Someone strummed a guitar as the tree was planted and people said their silent goodbyes. 'I'll look after your tree, Neema,' said Charlie through his tears.

Later, as the whole commune came together for a meal in the open air, Christian spoke to Molly about Charlie. 'Janine Jackson tells me that Charlie has money from his mother's life insurance,' said Molly. 'It's looked after by the council with Charlie's agreement, and he gets a weekly allowance.'

'Would it be enough to buy my caravan? I wouldn't want a lot for it.'

'Do you want me to talk to Charlie about it?'

'Let's ask Janine to join us and we'll all talk to him. Find out what he really wants. I want him to know that he's welcome to stay here if he'd like that.'

Molly was pleased. She and Blossom had grown fond of Charlie. 'Okay, I'll set that up.'

Janine Jackson had proved invaluable. She had established a rapport with Charlie and he obviously trusted her. Being aware that people had more or less told Charlie what to do for all of his life, Janine was keen that this big move should be Charlie's choice. First of all, she asked him to draw a picture of his dream home. While he was doing that, she gently probed him about his life in London and his flat. It became clear to everyone that Charlie was unhappy in his flat even though the men who had used him so badly were no longer around. Charlie said he was lonely and missed Neema.

Finally, Janine passed around the drawing that Charlie had done. It was the commune. That was clear to everyone. Christian told

Charlie that, if he wanted to live here, he would be very welcome, but that he would need a place of his own. Charlie looked expectantly at Janine, who nodded. 'That's possible, Charlie, if you want it.'

'Charlie wants to live here and take care of Neema's tree,' he said emphatically.

'That's a deal then, Charlie,' said Christian, and held out his hand for Charlie to shake.

Molly hugged him, tears in her eyes. 'Blossom will be so happy, Charlie. Me too.'

Janine smiled broadly. In her experience, these sort of fairy tale endings never happened for people like Charlie. She reflected that, on this occasion, some good had come out of the awful events of the last few weeks. All she had to do now was arrange for Charlie's money to be transferred to Cornwall Council, with the recommendation that a caravan on the commune was bought on his behalf. Janine would keep in touch for a month or two, but she was in no doubt that Charlie would be happy here and that her work with him was done. *Good job, Janine*, she said to herself as she walked over to her car. *Good job indeed.*

Chapter Twenty-seven

Peter and Cassie stood on the station steps, watching as Chief Superintendent Simon McKenzie took an impromptu press conference. He was obviously revelling in the announcement he was making that, through the hard work and diligence of his officers, the Devon and Cornwall Police had broken up a major paedophile ring, making a number of high-profile arrests.

Reporters clambered to be heard amongst the throng.

'Can you name the men involved?'

'How confident are you of convictions?'

'Was a police officer involved in the abuse of children?'

The Chief Super raised his hand to quell the shouting. 'All in good time, gentlemen and ladies. I can't say any more at the moment, so you'll have to be patient. I will say that we have a very strong case and are confident of a good outcome.'

'Is it true that you have a supergrass?'

The Chief looked away, ignoring the question. 'That's all for now,' he said, walking back into the police station.

The crowd broke up slowly, with some reporters angling to get a quote from Peter or Cassie, who merely smiled and followed the Chief into the station. Once out of earshot, Cassie said, 'I might just throw up.'

Peter laughed quietly. 'Shall we get back? We're supposed to be having the traditional drink at the pub tonight, but I'm not sure I'm in the mood.'

'Me neither. It leaves a sour taste when a criminal gets away with something, even more so if it's a bent copper.'

'True enough. We can only hope his exile proves as unpleasant as I think it will. I get the impression that Sunil has strong family ties. He may not fare too well without them.'

The drinks were set up on the bar as Peter and Cassie walked into the pub. Rachel came over to Peter and kissed him firmly on the lips. 'You okay?' she said quietly.

'I'll survive. It's good to see you, though. Let's make it a quick one and get home shall we?'

Rachel squeezed Peter's hand. 'That's a promise, then?'

Suddenly they were surrounded by the rest of the team and pushed and pulled towards the bar. 'Speech!' called one person, to a round of applause.

Peter reluctantly acquiesced. Raising his glass, he saluted the whole team. 'This was as fine an example of teamwork as I can imagine,' he said. 'We may have some misgivings about the result, but we mustn't forget that we have rescued a number of young girls from horrific abuse, and arrested the offenders, some of whom will raise a few eyebrows when it becomes public.'

'Here, here!'

'I think our new DI has had a baptism of fire,' he said, saluting Cassie. 'And that's exactly as it should be.' He paused until the laughter died down. 'I don't think she can now accuse us of being a sleepy backwater.'

'Did I ever say that?' quipped a smiling Cassie, looking incredulously around the room.

Peter continued. 'I think we all deserve a bit of peace and quiet now, but as my soon to be mother-in-law might say, *may you live in interesting times*, and, you know, I probably wouldn't have it any other way.'

Book Three

Snow Upon the Desert

The Worldly Hope men set their Hearts upon
Turns Ashes – or it prospers; and anon,
Like Snow upon the Desert's dusty face
Lighting a little Hour or two – is gone.

Rubaiyat of Omar Khayyam – second edition, 1868.

Chapter One

The night-time performance of Dracula at the Minack Open Air Theatre was always well attended. Tonight, with a full moon peeping out behind dark clouds, and the high spring tide crashing the surf against the rocks, the atmosphere guaranteed an unforgettable experience. This part of the Cornish coast was famous for two things. One, it was the launching site for the first undersea telephone cable between Great Britain and the United States, and secondly, it was the home of the remarkable open air theatre that was the Minack.

Carved out of the cliffside, creating an amphitheatre where the audience, seated on rough-hewn steps, looked down onto a stage beyond which was the wild Atlantic Ocean, the Minack attracted some of the best touring theatre groups in the country. Tonight, Detective Inspector Cassandra Wade sat transfixed alongside her two teenaged children, Micky and Tanya, as the players enacted the landing of the Prince of Darkness on the north Yorkshire coast at Whitby. They had secured seats just two rows back from the stage on the left, and had a great view of the action. Atmospheric lighting on a rock out at sea, plus the roaring sound of the surf, enhanced the dramatic experience.

'This is fab, ma,' said Micky.

'That's your best critique, is it?' Cassie replied, smiling at her son. She was glad that he wasn't one of those fifteen year olds who found anything other than gaming, Facebook and hanging with his mates, boring. She'd never tell him that, of course. Then there was Tanya. Just fourteen today. She would have been dressed to the nines and fussing with her hair if they had still been in Liverpool, but these last few months in Cornwall had worked its magic on Tanya, turning her from a dedicated *towny* to a beach babe. Cassie was now glad she had accepted the relocation to be the DI in the Special Incident Squad in Truro. At first she had kicked off against the placement but, seeing the effect it had on her kids, and having just been part of a major success for the Devon and Cornwall Police, she had to admit it wasn't half bad.

Just as the sounds of a shipwreck filled the auditorium, the stage lights went out and, above their heads, illuminated by needle spots, large paper bats swept down on zip wires, causing many 'Ooo's and 'Ahh's in the audience. Suddenly, on the left of the stage, almost right in front of Cassie, a bright flash threw a large bat-like figure into silhouette, arms outstretched in a menacing pose. Cassie chuckled as Tanya grabbed her hand. The figure suddenly started to move, staggering forward onto centre stage, face contorted, clutching his chest, before falling, face first, onto the stone flooring. Puzzled murmurings ran through the onlookers, but Cassie was on high alert. All her senses told her that this was no staged performance, but that something bad had happened. She believed that she may have seen some movement in the dying flashlight, or was that her imagination? Suddenly standing and shuffling past those seated by her, onto the aisle, she shouted towards the stage. 'Police! Stay back! Don't touch anything!'

The stage direction could have been, *enter stage left a large black woman with wild hair, coat tails flapping and waving her arms.* Some of the audience thought that this event was some curious adaptation to the plot, a modernised version of the classic novel perhaps? However, it soon became clear that something serious had happened. There was a hush over the auditorium, everyone being curious to know what would come next.

Cassie reached the stage, raising her warrant card. 'Detective Inspector Wade,' she said to the shadowy figures as she snapped on her latex gloves. 'Don't touch that body!' This to a small woman creeping forward towards the prone figure.

'But he might need help,' the woman pleaded.

'Stay back, as I told you.' Then, as an afterthought, 'If you wouldn't mind.'

Using the light from her phone, Cassie illuminated the head of the figure and placed her fingers on his neck. *Dead as a dodo*, she thought. *Maybe the other clue is the large knife sticking out of his back.* Standing, she took off her coat and placed it over the prone figure. She shouted out, 'Whoever's in charge of the lighting, please keep them off for the time being.' Then she dialled a number on her phone.

'No signal here, I'm afraid,' said a male voice. 'You have to go onto the car park.'

Cassie shook her head in amazement, then made a quick decision. She peered into the dark auditorium. 'Micky!' she shouted. 'Come down here!'

Micky jumped up from his seat and ran down the steps to his mother. He gazed transfixed at the body. 'Don't look there, Micky!' Cassie put her hands on either side of her son's face. 'Look at me. I want you to do something for me, okay?' Micky nodded. 'Take my phone and go up to the car park. The number is keyed in. It's Saroj Kapoor, you've met her, she's in my team.' Micky nodded again. 'Tell her to get the full murder squad down here now. D'you understand?' Micky nodded again. 'Tell me, then.'

Micky sighed. 'I'm to tell Saroj Kapoor to get the full murder squad down here now.' Micky glanced again at the prone figure. 'Is he dead?'

Cassie thought about making a funny quip about the knife being a give away, but realised that her son was in shock. 'Don't worry about that now, love, just make the phone call. Off you go.'

Turning to the back of the stage, Cassie asked the assembled cast, 'Is there such a thing as a screen in your props?'

A male voice said, 'Yes, there's one in the dressing room.'

'Thank you. Please go and get it now.'

The man returned in a minute or two with a large Victorian screen. Cassie nodded. 'That'll do nicely for the time being. Help me put it in front of the, er. . . in front of your colleague.'

The screen erected, Cassie was as confident as she could be that

261

the members of the audience were spared the sight of a dead body on stage. 'Okay, can we get some stage lights on now? And, if there's anyone backstage or in the wings, I want them out here. Will someone arrange that?'

'I'll go,' a male voice said. 'Do you want everyone? Even the scene shifters?'

'Yes, everyone, even the scene shifters, whoever they are. And quickly, if you don't mind.'

Turning to face the audience, Cassie, feeling rather foolish on a stage set, shouted instructions. She was taken aback by the natural amplification of the theatre setting. 'I'm Detective Inspector Wade. I want you all to remain in your seats. Do not leave the theatre.' There was a murmur of discontent. 'I know it's an inconvenience, but it's police procedure. We'll let you go as soon as we can.'

A shout came from the centre of the audience. 'Will we get our money back?' Cassie rolled her eyes.

The stage lights went up and Cassie shepherded the actors and scene shifters, who turned out to be black clad figures whose job it was to move scenery as unobtrusively as possible, to a spot away from the body.

'Is this everyone?' she asked, counting five actors and four scene shifters.

'No,' said the stage manager, 'there are the two costume ladies back stage and the lighting control man.'

'Not everyone, then?' said Cassie, with a hint of sarcasm. 'Could you get them out as well please.'

'Yes, sorry, I'll do that now, shall I?' Cassie nodded, reminding herself that these people were not used to experiencing violent death, and that she should cut them some slack.

The other three people joined the group and Cassie briefly asked them if any of them saw or heard anything unusual. She watched their faces carefully as they answered. There was a general shake of the heads and a murmur of 'No, nothing.' Cassie watched them for a while and then said, 'Well, it's not unusual to remember something later, so take a card each and call me if anything comes to you, even if you think it's not important.' They each took a card from her and smiled nervously as they shuffled their feet, obviously anxious to be away. 'Just wait there for a moment,' Cassie said, observing the looks of annoyance. 'I won't keep you any longer than necessary tonight, but I will want you back tomorrow.'

Fifteen minutes later, just as the audience was starting to get restless, sirens could be heard from the car park, followed by a group of uniformed officers making their way quickly down the steps. Cassie was relieved to have some help and wasted no time in organising them. She posted one officer at the exit to prevent anyone leaving and asked another to check backstage then cordon off the whole area. Seeing a WPC, Cassie beckoned her over. 'Do me a favour, would you? I've got my two kids here and I don't want them to have to wait around for me. Could you take them home and stay with them? They've had a bit of a shock.'

'Yes, ma'am,' said the officer, a little peeved that it seemed to always be the women that were asked to do child minding.

Cassie led the officer up the steps to where Tanya was sitting. 'Come on, love,' she said. 'Let's find Micky.'

It was clear that Micky wanted to stay where the excitement was, but Cassie placed her two children in the safe hands of WPC Taylor, and would hear no arguments to the contrary. The car park was now filling up with scene of crime officers and more police vehicles. Cassie directed them onto the stage, where a tent was quickly erected around the body. DS Saroj Kapoor parked her car and came over to Cassie. 'Interesting evening at the theatre, ma'am.'

'Too right, Saroj,' replied Cassie, pleased that her second in command was there to take charge of all these people whilst she got on with events on stage. The night was getting colder and a fine sea mist was rolling in. Looking at the audience shivering in their seats, she said, 'Let's get these people away. Organise some officers to take their details. Names, addresses, phone numbers, seat number and who they were here with. Get them to ask if they saw anything unusual.'

'Apart from a dead body?'

'Ha, yes apart from that. Did they see anyone leave their seat whilst the lights were out, that sort of thing. Put them on a priority contact list if they did. Then they can go.' Turning, Cassie saw the rotund figure of Dr Ben Samuels hurrying across the car park. 'Evening doctor.'

'Good evening, DI Wade. You have a body for me, I believe?'

'Well, technically, it's not a body until you say it is, but I couldn't detect any signs of life.'

'Right. Lead on Macduff,' Ben said, smiling to himself at his thespian reference.

As Ben leant over the body, shaking his head as he examined the prone figure for signs of life, Cassie remarked, 'Well, at least we can be certain about the time of death. I made it 10.45. And probable cause.'

'Yes, it looks like a fatal stab wound, but I'll be able to confirm that when I open him up.' Ben stood. 'Shall we say 10am tomorrow?'

Cassie nodded her assent. 'Thank you, doctor.'

As Ben hurried off, the SOCO team were arriving and the murder squad got into full swing.

Chapter Two

Cassie was in the squad room early the next morning. Her boss, DCI Peter Sanders, was away on honeymoon, and she was in charge of the Serious Incident Squad in the interim. As she organised Peter's desk to accommodate her own laptop and personal items, she reflected on the wedding. Peter had married his former DI, Rachel Morris, a beautiful woman of Asian origin. Peter himself was a striking man. Six foot three and muscular, with strong rather than traditionally handsome features, he towered over his petite bride. The event was a small gathering. Peter's parents were dead, leaving just his sister Jane to represent the family side of things. Rachel's father was a financier from London and her mother a Chinese woman with exceptional energy. Cassie smiled as she recollected Su-Lin fussing over Rachel and Peter, seemingly orchestrating every part of the event single-handedly.

The ceremony was held in a spectacular building which had been a guildhall in the fifteenth century, and had been restored by the National Trust to form a truly magnificent space. Large crystal chandeliers hung from the rafters, illuminating the ancient wooden structures which had been lovingly restored. The floor was laid with flagstones, again mostly original, but restored tastefully when this was not possible. Candles set in tall church candelabras flickered lightly in the breeze, giving a magical quality to the event. Partly responsible for this remarkable restoration was Sandra Parks, an architect who had barely survived a vicious attack in one of Peter's

m

previous cases. Sandra and Peter had formed a bond as he kept vigil at her hospital bedside, the two managing to communicate despite Sandra being in a deep coma.

Following the simple humanist service, the reception involved a great deal of eating, drinking and dancing, as it should, and Cassie had enjoyed every minute of it. The following day was Cassie's daughter's birthday and the trip to the Minack theatre was a treat. Who could have guessed it would turn out to be so memorable, and for all the wrong reasons.

Cassie heard the door and looked up to see DC Maggie Williams taking off her coat. 'Morning, ma'am,' she said brightly. Maggie was still something of an unknown quantity to Cassie. She knew, of course, that her DC possessed considerable IT skills and was a first rate researcher, but the young woman seemed to prefer sitting at a desk rather than being where the action was. Cassie thought she should have a word with Maggie soon, find out how she saw her future. Being very ambitious herself, Cassie couldn't imagine anyone being satisfied with a desk job when there was so much to be gained by taking a full part in investigations.

Cassie smiled. 'You heard about last night's events?'

Maggie shook her head. 'No, ma'am. Has something happened?'

Cassie was surprised. She was in the habit of checking the latest incidents on the police website before coming into work, and she expected the same of her colleagues. Then she reflected that it had been an eventful weekend and maybe not everyone was as dedicated as she was. As Cassie started to populate the whiteboard with information from the new case, she filled Maggie in on the details. 'Find out everything on the victim, Marcus Price. His family, friends and fellow actors, what his most recent productions have been, you know the drill.'

'Yes, ma'am. How awful that you were there with your kids.'

'Fortunate that I was on hand to take charge quickly, though. We gained vital time, preserved the scene and prevented possible suspects from leaving.'

'Yes, definitely, ma'am.'

Cassie watched as the younger woman settled herself at her computer and started to work. She reflected that in Liverpool

Maggie might have been called a bimbo, or even, God forbid, a slag. With her bleached blonde hair, extravagant make up and purple nails. 'Maggie?'

'Ma'am?'

'On second thoughts, you can come out to the Minack with me today. Robbie can handle the research. I'd like to see what you make of the scene.'

'Me, ma'am? Wouldn't you rather have Saroj or Kevin?'

When Cassie didn't answer immediately, Maggie felt flustered. She shouldn't have questioned the DI so directly. 'No. I mean I'd like to, if you think I could be helpful.'

'That's settled then. We'll be seeing Dr Samuels first at the PM, then straight on to Porthcurno.' Cassie ignored Maggie's slightly shocked expression. 'Weather looks like it's going to be foul, though,' she mused. 'I want to see all the cast and support staff on set, so it seems we may get wet. See if you can rustle up some waterproof capes.'

Maggie picked up the phone to organise the waterproofs, thinking only about the post mortem. She tried to avoid attendance at the morgue, avoid seeing dead bodies at all if she could. DCI Sanders understood this and chose to use her considerable admin and research skills, letting her off more onerous duties. Now DI Wade was winkling her out of her shell and onto the front line.

Maggie's parents were surprised when she decided on the police for a career. She had always been a studious girl, preferring reading to socialising. Not that she had no friends, but they did all seem to be of the same ilk. Needless to say, Maggie did great at school, gaining top grades in GCSE and A levels, and going on to study English at Exeter. As a secondary subject, she chose psychology, and became fascinated by criminology. After her degree, Maggie immersed herself in researching notorious cases like Jack the Ripper and Dennis Nielsen, and her parents became quite worried about her. 'You don't want to be reading about that sort of stuff, love. No thing for a young girl that,' her dad had said. 'Go out and have some fun. You should be looking for a job, too, instead of staying up there in your room all day.'

Being a dutiful daughter, Maggie searched job vacancies, finding nothing that appealed to her, until see saw an advert for the police academy. Seeing the image of a smiling young woman in a smart uniform convinced her that the police was where she wanted to be. No matter how her mum and dad tried to put her off, she was determined. 'Let her go, Jack,' her mum had said to her worried husband. 'Likely she'll change her mind, you know what they're like at her age.'

Mr Williams shook his head. 'Have you ever known our Maggie give up on anything once she's set her mind to it?'

Of course, she didn't. Excelling at all the assignments. Working her way through the ranks with an eye on only one thing. Becoming a detective. And here she was, in the Serious Incident Squad. A valued member of a valued team. The one thing she had hated about being a uniformed officer was that, every now and then, she would encounter a murder scene. Only liking to think of death in the abstract, and murder as a puzzle to be solved, Maggie managed to avoid getting too close to this aspect of police work and had found her niche in IT and research. As she grew in confidence, Maggie started to adopt a new style, as far away from the *nerd* image she had at school as she could manage. She had a new group of friends and liked nights out where vodka shots featured heavily. Now her new DI was asking her to get involved with front line police work. To get her hands dirty, so to speak. Not her bag at all. *Never mind*, she told herself. *The Chief will be back soon and we can get back to normal.*

Kevin and Saroj arrived together, chatting about the information they had just received concerning the murder at the Minack. 'Sounds like an Agatha Christie novel,' said Saroj, waving hello at Cassie and Maggie. *I wonder why Maggie's looking so glum?* She thought.

'Good job last night, ma'am,' said Kevin. 'I bet that took the perp by surprise.'

'Not so much that he or she couldn't get away, though, unfortunately. If I'd been a few seconds faster I could have nabbed him.' Cassie smiled ruefully at Kevin. 'Can you contact the cast and the support staff, and confirm that I want them at the Minack today, say about midday, after Maggie and I have finished at the morgue. There's a list on your desk.'

A light bulb went on in Saroj's head. *Ah, that's why our researcher is looking out of sorts. Didn't anyone tell Cassie that Maggie doesn't do PMs.*

'Yes, ma'am,' said Kevin, glancing at Maggie, clearly thinking the same as Saroj. 'No doubt the COD will be a stake through the heart,' he quipped.

Cassie smiled at Kevin's dark humour. 'Just as well I've got my garlic and crucifix then, just in case.' She turned to her DS, who was also chuckling at the joke. 'Saroj, when Robbie comes in, get him to contact Marcus Price's next of kin. I understand he has a wife and a daughter. I need to speak to his wife as soon as possible. And look into his background, we need to find a possible motive. And Robbie also needs to check out the rest of the cast. Any conflicts that we should know about, that sort of thing.'

Kevin nodded, as Cassie continued, 'Saroj, can you go through the information from the audience, see if anyone saw anything suspicious. We'll meet back here at four. Let's go, Maggie.'

Cassie hurried out of the squad room with a miserable looking Maggie on her heels. Kevin chuckled, 'I'd love to be a fly on the wall in the morgue, and it's raining.'

'Oh dear.' Saroj laughed, sharing the joke.

Maggie stood as far away from the dissecting table as she could. Fully kitted out in protective clothing, she felt totally out of place in this environment. She had a feeling that the DI realised this only too well and was enjoying her discomfort.

'Over here, Maggie,' shouted Cassie. 'You can't see anything from where you are.'

Ben Samuels raised his eyebrows. Was the detective being unduly harsh on the young woman? On the other hand, even new recruits had to get used to the sights and smells of the post-mortem if they were to be any good in the SIS. Turning back to the cadaver, Ben continued, 'Well nourished man. Possibly too well nourished, if his stomach contents are anything to go by. Last meal consisted of meat, fried potatoes, a sugary substance and fatty deposits.'

'Steak, chips and pudding?' said Cassie.

Ben nodded. 'Most likely. And there's a strong whiff of alcohol. Whisky, if my senses haven't deserted me.'

'Maggie, what do you think?' Cassie seemed determined not to let the researcher off the hook.

'I couldn't say, ma'am,' said Maggie, fighting down a strong feeling of nausea.

'COD Ben?'

'Stab to the heart without question. With a knife, not a wooden stake,' he said, smiling at his attempt at levity. *Everyone's a comedian*, thought Cassie.

When the two women didn't laugh, Ben shrugged and carried on. 'Very neatly done, too. No mean feat to pass through the ribs and straight into the centre of the heart, especially in the dark.'

'Specialist knowledge?'

'That, or sheer good luck. The knife could easily have struck a rib and missed a vital organ altogether.'

'Time of death we know, so unless there's anything else unusual. . ?'

Ben shook his head. 'I'll let you have the blood test results, but on the whole he was a fit man.'

'Thanks, Ben, let's go, Maggie.'

Maggie was relieved to get out into the fresh air of the car park. Cassie smiled at her. 'Well done in there. I know it's not your natural environment, but I want every member of my squad to take a full part in investigations. Okay?'

'Yes, ma'am.' Maggie put on a brave face. *Just let's hope it's not too often*, she thought.

'Have you eaten? I'm starving.' Cassie giggled to herself at the shocked look on Maggie's face. 'Let's find a café on the way, shall we?'

Chapter Three

Cassie stood in the third row of the stalls, surveying the fifteen assembled cast and crew. The rain had set in earnestly, obscuring the view of the sea. Only the sound of the waves betrayed the closeness of the wild Atlantic Ocean. Ignoring the murmurs of discontent, Cassie directed operations. 'Not wanting to come over all *Agatha Christie* or anything,' she smiled. 'But could you all take up the positions you were in when the lights went out.'

A collective sigh arose from the cast members. 'Is all this really necessary?' shouted a male voice.

'And you are?' Cassie enquired politely.

'Renfield. That's my character. I'm Steven Walker-Davis.'

'Yes, Mr Walker-Davis. It's necessary.'

The grumbling continued as the individuals shuffled around. The four scene shifters and the costume ladies remained in a bunch on the left. 'You four were there, were you?' said Cassie, directing her question at the scene shifters.

'We don't need to move. It is not necessary. We have nothing to do with this,' complained one man, putting his arm out to prevent the others from moving.

'And your name?' asked Cassie, narrowing her eyes.

'Alfred Marczak,' said the big man, in a pronounced middle Eastern accent.

Cassie walked over to where the four scene shifters stood. '*I* decide what is necessary, Mr Marczak. Let's have that quite clear. So, unless you want to be arrested for perverting the course of justice, I suggest you all take your places.'

Alfred Marczak shrugged resignedly and made a sweeping gesture. 'As you wish, detective.' His eyes were slits.

The two men and two women moved into their respective places without further comment.

Cassie turned her attention to the two young women. 'What about you two?'

One of them spoke up. 'In the dressing room, getting ready for the next costume change.'

'Did either of you notice anything unusual?' They shook their heads. 'Okay, I think you can go. If anything occurs to you, let me know.' The two women walked smartly away, relieved to be let off.

A hand was raised from the remaining group. 'How long are we going to be? Alicia Moore, playing Mina Harper.'

'We'll be as quick as we can, Ms Moore.' Going over to Maggie, Cassie said, 'Make a sketch of their positions and names.' Turning back to the stage, she continued, 'Did anyone notice any movement that wasn't scripted?'

All the cast shook their heads. 'What about you?' Cassie said to the scene shifters.

Alfred spoke up, 'I moved to check the flare but that is all.'

'And the rest of you. If you would like to speak for yourselves, did you notice anything unusual?'

There was a combined shake of the heads. But Cassie noticed that they glanced at Alfred nervously.

Just then, a man came rushing in from the wings. 'Sorry!' he shouted as he ran onto the stage. 'I only got the message an hour and a half ago and I had to travel from Camborne.'

'And you are?' said an increasingly frustrated Cassie.

'Colin Maynard. General factotum.'

Cassie shook her head. 'And that's what exactly?'

'Sorry. Been around actors too much. Dogsbody miss, or light and sound technician, on a good day.'

'Detective Inspector.'

'Sorry, Detective Inspector. That's three *sorrys* in less than a minute. I'm not doing very well, am I?'

'It's not a contest, sir,' said Cassie, liking the apologetic man, despite herself. 'Were you here on the night in question?'

'Yes. I was in the control room.'

'And did you notice anything out of the ordinary, just after the lights went out?'

'It was me who turned the stage lights off, and operated the bats. But no, I didn't notice anything.'

Cassie thought that Colin Maynard may be useful in getting her bearings around the theatre. 'Stay behind, Mr Maynard, I'd like to check a few things out with you.' The rest of you can go. We will want to speak to all of you individually in due course, so please stay available. And in the meantime, if you think of anything, however unimportant you may think it is, please get in touch with me.'

A distinguished looking man with white hair, carrying a large umbrella, separated himself from the rest of the cast, who were gratefully making their way inside. He put out his hand. 'Craig Williamson, playing Von-Helsing.'

Cassie reluctantly shook his hand, a questioning look on her face.

'I have to be in London tonight. Important audition.' He smiled conspiratorially. 'A poor jobbing actor must work.'

Cassie had no reason to keep him, so simply said, 'DC Williams will take your statement now, then. But we may want to speak to you again.' Turning to Maggie, 'Check his contact details, and when you're satisfied with his statement you can let him go.'

The rain had stopped and, as it often did in this part of the world, a bright sun took its place, glistening off the granite stonework. Cassie pushed back the hood of her waterproof cape, allowing her hair to spring outwards in an unruly mass. She ran her hands through the curls ineffectively. 'Now, Mr Maynard, a guided tour would be helpful.' Cassie smiled as she pulled off the waterproof and shook it, leaving it where she stood, confident that Maggie would collect it before they left.

Colin Maynard took in the woman before him. He thought she was majestic. Large, yes, but there was a lightness about her and a strength which appealed to him enormously. He also liked the way she conducted herself, taking charge, in total control. He had to admit, he liked strong women. He gave Cassie his most charming smile. 'No problem at all, Detective Inspector. Where would you like to start? And it's Colin.'

'You can start by telling me exactly what your job here is.'

'Like I said, a bit of a dogsbody, or multi-tasker, if I'm being kind to myself.' He chuckled ruefully. 'I work in the café and museum as well as operating the sound and lighting. I like to think I can turn my hand to most things, repairing scenery, fixing electrics, and so on. I also trained as a barista, so I make a mean coffee.'

At the mention of coffee, Cassie was instantly thirsty. She shouted over to Maggie, who was sitting with Craig Williamson, taking his statement. 'Just going to the café, DC Williams, seek me out there when you've finished with Mr Williamson.'

'Right you are, ma'am,' Maggie replied.

Seated in the bright café, looking out over the water, Cassie took a moment to appreciate her surroundings. In the October sunshine, the cliffs twinkled with raindrops. The rough grass and heather was interspersed with large black and grey rocks standing impervious against the strong westerly wind. Cassie had the sense of the timeless quality of this scene, *probably looked like this for millennia*, she thought, and could imagine pterodactyls swooping over the waves in search of giant fish.

'One cappuccino,' said a voice beside her, breaking her reverie.

Cassie accepted the cup, immediately sipping the creamy froth and chocolate sprinkles.

Colin laughed. 'You've got chocolate on you face.'

'Oops.' Cassie wiped her lips, suddenly wanting to distance herself from being a detective and simply enjoy a coffee.

'You don't come from around here, do you?' Colin said, sipping his own drink.

'If anyone else says that to me, I'll scream,' said Cassie, a laugh escaping, despite herself.

'I spent some time in Liverpool, that's all. I recognise the twang. A soft Liverpool accent though, more upper class. The Wirral, maybe?'

'Childwall. Not upper class exactly, but a bit posher than Toxteth, for instance.' Cassie was enjoying herself. Colin was very personable. He didn't seem to view her with suspicion as she had come to expect, but seemed genuinely interested in finding out more about her.

'What about you? I can't place your accent.'

'Scotland originally. Born there, anyway. Moved south to Guilford when I was two.' Colin's face became thoughtful, as if deciding whether to say more. 'I was adopted,' he suddenly said. 'Taken into care, off and on, and then adopted when I was five. The usual story in Glasgow, drugs and drink. Can't remember my mother at all, but I've been told that she died a year ago.'

Cassie watched Colin as he stirred his coffee. 'I'm sorry, I didn't mean to pry.'

'No, no. It's not painful, just sad that she died before I could see her. I was just curious, anyway, no bond there at all. I had great adoptive parents, the best.'

A comfortable silence fell between them as they both gazed out to sea.

'Look, we can do this another time, Colin. I have to get back to the station, anyway.' Cassie suddenly didn't have the appetite for questioning him. 'Will you be on duty tomorrow?'

Colin tipped an imaginary hat. 'Always on duty, ma'am.'

Cassie smiled warmly. 'Can we say eleven?'

Chapter Four

The squad room was a hive of activity when Cassie and Maggie returned. The white board had been populated with more information, including the results of the PM, which had been emailed through to the team. The victim's wife, Lucinda, had been found and contacted in the Caribbean. With her was her sixteen year old daughter Victoria, Marcus Price's step-daughter. This is not the sort of news the police would normally choose to break over the phone but, as they couldn't risk Mrs Price finding out another way, in the newspaper perhaps, Saroj had spoken to her, giving the briefest of details.

'Mrs Price and her daughter are travelling home tomorrow, ma'am,' Saroj told Cassie as she joined her at the whiteboard. 'I'm going to see her at their holiday cottage in St Ives. I'll arrange for a formal identification then, too.'

Cassie nodded to Saroj and surveyed the information before her. The eight cast members had been named, as well as the four scene shifters and the costume ladies. Cassie took up the pen and added Colin Maynard, noting his role with the theatre. Unusually in a murder case, the time of death, cause of death and the murder weapon were all known quantities. Cassie tapped the board with the pen. 'We need a motive,' she said, almost to herself.

'Robbie. What do we know about the cast?'

'They mostly work together regularly, ma'am. The exceptions being Marcus Price himself and Daisy Drummond, who was cast as

276

Lucy Westenra. Ms Drummond was brought in by Price according to the producer/director Christopher Steele. Mr Steele was unable to be present on the night of the murder, he had the flu, apparently. He certainly sounded rough on the phone, but then he used to be an actor, so. . . '

'Yes, quite. We'll have to see him, Robbie. You and Kevin interview him at his home, and don't catch the flu, we need you fit and healthy. Check out his alibi. If he had the flu, and not just *man flu*, find out who was looking after him.'

Robbie continued, reading from his notes: 'Mr Steele also said that Craig Williamson, who was playing Von Helsing, had expected the starring role, and was a bit put out when Mr Steele told him he had cast Marcus Price. Steele said that he wanted a *name*, and Price had just completed a successful tour of Julius Caesar with the RSC. A minor role in the play, but well received. Daisy Drummond was in the same production and Steele agreed to take her as well, at Price's request. He suggested that there was something between them.'

'I want to know more about this man, Alfred Marczak.' Cassie tapped his name with her pen. 'I've got a bad feeling about him. The other scene shifters were afraid of him. I want to know why. Bring the four of them in, and check out Marczak's background.'

'Saroj and I will see the other cast members tomorrow, except for Craig Williamson, who's in London on an audition.' Cassie looked thoughtful. 'Check that out too, Robbie. What was the audition, Maggie?'

Maggie checked her notebook. '*An Inspector Calls,* ma'am. At The Playhouse Theatre.'

'How apt,' Cassie smiled. 'I'm seeing Colin Maynard again tomorrow. I want to look around the theatre some more. Can people get in and out without being noticed? Could someone do the deed and then just disappear? Maynard seems to know a lot about the place, maybe he can throw some light on it.'

'Saroj, round up the cast members and the scene shifters and get them in for interviews tomorrow afternoon. I should be back by three, so any time after that.'

'Yes, ma'am,' said Saroj.

'Okay, get off home then. Good work today.' Cassie's eyes lingered on Maggie, and she smiled.

The following day was sunny but with a cold Easterly breeze. Cassie had wrapped up warmly but was now regretting the padded jacket and the woolly scarf, as the sun made the car's interior hot and steamy. Opening the window slightly, she unwound the scarf from her neck and threw it onto the back seat. *That's better*, she thought, breathing in the fresh air. As she drove, she reflected on the state of the Cornish roads and the lack of any real traffic. Her radio was tuned into Radio 2 and the traffic news reported holdups on all the major roads leading out of Liverpool towards Manchester. *Five car pile up on the A580*, the announcer said, *and a lorry has shed its load on the M60 causing a four mile tail back.* Cassie chuckled as she motored along the A30. Probably the busiest road in these parts, but still free flowing. She hummed along to the music that followed the report, feeling cheerful and looking forward to the day. Could it have anything to do with meeting up with the charming man she met yesterday? She shook this image from her mind. *He's still a suspect until I can eliminate him*, she thought. But still she looked forward to spending an hour or so in his company.

Bypassing Penzance, Cassie drove on through a couple of roundabouts, the roads becoming narrower and more shaded with trees. Branching off onto the B3283 Cassie passed through a small hamlet called St Buryan, *not changed in a hundred years, I bet*, she thought, taking in its closely packed granite cottages and ancient church. Seeing signs for places called Crows-an-Wra, Trewoofe and Trethewey, she mused that she could be in a foreign land. Of course, the true Cornish would claim that theirs was a totally separate kingdom to the rest of the British Isles, with its own traditions and customs. Many wanted independence for Cornwall and a resurrection of their language. Robbie had told Cassie that, in some pubs, Cornish was the only language spoken. This didn't mean that they were inhospitable. Depending largely on tourism for their income, most pubs, shops and hotels welcomed visitors, with open arms. But maybe they gave a sigh of relief when the summer was over and they could indulge in their unique fetes and festivals away from curious onlookers, many of these dating back to pagan times.

The road became the B3315 after the sign for Porthcurno, and Cassie was soon weaving her way towards the sea. Taking a left turn off the main road, she passed a small hamlet with a couple of shops and the Museum of Global Communications on her left, which told the story of laying the first underwater cable to America from the sandy beach below. Passing the car park for that beach, Cassie continued up a steep hill with a sharp left hand bend before arriving at the Minack car park.

Colin Maynard was waiting for her and waved her over towards a convenient parking spot. Cassie thought he was definitely a good looking guy. About six foot tall with dark hair and a slim build, *not too slim, though*, she thought, not like the super-skinny look young people seemed to want these days. He had a nice face, too. A ready smile, with even, white teeth, and clear eyes that met yours with a steady gaze. *Come on, Cassie*, she said to herself, *all business now*.

'Good morning, Detective Inspector,' Colin said, as she stepped out of her car. 'Lovely one, too.'

Cassie agreed, 'Certainly better than last time I was here. Now, let me tell you what I'd like.'

The tour of the site started with the theatre itself. It turned out that there was a private entrance for the players which led into the dressing rooms, bypassing the main auditorium. From the side of the car park, steep steps could be accessed that led down onto the beach below. A spectacular beach too, Cassie thought, with its white sand and lively surf. The stage area was approached from the dressing room which was to the left as viewed from the audience. Stone structures on the stage provided places for cast members or scene shifters to hide until they were required. To the extreme right were locked storage units and a gate leading out towards the cliffs.

Colin followed Cassie onto the stage, where she stood on the spot where Marcus Price had *appeared* as Dracula on that fateful night. 'Where would Price have appeared from?' she asked Colin.

'He would be hidden behind this pillar until he got his cue.' Cassie turned and saw a large stone structure about a metre away from where she was standing.

Taking a step back, she beckoned to Colin to take her place as Dracula. Standing behind him, she tried to imagine an escape route. *I could quickly duck behind the same stone pillar that Price had come from*, she thought. *With the lights out, it would be easy to go unnoticed.* Looking at her map of where everyone said they were standing at that time, she thought any one of a number of individuals could have moved undetected to the spot behind Marcus, stabbed him, dodged back behind the pillar and then to their place. She needed to narrow down the field. Individual interviews would help her determine who had a motive for killing Marcus Price, then she could concentrate her efforts better. Of course, it could also have been the work of someone not involved in the production. The cliffs which dropped away from the back of the stage were rugged and dangerous, but it wouldn't be impossible for someone with the right skills to climb up and, when the lights went out, stab Price and disappear the way they had come.

Colin had been standing stock still whilst Cassie thought things through. Now he turned slightly, looking over his shoulder at her. 'Okay,' she said. 'That'll do for now.'

'Could I tempt you to a coffee, Detective Inspector?'

'That would be lovely,' Cassie said warmly.

'Brilliant. And is there something else I could call you instead of Detective Inspector?'

'It's Cassie,' she said, feeling a little shy suddenly.

'Then let me take you for a coffee, Cassie. And maybe a spot of lunch? They do a great crab sandwich here.'

Cassie dabbed her mouth with a napkin, sneaking a glance at Colin, who was scooping up stray flakes of crabmeat off his plate with intense concentration. Their conversation over lunch had been lively and interesting, causing Cassie to wonder what this intelligent and attractive man was doing working as a general dogsbody for a theatre company. He told her he had no aspirations to be an actor, but surely he couldn't settle for this life for ever, could he?

She turned her gaze to the window. The sun still shone, but dark clouds were looming on the horizon. Cassie could see rain falling out to sea and a rainbow arching over the headland.

Colin caught her attention. 'Penny for them,' he said.

'It's really beautiful here. I can perhaps see why you stay.'

'You're perhaps wondering what I'm doing wasting my life making coffee and switching lights on and off.'

Realising how perceptive he was, Cassie decided to take the plunge. 'Well, it's none of my business, but you do seem to be worth more than this. Care to tell me how you come to be here?'

Colin was the one to then gaze over the waves thoughtfully. 'I had a brain tumour,' he said, suddenly turning to face Cassie. 'It was benign but was pressing on a part of my brain that affected my movement, especially my fine motor skills, hands and fingers.'

'Oh, I'm so sorry, Colin. I shouldn't have asked.'

'No, it's okay. I had the tumour removed and things improved, but I still have tremors in my hands. That's why you had coffee spilled in your saucer,' he joked.

'What did you do before?'

'Before the tumour? I was training as a doctor, in my final year at Edinburgh. My specialism was to be surgery,' he smiled ruefully. 'Doing the sort of operation that was done to me. Obviously, that was out of the question, given I had trouble even holding a dinner knife, let alone a scalpel. My supervisor suggested I switched specialism to be a GP, but I was so angry, Cassie, I couldn't accept what, for me, was second best.'

'You must have been devastated. I am so sorry.'

Colin smiled warmly. 'It was over two years ago now, and I'm coming to terms with it, as they say.'

'You've been here all that time?'

'God no. I sold up and took myself off around the world, much to my folks' dismay. I got involved in extreme sports. Rock climbing, sky diving, wind surfing, bungee jumping, anything that gave me an adrenaline rush. It took time, but I got it out of my system. Falling off a rock face in New Zealand brought me down to earth, literally.'

Colin observed Cassie's sad face. 'Don't look so glum, Cassie. I'm a different person now. I spent some recovery time with my parents in London, then came here for a holiday and just stayed. I have regular check-ups, which I kept to even when travelling, and there's no sign of the tumour returning so I'm well and truly in remission.'

'That's good to hear, Colin. What about the future, though? If you don't mind me being nosey, I am a detective, after all.'

'I don't mind. I'm going back to medicine. This time to train as a GP. I'm off to Edinburgh in January to complete my degree.' Colin held Cassie's gaze. 'I've not met anyone I wanted to tell that story to before. You're a good listener.'

'Also part of my job,' Cassie said. 'But this time it's been a privilege.'

'Look, I know this is out of order, me being involved in this murder business, but would you like to go out one evening? Dinner, or just a drink if you prefer?'

Cassie smiled and rubbed her forehead. 'I don't know, Colin. Strictly speaking I shouldn't.'

'It's okay, forget I asked. Maybe when it's over, before I have to rush off to Scotland?'

Cassie was quiet for a moment, thinking. 'Just a drink, then?'

'You mean it? I have to admit I've fancied you since that night you came rushing onto the stage, arms and hair waving madly.' Colin paused. 'You don't mind me saying that, do you?'

'No, I don't mind, Colin. I'm flattered.' Cassie looked at her watch. 'Look, I've been longer than I should have been, so I'll have to get going. I've enjoyed myself very much, and thanks for the lunch and everything. You've got my card, so give me a ring about that drink.'

Colin stood as Cassie did. He came over to her and placed a kiss on her cheek. 'I'll ring you, then.'

As Cassie was leaving the car park, she glanced in her rear view mirror to see Colin waving madly and running after her. She stopped and got out of the car.

'Cassie!' he shouted. 'There was something I meant to tell you.' As he caught up with her, he shrugged sheepishly. 'I was so enjoying our talk that I totally forgot why you were here, and that you'd asked everyone to tell you if there was anything at all that might have a bearing, even if we think it unimportant.'

282

'You have something, Colin?'

'Like I said, I don't know if it's important, probably nothing at all, but I think Marcus was having a fling with someone.'

'Daisy Drummond.'

'Daisy? No, not her, I saw him with Alicia. It was after everyone had gone from rehearsals. I was in the control room but then came down to the dressing room to find them. . . well, in an embarrassing position.'

'Well, what? Having sex or kissing and canoodling?'

'Looked like sex to me. He had her up against the wall.'

Cassie looked thoughtful. 'Thank you, Colin, that is interesting. Anything else you've remembered?'

'No, that's it.' He smiled.

'You'll have to come into the station to give a statement, anyway, as will the rest of the cast, so shall we say tomorrow at ten?'

'I'll be there. And thanks again for staying for lunch. I had a lovely time.'

Cassie simply smiled. 'I'll have to be off. Tomorrow at ten, then.'

Chapter Five

It was four o'clock before Cassie returned to the squad room. Saroj was out visiting Marcus's wife and daughter in St Ives. Kevin looked up as she entered. 'Ma'am, we have all the cast in interview rooms. They're getting a bit edgy, been here since three. The scene shifters and the costume women are booked to come in tomorrow, and I've just spoken to Colin Maynard, who told me he would be here at ten as arranged with you.'

Cassie nodded. 'Have we checked out Price's hotel room?'

'Yes, ma'am. Obvious signs of sexual activity on the bedclothes. They've been taken away for forensic examination, along with a pair of women's briefs which were in the bed.' Kevin checked his notes. 'Nothing else of much interest. He had an iPad which, along with his phone, is with the technical team.'

'Okay, I'll interview Alicia Moore and Daisy Drummond. Maggie, you can join me. Kevin, you take Steven Walker-Davis and Michael Gallagher with Robbie.' Cassie checked her watch. 'We'll meet back here at six for a catch up. Robbie, make sure the other three have tea and coffee before you start, will you, and apologise that they have been kept waiting. That might appease them a bit.'

Alicia Moore was showing signs of irritation. She was sitting side-on in her seat, legs crossed, fingers drumming on the table. 'At last!'

she exclaimed, as Cassie and Maggie entered. 'Is all police work like this? It's worse than auditions.'

Cassie started the recorder and introduced the session. 'Sorry to keep you, Ms Moore. Murder enquiries are necessarily intense, especially in the early stages. I'm sure you can appreciate that.'

'Yes, sorry. Poor Marcus, I can't quite believe he's dead, even though I actually saw his body.'

'You were close to Mr Price?'

'Well, we were colleagues. He's. . . he *was* married, you know.'

'So your relationship was purely professional?'

'Has someone said something? They can be a catty lot, actors, spreading rumours and gossip on the flimsiest of evidence.'

'So you deny a sexual relationship?'

Alicia sighed. 'A little indiscretion perhaps. One can feel very excited by drama, Inspector, and it's not unusual to lose control, as it were.'

Cassie decided not to pursue this line until they had stronger evidence, like the bed sheets. 'Have you remembered anything about that night? Anything unusual?'

'As a matter of fact, I have.' Alicia leaned over the table, relieved to get away from the question of her relationship with Marcus. 'It was the lights.'

'Go on.'

'Well, after the scene where Dracula landed, you know the darkness and the bats and the flare, the lights are meant to come on again straight away, low lighting depicting a night time scene at the docks.' Alicia looked from Cassie to Maggie. 'And they didn't. You asked for the lights to be kept off, I realise that, but they should have been on by then. That was strange. Colin's usually so reliable.'

The interview with Daisy Drummond followed much the same line as that with Alicia Moore. At first the actress denied a relationship with Marcus Price, only to accept that they had had an affair, but he had cooled off. 'I think he may have met someone else. He was certainly showing less interest in me.'

'Did you have any idea who he may have been seeing?'

'Not one of the cast, that's for sure. Not Alicia, anyway, she's not his type. And there's no one else, unless it was one of the guys. He can be bi you know.'

Cassie steered the interview away from personal relationships, thinking that actors were a strange lot. Lax morals didn't begin to describe it.

'Have you remembered anything unusual from that night?'

'Well, the dark scene went on a bit longer than it should have, and then you asked for lights to stay off anyway. And I thought I saw a shadow running across the stage while it was dark. A scene shifter, most likely, but they are supposed to stay behind the action. Anyway, as soon as poor Marcus. . . you know, everything happened in slow motion. You came running onto the stage, shouting something about a crime and telling us to stand back, it was surreal. Things got a little hazy after that.'

Meeting back in the squad room at six o'clock, the team compared notes about the interviews. All except Michael Gallagher mentioned that the lights were out for longer than usual. Colin Maynard was in the lighting control room and would need to explain why that had happened. Cassie thought it was fortuitous that the stage was in darkness until a screen was erected around Marcus Price's body. Imagine the images on Facebook, if not. That would have been a really terrible way for relatives to find out that their loved one had been murdered, not to mention the privacy that the police owed to the deceased.

'What about the person who mentioned a shadowy shape running across the stage?' said Kevin. 'That could be important.'

'That was Daisy Drummond. She thought it was probably a scene shifter, but if it was, he or she was out of place.'

'Okay everyone, we can't do any more today, so get off home. Bright and early tomorrow.' Just then Saroj came into the squad room, and she and Cassie moved into the office.

Sitting in Cassie's office with a coffee each, Saroj filled her boss in on the meeting with Mrs Price and her daughter.

'To be honest, ma'am, she didn't seem all that upset. I know she'd had a bit of time to get used to the idea on the way home from

Tobago, but I sensed a bit of relief, and the daughter was very nervous, kept looking at her mother, for guidance I thought.'

'Did she identify the body okay?'

'Yes, no problem, though she only gave a cursory glance, and seemed keen to get away. I've arranged to meet her again tomorrow and I'll get a bit more background. Price was her second husband, so there could be something there, with the ex, I mean.'

'Right, let's get off, Saroj. We could have the results of forensics tomorrow, find out who's been sleeping in Marcus Price's bed, amongst other things.'

Saroj rose and headed for the door. 'It's a queer one this, ma'am. We know the how and the where and the when, but not who. We need to establish possible motives as soon as we can so that we can concentrate our efforts a bit better.'

'Couldn't agree more, Saroj. We need to dig into people's backgrounds, do they have history with Price? Any reason to hate him so much they are prepared to murder him? And the method is puzzling. There must be easier ways to kill someone than in front of a live audience. Could our killer be a show off? Certainly a risk taker.'

'Food for thought, ma'am. Anyway, I'm off, don't work too late.'

'Yeah, see you tomorrow, Saroj.'

Cassie stayed behind at her desk, thinking about the day's events. Her mind was primarily occupied by thoughts of Colin Maynard. There was no doubt she was attracted to him and had, rather foolishly, agreed to have drinks with him. Now this lighting business was bothering her. If the lights should have gone up immediately following Dracula's appearance, then Colin was responsible for making that happen. What reason could he have for not doing that? For keeping the stage in darkness. Cassie wondered about her judgement of this man. Had she been so flattered by a good looking man's attentions that her professionalism was compromised? He was not yet eliminated as a suspect, after all.

She sighed loudly. *I'd better let Saroj interview him tomorrow,* she thought, *and I'll stick to the four scene shifters. We'll see what comes of that. I haven't made any firm arrangements with him, so nothing lost at the moment.*

That decided, Cassie picked up her briefcase and left the office.

Chapter Six

The next morning Cassie was on the phone to Saroj early. 'About today's interviews, can you take Colin Maynard and I'll make a start on the scene shifters. I particularly want to speak to Alfred Marczak, but I think I'll see the others first. See what it is they're afraid of.'

'Yes, ma'am. I'm seeing Price's wife and daughter today, but I can contact them and arrange for that to be this afternoon.'

'If you would. Did you find out anything about the ex husband?'

'Yes, he's called James Dunn. He has stage four cancer and is in and out of the hospice. He lives in Hayle. I'm making arrangements to see him today, as well.'

'No, leave that Saroj. I'll speak to him myself. Text me his address.'

'Yes, ma'am.'

Cassie hung up, picked out a smart suit and blouse and jumped into the shower. She was aware on some level that she was taking more care with her appearance, but quickly dismissed the notion that it was anything to do with Colin Maynard. As if to confirm her thoughts, Micky commented on Cassie's appearance as she came into the kitchen. 'Going somewhere special, ma?'

'No, what makes you say that?'

'It's just that you look like you're going to court.'

Cassie simply shook her head. Tanya walked in and made matters worse. 'Looking a bit posh there, ma.'

'Can you both stop commenting on my appearance please. I

normally dress smartly for work.'

The two teenagers exchanged a look. Changing the subject, Micky reminded Cassie that he was going surfing this weekend in Newquay. 'Robbie is picking me up early so that we can catch the tide.'

'Robbie will probably be working, love. We've got a murder investigation on the go.'

Tanya smirked. 'Poor Micky can't go surfing with his mate Robbie,' she said sarcastically.

Micky ignored her and left the room, calling over his shoulder, 'It would be good if someone could let me know what's going on. I've got a life too, you know.'

Cassie shouted after him, 'Sorry, love, I'll get Robbie to ring you.' Then, turning to Tanya, 'And you, young lady, can stop winding your brother up and get ready for school.'

As soon as Cassie left the house, she was all work, planning the day in her head as she drove down Morlaix Avenue from the house she was renting on the newly built estate on the hill overlooking Truro. It was a convenient location but not the prettiest area, as the builders were still very much in evidence on the site, and there was no planting completed. The garden of her own property was just a mud pile, and she had no inclination or time to make it otherwise. *Only temporary*, she reminded herself, without being at all sure about what her next step may be. Cassie had resented her posting to Cornwall, but was growing to see the advantages of living somewhere rural after the big city. Liverpool could be exciting, and the shops were definitely a bonus, but the crime rate was high and young people were often drawn into the gang culture that was rife in some areas. She thought that her two were too sensible for that, but Cassie had dealt with many families who thought the same as her, only to be devastated when their son or daughter became a victim of drugs or knife crime, or, worse still, a perpetrator of the same.

Putting these thoughts behind her, Cassie parked and went into the station. To her surprise, Colin Maynard was waiting in reception. He rose to meet her as she came through the doors.

n

'Hi Cassie. Sorry to be early, but I wanted to miss the traffic.'

The constable behind the reception desk looked up and raised his eyebrows, surprised at the familiar way that the man had addressed the DI.

Cassie glanced around then back to Colin. Realising his mistake, he corrected himself. 'Sorry,' he whispered, 'Detective Inspector Wade.'

This made matters worse in Cassie's view, as the whole episode was beginning to look conspiratorial. 'Good morning, Mr Maynard, DS Kapoor will be with you shortly.' She said loudly. 'Just take a seat.'

That said, she hurriedly made her way through the double doors into the heart of the police station. She was still muttering to herself and shaking her head when Kevin stopped her. 'The two women, Maddy Grant and Della Randi are in interview rooms. Saroj told me you wanted to deal with them.'

'Yes, Kevin. I want you to join me, but let's have a coffee first.' As the two of them walked to the squad room, Cassie asked, 'and the two men?'

'Not arrived yet, ma'am.'

'Okay, but if they're not here within the hour, have them brought in, arrested if necessary.'

'Ma'am.'

The interviews with the two female scene shifters revealed little except that they both thought that Alfred Marczak was not a very nice man. Neither of them admitted to having known him prior to taking the job at the Minack, and both said that they had only been working there for the summer and, now that the season was over, they would be moving on. They both insisted that they had been in the spot they had indicated to Cassie during the dark scene, and had not moved at all. Neither did they see anyone else move.

'It's as though they rehearsed that together,' said Kevin.

'Probably did,' Cassie agreed, 'but I don't think they had anything to do with the murder. They're clearly afraid of Marczak though, and I don't think they'd tell us if they suspected him of being involved.'

Kevin's phone vibrated and he answered it. 'Marczak and Kaczyorski are in reception, ma'am.'

'Okay, have them taken to interview rooms.' Cassie looked around the squad room as they entered. 'Saroj interviewing?' she asked.

Robbie replied. 'She's in room three with Maggie. They're interviewing Colin Maynard.'

Cassie nodded. 'Oaky, Kevin, let's go see Kaczyorski, we'll let Marczak stew for as bit.'

As Cassie and Kevin were leaving the squad room, Robbie called out. 'Ma'am, I've got some information about Alfred Marczak. He's wanted in connection to a murder in Slovakia. It's definitely the same guy, their police have sent me a photo.'

Cassie leaned over Robbie's desk to see the image on screen. 'In that case, we can keep him here until we contact the Home Office. Good work, Robbie. Get a warrant to search his flat.'

'Ma'am.'

'Mr Kaczyorski. Do you mind if I call you Bartek?'

Kaczyorski shrugged. 'And your given name is?' he directed his question at Cassie, smirking.

Ignoring the cheeky question, Cassie opened the file in front of her. 'You live with Alfred Marczak?'

'We share a flat, yes.'

'You're friends.'

'No, is a convenient arrangement. That is all.'

'And how well do you know Marcus Price?'

Bartek looked surprised. 'The actor who was killed? Not at all. I have never spoken to him. I am beneath him, I think,' he laughed.

'So, before this production you didn't know anything about Mr Price?'

'I tell you, we never met, and I am not a *theatre goer*, as you say, so I not hear of him, either.'

'Did you notice anything unusual that night?'

'No. The darkness was long, that's all.'

'And did you move during that time, when it was dark?'

'No. We stay back of stage.'

'Did you see anyone else move?'

'No. The women and Alfred were with me, no one move.'

'Where are you from, Bartek?'

'My home? It is Bosnia. I go back there soon, to my family.'

'And Alfred Marczak, where is he from?'

'We do not talk about these things.'

'Come on, Bartek, you live with a guy and don't talk about home?'

'It is convenient arrangement, as I said. We are not friends.'

'Why are you afraid of him?'

Bartek's eyes darted around the room. 'Afraid? No.'

'What *do* you know about Alfred? How long has he been in this country, for instance?'

'I don't know this. You should ask him.'

Cassie decided that she had had enough of these evasive answers. Perhaps an hour or two in the cells would soften him up. She was sure he knew more than he was currently saying. 'This constable will take you back to your cell. We'll speak again later.'

Bartek protested loudly. 'But I know nothing, as I said. You should let me go now.'

Cassie and Kevin ignored the protestations and left the room before the constable directed Bartek out after them.

Cassie was curious to know how Saroj was getting along in her interview with Colin. However, there was no sign of her DS in the squad room. Cassie casually asked Robbie. 'Is Saroj still interviewing?'

'Yes, ma'am. By the way, I have the warrant to search Marczak's flat.'

Cassie decided that she needed to be out of the station. 'Come on Kevin, let's see what Marczak has to hide.'

* * *

Cassie and Kevin snapped on their latex gloves. The flat was a slum. Empty take-away containers and beer cans littered the floor and the table in the living room. 'The way some people live,' said Kevin, screwing his face up. The smell of stale food and body odour was overpowering.

'I suppose you don't notice it after a while,' Cassie replied.

The room had one large grubby sofa, over which a blanket had been thrown. 'It looks like one of them sleeps in here.' Dirty socks and underwear were piled in a heap at one end.

If anything, the kitchen was worse. The smell from the overflowing wastebin was noxious. Cupboard doors were left open or broken, and there was no sign of crockery or food inside. The plates and cups that should have resided there were piled in the dirty sink. Any attempt at eating off them abandoned long ago.

Cassie opened the fridge. No food inside, but two bottles of Polish vodka lay on a shelf. Opening the small freezer compartment, Cassie took out a container with a bread wrapper inside. Unwrapping the parcel, she found a passport and a wad of cash. 'Marczak's passport,' she mused, looking through it. 'He came into the country six months ago.' Digging further into the icy interior, she found another package. Carefully opening the wrapping, Cassie could see that it was a knife. Immediately, she placed the knife and its wrapping into an evidence bag.

Finding nothing further in the kitchen, she wandered into the bedroom. There was a double bed with very dirty blankets covering it. No sheets as far as Cassie could tell. She flipped back the blankets to reveal a very stained mattress.

Under the bed was nothing but dust. The only other furniture in the room was a small chest of drawers and a chair next to the bed, on which a photograph of a woman and a small boy was given pride of place.

Cassie picked it up. 'Whoever slept in here, has a family. It could be Kaczyorski, he has mentioned a family.' She bagged this item also.

A search of the drawers revealed nothing of interest. 'Well, unless we want to arrest them for being a bio-hazzard, we can leave it there. We can always get the SOCO team in if we feel it necessary later.'

Kevin nodded, clearly relieved to get away from this oppressive flat. 'Right you are, ma'am.'

'What's our next step with these guys, ma'am?' Kevin asked as Cassie drove back to the station.

'We can hold Marczak until we find out more from the Slovakian police and the Home Office. But we've no reason to believe that Kaczyorski has done anything wrong. We'll have to let him go.'

'D'you think Marczak could be the killer? And what motive could he possibly have?'

'He's killed before, by all accounts, Kevin. We don't know under what circumstances yet though. He could be a contract killer, in which case we need to look for someone who had enough of a grudge to pay him to murder Marcus Price.' Cassie continued to speculate. 'I'm convinced that the key to solving this lies with Price himself. I'm not clear yet what sort of a man he was, who his friends, or more to the point, enemies were. We've a lot more digging to do, Kevin.'

The two travelled the rest of the way in silence, each with their own thoughts. Kevin was thinking about the case, but Cassie's mind was on Colin Maynard and what the interview with him had revealed. She couldn't see this personable man committing murder, or was that wishful thinking? There was the thorny issue of the lighting, for instance. Why did the lights not come back on when they should have done? Colin was responsible for that, so his explanation would be interesting. He'd told her that he'd been out of the country for two years, so how plausible was it that he had some kind of history with the dead man? Motive, motive, motive. 'We need to know a lot more, Kevin,' she suddenly said. 'An awful lot more.'

Chapter Seven

Not feeling ready to interview Marczak yet until they had contacted the Slovakian police, Cassie dropped Kevin off at the station. 'I'm going to visit James Dunn,' she told him. 'I want you to get this evidence over to forensics and then contact the Home Office and the Slovakian police. We need to know more about this murder he's wanted in connection with and our extradition arrangements. And tell Saroj I want to see her before she leaves.'

'Yes, ma'am.' Kevin thought that his DI was looking more agitated than usual. *I suppose it's because the DCI is away and she's in charge of a tricky murder investigation.* Kevin was looking forward to Peter's return in a few days, he always seemed to bring a sense of calm and order to the work, and it would be good to have a fresh eye cast over this situation. He watched as Cassie drove hurriedly away from the station, then set off at a pace into the building to carry out the tasks he had been set.

Cassie was thinking too that she had never felt so lost at the beginning of a murder enquiry. *Perhaps it's because it seemed so easy in the beginning, me being on the scene. There seemed to be a limited number of suspects and I was sure one of them would be caught quickly, given a confession or, at least have a strong connection with the murdered man that implicated them.*

Clearing her mind of these thoughts, Cassie made her way through the maze of steep streets at the back of the main road in Hayle. Finding the address easily, she parked and walked up the path of a neat and tidy bungalow. Turning, she saw that, from this high point, there was a spectacular view over the estuary with its wide beaches and rugged coastline, looking especially lovely with the low October sun glistening on the sea. Hayle was advertised as having *three miles of golden sand*, and, from this vantage point, she could see why. Cassie knocked at the door and was just about to repeat her knock when the door opened slightly. A man with wisps of grey hair and gaunt features peeped around the opening. His voice was, however, relatively strong for such an aged looking man. 'Can I help you?'

Cassie introduced herself and, opening the door wide, James Dunn smiled and allowed her access to a wide hallway. Cassie could see that he was quite frail as he held onto the wall for support. He was friendly enough, though, and indicated that she should go ahead of him into a comfortable sitting room. The room faced the front of the house and took advantage of the outstanding view. 'You've got a lovely spot here,' she said, turning to see James Dunn lowering himself gingerly into an armchair.

'Thank you. Not that I can take much advantage of it, apart from looking at it, of course.' He sighed deeply. 'I used to walk over the sands from Lelant to Carbis Bay and then to St Ives. Sometimes get the little train back when I first started to feel tired with the chemo. Michael Portillo did that ride when he was doing those train journeys on the telly. Said it was one of the prettiest train journeys in England. Couldn't argue with that.' He looked up at the large black woman in front of him. *Not your usual bobby in these parts*, he thought, and that accent is northern, Liverpool perhaps. 'Would you like some tea,' he asked.

'I'll make it if you like,' she said in reply. 'Not to intrude or anything, but I can see you're a bit infirm.'

'Ha!' he laughed. 'A bit infirm alright. Okay, me lover, you get on and do that. You'll find everything out, can't be bothered to put stuff away in cupboards these days. My ex-wife would go spare, I can tell you, but I don't get visitors as a rule these days, so what's the harm?'

Cassie was making the tea when there was a knock at the door. 'Shall I get that for you?' she shouted through from the kitchen.

'If you don't mind. Nobody calls for weeks and then two in the space of ten minutes.'

At the door were a woman whom Cassie guessed was a very well preserved fifty something, and a girl of around sixteen. The girl looked as if she had been crying, and was screwing up a tissue between her fingers. The woman was shocked to see Cassie. 'Is Mr Dunn in?' she said, believing the other woman to be a home help or something.

'Could I take your name and I'll see if he's up to visitors at the moment.'

'I'm Lucinda Price and this is my daughter, Victoria. He'll want to see us, I'm sure, so if you wouldn't mind. . . ' Lucinda made to step in.

'If *you* wouldn't mind waiting,' said Cassie firmly. Lucinda was taken aback by the impudence of, what was to all intents and purposes, a servant.

She was, however, always polite, even to servants. 'Very well. But we must see him, it's important.'

Well, well, well, thought Cassie. The ex wife, and so soon after her husband's demise. This could be interesting. 'Mr Dunn, there's a Mrs Price and her daughter at the door.'

'Blow me, what can they want?'

'Will it be tea for four, then?'

When she brought the tea in, Cassie thought she should make herself known to Mrs Price, even though she was enjoying the little unwitting deception.

'You could have told me,' complained Lucinda. 'I feel very embarrassed now.'

Victoria had made a beeline for her father's chair, kneeling beside him, with tears in her eyes. 'Oh daddy, I'm sorry. I should have come before, never mind what he said.'

'Hey, no need to take on so,' said James. 'You're here now.' He patted her hand, clearly emotional himself.

Lucinda was acutely aware of the inspector witnessing this scene, and tried to hush her daughter. 'Vicki, we're not alone.'

'I don't care,' shouted the teenager. 'It's my dad, we should have come before. It's all your fault.'

Lucinda turned to Cassie. 'I'm sorry, Inspector, you must excuse my daughter. What with her father dying. . . '

'He wasn't my father!' Victoria insisted. '*This* is my father, and he's ill. We should have been here for him, only that pig kept us virtually under lock and key.'

Cassie knew that she would have to dig deeper into this intriguing situation, but now was probably not the time. She turned to the highly embarrassed Lucinda. 'Mrs Price, I will need to speak to you and your daughter at some time, but, for now, I'll leave you to have your visit.' To James she simply said, 'Another time, Mr Dunn?'

'Always here lass, unless I'm at the hospice.' Victoria burst into floods of tears and clutched her father tightly.

Cassie took her leave, still trying to absorb the implications of what she had just witnessed. If Marcus Price was as controlling as Victoria seemed to suggest, that could be motive. Just how Lucinda Price could have managed it from Tobago was another issue. *I wonder if we can tie her to Marczak?*

Putting these thoughts on the back-burner, Cassie made her way back to Truro. Her thoughts now turning to Colin Maynard's interview with Saroj.

Maggie had other news which took Cassie's mind off in a different direction. The Czech and Slovak Federal Republic did have an extradition treaty with the UK, and Maggie had spoken to someone in the Home Office who was very interested in Alfred Marczak. She wanted to speak to the officer in charge of the case as soon as possible.

'I'll do that now,' said Cassie. 'But she will have to understand that he's ours until we can eliminate him from Marcus Price's murder.' Walking over to the white board, Cassie added the new information, some of it speculation at this point, like Lucinda Price's possible connection with Marczak. 'Maggie, check out the hospitals near the Price's home address, see if Mrs Price has ever been admitted with injuries which may be DV related.'

Maggie looked surprised. 'You think he was violent towards her?'

'Not sure. At the moment it looks like he was very controlling, and that may be the full extent of it. Doesn't hurt to check up, though.' Cassie looked around the room. 'Saroj about anywhere?'

'Just popped out for a sandwich, ma'am. I think she wanted to see you.'

'Send her in when she gets back.'

'Ma'am.'

Cassie went into her office, closed the door and picked up the phone. She was quickly connected to Diana Sharples, the Home Office contact, and wasted no time telling her that, although Devon and Cornwall Police were keen to cooperate in any way with the Home Office, her first duty was to investigate the murder which had been perpetrated on home soil.

Expecting a challenge, Cassie was pleased that Ms Sharples was very understanding. 'Well, it looks like he's not going anywhere at the moment, Detective Inspector, so I'll leave that with you. Please let me know if anything changes, I really wouldn't want him released into the community.'

'No chance of that, Ms Sharples. We are awaiting forensic analysis results on the items we procured from his flat, and he's going nowhere until I'm satisfied that there is no link between him and our investigation. I'll be in touch when I know more.'

Replacing the phone, feeling satisfied that she had events under control, Cassie looked up to see Saroj entering the squad room. After a word with Maggie, who indicated the DI's office, Saroj came briskly over to comply with Cassie's instruction.'

Knocking and opening the door, Saroj asked if her boss would like coffee.

'Not at the moment, Saroj. Come in and sit down. I want a blow by blow account of your interview with Colin Maynard.'

'He's very charming, and comes across as cooperative. I don't know why, but I'm always a little suspicious of too much cooperation.' Saroj smiled wryly, noting that Cassie was drilling into her with her dark brown eyes.

'He was very interested in how far we had got with the

investigation too, and asked if it was possible to speak to you. Of course, I batted that one off.'

Cassie was impatient and slightly irritated by Saroj's focus on her first impressions of Colin. 'Did you find out why the lights stayed off?'

Taken aback by the sharpness of Cassie's tone, Saroj became more businesslike. She checked her notes. 'He says he saw you stand and run down the steps, shouting to everyone to stop and not touch anything. He took this as an instruction to himself as well as the people on the stage, so backed off from the controls until instructed otherwise. Then you asked for the lights to remain off and he complied with that until you asked for them to be switched on again.'

'That sounds reasonable, don't you think?'

'Well, I think he's either very sharp, taking the order to not touch anything to mean him as well as the people on stage, or he's hiding something. I haven't made my mind up yet.' Saroj continued warily, not sure where her boss was coming from at the moment. 'He told me that the special effects could be operated on a timer which would have made the lights come on automatically after the flash, but that he often liked to override this and control the scene manually. He had set the bats off, I suppose you know what that was?' Cassie nodded. 'And then he waited for Alfred Marczak to throw the switch which operated the flash. He says he wanted to wait a few seconds after that for maximum effect before making the lights gradually come up. However, that's when you took charge and he stopped.'

Cassie looked thoughtful, leaning over the desk, her fingers steepled in front of her, still holding Saroj in her gaze. 'Have we found any connection between Maynard and Price?'

'No, ma'am. Maynard's been out of the country a fair bit, and as far as we can ascertain, their paths haven't crossed. Neither does he know Mrs Price, as far as we can tell.'

'So we have no motive?'

'None that we are aware of. I don't like his attitude though, too cocky if you know what I mean.'

'Or just confident and cooperative?' Cassie relaxed back in her chair. 'Where is he now?'

'He's still in the interview room.'

'Okay, I think we can let him go for now. Something may come up in our interviews with Marczak or Mrs Price which means we'll have to have him in again but, for now, there's no reason to hold him. Do you agree?'

'Yes, ma'am. And his request to see you?'

'Not at the moment. If he has anything to say, he can say it to you.'

Chapter Eight

The next day was Saturday and, as Cassie prepared to go into the office, she was acutely aware that Peter Sanders was due back on Monday. Cassie had hoped to make considerable progress by now to prevent her DCI taking over the case. However, after six days, she did not have a viable prime suspect. This case was going stale on her and she desperately needed a breakthrough. Perhaps Marczak would provide that for her. He was a strong suspect in a murder in Slovakia, thought to be a contract killing. He had the opportunity, and was certainly ruthless enough, to have also murdered Marcus Price for money. Cassie just had to find a connection between him and one of the people she suspected may have a motive for seeing the actor dead.

Her favourites for this were Mrs Price, who seemingly was under her husband's complete control and may want to see the back of him for good, and James Dunn, who had reason to hate Price for taking his wife and daughter from him. Of course, at this point she didn't know that Dunn did hate Price. Maybe he was glad to see the back of his wife, but witnessing the scene at Dunn's home yesterday, she didn't think this would be the case.

And then there were the unknowns. People from Price's past who bore enough of a grudge to want to see him eliminated. There was Craig Williamson, for instance. He had wanted the part of Dracula for himself. How aggrieved would he have to be to pay someone to kill his rival? Cassie couldn't quite see it, though. She thought that show business may be a cut-throat occupation, but not literally. She would ask Robbie to make contact with the actor and get him back for an interview, anyway. It was a loose end that needed tying up.

Today she would start the process with Marczak. She would have to tell him about the Slovakian connection and the UK's willingness to extradite felons to his home country. She was sure that, at this point, Marczak would demand a lawyer, but she was prepared for that eventuality. After these preliminaries with Marczak, Cassie intended to see Mrs Price and Victoria, before returning to Hayle to interview James Dunn.

By the time Cassie had thought all of these aspects through, she was dressed and ready to start the day, with a distinct plan of action. She was sure that today would be the day when things would become an awful lot clearer.

Saroj was at the white board when Cassie entered the squad room. Glancing at the new information being written up, she hailed Robbie, 'You remember Craig Williamson? The actor that went to London for an audition?'

'Yes, ma'am.'

'Well get him back here, Robbie. I want to speak to him.'

'Is he a suspect, ma'am?' asked Maggie.

'They all are, until they're not.'

Walking over to Saroj, Cassie noted the new information. 'So there's a match between the blood found on Marczak's knife and the Slovakian victim? That might give us some leverage. It means we can keep him a bit longer, at least.'

Cassie turned to Kevin, who was busy scrolling through his computer screen. 'Anything interesting?'

'Good morning, ma'am. It seems that Marcus Price wasn't well liked in the business, but was a good actor, by all accounts. I can't find anyone he crossed to the extent that they would want him dead, but who knows how people think, especially actors, they can be a hysterical bunch, I believe.'

'Okay, you can leave that for now, Kevin. I want you in the interview with Marczak. I think a male presence would send the right signals for the first interview. Saroj, I want you to be ready to take Kevin's place if I ask, but I expect that to be this afternoon.'

'Okay, let's get to it. Saroj, have Marczak brought up from the cells.'

Sitting opposite the surly Slovakian, Cassie had her first really good look at him. He was tall and wiry, his slimness belying the strength that she thought was hidden there. He had the dark, brooding looks of men from the eastern bloc, made more sinister by the scar which ran from his forehead, across his left eye, to his chin. A knife wound, undoubtedly. He stared fixedly at Cassie as she took up her position across the table from him, switching on the recorder and introducing the session.

Cassie looked steadily back at Marczak. 'Do you know why you are here, Mr Marczak?'

'You keep me under false pretenses. I have done nothing, except I am a foreigner, yes? And so I must be guilty.'

'You are here in connection with the murder of Marcus Price. You were on site when the murder occurred and had opportunity to kill him. We also have strong evidence that you are connected to a murder investigation in Slovakia, and the British government will be happy to comply with any request for extradition to that country should that be forthcoming. Do you understand?'

Alfred shifted his eyes onto the table, studying his hands. 'I want a lawyer,' he said quietly.

'That is your right, but you understand you have not been charged with anything yet?'

Marczak nodded. 'I still want lawyer.'

'Okay, do you want to contact your own lawyer, or shall we provide one for you?'

'I am not made of money, as you Brits say. You find lawyer for me.'

'The constable will take you back to your cell whilst that is arranged. Have you had breakfast?'

Marczak looked startled. 'Yes, thank you, I have eaten.'

'Okay, I'll see you again in due course.'

After Marczak had left the room, Kevin said, 'That was short and sweet.'

'To be expected. Find him a lawyer, Kevin.'

Cassie asked Maggie to drive as they went to St Ives to see Mrs Price and Victoria. The DI was deep in thought, pondering the interview with Marczak. How to establish a link between Mrs Price and the surly Slovakian? If Marcus Price really did keep her under a tight control, it was hard to see how she would have enough freedom to explore the murky underworld which held men like him. It's not as though they advertised. If not Mrs Price, then maybe James Dunn was the one who wanted the actor dead. She didn't know anything about him except that he had cancer. Kevin had been told to do background checks on key players, so maybe that would throw something up. Anyway, she was seeing him later and could press him on his contacts and see if she could establish a motive.

Cassie put her thoughts aside and gazed out of the window. She had received a text from Colin Maynard asking about the drink she had foolishly agreed to. Was it foolish, though? Cassie was ninety-nine percent sure that Colin had nothing to do with the murder and he may have information about Marczak. Was she just making an excuse to see him again? There was no doubt she was attracted to him, and it had been a long time since she had had a night out with a man, a reason to get dressed up. Impulsively, Cassie took out her phone and replied to Colin's text. Love to. Send me directions. X. Well, that's that, she thought, wondering if the kiss was too much. What the hell, she suddenly felt quite excited about the date, and kisses on texts were expected, they didn't mean anything.

Suddenly Cassie was aware of a change of scenery. They had left the A30 and, bypassing Hayle, were following the coast road to St Ives. Maggie told her that there was a beautiful sandy beach over on the right. 'It's Carbis Bay, ma'am, and well worth a visit. Your kids would love it, I'm sure, though this isn't the best time of year to appreciate it. There's a nice hotel and beach cafés, too.'

Cassie nodded. 'I'm quite stunned by the number of lovely places to visit. If only I had the time,' she laughed. 'Shouldn't have been a copper, should I?'

Maggie swept down towards the little seaside town of St. Ives.

'It's impossible to park in the town, and especially where Mrs Price's cottage is. I suggest we use the railway station car park, if that's okay with you?'

'Absolutely, Maggie. I would appreciate the walk.'

Coming down the steep steps from the car park, Cassie could smell the sea and hear the squawk of sea gulls. They walked down a narrow street, a hotel on the right and little cottages on the left, mostly holiday lets she noted from the signs in the windows. Art gallery, lifeboat station, sea front, with its shops and cafés. A real seaside town, Cassie thought. 'I bet this is busy in summer,' she said to Maggie.

'You'd guess right, ma'am. Hard to move down this street in the school holidays. The locals have mixed feelings, as you can appreciate. They rely on visitors for their livelihoods, but the price for that is the large number of second homes and holiday lets. The council are trying to enforce a limit on second home ownership, it pushes the property prices up and locals can't afford to buy.'

'It's not the same where I come from, but I can empathise about the tourists. Liverpool city centre is packed with them any time of year. There's a queue a mile long to see the Cavern Club most days.'

Turning off the sea road, they soon found the address they were looking for. A small but pretty cottage on a steep and narrow street. Geraniums, fading now the autumn had come, packed two tubs beside the front door. Cassie knocked and the door was quickly opened by Victoria. 'Come in, Mum's in the sitting room.'

Cassie thanked the teenager. 'If you wouldn't mind, Victoria, I'd like to speak to your mum alone. Maybe you and my constable could take a walk? Perhaps an ice cream or a coffee?'

'Yeah, great,' said Victoria. 'I was feeling cooped up in here anyway. I'll get my coat.'

Cassie found Lucinda Price lounging on an armchair, a glass of something that looked like whisky in her hand. She looked up as Cassie came in. 'Ah, Detective Inspector, come and join me.' Lucinda shook the glass towards Cassie. 'Drink? Or is it too early for you?'

'I wouldn't mind a glass of water, if that's okay.'

Lucinda nodded towards the kitchen. 'Would you mind?'

Cassie went into the small but fashionable kitchen. Finding a glass, she poured herself some water. *I hope she's not had too many of those*, she thought, noticing the half empty whisky bottle on the worktop.

Seating herself opposite Lucinda, Cassie got straight to the point. 'Tell me about your relationship with your husband.'

'God! Where to start? He was a controlling pig, if you must know. He used to hit me too, at first, but we went to a lot of social events and I couldn't always be in long sleeves and high necks, could I? Then he settled for controlling every move I made. Vicki too, when she was old enough to go out on her own. He had us followed, and not too discreetly, either. He wanted us to know that he knew our every move. Not that I could have gone far. He kept me short of money, too. Tobago was a special treat for Vicki when she finished her GCSEs, but even there his men followed us.'

Cassie had heard enough to get the gist. 'So you won't be too upset that Marcus is dead,' she said bluntly.

'Ha, upset? I'm celebrating, can't you see?' She held up the glass. 'Only thing is, poor James. I intend to look after him for the little time he has left, Inspector. At least Marcus had the good grace to get killed in time for me and Vicki to spend some time with James. I'm grateful for that.'

'Why did you leave your husband, Lucinda, if he means so much to you now?'

'Gosh, you are direct, aren't you? My head was turned by the showbiz lifestyle, I suppose. And Marcus was charming and good looking. James is. . . was a builder. Oh, he earned a good wage, never short of work, and I was an events organiser, well, an assistant – very junior. But that's when I met Marcus. He was guest of honour at a fundraiser and he swept me off my feet. We started meeting up in London. Once a month or so at first, then I started to make excuses to stay overnight. Needless to say, James was suspicious, and I fancied myself in love by that time. So I left, and took Vicki with me. James was devastated, of course, and he said some very cruel things. Vicki sided with me at first and refused to see her dad. By the time she wanted to, Marcus wouldn't allow it. So, you see, Inspector, it's a very sad story.'

'Did you ever contemplate getting away from him?'

'Oh yes. Many times. I couldn't do it. No money and nowhere to go. I didn't think for a minute that James would have me back. Besides, Marcus would have killed me. You're shocked? Well, I really believed it. He might have thrown me out, but he would never let me leave.'

'And now he's dead.' Cassie let the statement hang in the air.

'And you think I may have had something to do with that? I'm afraid not, Inspector. I am merely the beneficiary of someone else's hate for Marcus.' Lucinda raised her glass. 'And I'm grateful to whoever that is.'

'Speaking of beneficiaries, I guess you're quite a rich woman now.'

Lucinda gave a hollow laugh. 'That's your guess, is it? You'd be wrong there, Inspector. Marcus has three children from a former relationship. They get all of his money. I get the house in London and that's all.'

'Still, that must be worth a bit.'

Lucinda gave Cassie a puzzled look. 'What are you hinting at, Inspector? You think I may have paid someone to kill him?'

Cassie didn't reply, so Lucinda continued. 'Look, I have to have somewhere to live, and all mine and Victoria's friends are in London, so that's where we'll stay. And even if we move to a cheaper area, I still need money to live on. I don't have many marketable skills, so I wouldn't be able to find work easily. So you see, Inspector, my paying someone to get rid of my husband is out of the question.'

Lucinda gulped the remainder of her whisky and gazed out of the cottage window, looking quite forlorn. Cassie felt sorry for the woman, for the first time. 'I'm sorry, Mrs Price, but I have to ask these questions.'

'I understand, Inspector, but you'll have to look elsewhere for your killer.'

Maggie was very talkative as she drove to Hayle, with Cassie again happy to be a passenger. 'Victoria seems to be a troubled young woman. She clearly disliked her stepfather, and now she blames her mother for getting involved with him in the first place. Her dad is terminally ill, and she's obviously upset by that, blaming her mother again for not leaving Marcus Price years ago. I think those two have a lot of ground to make up.'

Turning off the main street, Maggie navigated her way through the steep streets to James Dunn's bungalow. 'It's a pretty spot this,' she said as she climbed out of the car.

Cassie agreed, taking in the view with appreciation. 'Too bad he won't be here much longer,' she said, with genuine sympathy. 'He's only fifty-two, but you'll be shocked to see him. It's a terrible disease, robs a person of dignity as well as everything else. Personally, I'd rather go to Dignitas than suffer in that way, but I guess we're all different.'

'People hang on to life for as long as possible, in my experience ma'am.'

Cassie shrugged. 'You may be right, Maggie, no one knows until they are in that position themselves, I suppose. Anyway, let's go and see Mr Dunn and keep our personal thoughts out of it. He's still a suspect in a murder investigation.'

James Dunn seemed even more frail than yesterday, if that was possible. 'Had a bad night,' he said, as he allowed the two women to precede him into the living room. 'Must have been all that excitement yesterday.'

Maggie offered to make tea. 'Make mine a coffee, would you,' said James. 'And put a tot of brandy in it, my lovely, it's not as though I have to worry about becoming an alcoholic.' He smiled ruefully at Maggie who was at a loss to find something lighthearted to say. She simply smiled and disappeared into the kitchen.

Turning his attention to Cassie, James said, 'We were interrupted yesterday sweetheart, what can I help you with?'

'If you wouldn't mind, you can tell me a bit about your life. What you did for a living, your friends and workmates and, if it's not too painful, how you and Lucinda split up.'

'Wow, I didn't expect you to want my life story. It's pretty boring, to be honest. My dad was a builder and I was a builder. Started with him when I was sixteen, before that if you count the weekends when I was still at school. I loved it, fresh air, physical labour, good craic with the lads.'

'How did you and Lucinda meet?'

The question hung in the air while Maggie set the tea and coffee on the table. Taking a sip of the hot brew, James continued.

'We did some work for her dad. They lived in West Penwith. Old cottage in Cott Valley it was. Beautiful spot, but the house was suffering badly from the damp. We put in a new damp course and replastered throughout, but nothing could really salvage it. They lived there for another few years and then sold it to a developer.'

'And Lucinda?'

'Can't say it was love at first sight. She was a bit on the snooty side, thought she was a cut above, if you take my meaning, but me and dad were there for a couple of weeks and eventually we clicked. We used to walk down to the sea, lovely walk that is, and talk about all kinds of things. I wasn't the wreck you see now, I was a handsome devil and cheeky with it, so I set my cap at her and she agreed to walk out with me.' James smiled at the thought. 'And if that sounds a bit old fashioned to you young folk, that's how we were round here in those days, a bit behind the times, not sophisticated, you could say.

'When we had Vicki she was pleased as punch, and I was a proud dad. We couldn't have been happier. But Lucinda liked to be occupied, said she wanted to be a role-model for Vicki. I didn't know quite what she meant by that, but I was happy to go along with it. So she got a job with an advertising firm in Penzance, they did promotions and stuff. That's how she met Price, at some event in London.' James's face fell and his voice became quiet as he recounted the days Lucinda spent away from home, and then the nights, until she eventually told him she was leaving. 'You could have knocked me down with a feather. I hadn't a clue, trusted her, you see. Then I was angry, I admit that, angry at her. I'm ashamed to say I called her some awful names.'

'So the divorce was acrimonious?'

'Aye, that's one way of putting it. I fought tooth and nail to keep Vicki, but nothing doing. Then Vicki didn't want to see me, that bugger, pardon my language, set her against me.'

'So it would be fair to say that you didn't like Marcus Price much?'

'Like him? I bloody hated him. I don't know if it works like this, but I started to be ill practically from the moment she left. I ignored symptoms for years, burying myself in work, the more physical the better. Until I collapsed one day and was rushed into hospital. I had peritonitis, my bowel had ruptured. Took weeks of antibiotics to settle me down and then they did a scan. Hopeless they said. One doctor simply said, "put your affairs in order", as blunt as that.'

'That's terrible, James.'

'It was a low point alright. But I've astounded them by still being alive.' James gave a hollow laugh. 'I'm on a special diet. I ditched the chemo when it made me more ill than the cancer. I eat healthy foods and supplements, a bit different to pies and pasties. And I stopped drinking until recently, but now I think, what the hell, I don't have long.'

'It must have been emotional seeing your ex-wife and Victoria yesterday, knowing what you've just said.'

'Emotional? Aye, it was that all right. But I'm glad I can see them for a while, especially Vicki, she's the victim in all this.' Cassie could see that James had tears in his eyes. 'All those wasted years. That bastard stopping her from seeing me. I'm glad the bugger's dead.'

'Do you get treatment at all?' Cassie asked, suddenly concerned about the man in front of her.

'I go to the cancer clinic for check-ups, that's all. Pain relief, as much as I want. That's when I get to have a social life,' he laughed. 'Sad bastards like me, but we have the craic. Morbid, dark humour, but surprisingly funny.'

'Does anyone visit you? You know, friends?'

James suddenly appeared guarded. 'It's just me, most of the time. Social Services send someone now and then, asking if I need help. All me old mates have lost interest. Can't blame 'em.' James drooped. 'Look, if you don't mind, I'm very tired.'

'Of course. Do you mind if we come to see you again? If we have any more questions?'

James nodded. 'That'll be alright. Can you see yourselves out?'

Cassie drove back to the station. Maggie had been clearly moved by James's situation and was a quiet passenger. Cassie wanted to get the mood back into work mode. 'What did you think of that?'

'The poor man. Losing his wife and daughter like that, then meeting them again when he's dying, it's very cruel.'

Cassie nodded her acknowledgement of the younger woman's empathy. 'Now, from a police perspective?'

'Oh, right. Well he clearly has a motive for seeing Price dead, he practically said as much, but means and opportunity?'

'He could have paid someone to do it.'

'I didn't get the impression he had a lot of money. And how would he find a hit man? Hayle is hardly the gangster capital of the world.'

'Point taken, Maggie, but we should dig around, see if he could possibly have known someone, like Marczak, for instance.' Cassie thought for a moment. 'Put a watch on him, Maggie, see who visits, he was quite guarded when I asked him about friends. I think there's something he doesn't want us to know. It could be that he pays prostitutes to visit and he's ashamed, as innocent as that. But he clammed up, so I'm suspicious.'

'Right, ma'am. Round the clock?'

'Not much use if it's not, Maggie.'

Chapter Nine

Cassie and Maggie had stopped off at a café on their way back to the station, so it was almost four o'clock when they arrived in the squad room. Cassie was stopped in her tracks as she saw Peter there, surveying the whiteboard. He turned at the sound of her and Maggie's voices.

'The very person,' he said, looking at Cassie. 'I need you to fill me in on where this investigation is up to.'

Cassie was clearly flustered. 'I didn't expect you back till Monday, sir.'

'We arrived back this morning, so I thought I'd get up to speed. I've been following the investigation as best I could through the usual networks, and I believe you have a prime suspect.'

Cassie was hesitant, 'Er, I suppose you mean Marczak.' She appeared anything but confident.

'Come on,' he said, indicating his office, 'take me through it.'

Cassie collected her thoughts, as Peter made some space on his desk.

'I'll clear my things out, sir,' said Cassie, coming forward to pick up papers which she had left strewn over the surface.

'Never mind that now, you can clear up later. Tell me about Marczak.'

Cassie filled Peter in on the Slovac's background, and about him being a prime suspect for a murder back home.

'He's obviously ruthless enough to be our killer,' said Peter. 'But what's his motive? I suppose you see him as a hired killer.'

o

'Yes, I'm hoping to tie him in with the widow or her ex, or both of them in cahoots. My interviews with Mrs Price and Dunn today confirm they had motive. They both hated his guts.'

'Okay, I can see your thinking Cassie, but if I was a hired killer I doubt if I'd perform the act on stage in front of a couple of hundred people. He would have had lots of opportunity to kill Price without attracting suspicion onto himself. It's all a bit theatrical, this murder, as if the risk was part of the attraction for the killer. You being there was an added bonus, maybe. The drama of it all – I wish I could have been there to see it.' Peter smiled at the thought, but noticed that his DI wasn't smiling.

'Okay, let's go through some of the other suspects. Is there anyone you have ruled out?'

'All of the cast had opportunity if you count them being on stage when Price was killed. And the two women, Drummond and Moore, had reason to feel some animosity.'

'They were both in a relationship with him?'

'We should have the forensics back on Price's bedsheets any time. That will tell us who was the favourite at the time, but I don't see either of them as suspects. They're more likely to drop him in it with his wife, anonymous letter or something, but not murder.'

'We can rule the women out, then. What about the rest of the cast?'

'There are six men, none of whom have motive as far as I can see. In fact, stopping the show was the last thing they would have wanted, by all accounts. A successful production was just what they wanted for the old CV. There's only one who seemed to bear a grudge, and that's Craig Williamson. He wanted the lead and was very put out when Price got it.'

'Jealousy is a strong motive, and it would fit the theatricality of the act, but I still think our killer was taking a big risk,' said Peter, thoughtfully. 'Do you think he was up to it?'

'I can't see it, sir. I had nothing to hold him on at the time, so I let him go to London for an audition. I'm having him brought back for further questioning, but I'm not hopeful.'

'So, the way you see it, you're left with Marczak? Is there anyone else? One of the support staff?'

314

'The director was sick and not there that night, then there's the two costume ladies and the light and sound man. That's the lot, unless you consider a totally unknown suspect. It is possible to gain access to the theatre from the cliffs. He or she would have to be a very accomplished climber and knowledgeable about the area, and it was dark.'

'Same thing goes for that theory as my thoughts about Marczak. Why go to all that trouble when you could catch Price in a dark alley or on the car park, for that matter. So let's rule that out for the moment.' Peter counted on his fingers. 'So there's two costume ladies – let's count them out, and the lighting man. What do we know about him?'

Cassie took a deep breath. The way that Peter had summarised the case had brought Colin into the frame, and she felt uncomfortable considering that. However, Cassie filled Peter in on her and Saroj's interviews with Maynard.

Peter flipped through Saroj's interview notes. 'Saroj didn't like Maynard's explanation for why the lights didn't come up, and she had him down as a cocky sod.' Peter looked up at Cassie. 'What do we know about his background?'

Cassie filled the DCI in on Colin's past. Painting him as a sympathetic character who was now getting his life back on track after a tragedy in his life.

Peter sensed that his DI had some empathy for this man and may be discounting him because of that. 'Have we checked out his story, Cassie? Medical history, for instance? And what about his friends at uni, what did they think about him? And we can easily check his passport to confirm his world travel.'

Cassie was flustered. 'So you'd see him as a significant suspect, sir?'

'You said he described himself as a thrill seeker, an adrenalin junkie, I could see him liking the risk of getting away with a murder in front of all those people. And he had the time when the lights were out, remembering that he was in control of keeping the auditorium dark, whilst he made his way onto the stage and back to the control room, perhaps.'

'What about motive, though?' said Cassie, all the time thinking that her boss had summarised a perfectly viable scenario.

'That's why we should look further into his background, Cassie. Have Maggie or Kevin do some digging, then get Maynard back in, I want to interview him myself. I don't like cocky sods who think they're fireproof, I want to rattle his cage.'

Cassie thought her boss was being unfair to Colin, but thought that she shouldn't defend him too much. 'When do you want him in, sir?'

'There's no rush, Cassie. I want all my ducks in a row before I interview him. Maggie and Kevin should be able to get something for us on Monday, let's look at that and decide our next step. In the meantime, have a Sunday off, take your kids out.'

Tonight, however, Cassie had a date with Colin. She could have called it off, and, quite frankly, didn't know why she hadn't. She couldn't believe that he had anything to do with the murder but she couldn't object to Peter's insistence that he was a viable suspect, and had set in motion the investigation into his background that her boss had asked for. Maggie and Robbie were very skilled at digging into people's past and Cassie had asked them to make the necessary enquiries into Colin Maynard's background as a matter of urgency. She knew it wouldn't be long before they came up with a complete picture of his childhood, his time at Edinburgh university, medical records and his subsequent travels. There was no doubt in Cassie's mind that what Colin had shared with her about his past was true, but she still felt a bit uneasy about meeting him tonight.

Sitting in her car on the car park, Cassie spotted Colin as he waited for her by a seafood restaurant. There was a queue snaking around one side of the building, with people waiting for take away fish and chips. The thought made Cassie's mouth water. Colin hadn't seen her car arriving, so she was able to watch him unobserved. He looked relaxed and a little vulnerable as he checked his watch and idly paced to and fro. He seemed to be humming quietly to himself, or was that just her imagination? His breath was white in the sudden chill of the November night. There was nothing furtive about his demeanor that Cassie could detect, and she was good at reading body language. Feeling more confident that this young man could not be guilty of murder, she allowed herself to smile and put thoughts of the investigation out of her mind. Cassie found herself looking forward to a pleasant evening.

She had dressed with care, finding a top and trousers that made the most of her full figure. The coffee colour of the silk blouse flattered her skin tone, its low neckline revealing the top of her ample bosom. Tanya had helped her with her hair, teasing the tight curls into a mound on top of her head, wispy tendrils trailing around her face and neck. Checking in her car mirror, Cassie knew she looked good. When she stepped into the light emanating from the restaurant windows, her feeling was confirmed by Colin's expression. 'You look amazing,' he said as he took her hands in his and looked her up and down. He pulled her towards him and kissed her lightly on her cheek. Placing his arm around her shoulders, he shivered. 'Let's get you out of the cold.'

Cassie didn't know Falmouth at all, so she was curious about the large open square she saw over Colin's shoulders. 'Shall we walk for a bit?' she said, linking his arm. Cassie smiled widely, revealing her perfect white teeth. 'Have you been waiting long?'

'However long, it was worth it, you look fantastic.' They strolled across the square over towards the marina, where several large cruisers were moored. Colin kept up a narrative about the history of Falmouth. 'One of the deepest natural harbours in the world,' he said. 'Even attracts cruise ships in the summer. This square has festivals all year round. You've missed the oyster festival by a couple of weeks. Massive marquees are erected and there's food and drink as well as crafts and such. All the festivals are well attended and good fun.'

Conversation with Colin was easy. They chatted about all kinds of things, but stayed away from the investigation. Colin asked about Cassie's children and laughed out loud at Cassie's descriptions of their antics. 'Our Micky has had one of those *footballer* haircuts. He went to a Turkish barber in Truro and had all of one side shaved, with two parallel lines cut in above his ear. Trouble is, his hair is so curly that the rest just sticks up like a cock's comb. Tanya teases him mercilessly.'

Colin smiled, but looked a little sad. 'I wish I'd had a sister to

317

tease me, and a mother who loved me as much as you clearly love your two.'

Cassie took his hand. 'What about your foster parents? They wanted you, must have done to adopt you.'

Colin became quiet and steered Cassie away from the marina. 'Let's talk about something else, eh? And it's time we got inside, you look freezing.' Colin led the way back across the square to a café bar where they could snuggle into a cozy corner.

Neither of them had eaten, so Colin ordered some tapas to go with their non-alcoholic drinks. 'Next time we should go for a nice dinner and get a taxi so that we can have wine.' Cassie smiled in agreement. Colin paused, his fork halfway to his mouth. 'You really are amazing looking, you know. Your skin is fantastic and those dark eyes. But d'you know what first attracted me to you?' Cassie shook her head, a little bemused. 'It was the way you took control that night at the Minack. You spoke, and everyone listened. You were magnificent, the way you organised everything, taking charge of all those people.'

'Look Colin, I'm flattered, but that's police training. Any of my colleagues would have done the same.'

'Oh, I don't know. You put Marczak in his place and dealt with all those actors and their massive egos. I adore strong women, Cassie. Even in this day and age, women defer to men too often, and what do they get for it? Taken advantage of, that's what.' Colin was clearly moved by his thoughts and Cassie felt that he was getting into a dark place, and this wasn't the occasion for that. However, he waved her protests away. 'You might realise that I am not a fan of my gender. In my experience, men use women for their own ends. Take Marcus Price, for instance. He steals another man's wife and, as if that's not enough, chases anything in a skirt just for his own selfish pleasure. That night I saw him with Alicia, I caught her eye as he was having his way with her. She looked resigned, Cassie, as if it was just one of those things that you had to do to get along in the business. Just like my mam.' Colin choked, his Scottish accent coming out with his emotion. 'Them bastards used her, knowing she was hooked on the drugs. I saw that look on her face as well, as she shooed me way up the stairs when I caught them at it.'

318

'Colin, look, this isn't the place. . . '

'Excuse me a minute,' he said, pushing his chair back and hurrying away from the table.

Cassie gave a long sigh. *We should probably call it a night*, she thought. But then Colin came back looking apologetic. 'I'm so sorry, Cassie. I didn't mean to bring a downer on the evening.'

'It's okay, Colin, but I think maybe we should go.'

'No, please, it's early. And I promise not to burden you with my troubles.' His smile was warm and genuine, and Cassie didn't have the heart to say no.'

'Okay, how about you tell me about your travels. Where was the best place?'

This did the trick, and Colin spent the next hour regaling Cassie with the splendour of New Zealand and the intensity of India. He was a good storyteller, peppering his experience with anecdotes about individuals he met. Colin was obviously interested in people, but didn't waste an opportunity to criticise the ruling classes, especially the British role in India. A listener could be in no doubt that Colin was a supporter of the underdog, especially women, whom he saw as oppressed in many of the countries he visited.

The evening ended all too soon for Colin and he pressed Cassie for another date. 'Let's get this investigation out of the way first, Colin,' she said, as they stood by her car. 'It's awkward for me at the moment, but I've had a lovely time tonight, thank you.' She leant and kissed him on the cheek.

Colin held on to her and placed a gentle kiss on her lips. 'I understand, Cassie, but I'll hold you to that promise.'

As Colin let Cassie go, he said, as an aside, 'I've been asked to come to Truro tomorrow to see Detective Chief Inspector Sanders.' Cassie turned to look at him, but didn't speak. 'Do you know what that's about?'

'I can't say too much about that, Colin. He's my boss and he's been away on holiday, so it's natural that he wants to get involved with the investigation now he's back.' She put her hand on his shoulder. 'Try not to worry, just answer the questions, I'm sure you'll be fine.'

However, as Cassie drove home, she couldn't help the niggling

319

feeling that Colin had said something tonight that was important to the investigation. *What was it?* She thought. *Something to do with Marcus Price being a womaniser.* She was feeling tired now, though, and had an early start tomorrow. *It'll come to me, I'm sure,* she thought yawning. *When did I get to be so lightweight? I used to stay up all night and get up for work the next day, no problem.* Cassie smiled. *Not getting any younger, Cass.*

Chapter Ten

Sunday morning in the squad room was surprisingly busy. Robbie and Maggie had arrived early, after working at home researching Colin Maynard's background. After fighting her way through hospital bureaucracy, Maggie had been able to confirm that Colin Maynard had surgery to remove a large non-malignant tumour in 2016. She had been lucky enough to speak to the surgeon who operated, and he confirmed that, although the surgery had been a complete success as far as removing the tumour was concerned, Colin had been left with some residual damage which affected his fine motor skills.

Maggie also found that Maynard had failed to attend three of his six monthly check-ups at The Royal Cornwall Hospital when he was travelling abroad. However, he had attended the last one two months ago, and was found to be in excellent health generally. The surgeon had hesitated, wondering how much he could share about his patient. This was a murder enquiry though, and he was not one of those medics who withheld information on principle. He told Maggie that he had detected a small growth in the same region as the last one. 'It will be a fairly simple operation to remove it,' he said, 'but I am disappointed that it has returned.'

Maggie asked to be rerouted to the hospital administrator, where she found that Maynard had given his next of kin as a Jean McIntire, not his adoptive parents as Maggie expected. Making a note of Ms McIntyre's's contact details, she asked if there was any mention of a Mr and Mrs Maynard as relatives. The answer was no. Strange, thought Maggie, maybe they're deceased. Something to pass on to Kevin for social services to answer.

Meanwhile, Kevin had found evidence from the passport office, that Maynard had travelled extensively for around eighteen months, countries including Australia, New Zealand, India and Russia. That all checks out with Maynard's statement, Kevin noted. The next step was contacting Edinburgh University to see if he could find anyone who was a particular friend of Maynard's before he had to leave. That would have to wait until tomorrow, he thought.

The situation was much the same with social services in Glasgow. Robbie wanted to know more about when the young Colin had been taken into care. What his family name was, what the specific problems were, and about the couple who adopted him. When interviewed, Maynard had been reluctant to give any information about his adoptive family, saying only that the couple were now quite elderly and in poor health and he didn't want them worried. Needless to say, he could find no one to speak to on a Sunday, but was able to get some contact details for first thing tomorrow.

Kevin turned to Maggie, who was typing up her short report for DCI Sanders. 'Why is it just us who work on Sundays, Maggie?'

Cassie had decided not to take the day off as Peter had suggested, and as she stepped into reception at the station, she was met by Jane Dunbarton, the solicitor assigned to Marczak. The two women shook hands as they introduced themselves, and retired to an interview room.

'My client wants to confess to the murder of Marcus Price,' the young solicitor said bluntly. 'I have tried to persuade him otherwise, as I have seen the evidence you have against him, and it amounts to nothing. But he is determined.'

Cassie was well and truly shocked. 'But he hasn't even been charged yet.'

'Well, I guess you'll want to do that now,' Jane paused. 'Look, it's not my place to say this, but I think him being wanted in connection to a murder in Slovakia has something to do with it. The sentence for murder there is life imprisonment, and life really does mean life. He would die in prison and, from what I know, the prisons there are a bit primitive, if you take my meaning.'

'So he'd rather go to prison here for a murder he didn't commit than be extradited back home to face trial there?

'Precisely. My guess is, if you pushed him on certain details, he would trip himself up.'

Cassie didn't like the young solicitor giving her advice on how to interview a murder suspect, but let the issue pass. 'Thanks for letting me know, Jane. Do you want to see him now?'

'Yes please. I'll have another crack at dissuading him from this course of action, but I don't hold out much hope,' Jane gave a wry smile.

Cassie stood and picked up her briefcase. 'I'll have him sent up, then I'll arrange an interview. Would thirty minutes be enough for you?'

'Plenty, I should think. Thanks DI Wade.'

Peter was one of the early birds that morning. His holiday had left him completely refreshed and he was eager to get to grips with the Marcus Price case. His office had been restored back to the neatness he liked, Cassie's untidy belongings having been removed by her the previous day. As he was thinking of asking his DI to join him, she walked through the door. 'Morning, Cassie,' he said, a bit surprised that she hadn't knocked, but the look on her face persuaded him to ignore that fact. 'Didn't expect to see you today, what's up?'

'Alfred Marczak is what's up. He wants to confess to killing Marcus Price.'

'And that's bad news because. . ?'

'His brief doesn't think he did it. She believes he's trying to avoid a tough sentence in Slovakia in exchange for a lighter one here, and better prison conditions.'

'I see. We'll have to test him on the details and see how he handles that.' Cassie gave a wry smile as her boss had echoed precisely the advice from Jane Dunbarton.

'I'll lead the interview this morning.' Cassie nodded her

acceptance. 'I'll press him hard on the facts and see if we can't break his story. He'll have to tell us why he killed Price and give us more details on his reason for choosing to do it the way he did. Are you ready?'

'Can't wait, sir. If there's something I really don't like it's criminals who think they can manipulate our justice system to meet their own ends.'

'But I thought you liked Marczak for this, Cassie.'

'I did. Still might, if we can connect him with someone who had a motive. So far that's proving difficult. And what you said about the way Price was killed – I can see that Marczak would have chosen something less public. And he would have disappeared pretty quickly after the event. He had the opportunity before we brought him in.'

'All good points, Cassie. Coffee before we start?'

Peter watched Cassie walk over to the coat rack, where she hung up her coat and removed her scarf, and then to the coffee machine. *There's something different about her*, he thought, *but I can't put my finger on it. Perhaps it's being in charge in my absence. I know she likes to control things, and me being back before this case has been put to bed may have put her nose out of joint, made her more vulnerable. But she looks different, too. More, what is it? . . . Sexy! That's what it is. I'd swear she's lost weight, and she's wearing perfume. I wonder if she's met someone?* Peter smiled, thoughts of Rachel springing into his mind. *I wonder if being in love has made me more perceptive?*

All thoughts of love and romance disappeared from Peter's thoughts as he faced the tough Slovakian over the interview table. Peter knew he had an intimidating presence. His six foot three height and broad frame, along with the remnants of a broken nose, had many a criminal losing their cockiness as they faced his piercing blue eyes. That being so, Peter was a little surprised to notice that the wiry, hard faced man opposite showed no signs of fear. In fact, he leant forward and squared up to the imposing detective. *Okay, game on.* Thought Peter, imagining a hard rugby game where we faced a fearsome scrum defence.

Peter switched on the recorder and opened his file. 'Interview with Alfred Marczak in connection with the murder of Marcus Price. I'm Detective Chief Inspector Sanders. Present are. . . '

The other players in the room introduced themselves. 'Now, Mr Marczak, do you know why we are interviewing you this morning?'

Alfred leaned back and crossed his legs. 'I would like to confess to the killing of Marcus Price. That is my statement.'

'I don't know how things are done in Slovakia, Mr Marczak, but I'm afraid we are going to need a lot more than that before we can take your confession seriously.' Peter consulted his file. Selecting a photograph of Lucinda Price, he passed it across the table towards Alfred. 'Do you know this woman?'

'No. I never seen her.'

'You're quite sure?'

'I never seen her. Who is she?'

Ignoring the question, Peter took back the photograph and replaced it with one of James Dunn. 'Do you know this man?'

'What is this? Do I know this person and that person.' Marczak said in a sing song voice. 'No. I never seen him too.' He pushed the photograph back.

'Again I'll ask you, are you very sure you have not met this man?'

'I. . . am. . . sure. Is that enough?' Marczak recrossed his legs and folded his arms.

'Okay, Mr Marczak. Now, have you seen this knife before?' Peter showed an image of the murder weapon to Alfred.

Marczak studied the photograph for a few seconds. Running his hands over the surface, he was thinking carefully before answering. 'And what if I have?'

Peter was not fooled by the ambiguous answer. 'Have you? Yes or no?'

'I may have.'

'Is it your knife?'

'I have many knives.'

Deciding not to continue with this game, Peter took the photograph back and replaced it with one of the knife found in Marczak's flat. 'Is this your knife?'

Alfred only glanced. 'Is my knife,' he confirmed.

325

Peter indicated to Cassie to take over. As she leant forward, Marczak looked directly at her and she held his gaze steadily. 'Mr Marczak, tell me why you killed Marcus Price.'

'He is not nice man, he insulted me and my country.'

Cassie paused and held Marczak's stare until he looked away. 'And why on the stage at the Minack?'

'Why not? I am. . . on impulse, you know? Big temper.'

'Why have you only now confessed?'

'I don't know. I am good man?' Marczak smiled broadly, showing brown stained teeth. He laughed loudly and scratched is head. 'You arrest me now?'

Peter ended the interview abruptly, leaving Alfred startled and seeking help from his solicitor. 'You wait!' he shouted. But Peter and Cassie had already left the room to be replaced by a constable ready to escort Marczak back to his cell.

Walking along the corridor, Peter turned to Cassie. 'You believe that?'

'Not a word.'

'Okay Cassie, if we eliminate Marczak, which I feel we need to do now, who else is in the frame?'

The two detectives were standing in front of the whiteboard. 'We've eliminated most of the cast, at least for now,' said Cassie. 'I still want to talk to Craig Williamson.' She tapped her pen on the photo of the actor.

'He's the one who had to dash of to London,' stated Peter. 'I can't help wondering why you let him go, Cassie.'

'It was a judgement call, sir. I had no more reason to hold him than any other member of the crew, and he is contactable. He's coming in tomorrow for an interview.'

'Right,' said Peter, underlining Craig Williamson's name in red. 'So, if we ignore the costume ladies – I really can't see either of them being involved – we're left with Mrs Price, James Dunn and Colin Maynard, with an outside possibility of Craig Williamson.' Peter turned to Cassie. 'Is that the way you see it?'

'Well, yes and no. Neither Mrs Price nor James Dunn could have committed the act themselves. Mrs Price was in Tobago and Dunn is far too ill, they would be accessories at best. And I haven't been able to find a motive for Colin Maynard.' Cassie thought that this was the time she should tell Peter about her connection with Colin before he found out for himself.

'There's something I need to tell you, sir. And it had better be in your office.'

After Cassie had filled Peter in on her liaisons with Colin, Peter tapped the desk thoughtfully. 'You've shown a remarkable lack of judgement, Cassie,' he said, looking up at her embarrassed figure standing silently by the door. 'Come and sit down, we need to discuss this properly.

'How far has this relationship gone? I mean, have you slept with the man?'

'No, sir,' Cassie protested. 'I had lunch with him when he was helping me with my investigations at the Minack, and a drink with him last night. That was an error of judgement, I admit, but it was just a drink.'

'I can't believe it, Cassie, what were you thinking? A suspect in a murder investigation and you go having dates with him!'

'One date, sir! And I didn't see him as a strong suspect at the time.' Cassie forced herself to calm down. 'If it's any compensation, I feel I know him a lot better than I would have done if I'd simply interviewed him.'

Peter laughed derisively. 'Go on,' he said.

'He is, as you have pointed out, a risk taker. He admits to loving the adrenalin rush he gets from living on the edge. I don't think he's a natural killer, if that makes sense, but I do think he's capable of ignoring the living person and treating the whole escapade as an adventure. He also admits to hating the sort of man who treats women as objects. . . ' Suddenly, Cassie recalled what it was the night before that had made her detective alarm bells ring. 'I've just remembered, he said that Price had *stolen someone's wife*. How could he know that unless he had it from the horse's mouth?'

Forgetting that he was on the verge of disciplining Cassie, Peter became excited by this new lead. 'So if we accept that he knows Dunn, that could be the missing piece, Cassie.' However, Peter was not the sort of detective who went off half cock. 'We'll take our time and get this right. You still have the round the clock surveillance on Dunn's house?' Cassie nodded. 'Okay. Maggie and Kevin have more background checks on Maynard to do, so we should wait and see what that throws up. And we've got the Williamson interview to do tomorrow. I want a strong case, Cassie, no mistakes on this one.'

'Right sir. And the other business?'

'We'll talk again, Cassie. When this is over.'

Chapter Eleven

The atmosphere in the squad room on Monday morning was electric. Maggie and Kevin were busy on the phones, following up on their research from the day before. Saroj and Robbie were about to leave to relieve the two uniformed constables who had been carrying out the night-time surveillance on James Dunn's house.

Peter called everyone to attention whilst he briefed them on the analysis that he and Cassie had done the previous day.

'I'm as certain as I can be at the moment that Colin Maynard is our killer. His motive is a bit unclear, I admit, but I'm guessing that James Dunn has offered him money, and Cassie believes that the enterprise would appeal to his sense of adventure. By all accounts, he's drawn to risky pursuits. That, and the fact that he proclaims his hatred of controlling and abusive men, leads me to believe that he would take this on. Cassie?'

Cassie stepped forward, any sympathy she might feel for Colin was pushed to one side. She was a detective first and foremost and wanted nothing more than to arrest him for this crime. 'I've not much to add to that, except that Maynard lied to me about his health. He told me that his tumour had completely gone but Maggie found out yesterday that this wasn't true. The reappearance of this growth could be a significant factor. We are fortunate to have someone on our team with medical training.' Cassie turned and signalled for Saroj to come forward.

'A tumour located near to the cerebellum,' said Saroj, 'which

Maynard's is, can affect a person's reasoning and decision making. In brief, it can make him or her less aware of the consequences to their actions. For instance, it can make someone, who was previously cautious, become reckless.'

Peter resumed his briefing. 'Thanks, Saroj. So putting all we know about Maynard together, I feel confident that we have enough to arrest him. I would like to tie him in with Dunn or Mrs Price, or find another link to Price that would give him motive, but we may have to wait until we interview him to establish that.'

'Cassie and I will also interview Craig Williamson today. He knows Price and may give us information that suggests a link between Price and Maynard, but in the meantime, we'll keep a watch on Dunn and see if he makes contact. Saroj and Robbie are on their way now to do just that.' This signalled the pair to leave, gathering their supplies of sandwiches and coffee.

Maggie and Kevin returned to their computer screens and telephones. Peter asked Cassie to join him in his office. 'I'm considering asking you to take a step back on this Cassie. Your relationship with Maynard could cloud your judgement and I don't want to take that risk.'

'No, sir, please don't do that. I don't have a *relationship* with him, and I am as keen as you or anyone on the team to bring him to justice, if he is indeed guilty.' Cassie stood her ground. 'Let me prove that to you, sir. I promise I won't let you down.'

Peter considered his options, and decided to give his DI an opportunity to redeem herself. 'Okay. I hope you're as good as your word, Cassie. I don't want to regret giving you this chance.'

Cassie breathed a sigh of relief. 'Thanks, sir. Don't worry, I'm rock solid.'

Craig Williamson was a graceful man. Well dressed and perfectly groomed. He sat in the interview room waiting for his *interrogators*, as he liked to think of them, taking off the part of a British war hero expecting the gestapo. His assumed a pose of arrogance with a stiff upper lip, and pulled his trouser legs up to save the creases. As Peter and Cassie entered, Craig stiffened his spine and stared at them defiantly. He almost said, *you'll get nothing out of me but my name and number*, but stopped himself, and suppressed a giggle at the thought.

'Mr Williamson, thank you for coming in today,' Peter said, taking up a position opposite the actor. 'We just have a few questions which shouldn't take long.'

Craig looked at Cassie. 'Hello again, DI Ward. Aren't you going to ask me how I got on with my audition?'

The two detectives exchanged a glance, but said nothing.

'Well, I got it! It's a great role for me too. . . '

Cassie cut in. 'I'm sure that's good news, Mr Williamson, but time is of the essence, as you will appreciate, so if we could stick to the matter in hand.'

'Oh yes. That ghastly murder. I never had much love for Marcus Price, but I would never wish him dead, just incapacitated, ha ha.' Seeing the serious faces of the detectives, he said, 'Just my little joke, we actors are very competitive, you know.'

Ignoring the actor's words, Peter went through the process of showing him the photographs of Mrs Price and James Dunn.

'I know her,' Craig said, picking up a photo. 'Not well, but one attends functions with other actors, you know. Marcus was always very jealous of her, guarded her like a precious antique. Not that she was antique looking, oh no, very attractive, in a mousy sort of way. Very quiet, as I recall, jumpy.'

He looked briefly at the other photo. 'Don't know him. Looks a bit rough, though, is he a suspect?'

Cassie took over. 'Did you know the backstage staff, Mr Williamson? This man, for instance?' She showed Craig a photo of Colin Maynard.

'Ye-e-es, I think so.' Craig examined the image. 'Technician, I think, lights, sound, that sort of thing.'

'Would Marcus Price have known him?'

'Don't know, dear, he may have done. Price was very fussy about special effects.'

'Did you ever see them together, after the show for instance?'

'What, socially? No chance, love. Never fraternised with the hoi polloi, did Marcus.'

Peter realised that they were getting nowhere with this interview. Williamson wasn't going to be any help, and Peter quickly discounted him as a suspect, even though he was an actor and may well be playing a part. He decided to stop and let Williamson go. 'Thank you again, Mr Williamson. We may wish to speak to you further, but for now you're free to go.'

'Well, that was short and sweet,' Craig sounded a little disappointed. 'but I'm happy to help any time, work commitments allowing.'

Chapter Twelve

It was just before seven-thirty on the Tuesday morning, and Maggie and Kevin were finishing their shift of surveillance outside James Dunn's bungalow. There had been nothing to report since Mrs Price and Victoria had left at eight o'clock the previous evening.

Kevin yawned widely. 'You know, Maggie, I'd hate to think that no one visited me when I was on my last legs. Apart from his ex and his daughter, James Dunn seems to be all alone in the world.'

'Yeah, and he's only got them since Marcus Price was killed. He's lucky in that respect, at least.'

'What if it wasn't luck, though? The DI seems to think he could have had something to do with it.'

'Not out of the question, is it though? Perhaps he was in cahoots with Mrs Price, no love lost there for either of them.'

'Who do you fancy for the hit man, then? He couldn't have managed it himself.'

Maggie shook her head. 'The Chief fancies Colin Maynard for it,' she said quietly, gazing out of the window.

Maggie reflected on the discussion she had had with Mrs Maynard yesterday. She had finally tracked down the couple who had adopted the young Colin Mc Leish, as he was then, at eight years old. Maggie had spoken to a social worker from the Glasgow Family Placement team who was really helpful. She remembered Colin as a sad and shy little boy. 'It's an all too familiar story these days, I'm afraid,' she had said. 'Single mother, drug user, on the

p

game when she needed a fix. Poor Colin was in and out of care since he was five. Eventually the police found him wandering the streets at midnight and took out an EPO, emergency protection order. We found him some foster parents pretty quickly. They had five other children placed with them and Colin wasn't happy. Fortunately we had the Maynards on our books. They really wanted a younger child, one that was less damaged, I suppose. Anyway, when they met Colin they just clicked, it can happen like that sometimes. He was a good looking lad who was eager to please, and Mrs Maynard, especially, just fell in love with him. The adoption went through quickly and we closed the case.'

Maggie held on as the line went silent. 'You still there?' she asked.

'Yeah, it's just that it's so sad. After eighteen months the Maynards asked us to take him back. Just for a break, they said at first, but then it was obvious, when they didn't want to see him at all, that it wasn't going to work. For Colin's sake we moved him permanently into a children's home.'

Maggie pondered over the life that some children had, comparing it with her own loving family. *If I ever have children,* she thought, *I will definitely keep them safe and loved.*

Mrs Maynard, when Maggie had reached her, confirmed the salient facts of Colin's adoption and subsequent rejection by her and her husband, who had since died from a heart attack. But she was able to give Maggie a more detailed picture of how it came about. 'We were desperate for a child of our own, but that wasn't to be. We were getting on a bit before we came round to the idea of adoption. We wanted a young child, we'd heard that there weren't any babies available but that didn't bother us. We thought a two year old would be nice. Then we met Colin and we thought he was just perfect. Good looking lad, quiet, intelligent and he seemed to like us. My Alan was looking forward to taking him to football matches and helping him with his homework, that sort of thing. Colin was a bit withdrawn at first, but only to be expected, the social worker said. It was after the adoption went through that he changed. The social worker said he was testing us, pushing against us to see if we would reject him like his mum had.' Mrs Maynard sniffed and blew her nose loudly. 'Sorry love. He refused to wash, called us awful names, trashed his room after we had it specially done out in Rangers colours. Worst of all, though, he wouldn't speak to us. He'd sit with his head down watching TV, and then just leave the room. We didn't try to stop him towards the end, it was a relief to have him gone. It wasn't long after that that we wanted him gone for good.'

Kevin too was in reflective mode. *It wasn't out of the question that Colin Maynard could have done it.* He thought. *He had opportunity, he was fit and he had medical training – Ben Samuels had said that it may have been someone who was familiar with anatomy.* There was no doubt that Colin was an unlucky man. After finding the right department in Edinburgh University, Kevin had tracked down Colin's ex girlfriend, Jean McIntyre. She was a GP in Glasgow now and happy to talk about her ex boyfriend, whom she seemed very concerned about.

They had met early on in their medical training and really hit it off. Colin was quiet, she said, and studious, but that was okay with her as she was much the same. They started living together and intended to get married when they qualified. 'It was a real bombshell when they found the tumour. Colin had been having mood swings and trouble sleeping, but we put it down to final year pressure. He collapsed one day and was rushed into hospital. The tumour was sizable and malign, but pressing on his cerebellum. The operation to remove it was successful, but it didn't end there.'

Jean told Kevin that Colin just wasn't the same after the operation. His personality changed, he became more adventurous and sought risky pursuits. 'Very out of character. The Colin I knew was afraid of heights and flying, amongst other things.'

After deciding to leave his course on account of his hand tremors, Colin took up sky diving and wanted Jean to join him climbing Ben Nevis. 'I was stressed enough with my finals looming so, inevitably, we had a blazing row and he moved out. One surprising thing happened, though. Colin was never a gambler, so I was shocked when I heard he had won money on the lottery. Not millions, about three hundred grand, I think. He disappeared then. Went travelling, I believe.'

Maggie had been leaning back in her seat with her eyes closed.

A nudge from Kevin brought her attention back. 'Who d'you think that is?' he said, focusing his camera on the figure walking down James Dunn's drive.

As the figure reached the door it turned. The man's face was illuminated by the street light which was still bright in the early dawn, so there could be no doubt, it was Colin Maynard.

Maggie reached for her phone and called Peter.

'Sanders,' came the quick reply.

Maggie filled him in on the latest development. 'Cassie and I were just on our way to arrest Maynard. We'll be with you as soon as we can. Don't do anything. Just watch and wait. Let me know if there are any developments.'

'They're on their way,' she told Kevin. 'The Chief and the DI. I'd like to be a fly on the wall in there,' she said, pointing to the bungalow. 'This is significant, Kevin. At last, confirmation that Dunn and Maynard know each other.'

Cassie became quiet when Peter filled her in on developments at Dunn's house. *It looks like we may be right,* she thought. *But why? Surely not out of friendship, and James Dunn didn't look like a man with the sort of money to pay to have someone eliminated.* Cassie still didn't want to believe that she could be that bad a judge of character, even though it was the only scenario that made any sense.

Peter's phone buzzed. 'Yes, Maggie?' he said. Turning to Cassie he told her that Maynard had left Dunn's bungalow in what looked like a right huff. He had slammed the front door and sped off in his car.

'They're following now. He's headed on the coast road towards Portreath.' Peter quickly turned off the A30 and took the road leading to Portreath, aiming to approach Hayle from the opposite direction, so as to intercept Maynard.

The phone buzzed again. Peter listened. 'Thanks Maggie. Just keep an eye on him, we'll be with you soon.'

'He's stopped in a café car park opposite Hell's Mouth. Maggie says he got out and walked over towards the cliff top.'

Cassie didn't like the sound of Hell's Mouth at all. She had a sinking feeling in her guts. 'Don't do anything stupid,' she said quietly.

Peter glanced over at his DI, suspecting, from the fervent plea he had just heard, that Cassie felt more for this man than she admitted to earlier.

Peter pulled in beside Maggie and Kevin and got out of the car to discuss tactics. However, Cassie didn't wait to talk about what they were going to do, she ran across the road and climbed up the rough path leading to the cliff top.

The wind whipped at her hair and the sound of the waves was menacing as the sea pounded into the steep sided cove that bore that awful name. She spotted Colin standing on the edge, his back towards her. He hadn't heard her approach over the crashing of the waves.

'Colin!' she shouted when she was a few metres away.

He turned slightly to look over his shoulder. 'Go away, Cassie!' he shouted.

'I'm not going anywhere. Not now and not in the future.'

'Ha! You expect me to believe that? It's all over, isn't it? You'll find out as soon as you speak to Dunn. He wants to come clean, salve his conscience before he dies.' Colin bent and looked over the edge. Cassie's heart was in her mouth. 'He was going to leave me everything. The house, his savings. I was going to pay for Edinburgh with that. Now he's suddenly remembered he's got a daughter,' Colin gave a hollow laugh. *Sorry Colin, I need to make sure she's alright.* He cried though, genuine tears, said he hoped I didn't hate him.

'I don't hate him, actually. This is perfect, just the way my life should end. It's been shite from start to finish.'

Cassie tried one last-ditch attempt. 'You can't say that. Colin. What about us?' Cassie knew she would be giving him false hope by saying this, but she would try anything to get him away from that cliff edge. Colin didn't answer, just swayed slightly in the breeze. 'Look at me, Colin. Look at me!'

As he turned, Colin took a small step away from the edge. Peter had been making his way along the cliff path, the rising sun behind him putting Maynard into bright relief and slightly concealing his own presence. Maynard's short step back from the edge was all that Peter needed. He knew he was pretty fast over ten metres, so he launched himself towards the man. Getting within a metre of Colin, Peter leapt, wrapping him in his two strong arms, holding onto him tightly. At the same time, he twisted and rolled away from the edge, clamping Colin with his whole body. His rugby mates would have called it a try saving tackle. Cassie called it a miracle.

The two men rolled to halt at Cassie's feet. Colin struggled weakly but soon stopped and began sobbing noisily. Peter sat up and cradled the younger man in his arms. 'It's all right now, mate,' he said kindly. 'It's over.'

Cassie helped pull Colin to his feet. Standing erect, she said, 'Colin Maynard I am arresting you for the murder of Marcus Price. You do not have to say anything, but it may harm your defence if you fail to mention when questioned something that you later rely on in court, anything you do say may be used in evidence. Do you understand?'

Colin looked up at Cassie, his expression unreadable. He nodded sharply. 'Yes, I understand.'

Maggie and Kevin were standing by. Kevin approached Maynard and cuffed him. 'Come with me, sir,' he said, leading the still shaky man away down the path.

Peter and Cassie stood looking out to sea. 'That was very brave, sir,' she said.

'Ditto, Cassie. I heard what you said to him, what I didn't know was if you meant it. Then when you arrested him I knew. I guess it hurt a bit, all the same?'

Cassie shrugged. 'Not at all, sir. He's a felon and I'm a cop. Couldn't be any other way, and, from what Maggie and Kevin found out yesterday, I realised he lied to me about practically everything. He's not the man I thought he was.' Cassie turned and made her way down the steep slope.

Peter followed his DI down the path, knowing that she was putting on a brave face. *She'll get over it*, he thought, *and be all the better for a lesson learned.*

Chapter Thirteen

Cassie told the duty sergeant that she would be a couple of minutes. It was a bit irregular to see a suspect in their cell alone, but he had been willing to turn a blind eye. Cassie waited for the door to be unlocked and then stepped into the unwelcoming room. Colin was sitting curled up on the end of the bench that served as his bed. He looked up as she came in.

'Hello, Cassie. I would offer you a seat but, as you see, it's a bit sparse in here.'

'How are you feeling, Colin?'

'After your boss thwarted my pathetic attempt to end it all, I was pretty depressed, but now? Not too bad, as it happens. My solicitor, paid for by James Dunn no less, tells me that my tumour is a cracking defence. Only downside is that, if she gets me off on a plea of diminished responsibility, I may have to spend my life in a mental hospital.'

Colin gave Cassie that lopsided grin that she had liked so much. She smiled back. 'My sources tell me that, if they manage to get all of the tumour out this time, you could be back to your normal self. So you would then be eligible for release. That's something to hope for, surely?'

'I've hoped for good things all my life, Cassie, but my dreams always seemed to disappear like snow on the desert. But you're right, of course, there's always hope. No return to medicine though, that's for sure.'

'You're an intelligent man, Colin. There are lots of options open to you. Just get better first, eh?'

'If I'd been more intelligent, Cassie, I would never have agreed to do this in the first place.'

'I don't really understand why you did, Colin. Was it just the money?'

Colin shook his head. 'No, not just that, although I wanted cash to get my life back on track. I felt sorry for James. We met at the cancer clinic and got talking. His mates seemed to have deserted him, so I met up with him a couple of times for a drink. Of course, he told me about Marcus Price and his wife. I wasn't lying when I said I hated men like that, Cassie. We laughingly talked about how James could take his revenge, and somehow the plan came together. I don't think James thought I would do it at first, but I became excited by the whole thing, getting away with murder – the ultimate risk.'

Cassie remained quiet, taking in what Colin had just said. She looked at him, an expression of sadness on her face. Colin recognised her hurt.

'Cassie, I want to apologise for using you. I thought I could stay close to the investigation and maybe steer you away from suspecting me.' Cassie remained silent. 'In other circumstances it might have been different, but. . . '

The duty sergeant popped his head round the door. 'Ma'am, I'm going to have to. . . '

'It's okay, Sergeant,' she said, turning her back on Colin. 'I'm finished here.' With that Cassie turned her back and walked quickly out of the cell, along the corridor and up to the squad room.

Epilogue

Six months later. . .

The early spring sunshine was warm on Cassie's back as she and her two children walked up the drive of the renovated farmhouse that was Peter and Rachel's new home. Either side of them were fields with borders of trees. On one side a mown path was evident, leading to a large summer house where bunting decorated the verandah. Cassie could see Peter in the distance, pouring wine into the waiting glasses of her team mates. She had hoped to find time with her boss alone, but her news would have to wait now for a more fitting moment.

Looking up from her place beside her husband, Rachel saw them and waved. *She looks happy*, Cassie thought as she waved back, walking through the small gate that Micky had opened. *And why shouldn't she be? Married to the man she loves and expecting his baby, as well as having all of this.* Cassie surveyed the three acres of fields and gardens and the impressive stone built house that occupied the centre ground. *I wonder if she misses the job?* Rachel had just started her maternity leave, and this party was in part an acknowledgement of that, as well as a housewarming. Tanya was carrying a box tied with a yellow ribbon. A selection of baby paraphernalia and a bottle of champagne seemed to Cassie to hit the right note.

As the small party neared the summer house, a large golden Labrador bounded forward to greet them. *Well, that's the cliché*

341

complete, thought Cassie. *I hope Peter's not going to be too domesticated. He might start taking weekends off to go to farmer's markets and the like.*

'Just in time,' shouted Peter, as he handed Cassie a glass of bubbly. 'Now, what can I get you two?' Micky and Tanya looked pleadingly at their mother. 'Just a small one then,' she said indicating the bottle, 'then it's lemonade.'

'Lemonade?' chuckled Micky. 'Is it the 1950s?'

'Okay, smart arse, Coke or whatever.'

Peter poured the drinks and tapped his own glass. 'Just a few words and then I'll shut up.' Looking around he smiled at his assembled team. 'I asked you to come before the others get here so that I could have a private word.' His arm was draped around Rachel. 'It's been a busy year, more interesting than we might have expected, perhaps. At one time I thought that Cassie had been importing crime from Liverpool.' Cassie raised her glass at the ripple of laughter. 'But you have all been exemplary and I'm so proud to have you as my colleagues. Today is a 'thank you' to you, as well as a celebration of my good fortune. So drink up, there's plenty more where that came from.'

'Cheers!' shouted Kevin, as everyone raised their glasses.

Cassie spotted Peter wandering off towards the barbeque, so she followed. 'A word, sir?'

'No 'sirs' today, Cassie.'

'Well it is business, I'm afraid,' she said. Peter looked up expectantly, raising his eyebrows.

Just then, Rachel joined them. 'Some more guests, love,' she said. 'Can you light that thing, Cassie?' Pointing to the large gas barbeque.

'I think I can manage, Rachel,' Peter allowed himself to be led away by his wife, whilst looking over his shoulder briefly, a quizzical expression on his face.

The party was swelled by Peter and Rachel's friends, all chatting away happily as they filled their glasses and accepted nibbles offered by Rachel. Cassie was content to take charge of the cooking. As she flipped burgers, her thoughts strayed to the decision she had come to in the last few days. The offer had come out of the blue, and she wasn't sure whether Peter knew anything about it yet. It would be unusual for him not to have been told, but perhaps the news went higher up the chain of command and he was kept in the dark until Cassie had made her decision.

Robbie strayed over to the barbeque, attracted by the smell of frying onions. 'Can I have a burger, ma'am?' he said, 'and then I'll take over from you if you like.'

'That's a great offer, Robbie, and it's Cassie when we're off duty.'

Cassie expertly built a burger, with the works – lettuce, relish and tomato, and a fat beef pattie. 'There you are Robbie, napkins are just here.'

Between mouthfuls, Robbie pointed towards Micky and Tanya, who were throwing a ball for the dog. 'They seem to be enjoying themselves.' Cassie nodded thoughtfully. Robbie carried on. 'I've enjoyed meeting your kids, they're good fun, and Micky is becoming an ace surfer. Could be competition standard in a year or two.'

'Mmm,' replied Cassie.

The party was coming to an end before Cassie had an opportunity to speak to Peter again. He was clearing leftover nibbles inside the summer house. 'Need some help, Peter?' she asked.

'You could pass me a bin bag, Cassie.'

Cassie walked over to him, holding the black bag open. 'Did you know I've had an offer of a transfer to the Met?'

Peter continued dropping waste food into the bag. 'I wondered when you were going to tell me.'

Cassie's relationship with her boss had been a bit up and down since she joined his team, and she thought she knew exactly what he hoped she would do. She had to tell him, though, whatever the consequences.

'I've decided to turn it down and stay in Cornwall, if that's okay with you.'

Peter's smile lit up his face. 'Yes!' he shouted. 'I couldn't be more pleased, Cassie. I really thought you were going to tell me you had taken it.'

'You're happy about me staying, sir?' said Cassie, incredulously. 'I thought you would be glad to see the back of me.'

'I'm more pleased than you can imagine. I'll not deny that mistakes have been made, but we're all human, goodness knows I am. But you're a first rate detective, Cassie, and I think we work well together, don't you?'

Cassie was relieved and happy. 'D'you think there might be a bottle of that bubbly left somewhere, Peter? I think I need a drink.'